P9-DEU-310

At the King's Command

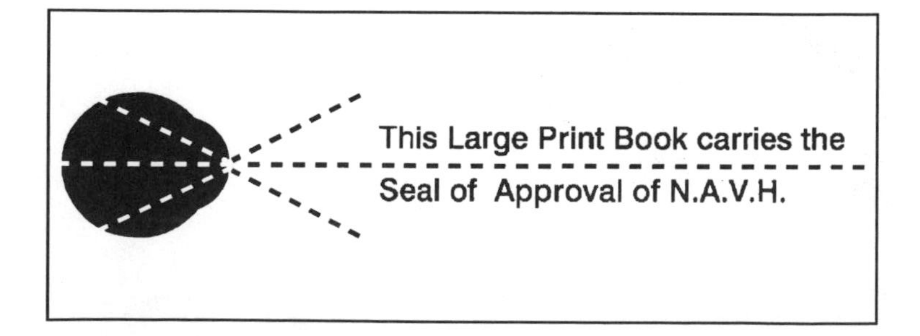
This Large Print Book carries the
Seal of Approval of N.A.V.H.

THE TUDOR ROSE TRILOGY

AT THE KING'S COMMAND

SUSAN WIGGS

THORNDIKE PRESS
A part of Gale, Cengage Learning

Detroit • New York • San Francisco • New Haven, Conn • Waterville, Maine • London

Updated from original publication CIRCLE IN THE WATER published by Harpercollins 1994.
Thorndike Press, a part of Gale, Cengage Learning.

Thorndike Press® Large Print Romance.
The text of this Large Print edition is unabridged.
Other aspects of the book may vary from the original edition.
Set in 16 pt. Plantin.
Printed on permanent paper.

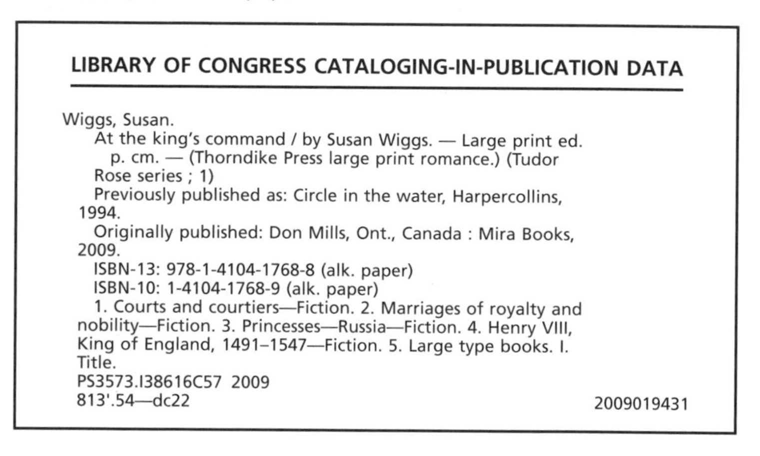
LIBRARY OF CONGRESS CATALOGING-IN-PUBLICATION DATA

Wiggs, Susan.
At the king's command / by Susan Wiggs. — Large print ed.
p. cm. — (Thorndike Press large print romance.) (Tudor Rose series ; 1)
Previously published as: Circle in the water, Harpercollins, 1994.
Originally published: Don Mills, Ont., Canada : Mira Books, 2009.
ISBN-13: 978-1-4104-1768-8 (alk. paper)
ISBN-10: 1-4104-1768-9 (alk. paper)
1. Courts and courtiers—Fiction. 2. Marriages of royalty and nobility—Fiction. 3. Princesses—Russia—Fiction. 4. Henry VIII, King of England, 1491–1547—Fiction. 5. Large type books. I. Title.
PS3573.I38616C57 2009
813'.54—dc22 2009019431

Published in 2009 by arrangement with Harlequin Books S.A.

Printed in the United States of America
1 2 3 4 5 6 7 13 12 11 10 09

This book is for Joyce Bell —
friend, fellow writer, voice of reason,
ear at the other end of the phone
and all-around fairy godmother.

ACKNOWLEDGMENTS

I owe a debt of gratitude to Joyce Bell, Betty Gyenes and Barbara Dawson Smith for their frequent and patient readings of the book in progress.

Glory is like a circle in the water,
Which never ceaseth to enlarge itself,
Till by broad spreading it disperse to naught.

— William Shakespeare

PROLOGUE

December 1533

The gypsy was hiding something. Juliana was sure of it. Even in the dimness of the barn, illuminated only by a wick burning in an oil-filled horn, she could see Zara's eyes dart nervously, her big-knuckled hands dive for cover in the layers of her tattered skirts.

"Oh, come, Zara," Juliana prompted. "You promised to read my future."

Zara's fingers came up to toy with her necklace of coins. "The hour is late. You should go back to the house. If your mother knew you'd sneaked out to consort with gypsies, she would beat you raw and turn us out in the snow to freeze."

Juliana fingered the garnet buttons on her cloak. "Mama will never find out. She never comes to the nursery at night." Juliana wrinkled her nose. "Besides, I shouldn't have to sleep in the nursery anymore. I'm getting too old for Misha's silly pranks and

Boris's night frights."

Zara's hand, large and heavy and smelling faintly of sheep fat, cradled Juliana's cheek with a gentleness the girl had never felt from her mother.

"Fourteen is not so old," Zara whispered.

Juliana peered at her through the dusty air, misted from the breath of the horses stabled in the back of the barn. The sweet, earthy smell of hay and animals drifted around her and insulated the small space from the blustering cold outside.

"Old enough to be betrothed." Juliana placed her hands upon her knees, the sable lining of her cloak soft beneath her palms. "Is that why you won't tell my fortune? Is Alexei Shuisky . . . Is he someone I can love?"

She thought of Alexei, a black-haired, fair-skinned stranger who had arrived only yesterday to settle the betrothal arrangements with her father. She had met him but once, for the house was vast and like everyone else, Alexei seemed to think she belonged in the nursery.

"After we are wed, will he beat me?" Juliana asked recklessly. "Take a new wife and send me to a nunnery? Grand Prince Vasily did exactly that. Perhaps it's all the fashion now."

Zara's lips parted in the beginnings of a smile, yet worry haunted her dark eyes. Gaps showed where she had sacrificed a tooth for each child she had borne. Her brood, now seven strong, slept upon straw and rough blankets in an empty stall. Her husband, Chavula, and her uncle Laszlo were presently out checking the traps for rabbits for the pot.

A feeling of comfort and belonging settled over Juliana. It was rare for a band of gypsies to travel this far north, yet each winter they came to Novgorod, high in the forested heartland northwest of Moscow. Juliana's father, Gregor Romanov, allowed the small tribe to shelter on his huge estate during the cold months.

The privilege was not lightly extended. At the age of three, Juliana had gotten lost in the thick, river-fed forest. Her father had mounted a frantic search. Hope dwindled as the cold northern darkness fell, and then a stranger had appeared.

Dressed in the bright breeches and beribboned blouse of a Carpathian, he had helped himself to a leash of three windhounds from Gregor's kennel. Searching tirelessly with the huge, fleet dogs, he had located Juliana huddled and weeping by an icy stream.

She remembered little of the incident, but she would never forget the ecstatic barking of the windhounds or Laszlo's wonderfully fierce face and the strength in his arms as he had lifted her up to carry her home.

Since that day, she had felt drawn to these mysterious, nomadic people. Her veins coursing with royal blood, she had been groomed from the cradle to be the wife of a powerful boyar. She was not even supposed to notice gypsies, much less associate with them. The fact that they were forbidden to her only made their secret meetings more delicious.

"Well?" she prompted Zara. "Have you seen such a vision of Alexei?"

"You know my visions are not so clear, nor so obvious."

"Then what?" Impatient, Juliana yanked a silver button off her hood. "Here, this is worth at least a hundred kopeks." Zara's hand closed around the bauble, and Juliana smiled slyly. "Ah. Does that help you see more clearly?"

Zara dropped the button into her bodice. "You Gaje," she said good-naturedly. "You're all so easily gulled."

Juliana laughed, the button no more valuable to her than a stick of kindling. Her family's wealth was a fact she accepted as readily as she had accepted her father's long absences in the service of Vasily III, grand prince of the neighboring city-state, Moscow.

The thought sobered her. A few weeks earlier, Vasily had died. He had left his son Ivan, a mere three years old, on the throne and his council of boyars quarreling bitterly amongst themselves.

Lately, Papa stayed locked in his study, writing frantic missives to allies in other cities. He was worried about the ruthless nobles who had begun to clamor for the power to rule now that the prince was dead.

Shaking off the image of her father's troubled eyes, his drawn face, she held out her hand, palm up. "Hold nothing back this time. 'Long life and happiness' might satisfy the superstitious Gaje, but I want the truth."

Zara reluctantly turned Juliana's palm toward the flickering light of the lamp. "Some matters are better left unknown."

"I'm not afraid."

Zara's eyes locked with Juliana's, veiled pools of black confronting clear emerald green. "It is good to be fearless, Juliana." Zara's nail, edged with ancient dirt, traced a sinuous unbroken line across Juliana's palm. Then the gypsy looked at the large brooch Juliana wore pinned at her shoulder.

The thin flame from the lamp gave the ruby a glow of life, making the precious jewel appear depthless in its cruciform setting of gold and pearls.

Zara's eyes glazed and her cheek — the one marked so wonderfully with a star — seemed to droop slightly. Without moving, she appeared to slip away, deep into a secret realm of intuition and imagination.

"I see three strong women." Zara spoke slowly, her Romany accent thickening. "Three lives entwined."

Juliana frowned. Three women? She was her father's only daughter, though she had innumerable Romanov cousins in Moscow.

"Their fates are flung like seeds to the four winds," Zara continued, still staring at the heart of the jewel, and always her fingers stroked and circled, discovering the unique topography of Juliana's hand.

Zara touched a delicate curved line. "The first will travel far." Her blunt finger continued, edging along until it encountered a broken line. "The second will douse the flames of hatred."

Zara's finger circled back, finding the point where the three main lines converged. "The third will heal old wounds."

A chill slid up Juliana's back. "I don't understand," she whispered, fighting the urge to snatch back her hand. Outside, the wind rattled through the bare trees, a lonely voice in a world of ice and darkness. "How can you see the destinies of two others in my palm?"

"Hush." Zara clutched her hand tighter, closed her eyes, and began to sway as if to a melody only she could hear. "Destiny falls like a stone into still water. The circles flow ever outward, encompassing other lives, crossing invisible boundaries."

In the distant kennels, the dogs added their voices to the howl of the wind. Zara winced at the sound. "I see blood and fire, loss and reunion, and a love so great that neither time nor death can destroy it."

The harshly whispered words hung, suspended like dust motes, in the dimness. Juliana sat motionless, part of her perfectly aware that Zara was a practiced trickster who could no more see the future than could her brother's favorite troika pony. Yet deep inside Juliana something moved and shifted, grew warm like an ember fanned by the breath of the wind. She sensed a bright magic in Zara's words, and for all that they were but vague prophecies, they embedded themselves in her heart.

A love so great. Is that what she would find with Alexei? She had met him only once.

He was handsome and youthful, merry eyed and ambitious. But love?

Questions crowded into her throat, but before she could speak, an owl hooted softly from the rafters of the barn.

"Bengui!" Zara dropped Juliana's hand. Fear shone sleek in her eyes.

"What's the matter?" Juliana asked. "Zara, what are you hiding?"

Zara shaped her fingers into a sign to ward off evil. "The owl sings to Bengui — to the devil." Her voice trembled. "It is a clear portent of . . ."

"Of what?" Faintly, Juliana heard the drumbeat of hooves. Not so much heard it as felt the deep rhythm in the pit of her stomach. "Zara, it's merely a barn owl. What could it possibly portend?"

"Death," Zara said, jumping up and running to the stall where her children slept.

Juliana shivered. "That's ridic—"

The barn door banged open. In a swirl of blowing snow, lit from behind by the icy glow of the moon, Laszlo entered. Behind him came Chavula, Zara's husband. Both men's swarthy faces appeared taut with terror.

Chavula spoke rapidly in the Romany tongue. Then he spied Juliana, and the color slid from his cheeks. "God!" he said in Russian. "Don't let her see!"

Cold apprehension gripped Juliana. "What's happening, Chavula?" She moved toward the door.

Laszlo stood in her way. "Do not go outside."

Anger rushed up to join with her fear. "You have no right to order me about. Step aside."

Juliana took advantage of his hesitation. She pushed past him and stepped out into the blustering snow.

The wind tore at her cloak. Swirling snowflakes pelted her face, and she squinted through the storm in the direction of the main house.

An eerie red glow lit the rambling mansion.

Juliana screamed.

The house was ablaze. Her family and all the servants were in danger. Her beloved windhounds and hunting dogs were confined to the kennels adjacent to the kitchen.

Laszlo yelled a command to Chavula. Lifting her skirts, Juliana raced toward the house. She felt Laszlo grab at her sleeve, but she shook him off.

She ran as if her feet had wings, skimming over the soft snow rather than sinking into the drifts. She saw flames lashing from the windows, heard the yelp of a dog and the whinny of a horse.

But the horses were all stabled for the night. The thought slid through her panicked mind, then disappeared like water through a sieve.

As she was crossing the broad lawn where snowclad bushes and arbors created soft hillocks, she heard heavy breathing behind her.

"Juliana, stop. I beg you."

"No, Laszlo," she called over her shoulder. "My family —" Papa. Mama. The boys and their nurse. Alexei. New urgency increased her speed.

Laszlo's hand gripped the hood of her cloak. He hauled back, and the sudden motion caused her feet to fly out from under her. She hit the ground with a muffled thud, landing beneath a snow-draped weeping mulberry. A shower of snow half buried her.

She opened her mouth to scream. Laszlo's hand, in a smelly leather mitten, clapped itself over her parted lips, and all she managed was a huff of frantic rage.

Pinning her to the ground with his own body, Laszlo spoke softly into her ear. "I am sorry, little Gaja, but I had to stop you. You do not know what is happening here."

She wrenched away from his hand. "Then

I must go and see —"

A series of loud pops punctuated the air.

"Gunfire!" Laszlo dragged her deeper into the cavelike shelter of the snow-covered mulberry. With a shaking hand, he parted the lower branches to reveal the front of the house.

Shock robbed Juliana of speech. She lay as motionless as a gilt icon. The flames were brighter now, fed by the high winter wind, roaring like giant tongues from the windows and casting bloodred shadows on the ground.

A group of horsemen rode up and down in front of the house. Their mounts were skittish, mist pluming from their distended nostrils and snow flying from beneath their hooves.

At the base of the stone staircase, a black shape lay on the ground.

"Gregor!"

Her mother's voice. The edge of tormented agony was one Juliana had never heard before. Natalya Romanov flung herself upon the shape. Even as her cries keened with the sharpness of grief, a broad-shouldered man in a fur hat and black boots strode forward. His wicked curved sword flashed in the firelight.

Natalya Romanov's screams stopped.

"Mama!" Juliana tried to scramble out from beneath the bush, but Laszlo held her fast.

"Be still," he whispered. "There is nothing you can do."

Nothing. Nothing to do but watch the murder of her family. She spied Alexei rushing to and fro, and for a moment hope crested inside her. Perhaps Alexei would save her brothers.

But as quickly as he had appeared, he faded from sight, surrounded by menacing attackers and roaring flames.

It was evil torture for Juliana to lie there, helpless, as if in the grip of the hideous nightmare. The assassins struck like a storm. They were no band of outlaws but soldiers, doubtless under the command of one of her father's many rivals. Fyodor Glinsky from across the river — only the week before, the rival lord had called her father a traitor.

"Shield your eyes, little one," Laszlo begged her.

She sobbed into her cold hands, but she would not look away. It was too late to help her loved ones, for the soldiers were swift. Their shadows loomed like demons on the fire-colored snow. In seconds she saw Mikhail's throat slit, little Boris fly backward as a man shot him at close range. Servants were herded like cattle into the courtyard and stabbed. The dogs, loosed from the kennel, were slaughtered as they lunged at the invaders.

Her entire glittering world, once so full of opulent promise, shattered like a house of spun sugar.

Juliana's mouth opened in a voiceless scream. Her hand closed convulsively around her pearl-and-ruby brooch. The priceless piece had been a gift from her father. The cruciform shape concealed a tiny stabbing dagger, but the weapon was useless against the swords and sabers and firing pieces of the soldiers.

The snap and hiss of the flames invaded the snow-insulated quiet of the night. Then a dog barked. Squinting, Juliana saw two men locked in a struggle. One of them was Alexei, she was sure of it! She closed her eyes and offered a brief, frantic prayer for his safety.

The baying of a dog caused her to open her eyes. One of the windhounds leaped out of the shadows and clamped its jaws around a booted leg. Juliana heard a muffled curse. *"Be damned to hell!"* As one man fell to the ground, she saw the stark outline of his cheek above a thick beard and felt a stab of awareness, but the feeling quickly dissolved into the eerie horror of blood and flame.

A blade flashed, met the animal's shoulder. The dog sped yelping into the night.

Through a drumbeat of shock, Juliana heard male voices rolling across the lawn.

". . . find the girl?"

"Not yet."

"Devil take you. Look again. We can't let a child of Gregor Romanov live."

"I'm here," Juliana called to them, but her voice was only a dry whisper. "Yes, I am here. Come for me!"

"Fool!" Laszlo covered her mouth again. "What will it serve to sacrifice yourself to these boyars, as well?"

Like the bitter winter wind, comprehension swept over Juliana. Boyars. Jealous, power-hungry nobles. They had killed her father, her family, her fiancé.

She remembered the whispered arguments between her parents. Over the fearful objections of her mother, Gregor had helped the grand prince draw up a new will on his deathbed, one that slashed the powers of the boyars. Now Juliana understood her mother's fear. The nobles would murder even women and children to seize control of the realm.

"Search the outbuildings," one of the soldiers called.

She turned her tortured gaze to Laszlo and whispered, "Help me."

"We must hurry." He dragged her from beneath the bush. "Keep low and to the shadows," he said, taking her by the hand. They skirted the lawn, her neck prickling in anticipation of the sting of a razor-edged blade.

They reached the barn and slipped inside. Moonglow shone through gaps in the wood siding.

Zara, Chavula and the children were gone. Only the faint scent of burnt oil from the lamp lingered.

Yet in the crossties between the stalls stood Gregor's two swiftest horses, bred for speed and endurance in the vast and distant steppes. The mounts had been saddled, and they stood with heads low, blowing softly into the chill air.

"Quickly, get on," Laszlo said, cupping his linked hands to receive her booted foot.

A muffled explosion sounded. Juliana looked through the open door to see that part of the palace roof had caved in, shooting a plume of sparks into the night sky. The sudden rush of firelight outlined three figures jogging toward the barn.

"We'll leave through the grazing pasture,"

Laszlo said, shouldering open a door in the rear.

Juliana bent low over the neck of her mount and slapped the reins. Her mind retreated and cringed in agony. The winter darkness swallowed the two riders as they headed toward the river Volkhov. They skirted the earthwork ramparts and walls of the kremlin of Novgorod, its torchlit towers speeding past in a blur of light.

The snow-muffled thunder of hooves startled the sleepy tollman at the wooden Veliky Bridge, but Juliana and Laszlo had stormed across by the time he roused himself to demand payment.

They galloped through the small merchant district of the town. Dogs barked and someone shouted, but the riders paid no heed. Not until the road had diminished to a snow-covered track and the naked woods walled them on two sides did they slow their pace to a lope.

"Someone is following us," Laszlo said.

Juliana whipped a glance over her shoulder. A narrow shadow slipped toward them.

Laszlo yanked a dagger from his sleeve.

"No!" Juliana said, dismounting in a billow of skirts and cloak. "It's only Pavlo." In moments the huge *borzoya* filled her arms. Pavlo was but a year old, her favorite and one she had been charged with training. She was not surprised the dog had caught up with them. The windhounds were bred to run with breathtaking speed, tirelessly, for miles, to exhaust a wolf so the hunters could bring it down.

"Pavlo." She buried her face in the deep fur of the dog's neck.

And smelled blood.

"He's been hurt, Laszlo." She plucked an image from the midst of her nightmare — a dog leaping, the slash of a blade, a forgotten curse followed by a pitiful animal yelp.

Laszlo was crouched in the path, examining something. "He's left a trail of blood, Gaja. I am sorry, but we must leave him."

Juliana struck away his sharp dagger. "Don't you dare." Her voice held a hardness, a note she had never heard before. It was the voice of a stranger, no longer a girl but a woman who had seen hell. "By God's light, Laszlo, he's all I have now."

The gypsy muttered something in Romany. He found a strip of material and bound the wound in the dog's shoulder. Moments later, they were on their way again.

Laszlo pushed ahead with unwavering purpose. Only when the silver thread of dawn glittered on the snowy horizon did

Juliana ask the obvious question.

"Laszlo, where are we going?"

He hesitated, then cast his gaze west, away from the rising sun. "To a place I have heard of in the songs of my people. A place called England."

England. It was but a vague idea in Juliana's mind, a few words on the page of a book she had once read. A murky, misty land of barbarians. Her tutor, a glib and gifted man, had taught her the language so he could read her odd poems of adventure and virtue triumphant.

"But why so far?" she asked. "I should go to Alexei's family in Moscow to tell them what befell their son."

"No." Laszlo spoke harshly, and the shadows hid his face. "It is too dangerous. The assassins could be neighbors, people you once trusted."

Juliana shivered, thinking of Fyodor Glinsky and all her father's rivals. "But . . . *England,*" she said in a dazed voice.

"If we stay here," Laszlo said, "they will hunt you down and kill you. You *heard* them, little one. I dare not risk a journey to Moscow."

Exhausted by loss, she closed her eyes and drew a deep breath. But in the darkness behind her eyelids she saw it again — death, blood, fire, all painted in the bright red hues of savagery.

Juliana forced her eyes open. The rising sun cast a ray of weak winter light on a dead snow-covered leaf that lay in the path.

Then she remembered the prophecy. Zara had whispered it to her only the night before, but an eternity had passed since then.

The first will travel far.

One

Richmond Palace, England
1538

Stephen de Lacey, baron of Wimberleigh, walked into the Royal Bedchamber to find his betrothed in bed with the king.

His face as cold and unflinching as a Holbein portrait, Stephen stared at the dark-eyed Welsh beauty all but hidden beneath the quilted silk counterpane. A hissing tide of resentment roiled deep inside him, threatening to drown him. Clenching his fists at his sides, Stephen conquered the turmoil within. Through deliberately blank eyes, he looked at King Henry VIII.

"My liege," he said, bowing stiffly, inhaling the scent of dried lavender and bergamot from the sachets in the bed hangings. By the time he straightened up, the king's attendants had arrived to groom their sovereign for the day.

"Ah, Wimberleigh." The king put out his

arms as an attendant scurried forward and helped him don a loose silk jacket. Henry smiled. In that smile there lingered yet a hint of the old charm, the derring-do of a golden young prince. A prince whom Stephen, as a boy, had idolized as the second Arthur.

The legendary Arthur had died young, in a blaze of glory. Henry had made the mistake of living on into the corrupt mediocrity of middle age.

"Come, come," said Henry, beckoning. He swung his swollen legs over the side of the bed and pushed his pale feet into a pair of brocade slippers held by a kneeling servant. "You may approach the royal bed. See what I've found you."

As he crossed the huge room, Stephen felt the searing curiosity of the sovereign's attendants. By now the chamber was crowded with titled gentlemen, all engaged to supervise the most intimate bodily functions of the king — and also to influence the policies of the realm.

Sir Lambert Wilmeth, groom of the stool, took His Majesty's bowel movements as seriously as Scottish border disputes. Lord Harold Blodsmoor, surveyor of the wardrobe, regarded the king's collection of shoes as highly as the crown jewels. Yet at the moment, the attention of these great gentlemen burned into Stephen de Lacey.

The girl smiled shyly and even managed to summon an artful blush. She stretched with catlike grace, a bare shoulder emerging from the bedclothes. Like most of the king's mistresses, she took a perverse pride in sharing the bed of the sovereign.

After so many betrayals, Stephen should have known better than to trust the king. Should have known that the summons could only mean more petty cruelty.

"I was feeling frisky today." Henry's grin held both mischief and subtle rancor. Limping slightly, he went to the royal stool, speaking over his shoulder as he relieved himself. "I decided to exercise the droit du seigneur — again. An antiquated notion, to be sure, but one that has its merits and deserves to be revived from time to time. Now, make a gracious greeting to your lady Gwenyth, and then we'll —"

"Sire," Stephen broke in, heedless of the gasps from the noblemen present. No one interrupted the king. In the thirty years of his reign, Henry VIII had put men to death for lesser offenses.

Instantly Stephen regretted the risk he had taken. With that one blurted word he might have jeopardized everything.

"Yes?" The king seemed only mildly annoyed as his gentlemen helped him into doublet and hose. "What is it, Wimberleigh?"

Stephen couldn't help himself. A killing rage rose like a fountain of fire inside him. "To hell with your droit du seigneur."

He turned on his heel and strode from the Royal Bedchamber. Though well aware of the infraction he was committing, he could not be a willing player in the familiar, vicious diversion that so delighted Henry.

The red-and-white livery of the king's Welsh yeomen passed in a blur as Stephen strode out into the paved central court. Seeking a place to cool his temper in private, he stalked into a walled garden. A pebbled path led him through tortured little plots of whitethorn and sweetbriar. The flower beds had been arranged geometrically, so that they resembled rather coarse mosaics.

Stephen wished for the hundredth time that he had ignored the king's annual summons and stayed in Wiltshire.

But to refuse the command was to risk the one thing Stephen would kill to safeguard. If the price of keeping his secret was to have his heart ripped out and his pride publicly shredded, then so be it.

His conviction that the king hadn't finished with him proved correct, for an hour later, a haughty majordomo summoned him to the Presence Chamber.

An open-timbered ceiling arched high over the hall. The watery sunlight of early spring streamed in through twin banks of mullioned windows. Colored glass made a shifting, jeweled pattern on the walls and floor. Somewhere, an unseen lute player strummed softly, the shimmering music a sweet undercurrent to the murmur of voices.

Members of the Privy Council stood by, sharp eyed, their shoulders hunched beneath heavy, long robes.

Stephen paced over the smooth flagstones to the gold-and-scarlet-draped dais. There he stopped, swept his satin-lined cloak back over one shoulder, and sank into a formal obeisance. Even without looking at the king, he knew Henry relished the submissive pose of a man of Stephen's height. Henry took pleasure in anything that made Stephen feel smaller.

He rose with hatred and defiance clear in his eyes, and a gift in his extended hands.

Henry sat upon his massive carved chair, looking like Bacchus clad in silver and gold. In recent years, his face had grown as large as a haunch of beef.

"What's this?" he asked, nodding to a

page. The lad took the small wooden coffer from Stephen and offered it to the king. With childlike haste, Henry opened it and extracted a tiny watch on a golden chain. "Marry, my lord, you never fail to amaze me."

"A trinket, no more," Stephen said in a flat, dead voice. Henry had many appetites, most of them insatiable. Satisfying his craving for unique gifts was no challenge.

Henry slipped the chain through the baldric that encircled his ample girth. "I assume the design is original."

Stephen nodded.

"You've a rare talent for inventions of all sorts, Wimberleigh. A pity you are so lacking in plain manners." The breadth of his cheeks made his eyes look beady, his mouth thin lipped and tight. "You left the Royal Bedchamber without begging leave, my lord."

"So I did, sire."

Henry's hand, pudgy and sparkling with rings, smacked down on the arm of his chair. His fingers strangled a carved gargoyle. "Damn your eyes, Wimberleigh. Must you always breach the limits of propriety and decorum?"

"Only when provoked, sire."

The king's expression did not change, yet

his small bright eyes took fire. “Has it never occurred to you,” he asked in a soft, deadly voice, “that you might do better to dance with your betrothed rather than with my patience? Lady Gwenyth is beautiful. She’s well-bred and reasonably wealthy.”

“She is also ruined, sire.”

“I did honor to the wench,” Henry snapped. “There is only one king of England, just as there is only one sun. My favor is not for one alone.”

Stephen bit his tongue to stop himself from responding. It was useless to quarrel with a man who likened himself to a heavenly body. He could satisfy his every whim all too easily, for what sane man or woman would dare refuse him?

“For God’s sake, Stephen,” Henry thundered, “your evasiveness bedevils me. I’ve found you four eligible ladies in the past year, and you’ve refused them all. What is it that makes you so much better than any other noble?”

“I do not wish to marry again,” Stephen stated. He could not resist adding, “My favor is for no one, not even that silly Welsh comfit I found in your bed.”

“Comfits are sweet and agreeable to the palate,” Henry pointed out.

“Aye, but when handled by too many

fingers, they lose their savor. And when left long enough to themselves, they rot."

Without taking his eyes off Stephen, the king held out his hand. A servitor stepped forward and placed in it a silver cup of sack. Henry drank deeply of the Canary wine, then said, "Ah. Still you pine for your Margaret, now seven years cold."

With all that he was, Stephen resisted the urge to bury his fist in his sovereign's face. How blithely Henry spoke of Meg — as if he had never even known her at all.

"Was she so very dear to you, then," the king went on, twisting the knife, "that you cannot love another?"

Stephen held himself motionless as his mind filled with memories of Meg. Peeking at him timidly from behind her veil on their wedding day. Weeping in pain and fear in their marriage bed. Hiding her secrets from the husband who adored her. Dying in a sea of blood and bitter curses.

"Margaret was —" Stephen cleared his throat "— a child. Gullible. Easily impressed." With terrible, blade-sharp guilt, he knew he had forced her into womanhood and then into motherhood. And finally and most unforgivably, into death.

"I know well what it is to mourn a wife," Henry said, an unexpected note of sympathy in his voice. Stephen knew he was thinking of quiet, dutiful Jane Seymour, who had died giving the king the one gift he craved above all others: a male heir to the throne.

"However," Henry continued, imperious again, "a wife is a necessary ornament to a man's station, and old memories should not make you balk at duty. Now. As to the Welsh lady —"

"Sire, I humbly beg your pardon." He dropped his voice so only the king could hear. "I will not take any man's leavings — not even those of the king of England. I'll not be a salve to your conscience."

"My conscience?" Henry's mouth curved into a cold sickle of amusement. His voice was a whisper meant for Stephen alone. "My dear lord of Wimberleigh, where on earth did you get the notion that I had one?"

Stephen's neck tingled. He reminded himself that Henry VIII had put aside his first wife and brought about the execution of the second. He had appropriated the authority of the church, taken possession of monasteries, driven the poor from their lands. The mere ruining of a young virgin would hardly trouble a man like Henry Tudor.

"My mistake," Stephen replied softly. "But never mind, the Lady Gwenyth would not want me anyway."

"Ah, your tarnished reputation," Henry said, waving his now-empty cup. "Wild revels, gambling and rapine. The gossip does find its way to court. Marry, sir, every maiden in the realm quails in fright at the very thought of you."

Stephen preferred it that way. He had worked hard to hide his few good qualities beneath a patina of ill repute. "I am a man of low morals. An unfortunate flaw in my character. And now if it please Your Majesty, I must withdraw from court."

With a swiftness that belied his age and bulk, the king came out of his chair. His thick-fingered hand closed in the front of Stephen's quilted doublet. "By God, it does *not* please me." He put his face very close to Stephen's, so close that Stephen could smell the warm sweetness of sack on his breath. "Get you a wife, Wimberleigh, and then get you a proper heir, else all of England will know what you hide at your Wiltshire estate."

An animal roar of denial surged to Stephen's throat. With an effort born of years of iron control, he forced himself to keep from tearing into the royal face. How Henry had come to know Stephen's terrible secret was a mystery; how he intended to use the knowledge was becoming painfully obvious.

With a will, Stephen expelled his breath slowly and stepped back. The king no longer gripped him, yet the hold lingered invisibly — would linger until Stephen shed himself once and for all of the king's ire.

"To your knees, Wimberleigh."

His cheeks on fire with rage, Stephen sank down.

"Now swear it. Let me hear you vow that you will obey me." The king's voice rang loud. "Let me hear that you will wed — if not Lady Gwenyth, then another."

The command hung, suspended, in the deafening silence that followed. From his low perspective, Stephen caught details with uncommon clarity: the ancient dust clinging to the hem of the king's cloak, the faint, septic smell of the ulcer on Henry's leg, the soft *chink* of the sovereign's chain of office as his massive chest rose and fell, and the dying echo of a plucked lute string.

All the court waited in a state of breath-held anticipation. The king had flung down the gauntlet, had challenged one of the few men in the realm who dared defy him.

Stephen de Lacey was no fool, and he valued his neck. The years, at least, had taught him to equivocate. "Your will be done, sire." He spoke clearly so all could hear, for he knew if he mumbled the pledge, the king would make him repeat it.

A collective sigh came from the Privy Councillors. How they loved seeing one of their own humiliated.

Henry lowered his vast bulk onto the throne. "I trust you'll obey this time."

Stephen stood. The king dismissed him with a curt nod. Almost immediately, Henry began to bellow for his attendants. "Saddle my horse, I wish to go riding."

Stephen left the Presence Chamber and passed through the antechamber. The air of corruption lingered even here, in the heavy scent of sandalwood burning in a corner brazier, in the stale mats of rushes that had not been changed in months.

Prior to his audience, Stephen had requested that his horse be brought out, for he wanted to be away swiftly. The grooms of the royal stables had promised to have the tall Neapolitan mare ready outside the west gate.

Stephen strode across the courtyard and passed between the octagonal-shaped twin towers. He paused beneath the ornate portcullis, the pointed wrought-iron bars aimed straight down at his head.

As promised, his mare stood ready in saddle and trappings, tethered to an iron loop in the shade of a spreading oak some distance beyond the gatehouse.

He frowned at the negligence of the grooms. Didn't they know better than to leave a valuable animal unattended? And where the devil was Kit, his squire?

Cocking his head, Stephen saw a movement beside the mare. A wraithlike shadow, secretive as an unconfessed sin.

A filthy gypsy woman was stealing his horse.

Juliana could not believe her luck. So desperately had she needed a horse for the fair in Runnymede tomorrow, she had been prepared to enter the very walls of the riverside palace and boldly steal an animal.

Instead, as she crouched in a stand of copper beeches and regarded the glistening walls and gilt turrets of Richmond Palace, a groom had emerged with one of the most magnificent beasts she had ever seen. The horse was fitted out with trappings of silver and Morocco leather that would, if traded, feed the gypsy tribe for a decade.

Pavlo, her windhound, had scared the lad off. By now it was a common ploy. No Englishman had ever seen a *borzoya,* and most thought the huge white dog some sort of mythical beast.

She glanced around to gauge the chances of being caught. A pair of guards in Kendal green-and-white livery stood sentinel in front of the twin gate towers about two hundred paces distant. Their blank gazes were trained on the horizon of the hills that rose above the river Thames; they paid no heed to the horse standing quietly in the shadows.

Juliana paused to touch her luck token — the dagger brooch she wore pinned inside the waistband of her skirt. Then she crept out of the beech grove. The matted grass was damp and springy beneath her bare feet, and her anklets of cheap tin clicked softly with each step. Her skirts, constructed of pieced-together bits of fabric, brushed the ground.

After five years of living among the gypsies of England, she had grown accustomed to looking like a beggarwoman — and to behaving like one when necessary. She accepted her lot with a sort of weary resignation that belied the purpose that still burned in her heart.

Never had she forgotten her identity: Juliana Romanov, daughter of a nobleman, betrothed to a boyar. One day, she vowed, she would return to her home. She would find the men who had murdered her family.

She would see the killers brought to justice.

It was a grand undertaking for a penniless girl. The early months in England had been almost hopelessly hard. She and Laszlo, who posed as her father, had bartered her clothes and jewels, bit by bit, on the long journey to England. She had arrived with nothing save her precious brooch, the glittering jewel encircled by twelve matched pearls, the secret blade inside, and the Romanov motto etched in Cyrillic characters on the back: *Blood, vows and honor.*

It was her last link with the privileged girl she had been. Never would she trade it away.

In time, the shock of losing her family had become a dull, constant ache. Juliana threw herself into her new life with the same determined concentration that had so pleased her riding and dancing masters, her tutor and music teacher, in Novgorod.

She had learned how to barter for a horse in apparently ill health, heal the animal, conceal its defects, and then sell it back to the Gaje for profit. How to appear at a market square looking like the most bedraggled, afflicted of creatures, so filthy that people gave her coin simply to be rid of her. How to perform breathtaking carnival tricks on horseback and afterward, with a lazy, seductive smile, collect coins thrown by her rapt spectators.

Life might have gone on like this indefinitely, but for Rodion.

Juliana shuddered as she thought of him — young, crudely handsome, glaring across the campfire at her with a sort of cruel possessiveness hard on his features.

The inevitable marriage proposal had come last night. Laszlo had advised her to accept Rodion. Unlike her, Laszlo had long since surrendered any dreams of returning to the old country.

Not so Juliana.

Rodion's plans had spurred her on her quest. The time had come to leave the gypsy train, to present herself to the king of England and request an armed escort back to Novgorod.

Her first order of business was to obtain a set of proper attire. She had become adept at pilfering food from market carts and washing pegged out on lines. A fancy court dress was much more of a challenge.

In the past, the men of the tribe had taken all her earnings. This handsome mare was for her alone.

A smile tugged at the corners of her mouth. The town of Runnymede held its horse fair starting at dawn tomorrow. She would make the sale quickly, then put her plan into motion.

"Stay here, Pavlo," she whispered. The large, shaggy dog cast a worried look at her, but lay down and settled his long muzzle between his front paws.

Crouching low, Juliana approached the horse from the front, slightly to one side. "There, my pretty," she whispered to warn it of her presence. "You're a pretty mare, that you are."

The horse ceased its browsing in the tufts of clover at the base of the tree. Its nostrils dilated, and Juliana heard the soft huff of its breath. The well-shaped ears lay back.

Juliana made a low clicking sound with the back of her tongue, and the ears eased up a little. She held out her hand, palm up, offering the horse a pared turnip she had filched from someone's kitchen garden.

The mare devoured the raw turnip and nudged Juliana's hand for more. She smiled. For all their strength and speed and endurance, horses were simple creatures easily led by their appetites. Not unlike men, Catriona would say.

Though tension burned in her shoulders and the need for haste pressed at her, she fed the mare another piece of turnip and moved close, running her hand down one side of the smooth, firm neck and up the other. All the time, she kept up a soft patter of speech, English words, mostly nonsense, the lulling language of a mother soothing a child to sleep. In moments, she knew the horse was relaxed and docile.

She glanced at the gate; the guards had neither stirred nor noticed her. A man appeared beneath the portcullis. From this distance, she had only the swift impression that he was tall, broad and tawny haired.

Filled with a sense of impending triumph, Juliana untied the braided cord that secured the horse to the iron loop. She placed one bare foot in the stirrup and reached for the raised cantle of the saddle to hoist herself up.

"Stop, thief!"

For a fraction of a heartbeat, the shout froze her. But in the next instant, Juliana swung up as if lifted by the hand of God and landed astraddle. Without breaking the flow of motion, she slammed her heels against the sides of the horse and made a loud smooching sound.

The horse took off like an arrow shot from a bow. Juliana gloried in the sensation of riding the best horse she had mounted since her frantic flight from Novgorod five years before.

■ ■ ■ ■

"I see the gypsy's stealing your horse, Wimberleigh."

Stephen was so shocked to see the woman galloping off astride Capria that he had not realized King Henry, surrounded by his entourage, had appeared on the high walk between the gate towers.

"She'll not get far," Stephen stated loudly. He whirled toward the stables where a groom was leading a saddled hunter out into the yard. "Bring me that horse at once," he shouted.

The groom looked momentarily confused. Then, apparently convinced by the thunderous scowl on Stephen's face, he hurried toward the gate with the horse.

"I'll make you a wager." Henry shaded his eyes and squinted at the fleeing figure of the woman, tattered skirts and tangled hair flying on the wind. "A hundred crowns says you'll never see that mare again."

"Done," Stephen snapped, mounting the hunter. He dug in his spurs and clattered across the bridge, out onto the open road. The horse had an indifferent gallop and a hard mouth. Stephen would have a bit of a chase on his hands, for Capria was the superior animal. And, he conceded, the gypsy wench was a skilled rider.

She flew past a grove of copper beeches, and a large white dog joined her on the road. Surprise stabbed at Stephen. The lanky, long-haired dog was nearly as swift as the horse.

He bent low over the pumping neck of the hunter. The brown clay road streaked beneath him in a blur. The gypsy whipped a glance back and banged her bare heels against Capria's sides.

Stephen closed a bit more of the distance between them. A sense of certainty surged up in him. He did not have to ride the woman down. He knew another way to bring Capria back. He needed only to get within earshot.

When he was sure his quarry lay close enough, he put his fingers to his lips. Shaping his mouth with his fingers, he emitted a long, ear-splitting whistle.

The mare jerked her head to the side. The reins slipped from the gypsy's grasp. Capria slid to a stop, wheeled, and charged back the way she had come.

"No!" The thief's faint cry carried across the undulating downs along the river. She groped for the flying reins, but the whiplike length of leather eluded her.

Stephen took a dark pleasure in her struggle. A lesser rider would have fallen, possibly to her death, but the woman's legs stayed tight around the horse's girth, her feet firmly in the stirrups.

With her throat locked in terror and her hands gripping the mare's gray mane, Juliana exhorted the horse to turn, or at the very least to stop.

But the stubborn creature only did so when it reached a large man standing beside a horse in the middle of the road. Catching the loose rein, he held out a treat in his other hand.

A crushing sense of defeat caved in on Juliana, but she gave herself not a moment for regrets. Even before the mare came to a full stop, she hit the ground running.

Her head jerked back, and she felt a tearing pain. She loosed a low, throaty scream. The villain had hold of her long braid.

She kicked out with her bare feet, bruising them against the man's tall boots. She scratched, digging her claws into his neck, his ears, anywhere she could reach.

The fight lasted mere seconds. With perfunctory swiftness, he used the leather reins to lash her wrists together.

"Now then." His voice was a deep rumble

of anger.

"Pavlo!" Juliana screamed.

The dog lunged. A hundredweight of muscle and fur hurled itself at the unsuspecting man.

Pavlo's yelp of pain pierced the air. Juliana blinked in amazement. Somehow, the man had grabbed Pavlo's crimson vellat collar and twisted, choking off the dog's windpipe.

"It would be a pity," he said, his tone infuriatingly blasé, "to destroy so magnificent an animal. But I shall, wench, unless you command it off the attack."

Juliana did not hesitate. Nothing, not even her own freedom, was more precious to her than Pavlo. "Let up, Pavlo," she said in Russian. "Easy, boy."

The dog submitted, relaxing his knotted muscles and emitting a strangled whine. The man eased his grip on the collar and then let go. "I wonder," he said. "Is this a case for the sheriff or the palace warden?"

"No!" Juliana had learned to loathe and fear the sheriffs of England. She plunged to her knees in front of her captor, her bound hands held high in supplication. "My lord, I beg you! Do not turn me over to the sheriff!"

"Christ's bones, woman." His face flushed with chagrin, he gave her sleeve a tug. "Get up. I mislike begging."

Heaving a sigh of resignation, Juliana stood. Vaguely she became aware of movement high on the walk between the two towers of the distant palace gate, but her gaze stayed riveted on her captor. He was garbed as a gentleman, in a costume of such exaggerated virility that she blushed. An abbreviated doublet allowed his white shirt to billow forth. Huge sleeves with clever slashings bloomed from the armholes. Tight particolored hose hugged his long legs, his muscular thighs, and culminated in an immense codpiece all decked with silver braid.

A large hand, surprisingly gentle, touched her under the chin and drew her gaze upward. "Nothing but trouble there," he said, a faint note of cynical amusement in his voice.

With the fire in her cheeks intensifying, she studied his face. He was clean shaven, an attribute that never failed to shock her, for Russian and gypsy men alike always wore full beards. Framed by a mane of wheat-colored hair, this man's face was smooth and stark, with chiseled angles that bespoke strength — and intimidating power.

Fear fluttered in her chest. It was his eyes that discomfited her. They were unusual, of the palest, opaque blue, cold as moonstones.

She peered into the icy blankness and was startled at what she saw there. A hard, tight pleasure. As if he had enjoyed the chase.

Suddenly the thought of being handed over to the sheriff did not seem so dire as tarrying in the company of this huge, forbidding lord.

But instinct told her not to show fear. She tossed her head. "You've got your horse back. She's a disobedient nag anyway, so why don't you let me go on my way?"

The man's mouth tightened. His version of a sardonic smile, she decided.

"Disobedient?" Absently he fed the mare a morsel from a pouch that hung from his wide, ornate belt. "Nay, just greedy. Capria learned long ago that to come to my whistle meant to win a bit of marzipan."

Before she could catch herself, Juliana mouthed the unfamiliar word.

"Almond sugar," the man said pleasantly enough. He held out a pasty-looking morsel. "Would you like some?"

She turned up her nose in resentment. The horse snatched at the tidbit.

"Where did you learn to ride like that?" her captor asked.

Juliana hesitated, wondering which lie to tell. If she admitted she had polished her considerable skills with the gypsies, it would endanger the band, for the Romany people were rarely welcome among gentlefolk. Unexpectedly, she heard herself blurting out the truth. "I learned from my father's riding master. In Novgorod, a kingdom of Russia north of Muscovy."

The man lifted one tawny eyebrow. "Not only a horse thief, but a lunatic, as well. How long has it been since you escaped Bedlam?"

"Not only a bully, but a braying ass, too," she shot back.

"Lord Wimberleigh!" A man in palace livery came pounding along the road. "You've collared the horse thief, then."

"It appears that I have, Sir Bodely."

"Well done, my lord, and you gave His Majesty a few moments of diversion in the process. Though I trow he'll not look kindly on losing the bet."

"Your prisoner, Sir Bodely," Wimberleigh said with a mocking bow. He grinned at Juliana. "The palace warden's thief taker, at your service."

Sir Bodely's brows beetled together. "A wench, is it? Looks gypsy to me." With swift, jerky movements, he bound her hands with coarse rope and gave the discarded reins to Lord Wimberleigh.

From a belt overhung with an ale-swiller's

gut were the tools of the thief-taker's trade: a black whip, manacles, and hobbles.

Wimberleigh's gaze fixed on the savage utensils. His eyes turned flinty, and beneath his billowing sleeves, his shoulders hunched. He turned away. "I'd best be on my way, then."

In a red haze of fury and fear, Juliana called out, "Are all great lords as cowardly as you, sir?"

His back stiffened, and he swung around to regard her with the respect he might afford a spider. "Were you addressing me?"

"You are the only cowardly lord present at the moment."

His eyebrows slid upward. "So. You find me cowardly, do you?"

Gingerly she lifted her bound hands. "You are quick to accuse me of stealing your horse, yet you balk at staying to see me punished. What is the penalty for my crime? Hanging? Or perhaps since I failed in my endeavor, I shall merely have my nostrils slit or a hand or an ear cut off. A true man would not lack the stomach to watch."

His squarish jaw tightened. He addressed the palace official. "Will the wench have a chance to face her accuser in a court of law?"

Juliana held her breath. *The law always*

reads against the gypsy. Laszlo had drummed that lesson into her head. But despite the past five years, she was not a gypsy. She was of noble birth. Her kin had been great princes and rulers. She would convince the court of her true identity and soon have the insolent Wimberleigh groveling at her feet.

The brassy blare of a horn scattered her thoughts. Out of the gates came a party of mounted noblemen, their persons arrayed even more sumptuously than Lord Wimberleigh's. Retainers swarmed around the gentlemen, boys trotting at their stirrups, a few clutching lead reins.

Sir Bodely doubled over in an obeisance so deep it looked painful. Even Wimberleigh bowed. Juliana simply stared, and with unerring instinct she picked out the king of England.

He rode a roan hunter. His saddle was huge, no doubt specially constructed to accommodate his ponderous weight. Henry of England was as impressive as Grand Prince Vasily had been. Like a proper boyar, the English king wore a full beard. His raiments glittered with gold and silver threads, and his mantle was edged with the black fur of the civet cat.

"My lord of Wimberleigh." The king's

voice was cold and full of hate. "It seems you made the better wager. I thought your mare a lost cause."

A wager?

Juliana felt a hot stab of anger. Her life hung in the balance, and the king and Wimberleigh were settling wagers?

"Tell me, my lord," said the king. "What trick did you play?"

"No trick, sire. I've trained the mare to come to my whistle regardless of her rider. She's as obedient as she is swift."

"The beast is a wonder," cried one of the king's men, clutching his velvet hat to his chest.

"Indeed she is, Francis," Henry replied. "No need to get yourself overwrought." His gaze flicked to Juliana. His small eyes were black and impenetrable. His thin mouth, enclosed in the graying red-gold beard, pressed tight; then the corners lifted in a grin. "An Egyptian wench. Well done, Wimberleigh."

A fresh wave of fear struck at Juliana. "Egyptians," as folk called the gypsies, were considered outlaws. In some areas, they were hunted for sport with prizes awarded to men who managed to kill or wound one.

"Your Majesty." Juliana spoke clearly, aware that a faint accent tinged her words.

"I am no gypsy." Her resonant voice, the carefully formed words, attracted the attention of all. Her goal had been to win an audience with Henry of England. True, she had not anticipated these precise circumstances, but now that she had his attention, she would make the most of it.

Henry loosed a bark of laughter. "It speaks! And rather prettily, I must admit." He reached out his gloves and jeweled hand. "Come here, wench."

"Your Grace, no!" A dark-haired lady on a palfrey beside the king gasped. "She's probably crawling with lice and vermin."

"I don't mean to touch it, Lady Gwenyth. I merely wish to look at it."

With her head held high, Juliana stepped forward. To her constant mortification, she did indeed suffer from frequent infestations of lice, and at the moment she itched from a light case. Still, she refused to surrender her moment with the king. Rope dragging in the powdery earth, she made a graceful, flawless obeisance. A murmur of new interest rippled through the fast-swelling crowd.

Juliana took a deep breath. Borrowing the storyteller's art she had learned from nights around the gypsy campfire, she began to speak.

"My name is Juliana Romanov. I was born

in the kingdom of Muscovy to the royal boyar Gregor Romanov of Novgorod."

From the corner of her eye, Juliana saw two ladies put their heads together and whisper. One of them pointed at Juliana's cold, bare feet.

She ignored them. "It is true that I tried to, er, borrow the horse of Lord Wilberford." She hoped she'd got his name right. "I knew not what else to do. Your Majesty, I am the victim of a terrible injustice. I meant to seek your protection and ask your help for a lady of the blood royal."

Low laughter came from some of the courtiers. Juliana knew they could not see past her tattered gown, her tangled hair, the smudges of ash and road dust on her face.

Yet she had the king's attention. She meant to seize the moment. "Five years ago, Grand Prince Vasily died, and the boyars — whom you call councillors or nobles — warred against each other. A band of mercenaries burned my father's house and murdered my family." She dropped her voice, amazed that even after five years, the nightmare memories still held her in a grip of horror and grief. For a moment, she was back in Novgorod, watching the bloodred flicker of flames on the snow, the tall boots crunching over the drive, the cruel blade of a killer. She heard again the yelp of a dog and a man's muffled curse.

As quickly as it had come, the vision vanished, leaving her drained. "I alone survived, and by God's grace escaped to England."

"Cromwell!" the king bellowed.

The dark-robed man, his clean-shaven face pale, dismounted and stepped forward. "I am here, sire."

"What think you, Sir Thomas? Can this barefoot wench truly be a daughter of Muscovy royalty, or has Wimberleigh bagged us a madwoman?"

Sir Thomas steepled his long, pale fingers. "It is true that Vasily the Third died five years ago, that there was infighting among the boyars. I had it from the Prussian ambassador."

Encouraged, Juliana nodded vigorously. "Then you understand my position. No doubt a prince as lofty as yourself would feel honor bound to give me your full support."

The king chuckled, a charming, musical sound. His mount shifted beneath him as if straining from the burdensome weight. "What sort of support, my lady?"

"A naval escort. Well-armed, of course, for I shall need help in bringing the murderers to justice."

Someone in the riding party laughed outright. Others joined in the mirth. Wimberleigh raised his eyebrows in skepticism. Furious, Juliana did the unthinkable. She plunged her bound hands into the waistband of her skirt and drew forth the Romanov ruby brooch.

"This is proof of my identity," she declared. "My father gave it to me on my thirteenth name day."

" 'Tis paste," Lady Gwenyth declared with a bored sniff.

"Or stolen," said someone else. "We already know she is a thief."

The dark man called Cromwell addressed Sir Bodely. "Take the cozening wench away and hang her."

Though her fingers were numb with terror, Juliana had the presence of mind to slip her brooch back into its hiding place.

Chains and manacles clanking, Sir Bodely advanced. Wimberleigh planted himself in the warden's path. "Free her," he said.

"But, my lord —"

"I said free her," the huge, brooding man repeated. "Her offense — such as it was — is against me. I say she goes free."

The king stroked his beard. "You always did have a soft spot for downtrodden females, eh, Wimberleigh?"

"She's naught but the bride of calamity," Cromwell said, his voice nasal with annoyance. "Surely the baron of Wimberleigh has better causes than —"

"Peace, Thomas." The king held up his hand, then gave a curt nod to Sir Bodely. The warden loosed Juliana's bonds. Her first instinct was to flee, from the crafty king and his court, and most especially the forbidding man who all but held her hostage with his cold glare.

"What say you, Wimberleigh?" the king asked. Cruel laughter danced in his eyes. "Shall we send the wench on her way, or do you want to keep her for yourself?"

Lady Gwenyth tittered behind her hand.

Juliana watched the tall, tawny-haired lord. He did not move a muscle, yet she sensed that he was torn. His craggy face was a mask of sheer dislike — whether of her or the king, she could not tell. She held her breath, waiting for his answer.

Stephen expelled his breath, wondering how he should answer. Knowing that any response would be the wrong one.

Murmurs of laughter rippled from the crowd. As far as they were concerned, this was a farce put on for their entertainment.

In spite of himself, Stephen had to admire the way Juliana bore up under the humiliating mirth of the king and his court. Henry's black-eyed glare had taken down fiercer adversaries than an addlepated gypsy girl, yet she returned his stare with unflinching ferocity.

Almost as if she viewed herself as his equal.

All of Stephen's instincts urged him to send the girl on her way, back to her coarse gypsy people. Then he committed a grave error. He looked into her eyes.

What a world of torment and yearning he saw there, in the flickering green depths. He thought of the husky, exotic cadences of her voice, the curiously accented words. *Your Majesty, I am the victim of a terrible injustice.* He told himself it should not matter; he had no business to concern himself with the troubles of an unwashed half-mad gypsy.

And yet a voice rose inside him — alien, yet wholly from the depths of his heart. "Sire, the choice should be hers."

"Nay," cried Henry, and his tone raised a prickle of suspicion on the back of Stephen's neck. "The choice is mine. If we let the wench wander free, she'll doubtless revert to her thieving ways. This girl, wild as she is, must wed."

A chill touched the base of Stephen's spine. In his mind he heard the echo of the king's command: *Let me hear that you will wed — if not Lady Gwenyth, then another.*

Henry was angry at losing the wager. He had ruined a handful of maidens and his patience was wearing thin. Stephen knew, with a leaden sinking in his gut, that the king had found a new way to indulge his malice.

"*You,* my lord, will marry the wench," Henry proclaimed.

Two

While the courtiers gasped in scandalized disbelief, and Lord Wimberleigh seemed to turn to stone, Juliana folded her arms to contain the frenzied beating of her heart.

"I cannot marry him," she said in a rush. She tried to suppress her accent, but when she was nervous it became more pronounced. "He — he is beneath me."

Uproarious laughter filled the air, and the sound stung like a glowing brand.

"Have you heard nothing I have said?" she shouted. "I am a princess. My father was a Romanov —"

"And mine is the Holy Roman Emperor," said Cromwell, his thin mouth pinched with dry humor.

Sir Bodely nudged her, none too gently. "Show a bit of gratitude, wench. The king just saved you from the gibbet."

She fell silent and still. Marriage to an English lord? But that would mean abandoning the goal that had driven her for five harsh years. It would mean putting aside her plan to return to Novgorod and to punish the assassins who had murdered her family.

King Henry brayed with laughter. "I did nothing of the sort, my good Bodely. I simply left the choice to Wimberleigh. And he chose to let her live."

"So I did," came Wimberleigh's quiet answer. He stood close to her, his presence as threatening as a rain-heavy storm cloud. His light hair swirled about his face, and she noticed tiny fans of tension bracketing his eyes. "But I think we'll both soon find, sweet gypsy, that some things are worse than death."

She stiffened her spine in response to the chill that suddenly touched it. She tore her gaze from Wimberleigh. There was something disturbing about him, a ruthlessness perhaps, and deep in his eyes lurked a glint of raw panic. A dread that matched her own.

"A charming observation, Wimberleigh." King Henry wore a jovial smile that Juliana instinctively mistrusted. Of all the men in England, only this king came close to the splendor she had known every day of her life in Novgorod. The dark raisin eyes darted from her to the baron. "This is an apt way for you to fulfill your vow to me, my lord. You promised to take a wife, yet insisted on a chaste woman. Why not the Egyptian princess, then?"

A fresh wave of laughter burst from the courtiers.

As Stephen watched the small bedraggled captive, she did a most amazing thing. Her dirt-smudged chin rose. Her narrow shoulders squared, and her hands balled into fists at her sides.

It was that stern pride, so incongruous in a girl in tattered skirts and matted hair, that caused Stephen to betray himself.

Summoning his massive frame to its full height, he glared the courtiers into silence. Even as he did so, he cursed himself for a fool. He shouldn't ache for her. He shouldn't defend her.

"Sire," she said, her voice composed, yet still lyrically rhythmic, "it is a great compliment that you find me suitable for so lofty a lord, but I cannot marry this stranger."

"Will it be the gibbet, instead?" the king asked, a cold smile on his face.

Though she did not move a muscle, she turned pale. Only Stephen stood close enough to see the pulse leap at her temple. He wanted to turn away, to shield his eyes from her. He did not want to see her courage or her desperation. He did not want to pity her or — may God forgive him — admire her.

He felt like a blind man in a thorny maze, unable to find a way out. Henry had aged rapidly and badly. He had grown as volatile and unpredictable as the Channel winds. Yet his craving for revenge was as sharp as ever.

"My lord of Wimberleigh," Henry shouted in his most blustery I-am-the-king voice, "I have offered you true English beauties — ladies of breeding and wealth. You have refused them all. A gypsy wench is no better than you deserve. The de Laceys were ever a mongrel lot anyway."

More laughter erupted. Yet some of the mirth began to sound forced. When the king lashed out with cruel insults, all feared the razor edge of his choler turned next upon themselves.

Thomas Cromwell cleared his throat. "Sire, for a nobleman to wed a common gyp—"

"Be silent, you spindle-shanked little titmouse," King Henry thundered at Lord Privy Seal. "Better men than Wimberleigh have wed women of low station."

Anne Boleyn, Stephen thought darkly. The

woman who had shaken the monarchy to its foundations had been naught but the daughter of an ambitious tenant farmer.

Cromwell flinched, but with his usual aplomb, he said, "Perhaps, then, 'tis a matter for the clergy to debate."

"My dear Cromwell, leave the canon lawyers to me." Henry turned to Stephen. "Your choice is clear. Marry the wench, or see her hanged for thieving."

"She'll need cleaning up," Stephen blurted. "And it will take her months to learn the new catechism. Then perhaps —"

"Nay, bring a cleric!" Dismissing Stephen's attempt at stalling, King Henry gave a regal wave of his hand. "To hell with banns and betrothal arrangements. We'll see them wed now."

Evening mantled the knot garden outside the chapel. Like a flock of gulls after a fishing boat, the courtiers moved off in the wake of the king. Hushed whispers hissed through the fragrant night air, seductive and yet somehow accusing.

Feeling numb and emotionless, Juliana stopped beneath an arbor and fingered a long, spiny yew leaf. Its rough edges abraded her fingertip. She had no idea what to say to this stranger. A king's caprice had made him her husband.

Stephen de Lacey turned to her. Stephen. Only during the hasty, almost clandestine ceremony had she learned his given name, learned it when she had been obliged to pledge a lifelong vow to this tall, unsmiling English lord.

Those whom God hath joined together let no man put asunder.

She wondered if the cleric's awesome words still rang in his ears as they did in hers.

He stood between two shadowy hawthorn hedges. The breeze ruffled his gold-flecked hair, and for a moment the thick waves rippled as if disturbed by the fingers of an invisible lover. He had the most extraordinary face she had ever seen, and the play of light and shadow only made it more so. His eyes caught an errant gleam of waning light, and she saw it again: the pain, the panic. The stark, lurking fear.

"Is he always this cruel?" she asked.

He cleared his throat. "The king, you mean?" He spoke in low tones, though his deeply resonant voice carried.

Juliana nodded. "Who else maneuvers lives like chess pieces?"

Wimberleigh pressed his palms against the railed border of the garden. He stood quietly for a moment, seeming to study the razor-clipped hedges. "He possesses both passion and whimsy. He grew up the second son, nearly forgotten by his father. Then his elder brother's death launched Henry into the succession, and he seized power as if he feared someone would snatch it away. When a man of such qualities also happens to be king and pope alike, it can make him unspeakably cruel."

"Why does he take pleasure in tormenting you?"

A bitter smile tightened Wimberleigh's lips, and she knew she would get no honest answer to her question. "Your complaint surprises me. The king saved you from death."

"I would have fought my way free," she declared.

"For what?" His voice had a taunting edge. "So you could return to the gypsies, who would make you a serving wench and a whore for the rest of your days?"

"And you, my lord?" Juliana shot back. "What will you make of me?"

Stephen de Lacey stepped closer, his large shape filling the twilit path. She stood her ground, though instinct warned her to flee. There was danger here, close to her, just a whisper away.

"My dear slattern," he said gently, in the voice of a lover, "I have just made you a baroness."

His mockery cut at her pride. "And for that you expect gratitude, yes?"

" 'Tis better than hanging as a horse thief."

"So is having one's nostrils slit, but that does not mean I relish the reprieve. Why did you save me? Clearly you like me not."

Dark laughter stirred his broad shoulders. He leaned close, his breath warm upon her cheek. "Your powers of observation are keen, my gypsy."

"You have not answered my question. You seem to be a man fond of his independence, yet you jumped like a trained spaniel when the king gave his orders. Why, my lord? I sense King Henry has a lance aimed at your heart."

His chin came up sharply, and she heard his breath catch. "Do not amuse yourself with idle speculation. My affairs are hardly your concern."

Resentment and frustration built inside her. She was supposed to be on her way to a horse fair now, planning her first audience with the king, who would help her win back her birthright. "It is my affair since you just took me as your wife."

"In name only," he snapped. "Or did you truly think I would take this marriage seriously?" With frigid disdain, he glanced at her from head to toe. "That I would honor vows wrung from me at the whim of King Henry?"

Juliana thanked God he did not mean to treat her as a true wife. She decided in that instant to stay in the tattered, lice-ridden guise of a gypsy wench, for it obviously disgusted him.

Still, a perverse sense of injured pride darkened her spirits. "I am free to go, yes?" she inquired. She fought an urge to clutch at the neckline of her blouse, to hide from him. "Well?"

"Not yet. I'll take you to Wiltshire. Once the king tires of his trick, we'll get an annulment and you can go back to — to fortune-telling or pocket picking or whatever it is that you do when you're not off thieving horses."

Juliana gritted her teeth. "I happen to do a good number of things. Some of them are quite clever. Tarrying in Wilthouse —"

"Wiltshire, my tenderling. 'Tis a few days' ride west of here."

She planted her hands on her hips. "Tarrying in Wiltshire was not part of —"

"Of what?"

She could not tell anyone, especially this stranger, of her secret schemes. "My plan," she stated simply.

He bowed from the waist. "I regret the inconvenience, then. Perhaps you'd be more pleased had I left you swinging from the gibbet."

She hated him for being right. Though she did not want to acknowledge the truth, he was as much a victim of the king's wrath as she.

A sigh of resignation gusted from her. Darkness now filled the knot garden, and the first stars of evening pricked the sky. "What about tonight?"

"I managed to dissuade the master of revels from leading the bedding ceremony."

"What is the bedding ceremony?"

"We would have been escorted to bed by a group of drunken revelers and . . . never mind. You may stay alone in my chamber. My squire and I will take the anteroom. Be ready to ride out at first light." He turned to leave.

"My lord." Juliana lightly touched his sleeve. The fine lawn fabric covered a hard, masculine warmth, and the sensation startled her.

Apparently it startled him, as well. His eyes widened, and a look of revulsion broke over his shadowed face.

Searingly aware of how long it had been since she had bathed, Juliana snatched her hand away. "I am sorry."

"What were you going to say?"

"I . . . forget." But as he showed her to the chamber where she was to sleep, she acknowledged the lie. She was going to thank him for saving her from the noose. For glaring the courtiers into silence when they would have made high sport of her. For speaking his vows loudly over the titters of the ladies.

But his look of disgust when she had touched him drove any sense of gratitude from her.

It was her wedding night, and save for the company of a large white windhound, she lay alone. More alone than she had ever been before.

As if the king had commanded it, the next day dawned clear and brilliant, the weather a sharp contrast to Stephen's gloomy mood. He should have let the gypsy girl flee on his horse, should have forfeited the wager to King Henry. Capria was precious to him, but not nearly so precious as his freedom.

Instead, he had foolishly allowed himself to be captivated by the horse thief's wide eyes, so clear and disarming in contrast to the dirt on her face, the tangles in her hair.

Gypsy eyes, he told himself. As false and full of lies as her Romany soul.

"Ah, Kit," Stephen said, sitting on a heavy box chair and holding his head, "say it was all a bad dream. Say I'm not truly shackled by God's law to a wild, half-mad gypsy."

Kit Youngblood's mouth quirked in a curve that suspiciously resembled a stifled grin. He held out Stephen's plain frieze jerkin. "It was no dream, my lord. The king waived the banns and called for a clerk. You are well and truly married to the strange girl."

Stephen lifted his head, rubbed his hands over his stubbled cheeks, then pushed his arms into the jerkin. "Must you always be so blunt?"

"My lord," Kit said, lacing Stephen's sleeve to the armhole of the jerkin, "why did you not simply refuse?"

Stephen did not answer, for not even Kit knew the truth — that if he had dared to cross the king once more . . .

"She would have been hanged," Stephen said brusquely. "We shall collect my gypsy baggage and get ourselves home. Then I'll find a way out of this mess. Where is the wench, anyway?"

■ ■ ■ ■

Juliana was already mounted and ready to ride when Stephen came out to the park beside the river Thames.

"My blushing bride," he muttered under his breath. She sat frozen upon a gray gelding, her cheeks still smudged with dirt, her eyes wide and wary with pain and uncertainty.

The look brought on a flash of remembrance. A few years earlier, Stephen had come upon a poacher's trap. The sharp-toothed iron jaws were clamped around the foreleg of a young doe. The dying creature had gazed up at him, that same look in its eyes, begging for a quick death.

Stephen had slit its throat.

"The lady," he said with a mocking bow, "does not seem to take joy in seeing her new husband."

"I take no joy in riding off with my jailer," she spat. "I'd no more pretend to like you than I would care to warm your bed."

He slid his gaze slowly over her. She sat astride, her patched skirts hiked up and billowing over the saddlebow. Long bare legs and dusty feet clung expertly to the horse's sides.

"Believe me," Stephen assured her, "I have higher standards for the women I bed." His fury at the king honed an edge of cruelty to his words. "You seem better suited to certain other domestic tasks."

She glared at him with loathing hot in her eyes. "I will not do your Gajo washing, nor work in your Gajo fields." With her strange dog trotting at her horse's stirrup, she rode stone-faced, looking disturbingly like a scatterling from a siege. When they stopped at wayside inns along the way, she ate and drank mechanically. At night she lay unmoving on a pallet. The dog never left her side, and while she slept he remained vigilant, lifting his black lip and growling if Stephen even so much as blinked at Juliana.

Kit, understandably discomfited by the tension, kept up a constant, mindless chatter as they trudged through the terraced green west country: King Henry had sent aides abroad in search of a new royal bride. At the royal court of France, people drank from cups that, when drained, revealed a man and woman in flagrante delicto. Sebastian Cabot, the mariner, had sent a savage from New Spain to London, and the creature was on display at the Bear Garden.

By the time the broad fields, scored by stone fences and thorny hedgerows, yielded to the ancient bounds of Lynacre, Stephen's shoulders ached with strain.

He glanced back and caught a familiar sight. Juliana had ridden too near the roadside hedgerow, and the hem of her skirt had snagged on the spiny bush. She yanked at it, and a piece tore off.

He knew her to be an excellent rider. Yet throughout the journey she had been careless with her person, leaving bits of thread or fabric or a few strands of her unkempt hair in the hedgerows.

She was clearly up to mischief and would bear watching.

"Ride ahead and announce us, Kit," Stephen said to his squire. "Let the kitchen know we've not eaten since breakfast, and tell Nance Harbutt the baroness will require a bath."

Kit kicked his mount into a canter and rode off, a plume of dust filling his wake. Stephen started off again — slowly, knowing with dread certainty that he was bringing havoc into his well-ordered world.

A lark in the hedge trilled, then fell silent. Only the soft thud of the horses' hooves and the creak of saddle leather punctuated the heavy stillness.

Moments later the gypsy's dog snarled and bounded across a field, a white streak flowing over the ancient barrows and undulating downs.

"Where's he off to?" Stephen muttered.

"He heard something." Juliana cocked her head. "Other dogs — I hear them now."

Stephen scanned the horizon, looking past the clumps of bright, blossoming furze and stands of thorn and holly to the chalk heights in the distance. When he spied the rider, he cursed under his breath. "Of all the people to encounter . . ."

Juliana followed his glare. "Who is it?"

"My nearest neighbor, and the loudest gossip in Wiltshire."

"You are afraid of gossip, my lord?"

Juliana watched Pavlo set upon the lurchers that accompanied the rider. The baying and yelping startled a flock of rooks from a stand of ash trees. The birds rose like a storm cloud, darkening the sky before wheeling off over the chalk hills.

Somewhat pleased that Pavlo had broken the monotony of the journey and the strain of their silence, Juliana clapped her hands, then cupped them around her mouth and called a command in Russian. Pavlo came bounding back, his narrow head held high, his feathery tail waving like a victor's banner.

While the lurchers ran for their lives, the rider cantered down a sheep walk that joined the road through a break in the hedge. He pulled his horse up short and glared at the huge dog. "The blighted beast should be garroted," he grumbled.

"He'd probably fight back, Algernon," said Lord Wimberleigh.

"God's holy teeth." The young man peered past Stephen and stared at Juliana. While he studied her tattered clothes and matted hair, she stared back, taking in the fine cut of his doublet and riding cloak, the slimness of his gloved hands on the reins. Beneath a velvet cap, a wealth of golden curls framed his narrow, comely face. "What the devil have you got there, Wimberleigh?"

"A very large mistake," said Stephen de Lacey, "but one I fear I am saddled with until I make some arrangements."

Saddled with! As if she were a mare with the botch, to be foisted on some unsuspecting gudgeon at a horse fair. Juliana's esteem for Lord Wimberleigh, never particularly high, slipped another notch.

"Marry, I forgot my manners," he went on in that blithe, sarcastic way of his. "Algernon, this lady calls herself Juliana Romanov. Juliana, this is Algernon Basset, earl of Havelock."

The jaunty young man flashed her a smile. He removed his cap, the long feather fluttering as he held it against his chest. "Charmed, Lady Error," he said with a merry laugh.

Juliana felt a small spark of recognition. Havelock was a man of humor, breeding and manners. He would not have been out of place in her father's elite circle of friends. Havelock was very unlike Stephen de Lacey, the brooding man who had, on a cavalier impulse that he clearly regretted, married her.

She gave the carl a cautious smile. "*Enchantée,* my lord."

Algernon's pale eyebrows lifted. Juliana was not certain what surprised him — her accent, her voice . . . or her smile. "And what brings you to our district?"

Juliana sent him the sly trickster's grin she had learned from Rodion's younger sister, Catriona. "Marriage, my lord."

"Ah. You look to wed a sheepman, perhaps, or one of the dyers from the village?"

Though Juliana would have enjoyed cozening him awhile, Wimberleigh gave an impatient grunt. "She's married to me, Algernon, and the tale is long in the telling, so I —"

"To you?" Algernon's eyes bugged out.

Juliana imagined she heard a clanking sound as his jaw dropped. "To *you?*"

"By order of the king," Stephen explained, his voice tight, as if each word were wrung from him. "And Algernon, I'd appreciate it most highly if you could silence yourself —"

"Silence myself? Not for a third ball, Wimberleigh," Havelock said, grinning broadly and resting a hand on his codpiece. "A Tower warden couldn't muzzle me." With a guffaw of sheer delight, he jammed on his hat, spurred his mount, and galloped back the way he had come.

Wimberleigh squeezed his eyes shut and pinched the bridge of his nose. He uttered a strange word that probably referred to some disgusting body function.

During the remainder of the journey, Juliana fought to remain calm and rational. She was a nobleman's wife. His charming disposition notwithstanding, she might turn her new status to advantage. Her role as a baroness might help her bring her family's murderers to justice.

Regrets rattled in a small, hollowed-out place inside her. She was to have married Alexei Shuisky. Her memories of the young boyar had been gilded by yearning dreams, and in her mind he had grown more handsome and engaging with the passage of time. How happy they would have been, living at one of the splendid Shuisky estates, raising their children amid beauty and splendor.

Juliana scowled at Stephen de Lacey, who sat his horse like a commoner, his broad shoulders clad in the simplest of garments, his golden hair overlong and in need of trimming. He had ruined any chance she might have had at a future in Novgorod.

Unless . . . Insidious as the wind through the hood of a caravan, an idea took hold. The king of England himself had claimed the power to end a marriage. It had been all the talk when Juliana first arrived in England. King Henry had put his Spanish wife on the shelf in order to wed a dark-eyed court lady. Even the gypsies had been impressed by his boldness.

They had been even more impressed by the eventual fate of Anne Boleyn: death at the block.

As a tall, turreted gatehouse hove into view, Juliana shuddered. Englishmen who did not want to keep their wives were very dangerous indeed.

An unearthly screech sent Stephen pounding up the stairs to the second story of the manor house. He hurried along the half-open passageway that ran from gable end to gable end, ducking low beneath slanting timbers.

What the devil could be amiss? They had arrived only minutes earlier. Yet the terror in the woman's voice indicated nothing short of murder.

He passed the gilt-framed portraits of his grandsires, his father, his mother, himself. From long habit he averted his eyes from the last painting. The portrait of Meg. Even though he did not let himself look, it touched him — a quick, searing arrow wound to the gut — then he hurried on to the chambers of his gypsy bride.

Though somewhat small of stature, she had a rather robust set of lungs. Her cries were long and harsh, probably loud enough to carry to the village beyond the river that bordered the estate.

Stephen stopped in the doorway and surveyed the scene.

Juliana stood backed up against a gargoyle-infested cupboard. The carved, leering faces with their wooden eyes and lolling tongues surrounded her dirt-smudged face as if they recognized her as one of their own.

Nance Harbutt advanced like a besieging

force on the gypsy. Nance had been part of Lynacre for as long as Stephen could remember, as ever present and unchanging as the gargoyle cupboard. The goodwife wore a starched wimple tied with a strip of cloth knotted beneath her well-fleshed chin.

"Stay away from me, you old gallows crow," Juliana yelled.

Nance gestured at Juliana's tattered skirt and blouse. "I know you felt pressured to wed, my lord, but where in God's name did you find this slattern cat?"

"Long story," Stephen said, perfunctorily searching Juliana for signs of physical abuse. Old Nance had never been averse to applying the switch or the rod where she deemed it necessary. "What's the trouble?"

Juliana tried not to wince as a knob from the cupboard pressed into her back. What manner of man was Stephen de Lacey that he would come barging, all unbidden, into a lady's chamber?

"She's trying to make me sit in that — that —" Feigning horror, Juliana waved her hand at the trunklike bathing tub on the hearth. "That cesspool!"

" 'Tis a fine, hot bath and you're in sore need of it," Old Nance snapped, scrunching her doughy face into an expression of disgust. "Jesu, you reek like a jakes-farmer."

Juliana recoiled from the tub, when in sooth, she yearned to plunge into the steaming water. It was a singular arrangement with an open conduit that could be connected with a cauldron over the hearth fire for a steady supply of hot water. Steam rose from the tub. Bits of harsh-smelling herbs floated upon the faintly oily surface.

For Juliana, dirt and grime had been a shield from lusty men for five years. With the exception of Rodion, she had managed to keep all interested males at bay, and she meant to continue with the disguise.

"*That* is what all the yelling is about?" Stephen said with a short laugh. "A bath? I view it as an occasional necessity, not a cause for panic."

Juliana shuddered. "I have seen people catch fever and die from sitting in stagnant water."

"You never bathe at all?" Stephen asked calmly.

Juliana sniffed, folding her arms protectively. "I bathe once a twelvemonth in running water. Not —" she pointed a grimy finger at the tub "— in a stagnant vat that reeks of poison simples."

"Poison simples!" barked Nance, all a-quiver. "Those are my own good herbs.

I'm no necromancer, not like that Jenny Fallow, who done in her husband with mandrake. Told him it'd prolong the sex act, see, and —"

"Nance," Stephen said, and Juliana suspected the woman had a penchant for meandering bits of gossip.

"And she said it did for a time, but —"

"Nance, please." Stephen's tone was edged with impatience.

"Ah, I do go on, don't I, my lord?" She glared at Juliana. "God blind my eyes, she's a pert one." Scowling, she planted her fists on her hips and leaned menacingly toward Juliana. "If you want running water, go bathe in the millstream."

"Never!" snapped Juliana. "I take orders from no one." For good measure, she kicked out with a grimy bare foot, knocking over the ewer beside the tub. Several gallons of water spread over the rush-strewn floor. Not yet satisfied, she ducked past Nance, grasped the edge of the tub, and upended it.

As Nance yelled to the Catholic saints and reeled back against the wall, a tide of scented water flooded the room.

A blur of motion streaked toward Juliana. Stephen cursed — another disgusting body-part word — and she felt herself being lifted and slung with dizzying speed over his shoulder.

She screeched, but it did no good. She pounded on his broad back and earned a slap on the rear for her troubles.

Pushing past Nance, Stephen grabbed a stack of linen toweling, a cake of lye soap and a vial of dark liquid and marched toward the door.

Her great bosom bobbling, Nance ran after them. "My lord, have a care —"

"I'll be all right," Stephen said. "She doesn't bite." As he hastened from the room, he added, "Actually, she probably does, but I haven't caught her at it yet."

When they emerged from the manor house, Pavlo launched into a barking frenzy. Slung upside down over Stephen's shoulder, Juliana called a command to the *borzoya,* but saw that he had been tethered to a hitch rail.

She felt the ground slope as Stephen stalked on, muttering under his breath, toward their destination — a swift running river.

"You would not dare," she said through clenched teeth.

"Your charms give me courage, darling," he said. Handling her like a sack of cats he wished to drown, he threw her into the stream.

A mouthful of water silenced Juliana's screams. The cold shocked her, but not nearly so much as the cruelty of the man she had married. She planted her feet on the pebbly bottom and surfaced, her hand on her dagger, ready to do battle.

He gave her no chance. He had waded out, fully clothed, and he, too, was armed — with a block of soap.

Juliana howled like Pavlo when he was confined to a cage. She bruised her hands and feet against her husband's hard body, all to no avail. Stephen de Lacey was relentless. He drenched her hair in a witch's brew of noxious herbs, then scrubbed every thrashing, squirming inch of her, and dunked her as if she were an armful of soapy bed linens.

When he finished, he did not even look at her, but turned and sloshed his way to the riverbank. "The towels are there," he said, indicating them with a jerk of his head. "And supper is at the toll of six. We're having company."

"I hope I gave you lice," she yelled after him.

Old Nance tucked a finger up under her hat

and gave her head an idle scratch. Then she sighed heavily, the sound of a woman who was absolutely convinced of her own saintliness.

"I've set the lady's chamber to rights, my lord." She waved her chubby arm, showing off the fresh rushes. "It were no small task, I might add."

Stephen offered her a straight-backed chair, and with a self-important rustling of fustian skirts, she lowered herself to the seat. He had hastily donned dry clothing and combed his damp hair.

"Well," she said, her manner brisk. "I'll not devil you with questions, my lord. We'll leave the gossips to mull over how it is that the baron of Wimberleigh came to wed a wild gypsy."

"Thank you." Stephen pulled up a chair of his own, straddling it and folding his arms over the back. He was grateful she did not demand an explanation. Yet at the same time, he realized she alone would have understood, for she alone knew the nature of the blade King Henry held poised over Stephen's neck.

"Aye, 'tis not my place to ponder the whys and wherefores of your new wedded state. Lord above knows, my poor old mind is too feeble to grasp how you got in such a fix."

She clasped her work-reddened hands. "Now that you've seen to the bathing, my lord, the gypsy needs a set of clothes. As to her savage ways, we'll see about them later."

"*Is* she truly strange, Nance?" Stephen asked, trying hard not to relive the tempest in the millstream. "Sometimes I glimpse something in her manner, hear a note in her speech, and I wonder."

"She's a gypsy, my lord, and everyone knows gypsies are great imitators." The goodwife sniffed and poked her broad red nose into the air. "Much like a monkey I once saw. 'Twas a mariner at Bristol, see, and he . . ."

His attention fading, Stephen nodded vaguely and planted his chin in his hand. It struck him that he had not entered this room in eight years. The chamber, with its adjoining music suite and solar, wardrobes and close-rooms, had been Meg's domain.

Though hastily aired and dusted for the new baroness, the room still bore Meg's indelible imprint — the fussy scalloped bed draperies of fading pink damask, the blank-eyed poppet propped on the window seat, the mirrored candle holder Stephen himself had designed. And on a slim-legged table lay a bone hairbrush, its back etched with a scene of the Virgin guarded by a unicorn.

Fearful of the emotion building inside him, he scowled at the floor. And spied, half-hidden by the fringe of the counterpane, a bright bit of string. Distracted by the out-of-place object, he stood and crossed the room to pick it up. "What is this?"

Nance caught her breath. "Milady was playing at Jacob's ladder the very night —"

Stephen turned toward Nance. His icy glare stopped her cold.

Nance's hand fluttered at her bosom. "Ah, the sweetling. Ever the child, she was."

The memory stung like salt on the wound of Stephen's guilt. He thought of his vagabond bride invading this room, sleeping in Meg's bed, handling Meg's things.

Like a weed, Juliana would blight the perfectly ordered chamber.

I'm sorry, Meg. Sorry for everything. The regrets poured like quicklime through him.

". . . burn the clothes, of course," Old Nance was saying, having slipped back into her matter-of-fact manner.

Stephen shook his head, drawing his mind from painful remembrances. He stalked back and forth in front of the windows. "What's that you say?"

"The gypsy, my lord. Her clothes are no doubt infested with vermin. 'Tis best they are burnt."

"Aye, but then she'll have nothing to — oh." Stephen pressed his fist on the window embrasure. "She is of a size with Meg."

"Not quite so plump as your first wife, my lord, but I could take a tuck or two in some of the gowns. Er, that is, if you don't mind —"

"I don't." He slammed the door on his memories.

"And about a lady's maid, my lord —"

"She doesn't need a maid, but a warden."

"That's what I thought, too," Nance said. "While you was occupied with your wife, I sent to the village for Jillie Egan, the dyer's daughter."

"Jillie Egan?" Stephen aimed a mocking scowl at Nance. "Oh, you are naughty, dear lady. The Egan girl's the size of a bullock, and has a stubborn will to match."

Nance winked broadly. "She'll not tolerate any stomaching from the gypsy."

Stephen strode to the door. "Do as you see fit. I've a pressing engagement elsewhere."

Nance Harbutt nodded in complete understanding. "My lord, what will you tell your new wife about —"

"Nothing at all," he cut in, his voice as

sharp as a knife. "Not a blessed, solitary thing."

THREE

"I trow that particular shade of blue is called woad," said a faintly amused voice.

"Eek!" Juliana nearly came out of her numb, chilled skin. She spun away from the polished steel mirror to face the intruder. "Dear Lord," she whispered in rapid Russian, "my jailer is a giantess."

Her gaze traveled from the boatlike feet clad in sturdy clogs to the ruddy face framed by coarse yellow hair. The distance was at least a score of hands — the height of a grown plow horse.

"I don't speak Egyptian, milady." The giantess placed her pawlike hands on her hips and leaned forward, peering frankly at Juliana. "I assumed you was trying to decide what shade of blue your lips turned from the cold bath. I'd say woad, from the mustard leaf."

"Woad," Juliana repeated stupidly, shaping her lips around the difficult *w*.

"Aye, I knows me colors. Me da is a dyer. Blue as a titbird's throat you are, milady."

Clutching a robe around her shivering form, Juliana blinked in astonishment. The fact was, she *had* turned blue from the icy bath in the churning, spring-fed millstream. After the heartless dunking Stephen had subjected her to, she had slogged back to the house, cursing him in a patois of English, Romany, and Russian. When the ogress arrived, Juliana had been staring into the mirror and wondering if her coloring would ever return to normal.

"Who are you?" She managed to force the question past her chattering teeth.

"Jillie Egan." The woman bobbed an awkward curtsy. "I'm to be your new lady's maid."

A lady's maid. Juliana closed her eyes for a moment and surrendered to memories she usually kept locked away. As a girl, she had been attended by no fewer than four maids — all of them pretty as daisies, impeccably groomed, and nearly as accomplished as their young mistress.

"Milady?" The ogress interrupted her thoughts. " 'Tis nigh time for you to be getting to supper."

Jillie led Juliana close to the hearth fire and unwound the linen toweling from her hair. The damp locks reeked of strong herbs Stephen had used to kill the lice. Jillie untied the shapeless robe, replacing it with a long, fine shift. The sheer fabric was gossamer to Juliana's skin, so deliciously different from the coarse homespun of her gypsy garb.

"Belonged to the first baroness, this did," Jillie commented, shaking out the scalloped hem of the shift.

"Lord Wimberleigh's mother?" Juliana inquired.

"Heavens, no. That one turned up her noble toes a score of years ago. Lord Wimberleigh's first *wife.*"

Juliana caught her breath. It had never occurred to her that Stephen de Lacey had been married before. A wife. Stephen was a widower. Suddenly the thought colored everything she knew about him: the hooded sadness deep in his eyes, his bitter resentment of Juliana, his long, brooding silences and searing moments of high temper.

"Where are my own clothes?" she demanded.

"Nance said they was dirty past washing, crawling with vermin and such. She had them burned."

"No!" The shout broke from Juliana on a

wave of panic. "I must find them. I need my —"

"Bauble, milady?" Jillie handed over the brooch. "I spied it pinned inside the waist of your skirt."

Juliana went weak with relief; then hope began to warm her blood. The ogress might be someone she could trust. Perhaps the only one she could trust until . . . She thought of the *vurma* trail she had left during her journey to Wiltshire, the bits of thread and fabric she had left to mark her way. *Hurry, Laszlo.*

Praying her guardian would rescue her from her own foolishness, she closed her fingers around the brooch. "Thank you." In spite of herself she was beginning to like the big bossy maid. As her tension and suspicion relaxed, she decided to give up her gypsy disguise. Her plan to exhort King Henry for help had failed, but perhaps here she'd find help from Stephen de Lacey. How far would he go, she wondered, and how much would he risk to be rid of her?

"Jillie," she said speculatively, "can you do hair?"

The maid grinned. "Like I were born to it, milady. By the time I've done, your new husband won't know you."

■ ■ ■ ■

"Well, Wimberleigh," said Jonathan Youngblood. "Don't keep me on tenterhooks like a side of pork. What's she like?"

Stephen squeezed his eyes shut, silently cursed Havelock's wagging tongue then opened his eyes to glare at his best friend. Jonathan sat easily in a carved box chair at the opposite end of the trestle table. Older than Stephen by a decade, he bore the scars of the Scots wars and the ample girth of good living. His bristly gray hair stuck out in spikes around a florid face, and he dressed like a ploughman, for he was never one to bow to fashion. A knight of the old order, Jonathan Youngblood had no use for the perfumed, posturing gentlemen who now dominated the court.

His warm brown eyes were the kindest Stephen had ever known. Blessed with an even dozen sons, Jonathan had sent Kit to live with Stephen, thinking the lad would fill the void of Stephen's childlessness.

If he only knew the truth . . . Stephen batted the thought away. "I ought to give you no preparation at all," he declared.

"Just a hint, then. Otherwise I shall spend the evening gaping like a visitor to Bedlam."

Stephen sighed and took a sip of malmsey from his pewter goblet, then set the cup down. The metallic *clank* echoed through the cavernous dining hall, with its tapestry hangings and the hammer-beam ceiling arching like giant ribs high above. The table was laid with fine plate and crockery for a sumptuous meal. Spiked on wrought-silver holders were beeswax tapers, their flames bending gently from the breeze through the tall, slender windows.

Great princes, learned scholars and dour clergymen had dined at this table, Stephen reflected. But never a half-wild vagabond. No doubt she had the manners of a sow.

Blowing out a sigh, he decided to tell Jonathan the truth. "Her name is Juliana, and she claims to be from the kingdom of Muscovy or Rus. No doubt 'tis a fiction she invented. She has been traveling with a band of gypsies."

Jonathan's eyes widened. "I had heard the king saddled you with a foreign wench, but I thought 'twas another of Havelock's embellishments. Or a jest of the king."

"To Henry, it *was* a jest."

"The king has a passion for amusement — at the expense of a good man's pride." Jonathan rested his thick forearms on the table and leaned forward. "So what's she like? Sloe-eyed and passionate? I've heard the Romany folk are a hot-blooded race." He jiggled his eyebrows.

Stephen scowled over the rim of his goblet. "She is rather . . ." He groped for a polite term. "Rustic."

"Ah. An earthy beauty, then."

"Not quite."

"She's not earthy?" Jonathan's gaze moved past Stephen; he seemed to be studying something behind his friend.

"She's not a beauty." Stephen realized he had little notion of what his wife truly looked like under all the grime and tangled hair. She had been too wild during the bathing, and he had glimpsed only raking fingernails and a red mouth spitting foreign curses.

In his mind's eye he pictured her: dark strands escaping two thick braids, a dirt-smudged face, a small shapeless form draped in rags. "Her looks hardly matter to me. I intend to be rid of her once the king has had his fill of tormenting me."

"I see." Merriment gleamed in Jonathan's eyes, and his lips thinned as he tried not to smile. "She is truly a humiliation, then."

"Aye, a bedraggled wench with all the appeal of a basin of ditch water."

"Why, thank you ever so much, my lord,"

said a soft, accented voice behind Stephen. "At least I haven't the manners of a toad."

Jonathan wheezed in an effort to stifle a laugh.

The gypsy. How much had she overheard?

Slowly, still clutching his cup, Stephen rose from the table and turned. His fingers went slack. The pewter goblet dropped to the table, spilling wine across the polished surface. Stunned into silence by the vision that had entered the room, he could only stare.

She wore a gown and kirtle of dusky rose brocade with a high-waisted bodice and fitted sleeves, and an overgown with a long, trailing train. The square neckline of the bodice revealed her bosom — fine-textured and rosy, as inviting as a ripe peach.

Had it not been for her vivid green eyes, he would not have recognized the face. Every trace of dirt and ash had been scrubbed away to reveal a visage as exquisite as the delicate blossom of a rose in springtime.

Eschewing the usual fashionable French hood, she wore her hair long and loose, dressed with a simple rolled band of gold satin. A thorough cleansing had turned the indistinct dark color to deep, rich sable ablaze with gleaming red highlights. The endless length and fine, billowy texture of it made Stephen's hands itch to bury themselves in it.

If I were to touch her now, he caught himself thinking, *I would touch her hair first.*

And with a dreadful, sinking awareness, he knew he would not stop there.

"You must be the lady Juliana, the new baroness." Jonathan bumped against his chair in his haste to get up. He swept into a dramatic bow. "I am Sir Jonathan Youngblood of the neighboring estate of Lytton Mount."

"Enchantée." With a slim white hand, Juliana swept back a glorious lock of soft hair. Pinned to her bodice was the large brooch she had brandished in front of King Henry. She gave a faint smile. The color stood out high in her cheeks. "It appears my husband was entertaining you with his vast charm and wit."

Stephen hated himself for recognizing the hurt in her voice. He hated himself for caring that his words had wounded her.

She faced him squarely, dipped her head in greeting, and said, *"Le bon Dieu vous le rendra."*

Her French was impeccable. *The good Lord will repay you.* He did not doubt it for a moment.

Moving cautiously, as if navigating a snake pit, he took her hand to lead her to the table. Her easy grace surprised him. She took her place in a nobleman's dining hall as effortlessly as if she had been doing it all her life.

The servitors came in their usual formal parade, with river trout and salad, venison pasty and loaves of dark bread, cold blood pudding and soft new cheese. Juliana received them with unexpected poise, nodding at the spilled malmsey and whispering, "His lordship needs more wine."

Stephen scarcely tasted the food he ingested mechanically.

He could not tear his attention from his wife.

Her manners astonished him. Where had she learned to wield knife and spoon so deftly, to sip so daintily from her cup? And, Christ's bones, to murmur such apt and discreet instructions to the servants?

Everyone knows gypsies are great imitators. Much like a monkey . . . The words of Nance Harbutt echoed through his mind.

But that wasn't the answer. It couldn't be.

Stephen barely heard the bluff, easy conversation of Jonathan, barely heard Juliana's soft replies as they discussed Kit, the weather, and her wild claims about her past. Caught in the grip of amazement, Stephen could do no more than stare at his wife.

He had expected the crude gypsy wench to be overwhelmed by the opulence of his home, crammed with the spoils of battles fought by his ancestors, church treasures plundered by his father, and the rich yields of his own endeavors as baron of Wimberleigh.

Instead, she seemed only mildly interested in her new surroundings. It was as if the plate tableware, the Venetian glass cups and art treasures adorning the hall, the solicitous servants, were commonplace to her. As if she had found herself in these circumstances before.

Nonsense, Stephen told himself. Perhaps the treasures were so alien to her that she could not begin to grasp their value.

He forced himself to attend to what Jonathan was saying. "You tell a most singular tale about your past, my lady," said the older man.

Juliana took a dainty bite of salad, then with a slender finger traced the rim of her glass fingerbowl. Just for a moment, sadness haunted her eyes, a melancholy so intense that Stephen's breath caught.

Then her eyes cleared and she gave Jonathan a serene smile. "It is no tale, my lord, but the absolute truth."

Stephen suppressed a snort of derision. Small wonder gypsies were outlawed. No one should be so adept at lying.

"The unexpected marriage to Lord Wimberleigh must have given you a bit of a turn."

"Indeed it did," she admitted with a pretty shrug. "I confess that I felt like the lady of Riga."

"Riga?"

"A small principality to the west of Novgorod. My old nurse loved to tell the story. The lady of Riga found herself on the back of a tiger. Once mounted, she had no way to go but onward, for if she tried to get off, she would be eaten alive."

"So you liken marriage to Stephen to a ride upon a tiger." Jonathan seemed to be enjoying himself enormously.

Stephen vowed to ignore this foreign woman, ignore the garish beauty that so overpowered Meg's demure costume. He would ignore Juliana's captivating smile, her low-toned, beguiling speech.

To do otherwise would be to open his heart to unspeakable pain. He endured the meal in silence, then said his farewells to Jonathan.

"She is charming," Jonathan said as they waited in the darkening yard for Kit to bring round his horse. "Tell me, where would a gypsy wench learn such manners?"

"I know not. Nor do I care."

"She is fascinating to watch."

"So is a poison asp," Stephen stated. "Here's Kit."

The tall, sturdy lad approached with Jonathan's horse in tow. "You're good to the boy. He was getting lost amidst my wild brood."

"No chance of that here," Stephen said, and a familiar ache flared to life inside him. "Kit is quick of wit and masters every art I introduce." He forced a smile. "Though I trow, other arts will interest him before long. He can hardly pass through the hall without setting the maids and scullions to sighing."

Jonathan laughed. "Teach him chastity, Stephen. I'd not have him siring a brood before his time."

"He'll learn no bad habits from me." Stephen stood watching as Jonathan bade Kit good-bye and trotted off down the lane. Chastity. Stephen was reputed to be the most profligate of noblemen, frequenting the dives of Bath, the harborside stews of Bristol, the gaming houses of Southwark.

He took no pride in his reputation, only a bleak satisfaction that it had made him distasteful to marriageable maidens. Now that Juliana had come into his life, he wondered what would become of the bad habits he'd cultivated so assiduously.

For a long while, he stood in the formal garden with its cruciform walks enclosing fragrant beds of foxglove and woodbine. The clean fragrance of springtime enveloped him, and he paused near a fountain to gird himself for the coming hours. The stone basin still held the warmth of the sun.

He pressed his fists against the basin, trying to banish all feeling, all emotion, forever. Yet he was like a rock in the sun, holding its warmth even as darkness surrounded him. He remembered Juliana's smile when he had no business thinking of her at all.

The sun slipped below the horizon. A few more minutes, and it would be time for him to go.

Shuddering, he turned and went back inside.

Juliana stood waiting in the entrance to the hall. She held a hooded candle in one hand. The diffuse light showered her eyelashes and hair with gold dust and carved mysterious shadows in the hollow of her throat, between her breasts.

God Almighty, Stephen thought. Didn't Jillie know a lady should wear a silken partlet there for modesty?

Just below the overtly feminine hollow, the jeweled brooch winked, its large center stone as darkly brilliant as fresh blood.

"What do you do after supper, my lord?" she asked softly.

Her question panicked him, and he lashed out in anger. "I'm sometimes wont to tumble a wench or two." Narrowing his eyes, he let his burning gaze sweep over her. "Three are even better."

Her small teeth caught in the fullness of her lower lip. "I do not believe you."

"You know nothing about me," he said.

She shrugged, the motion of her shoulders as graceful as a waterfall. "How much I learn is up to you. I noticed a music room connected to my chambers. Perhaps I could play for you —"

"The collection of instruments does not include gypsy bells and guitars." Stephen saw the look that crept into her candlelit eyes. *I have to hurt you, Juliana,* he thought, wishing he could explain, knowing he could not. To show her kindness would be a far greater cruelty.

Juliana came awake slowly. Just for a moment, she was confused by the lavish bed hangings that soared above her, the silky warmth of the fur-lined covers blanketing her.

In that distant, half-aware realm between waking and sleeping, she fancied herself in the nursery at Novgorod, waiting for Sveta to come with a cup of warm honey-sweetened milk and a tray of soft bread and herbed sausages.

The image drifted away and Juliana came up on her elbows. Lynacre Hall. She was here in this noble house, not in a bedroll under a tree, nor beneath the rank mildewed covering of Laszlo's caravan. She lay in a strange, beautiful chamber that had once belonged to the wife of Lord Wimberleigh.

What had the first baroness been like? Had he loved her, hated her, regarded her with cool indifference?

Had she been responsible for making Stephen into a cold, angry man, or had he always been that way?

Juliana decided to find out. In the cool morning breeze through the open window, she called Jillie and then waited, absently petting Pavlo's long, sleek head and listening to the manor come to life — the call of the goose girl, the sound of shutters being opened, the scolding of chickens, voices from the bakehouse. A few moments later, Jillie came into the room, balancing a salver between her arm and hip.

"Ah, you're awake, then," she said briskly, thumping the tray down on a spindly gaming table. "Good morrow, milady. Hungry?"

"Always," Juliana admitted, throwing back the counterpane. During her years with the gypsies, she had often gone to sleep with hunger gnawing at her belly. Begging, pilfering and poaching had their limits.

Jillie rummaged in the carved chest at the foot of the bed and emerged with a long wrinkled robe of finely woven wool. As Juliana put her hands through the gaping armholes, the scent of lavender and bergamot rose from the garment.

"Uneven dye job," Jillie muttered, shaking out the folds. "Me da does better work — when he can get it."

"Is there no work for a dyer, then?" Juliana peered at the thin brown liquid in the cup.

"Time was, he had the vats in the dying shed bubbling day and night — year 'round. But the trades have been moving to the cities — to Bath, to Salisbury and even London town."

Juliana took a sip. Small ale. Hardly her favorite for breaking her fast. She bit into the bread. The flour had been coarse ground and was mealy; her teeth crunched down on a hard piece of chaff. She was going to have to make some changes around here.

With elaborate casualness she said to Jillie, "Didn't the former baroness patronize local tradesmen?" She crumbled the bread crust between her fingers. "Dyers, millers and such?"

"No." Jillie looked down at her large red hands. "The lady Margaret never seemed to . . . to think of such things."

Margaret. Her name was Margaret. "I see. What sorts of things did she think of?"

"Don't know, rightly. Fashion things, music, needlework, mayhap gaming in the hall."

"And her husband." Juliana hated herself for wanting to know. "Did she think of him?"

Jillie slapped her hands on her thighs. "Blind me, but I forgot to draw your water, milady. I'll be back in a trice." Moving with surprising swiftness, she left the chamber. When she returned with a ewer of warm water for washing, she seemed disinclined to speak.

Juliana did not press her. She had not a single friend in this place, and she was loath to test the loyalty of her only prospect.

Jillie helped her dress in a pale peach-colored bodice and gown. "Nance was up late tucking this to fit you, taking up the hem." She stepped back to survey her mistress. " 'Tis a good fit."

Juliana heard the flatness in her tone. "But?" she prompted.

"Ah, listen to me. 'Tis not my place to judge my betters —"

"Jillie." Juliana spoke the name carefully. "You must always speak your mind to me." It felt strange inviting intimacy with a servant. Yet in her present circumstances, she had sore need of an ally.

"The color's wrong, milady," Jillie blurted out. "You've a fine rich mass of hair and roses in your lips and cheeks. 'Tis the jewel tones you'll favor, not this pale washed-out stuff."

"Then dye my gowns," Juliana said simply.

Jillie's jaw dropped. "Truly?"

"Truly. Tell your father I'll gladly pay his price."

"Ah, milady, you're —"

A loud clanking sound rattled through the open window. Juliana hurried over, followed by Jillie. In the courtyard below, on the gravel drive, rolled a sturdy cart laden with crates and oddly shaped parcels.

"What is this?" Juliana asked.

"The new shipment. His lordship's always

bringing things from London town." Jillie sighed and propped her chin in her hand. "The world is so big," she said wistfully. " 'Twould be a rare blessing to see it. I ain't once been out of the shire."

"Never?" The very thought made Juliana feel cramped and restless. "I'll tell you about it someday." She moved toward the door. "For now, we must receive our guest."

An hour later, she stood in an airy solar and looked through oriel windows over the apple yard, enclosed by a high brick wall and white with May blossoms. Lynacre was a strange and beautiful place. She had yet to make sense of the house, with its gable-ended great and small wings, the porches, the clusters of chimneys, the crenellated parapets. The grounds provided a puzzle of their own. Thus far she had noticed at least three separate walled gardens, thick woods rearing almost menacingly to the west, and layer upon layer of soft green fells leading down to the river.

She lowered herself to the window seat, drew her knees to her chest, and rested her temple against the sun-warmed leaded glass. Aye, the estate was strange and beautiful — much like its master. The thought of him reminded her of the old Russian story of Stavr, an enchanted prince who was trapped in his forest kingdom. He could only be freed by the kiss of a princess, freely given.

"What the devil are you doing?" snapped a furious voice from the doorway.

Juliana froze. To her mortification, she discovered that she had pressed her fingers to her lips and closed her eyes, lost in the fantasy of a magic kiss. With as much dignity as she could muster, she jumped up and shook out her skirts.

Stephen stood there in the same trunk hose and jerkin he had worn the day before. A light golden stubble softened the hard lines of his cheeks and jaw. His pale hair looked mussed, as if long fingers had run through it. The disarray gave him a certain rakish charm that made her breath quicken and her cheeks grow warm.

It struck Juliana, disturbingly, that he had not yet been to bed — unless it was with one of the wenches he had so pointedly mentioned last night.

She silenced the jangle of alarm in her mind. If it was his habit to carouse each night away, that was his affair. She'd be a fool to let herself be hurt by it.

"My dear," he said in a gravelly voice, "you've not answered my question."

"A carter arrived with goods from London. I received them and sent the carter round to the kitchen for a meal. My lo — Stephen," she corrected, boldly using his familiar name. She took an ivory whistle from a box and blew a high note. "What is this? For a shepherd, perhaps?" Before he could answer, she drew a light shroud from a dome-shaped cage to reveal a bright yellow canary perched inside. "And this . . . an addition to your dovecote?" She flipped through the stiff pages of a small, fat book, noting a few block-printed illustrations. "I do not read English well. Perhaps you could tell me what this says. And this —" She reached for a wooden box made of interlocking pieces.

A large male hand snatched the box away. "Are you quite finished?" Stephen demanded in a low, lethal whisper.

"These are children's playthings," she said, refusing to flinch. "I just wondered —"

He paced the length of the solar, his booted feet kicking up dust from the rushes. "I've a fondness for invention. My own, and those created by others. You need not read any further meaning into it."

Perhaps the toys were gifts for the children of the nearby village. Perhaps Stephen de

Lacey concealed a heart of gold behind a facade of stone.

Prodded by a devil of mischief, she picked up a tiny reed pipe and blew, her fingers covering the holes to vary the pitch.

"Stop that." He stood inches away, glaring down at her.

Juliana continued to play. She would rather suffer the heat of his anger than the chill of his indifference. She picked out the first few notes of an old Russian song about a cherry tree. There was something compelling about his nearness.

"Damn it, Juliana!" He took her wrist, bringing her hand up between their bodies.

Never had she stood so close to her new husband — close enough to hear the labored rasp of his breathing and feel it warm on her cheek. Close enough to catch his scent of leather and lye. Close enough to study the faint lines that fanned out from his exquisite pale eyes.

She stood riveted, staring up at him, feeling her pulse leap wildly beneath the firm grip of his fingers. And suddenly she knew. He, too, had felt the shock, the heat, the awareness. The recognition.

Of what? she wondered crazily.

Of desire.

The answer came to her like an arrow shot

out of the dark, hitting home with stinging accuracy.

"Stephen?" she whispered.

For a moment, he seemed to waver, caught up in the same unbearable tension that held her breathless. His sculpted, unsmiling mouth twitched and he bent his head, golden hair falling forward, almost brushing her brow.

Closer and closer, until a mere whisper of distance separated their hungry lips, until anticipation thundered in her blood.

And, just as suddenly, Stephen plucked the reed pipe from her hand and stepped back.

"I'll see to the parcels," he snapped. "You need not trouble yourself with them. And in the future, Baroness, *I* shall receive all goods and dispatches."

He withdrew quickly, his footsteps ringing on the flagged floor outside, then stopping.

Juliana hurried to the solar door and peeked out.

He stood in the narrow, dim passageway, his big hands pressed against the stone wall. His head was thrown back to reveal a taut brown throat. His teeth were clenched, his eyes tightly shut. It was a posture of such anguished frustration that Juliana felt like an intruder.

She slipped back into the solar. She had learned something about her husband this morning. He wanted her. That was one secret he could not keep from her.

Faintly, through a thick blanket of sleep, the sounds came to Stephen. A cry in the dark. A ragged sob of terror and depthless despair.

His awareness weighted by the quantity of sack he had drunk the previous evening to forget the startled hurt in Juliana's eyes, he barely acknowledged the sounds. And then, slowly, like a stalking sneak thief, realization crept over him.

The moment had come. For years, he had dreaded this night. And yet a small dark part of him had craved it. This was the end of the waiting, the uncertainty. At last, he would be free —

"No!" Denial broke from him, loud and fierce and anguished. He leaped from his bed, tearing back the covers, bare feet slapping the chilly flagged floor.

No, please God, no . . . With jerky movements he groped for his leather leggings, his billowy cambric shirt, and in seconds he flew out the door of his chamber and into the night-black passageway.

He expected to find Nance Harbutt, come

to impart the long-dreaded tidings, but no one waited in the gloom.

Still the weeping sound that had awakened him reached out, drew him along the passageway. . . .

To his wife's room.

The fog of sleep and wine blew away on a cold, knife-sharp wind.

Juliana. It was his gypsy wife, with her weeping and strange mutterings, who had roused him.

Both relief and annoyance eddied through him as he stepped into her chamber.

A low, throaty growl greeted him. Her lethal weapon of a dog stood stiff-legged in the middle of the room, glaring with malevolent eyes.

Stephen glared back.

The dog looked away first and crouched down, warily letting him pass.

For a moment Stephen stood still, uncertain. Watery moonlight, faint as fairy's breath, streamed through the open window and fell upon the imposing draped bed.

Juliana had been at Lynacre Hall only a week, yet already her presence pervaded what had once been Meg's domain. The fragrance of lavender haunted the air; gowns and shifts made a cheerful disarray on the stools and chests; an old lute stood propped in a corner.

Stephen noticed this only in passing. He stood spellbound by the soft, terrible sounds coming from the figure on the bed.

Though she spoke in a foreign tongue, his heart constricted, for he knew the meaning well. In her sleep, she uttered the words of a soul that knew the icy black depths of despair and hopelessness, the supplication of a heart yearning to be healed.

Praying the dog would behave, he swiftly crossed the room to the bed. He of all people knew not how to comfort an unquiet soul, yet he could not stand to watch her suffer.

He sat on the edge of the bed, the heavy frame creaking under his weight. His large hands came to rest on the one shoulder that protruded from the twisted bedclothes.

She held herself curled up like a child shivering from cold. Her arms were hugged tightly around her torso. The trembling that emanated from her tore at Stephen. With a low, helpless curse, he pulled her against him. He felt her warmth, the wild tattoo of her racing heart, the hot dampness of her tears seeping into his shirt.

"Hush," he whispered into her hair. His lips brushed the silky strands. He breathed in the faint herbal fragrance. "Hush, Juliana, please. 'Tis a night fright, no more. You are safe."

She came awake with a loud, air-swallowing gasp. "Stephen?"

Feeling awkward and ungainly, he held her away from him and peered at her face. Her eyes were wide and staring, her cheeks wet.

"I heard you cry out," he explained, gruff-voiced and struggling to sound matter-of-fact. "I thought to quiet you before you awakened the whole household."

"Oh." She scrubbed the voluminous sleeve of her nightrail over her face. "Didn't Pavlo try to stop you?"

"He understands I mean you no harm."

She nodded. "I — I am sorry I awakened you."

"Are you all right now?" It was too dangerous to be alone with her like this — in the darkened bed, with her all warm and soft and tumbled from sleep. And vulnerable.

"Yes," she said. But her voice was hoarse, her eyes tearful.

He knew he should make haste away, but it was contrary to his nature to leave a creature in pain. "It's over, Juliana. You're safe. 'Twas only a nightmare."

"But the nightmare is real," she whispered. "I see things that happened to my family, hear things —"

"What things?"

"Fire," she said, starting to tremble again. "Hoofbeats and screaming, flames shooting from the windows —"

"The windows?"

"The house at Novgorod. My father's house." She tipped up her head, for a moment looking almost haughty. "It was a place that makes Lynacre Hall look like a peasant's dwelling."

Stephen felt a sinking sense of disappointment. This was yet another part of the fiction she had created to support her wild pretenses. Another thread in the web of lies.

"In the dream, I am looking at the snow," she went on, oblivious to his skeptical thoughts and seemingly immune to his touch, to the hand that moved from her chin to her shoulder, his thumb tracing whorls in the hollow of her throat.

"The fire casts bloody shadows on the snow. And then I see my family gathered in front of the steps. The blades of the attackers flash. Alexei, my betrothed, is fighting."

Her betrothed? Stephen opened his mouth to ask her about this Alexei, but she gave him no chance.

"The steel blades are red in the firelight. My brother shrieks in pain. They do not cut him cleanly but —"

Her voice broke. She buried her face in her hands. "They have to hack and hack, and his cries become gurgles, and I can hear no more. And then, at the last, while Laszlo is holding me back . . ." She swallowed, seemed to force herself to go on. "I see Alexei fall. The leader is about to order his men to search for me. And Pavlo leaps out of nowhere."

"Pavlo?"

She nodded. "He had gotten free from the kennels. He is a very protective dog."

Stephen lifted a strand of hair from the nape of her neck. How soft it was, how fragrant. "I noticed."

"The rest, in my dream, is confusion. I see Pavlo leap, I hear muffled words. A curse. I cannot make it out over the roar of the fire, the sound of horses blowing, the other dogs baying. Pavlo yelps, and the man turns. He cannot see me, but the fire flares suddenly, and I wait, knowing I will see the face of a murderer."

Stephen held his breath. In spite of himself, he had gotten caught up in her tale of horror. Dream or not, it had an immediacy that seized him.

"And?" he prompted.

She sighed and pressed her brow to his

shoulder. "And nothing. It always ends the same. A flash, as if a firearm is being discharged. And then I awaken."

"Without seeing the villain's face?"

"Villain?"

He almost smiled, half enjoying the light pressure of her head against his shoulder. "The murdcrer."

"I always awaken before I see his face."

"You have this dream often?"

"At first, just after the massacre that forced me to flee Novgorod, I had this dream every night. Now, not so often. But it is like opening a wound. I feel it all again. The grief, the rage. The helplessness. The loss of everything." Her hand closed around his. Her palm was cool and damp with sweat. "The terror."

"Ah, Juliana." He smoothed his free hand over her head, tucking it more securely against his shoulder. He did not know what to believe.

"I'm frightened, Stephen. Always, Laszlo has been nearby to quiet my fears. Now I am alone. So alone."

"No, you're not," he heard himself say. "I'm here, Juliana."

The tension flowed out of her at his words, and for a moment he was struck by the wonder of it. That mere words and a soothing touch could bring comfort was a foreign notion to him.

"Stay with me," she whispered. "Stay with me and hold me while I sleep."

He was so stunned by her request that he forgot to be cautious. Before he knew what was happening, he stretched out beside her. He pulled the coverlet over her and held her tightly, her cheek against his chest, his chin resting lightly on her head.

He told himself this was only for a moment, only until she was calm and able to sleep again.

But an hour later he was still there.

Juliana slept peacefully, her breath soft against his throat, her small hand resting in the curve of his waist. Her slim leg draped over his thigh.

Stephen tried not to think about the fact that he was in bed with a beautiful woman. His wife. He had every right to kiss her, to touch her, to slide his hands beneath her nightrail and — He cut the fantasy short, and the effort made him ache. It had been so long since he had felt the softness of a woman's breasts loose beneath thin lawn fabric. So long since he had listened to the breathing of someone slumbering nearby. So long since desire had stirred within him and then, lancelike, had stricken him with sharp arousal.

As Juliana relaxed more deeply into sleep, Stephen tensed more painfully into wakeful awareness.

Damn! He should have left the moment she had awakened. He had no business listening to her fearful dream. No business offering comfort to a woman he had married so reluctantly. No business feeling this ache of longing for a Romany wench.

To draw his mind from his burning need, he concentrated on the tale she had told. It was the same one she had related to the king and his court.

The one he had deemed a pack of gypsy lies.

The flowing moonlight caught at something on the stool beside the bed. Her brooch.

Moving his arm slowly, he picked up the jeweled cruciform bauble. It felt heavy and substantial in his hand. The pearls were as smooth and round as glass beads. The large central ruby had as many glittering, mysterious facets as Juliana herself. At first he had supposed the jewel to be paste or, at the very most, garnet. A pretty enough stone but hardly rare. Now he wondered.

He held the brooch high in the stream of moonlight. He saw blood and fire, the same elements that had haunted her dream.

If it was a real ruby, then she was either an artful thief or a desperate woman who had lost her family and fortune to tragedy.

The long part of the cross curved slightly at the end, and on the back Stephen felt a tiny hinged catch.

Freeing it, he felt two parts of the brooch separate. To his astonishment, he held a tiny razor-sharp dagger.

Intrigued, Stephen studied the small blade, then sheathed it again. Working his thumb over the polished surface of the brooch, he felt a roughness on the gold. He squinted, angling it toward the light. Strange symbols were etched there — odd curls and angles, reminiscent of the ancient runes carved in the rock dolmens hidden in the secret dales of the Welsh marches.

A shiver passed over him. Holding the brooch gave him the strangest sensation. An uneasy feeling of portent.

He put the brooch down. Juliana stirred, settling closer.

Don't feel, he told himself. *Think.*

What was it about her? She was like the ruby, winking in the light, revealing one shining facet after another.

She was a gypsy horse thief one moment, a teller of tales the next. She spoke clear, melodic English but had trouble reading it. Her French was impeccable; she had demonstrated that during Jonathan's visit. Her commanding yet gracious way of dealing with the household retainers seemed odd in a girl raised amid a tribe of itinerant beggars.

Could she have acquired such accomplished skills simply by imitation?

It was the last unanswerable question that occurred to Stephen before he turned to his wife and held her close, and before sleep claimed him, he wondered exactly who it was he held in his arms.

Four

"Gajo!" roared a furious voice. "When I finish with you, there won't be enough left of you to feed to the swine!"

Juliana sprang up in bed and blinked at the sunlit chamber. Between half-open curtains, she spied a familiar figure. Beside her, she felt Stephen stir.

In the endless, frozen seconds, she remembered.

Stephen had stayed with her last night.

He rubbed his eyes, then narrowed them in shock when he glimpsed their guest.

Juliana held the coverlet to her chest. "Hello, Laszlo." She ran her fingers through her rumpled hair. "I knew you would come. Did you follow my *vurma?* What took you so long?"

Laszlo ignored her. With fire in his eyes, he glared at Stephen while rolling up his sleeves with slow and menacing deliberation.

"Milady!" Jillie called from the doorway. "Ah, forgive me, ma'am, but 'twas Meeks who let the blighter in. Here, I'll be rid of the baggage in no time." She grabbed the back of Laszlo's collar.

He jerked away from her. His dark eyes widened, and his thick beard seemed to bristle with a life of its own. "Name of God!" he burst out in Romany. "She is a giant troll!"

Untimely laughter tickled Juliana's throat. "She is my maid." She, too, spoke in Romany, then switched to English. "Jillie, this is Laszlo. Our guest."

"Guest!" he barked. "I would not sully myself under the roof of a tub-bathing Gajo swine." He addressed Stephen in English. "Tell me your name. I would know at least that much before I kill you and send you to hell."

Stephen leaned against the bank of pillows and bolsters. There was a look of lazy ease about him as he lifted an eyebrow. "You certainly seem capable of doing so. Might I ask why?"

Laszlo shook a furious fist at Juliana. "You ruined her! I would give my life to keep her safe, but you . . . you . . ."

Heaving a sigh, Stephen stood. He was fully dressed in rumpled breeches and shirt.

"Here now, wait —"

With a roar of frustration, Laszlo lunged.

Though Stephen was larger and heavier, the sudden attack unbalanced him and sent him crashing to the floor. The bed hangings quivered with the impact.

Gypsy curses streamed from Laszlo as he grappled with his opponent. He cursed the air Stephen breathed, the ground upon which he trod, and the color of his liver. He questioned the virtue of Stephen's mother and the virility of his father. He likened Stephen himself to something stuck to a wagon axle.

As the air turned blue with curses, Jillie sent Juliana a pleading look. With one shake of her head, Juliana held the burly maid at bay. Laszlo had suffered insult enough without his being bested by an unarmed woman.

"Laszlo," she said as his fists struck about Stephen's head. She grabbed his shoulder and tried to drag him off. "Laszlo, please."

"What?" His glance up was his undoing. With one swift shove, Stephen pushed him off and pinned him to the floor. Under Stephen's knee, Laszlo bucked and strained, his bearded face red with exertion.

"I had no idea sleeping with you was so hazardous, Baroness," Stephen said through gritted teeth. Then, to Laszlo, he added pleasantly, "I think the lady wants you to yield to me."

"I came here to kill you. Why should I yield?"

"Because if you don't, I'll have to hurt you."

"Pah!" Laszlo exploded.

"And because," Stephen added in a voice tinged with regret, "I am her husband."

Stephen sat in a leather-slung chair in his estate office, facing the gypsy called Laszlo, who refused to sit. The robust old man peered suspiciously into the cup Stephen handed him.

"It's malmsey," Stephen said. "A sweet Madeira wine. You'll like it."

"Gajo witch's brew," muttered Laszlo, but he tipped the cup and tossed back the drink, then wiped his sleeve across his mouth.

Stephen felt the cool prickle of tension on the back of his neck. Without either of them moving, he and Laszlo seemed to be circling one another, each gauging the other's power and strength.

"There is no need," Stephen said, "to make this unnecessarily complicated."

The man struck his thumb into his wide silk sash. His dirty fingertips rested lightly on the bone hilt of a long knife. "Tell me about yourself, Gajo."

"My name is Stephen de Lacey." He did not add his title, for he doubted the gypsy would be impressed. "And you are Laszlo. Tell me, do you often barge into private bedchambers like an outraged father?"

The stranger drew himself up proudly, his chest filling the embroidered vest he wore, his hawk nose poking the air. "Only for Juliana do I act the outraged father."

Stephen blinked. Her *father.*

Beyond his office window, the morning sun dropped behind a puff of low-hanging clouds. The room filled with shadows, and the eyes of the gypsy turned as dark as mortal sin.

Any hope that the girl might have told the truth died a quick death. Daughter of a Russian nobleman, indeed.

Stephen searched Laszlo's long, spare face for a family resemblance. Instead, he saw only stark contrast. Laszlo had high, bony cheeks while the girl's were smooth and sweetly rounded. Laszlo's hair was coarse and, though threaded with gray, had once been pure black. Juliana's was a sable-rich, sun-catching brown. And then there were the eyes — Juliana's wide pools of clear green bore no likeness to Laszlo's.

"She must resemble her mother, then," Stephen concluded.

Laszlo lifted his chin, the thick pronged beard jutting forward. "She does. In every way."

Stephen sensed something cryptic in the statement. "So Juliana is your daughter. Why did she run away from you?" His hand curled into a fist. "Did you beat her?"

"No!" Laszlo's ruddy face paled a shade. "I would never lay a hand on such as her."

"And yet she strayed from you. I caught her stealing my horse."

A scowl darkened Laszlo's brow. "Caught her, did you? Hmph. I taught her better."

Stephen rolled his eyes. There was simply no reasoning with this angry foreigner. In that, at least, Juliana resembled him. "How did you know to come here?"

"The girl left signs."

Stephen frowned into his cup. "Signs?"

"We call it *vurma.* Signals along the way."

"Bits of cloth?" Stephen inquired. "Thread? Hair? Things like that?"

Laszlo helped himself to another cup of malmsey from the jug on the table. "Yes."

Now Stephen understood why Juliana had ridden too close to the hedgerows, torn her skirts along the way. The wily female. He should have known. He could not trust her at all.

"She was to have married Rodion, the bearward and captain of the *kumpania,*" Laszlo commented. He watched Stephen's face closely as if trying to read it like a map.

"Then she must have fled to escape the marriage," Stephen concluded. "Is it not true that your people allow a woman to make up her own mind on such matters?"

"Yes. If she knows her own mind." Laszlo shook his head, and for a moment he seemed to forget where he was. "Juliana did not. Always dreaming, that one. Always planning to go back."

"Go back? To where?"

"To her Gajo home."

"I thought you said you were her father."

"*You* said I was her father."

"And you did not deny it."

Laszlo picked up a clockwork horse made of tin. He frowned at the movable joints. Stephen had invented it to amuse the tenants' children.

"Well?" His patience thinned. "Are you?"

Laszlo cranked the spring mechanism on the underside of the horse. "Am I what?"

"Juliana's father!" Stephen's voice rang with frustration.

"Are you truly her husband?" Laszlo set

down the toy. It skittered across the tabletop and crashed to the floor. With a startled yelp, the gypsy backed off, muttering and making signs against evil.

In spite of himself, Stephen felt a glimmer of humor. "By order of the king, we were formally wed."

"And why would the Gajo king give such an order?"

Stephen hauled in a deep breath. He did not want to insult Laszlo by admitting that, for him, marriage to Juliana was a punishment. "It's a long story."

"But you wasted no time bedding her."

Stephen thought of how soft she had felt to him last night. How sweet she had smelled. How very much he had wanted her.

Fool, he told himself. That was undoubtedly part of her plan — to entice him into her bed so that he would have no grounds for annulment later. "That is none of your affair."

"If she is to be your wife," Laszlo said stolidly, "you must perform the *plotchka.*"

"Laszlo, no!" Juliana said from the doorway. Her maid had done something artful with her hair, pulling it back with combs and letting the great length of it cascade down her back. Before he could stop himself, Stephen imagined touching her hair as he had done last night, while she slept.

Ungainly as a roe deer, Pavlo bounded into the room and launched himself joyously at Laszlo. The old man laughed and scratched the dog's ears.

"Laszlo, no *plotchka,*" Juliana said, folding her arms beneath her breasts.

Stephen stared at her. Each day she looked more lovely than she had the day before. She wore a gown of vivid peacock-blue, and he wondered where she had gotten it. Meg had never owned anything in that garish color.

"It is not good!" Laszlo yelled, pushing the eager dog down. "You are not properly wed until you perform the rite."

"Exactly!" she said. "I don't want to be properly wed." She let forth with a stream of conversation in her strange tongue. Laszlo responded rapidly in kind, poking the air with his finger. Her chin came up, and she replied, but he seemed unmoved and, finally, ended the argument in a ringing shout.

Juliana's face drained of color. A hunted look haunted her eyes. She glanced at Stephen and then back at Laszlo. Her narrow shoulders seemed to constrict. Though he had not understood the exchange, Stephen sensed her torment, and for once he did not question his own need to end it.

"What did he say to you, Juliana?" he asked softly.

"I told him the king ordered our wedding as a jest, and that we will get an annulment. But Laszlo refuses to listen. He says I shamed him. Shamed the man who risked everything to protect me."

"What is this *plotchka?*" Stephen asked.

"A Romany marriage ceremony," said Juliana.

Stephen raised his eyebrows. "Is that all?"

"All?" Laszlo slammed his cup on the table. "Are you so grand, then, so lofty that a gypsy's pride means nothing to you? Are you so great a man that I am but dung beneath your boots?"

Stephen recoiled inwardly at his thoughtlessness. Sweet Jesus, he had become as intolerant as his king.

"I of all men," he said quietly, "should know the fragility of a man's pride, sir. I would not presume to tread upon that of another."

"Then agree to the *plotchka,*" Laszlo said simply.

"We are married in name only." Stephen did not know why, but his own words bothered him. "Last night was not . . . as it must have looked to you. She had a nightmare and cried out, and I comforted her. Nothing more."

For the first time, Stephen saw approval in Laszlo's eyes. Before the gypsy got the wrong idea, Stephen added, "I mean to give Juliana her freedom as soon as the king tires of the trick he played."

"So. When she is no longer of use to you, you will discard her like a horse with the slump?"

"I'm trying to help her, for God's sake," Stephen burst out. "She doesn't want this marriage and neither do I!" He turned to Juliana. "Or do you?"

She twisted her fingers together, her hands pale against the bright blue-green of her gown. "I wish to please Laszlo. He was so disappointed when I refused to wed Rodion. Laszlo alone protected me when evil men would see me dead. He left his family on my account, defended my honor when men would have taken it from me."

"I would expect no less from a father," Stephen said.

Suddenly she seemed to find her pride again, and she sent a look of fervent affection at Laszlo. "He is not the man who sired me, but these five years past he has been my father."

Stephen did not know what to believe. Was

this all a farce to dupe him? For what purpose — to snare a noble husband for a sly gypsy? And why could he not see the lie when he looked into her proud, beautiful face?

"So you want this . . . *plotchka,*" he said, stumbling over the word.

"It is my duty to Laszlo," she stated, rather neatly hiding her own feelings about the matter.

A denial formed on Stephen's tongue, but he made the mistake of looking at her a heartbeat too long, of seeing just a little too much — the barely detectable quiver of her chin, the diamond glitter of a tear in her eye, which she quickly blinked away.

And then he made his fatal mistake. He remembered, once again, how it felt to hold her all night.

"What does this rite entail?" he heard some fool asking. Belatedly, he realized it was he, the baron of Wimberleigh, playing like a willing gull into the hands of a pair of gypsies. But this ceremony was pagan, hardly legal. Why not humor the old man? No court or cleric would let it impede an annulment.

"First," said Laszlo, lifting his swarthy face like a hound scenting victory, "we must gather the whole *kumpania.*"

"But you came alone. There's not another gypsy within miles of —"

"Lord Wimberleigh!" Nance's horrified screech preceded her cumbersome figure into the office. She pressed her back against the wainscoted paneling inside the door. Her jowls and bosom heaved in tandem as her gaze fixed on Laszlo. "Eek!" she squealed. "There's another one!"

His patience nearing its limit, Stephen squeezed his eyes shut for a moment. "Yes, Nance? What is it?"

"The gypsies are upon us, milord!" Bringing up the hem of her apron, she fanned her florid face. "I had it straight from the chandler's boy when he came round to deliver tapers. Nasty, greasy things they are, too, I might add. All tallow and nary a drop of beeswax if you ask me. And the wicks all be —"

"Yes, yes." Stephen waved his hand. "We'll speak of the candles later, Nance. Now. You say the lad has seen gypsies."

Laszlo and Juliana exchanged a look of amusement.

"A whole ragged rabblement of rakehells, milord." She clapped a chubby hand on her forehead. "The countryside's crawling with them. They be coming in a long train up the Chippenham road — right toward the manor house, mind you." She paused to catch her breath. Stephen had never known anyone to enjoy a great fright as much as did Nance Harbutt. "Ah, we'll be plundered for certain," she rushed on, "the plate carried off and Lord knows all the mothers had best hide their babes, for 'tis common fact the Egyptians are child stealers." She finished with a challenging glare at Laszlo as if defying him to suggest she was wrong.

"Why would we steal Gajo babies?" Laszlo grumbled. "We have plenty of our own."

Nance dropped her apron and planted her fists on her hips. "Hmph! Blind me, milord, but we'd best be about securing the place before —"

"Nance," Stephen said with the patience he always managed to find for her.

"— the punks and rapscallions be in our very midst —"

"Nance."

She blinked. "Aye, milord?"

"I believe it's true," Stephen said gently. "The gypsies are coming."

"Eek!" The apron started flapping again with new vigor. "And didn't I tell you the apple-squires, the runagates —"

"They aren't here to steal plate or babies, Nance."

"Then what —"

"They've come, my dear Nance —" Stephen watched Juliana, her impossibly comely face alight with anticipation "— to witness my wedding."

"My lord," Kit Youngblood said, stepping back to survey Stephen's costume, "forgive me for asking, but why?"

Stephen examined his tightly laced velvet sleeves, the cambric undersleeves peeking artfully through the gaps. "I thought a festive costume would be in order, since our guests take this ceremony so very seriously. Should I have worn the murrey doublet, then?"

Kit scowled in frustration. "You know I don't mean the costume, my lord. Why are you going through with this gypsy ceremony? 'Tis pagan!"

So are my feelings for the bride. Stephen pressed his lips into a firm line of resolve. He would not admit that he had been seized by a desire to please Juliana, to ease the torment he saw in her eyes. Instead, he ran a hand through his freshly washed hair and said, "Some things, my young friend, are better compromised. If I had refused, Laszlo would have unleashed the mischief of his people on the villagers. Better I should go through their pagan rite and send them on their way."

Kit's throat bobbed as he swallowed. "And the baroness, my lord? Will she go with them?"

"Alas, no." For the sake of his own peace of mind, Stephen truly wished he knew a way to send Juliana out of his life. But it was too soon. The king was still savoring his prank. "I fear that after this *plotchka* event, the gypsies will expect me to keep her."

A flush crept up Kit's face, coloring his cheeks and ears. Stephen could have sworn the lad grinned as he bent over a carved chest, searching for Stephen's best hat.

"This pleases you?" he demanded stonily.

"Er, my lord, 'tis hardly my place to comment on the lady — or your . . . er, circumstances."

"You'd not be your father's son if you failed to speak your mind."

With Stephen's hat in hand, Kit straightened and made no attempt to hide his adolescent grin. "After Jillie did her up in proper gowns and hair, my lord, I saw that the baroness was truly . . ." His voice trailed off. He stared up at the ceiling as if seeking to pluck a word from the rough beams.

"Truly what?" As always, Stephen held the boy in secret fascination. Jonathan Youngblood had no idea what a gift he had given

Stephen in sending Kit to him for fostering.

" 'Tis hard to say." The lad tugged at a few prized whiskers sprouting from his chin. "There's a look about her. She's . . ."

"Pretty?" Stephen could defend himself against a pretty woman. He was adept at it.

"No, my lord. *Pretty* is not the word."

Stephen ground his teeth, then suggested, "Beautiful?" Beauty was more dangerous, but not insurmountable.

"One might say so, my lord, at first glance, but she is more than that."

Stephen wanted to tell the lad he had no business scrutinizing another man's wife so closely. But Stephen's throat was suddenly dry and tight, and he could not speak. Though Kit was almost a man, he had not yet mastered the most manly of arts — deception.

"She is not simply beautiful, my lord," Kit went on, all artless honesty. "She's . . . luminous. Aye, she shines with a light all her own. 'Tis a most magical thing." Satisfied with his summation, Kit handed Stephen his hat, a velvet toque with a silver clasp securing a jaunty pheasant feather to the rolled brim.

Stephen took it with numb hands. Kit spoke the truth as only a guileless youth could. There *was* something special about

Juliana. If she were merely pretty or even beautiful, he would have no trouble keeping his distance.

Luminous and magical were something else entirely. He had never before faced such perils. As Kit secured a dress sword to Stephen's baldric, he felt as if he were being girded for battle.

As indeed, he thought grimly, he was.

Juliana stood surrounded by gypsy women. With their usual speedy efficiency, they had set up a camp in the east park, with the caravans and animals sequestered in a grove of trees and a bonfire built in the middle of a clearing by the river Avon.

Long lengths of cloth formed a crude pavilion around Juliana and the women. Before the *plotchka,* the bride's privacy was scrupulously guarded.

"Hold still," murmured Leila, one of the elders. "Here's a bit of sparkle." With delicate movements of her hands, she clasped a thin gold wire to the side of Juliana's nostril.

Juliana suppressed a smile. Even before tonight, her husband had thought her strange. He did not know the half of it.

"And now the necklace of coins," said Mandiva. In keeping with tradition, the women had collected a coin from each man in the tribe. Juliana would go to her husband with a token of goodwill from each.

Juliana fingered the pennies and farthings. There was even a gold noble, probably from Laszlo. She felt guilty taking money for a marriage that was no marriage at all. But the alternative was to let Laszlo suffer disgrace, and she could not let that happen.

"Did Rodion contribute?" she asked.

Mandiva shook her head. "Not yet. Though I'll box his ears if he balks."

"Let me through, damn your coney-catching eyes." The English words came from outside the tent. With an apologetic shrug at the women, Juliana held back the flap. Like a cog under sail, Jillie Egan pushed her way through a group of men and children.

The little ones stared in awe at the giantess. "Jofranka!" one cried, naming her the witch of Romany legend.

Someone else shook a braid of white garlic at her — a sure way to banish a sorceress. Jillie grabbed the garlic, gave it a sniff, then handed it back. "Thank you, but I've already eaten."

Someone else shook a bat bone charm in her face.

"Boo!" she shouted.

The gypsies backed off, their faces watchful. "A witch unafraid of the charm must be powerful indeed," someone whispered.

"Let her by," Juliana called. "She's a friend."

Though Leila and Mandiva grumbled, they allowed Jillie to enter the tent, casting slitted stares of suspicion before leaving.

"Well now," Jillie boomed, taking in Juliana's borrowed silk skirts, her blousy bodice and clanking necklace, the ring in her nose. "Don't you look fine."

Juliana smiled. "You think so?"

"Oh, aye. Passing strange, though." Jillie reached down and touched the wreath that circled the crown of Juliana's head, holding the veil in place. "What's here?"

"A wreath of wheat for bounty, wild rosemary for remembrance, lavender for love. It's traditional."

Nodding in approval, Jillie inspected Juliana's hair, which fell free below the veil almost to her knees. Juliana pulled the gauzy length of raw silk down and forward. "His lordship is not to see my face until we have exchanged vows."

"Too late for that. He's seen your face and a good bit else besides." Jillie winked broadly. "Now all we have to do is wait for the bridegroom." She went out to stand by the bonfire, arms akimbo, face alight with a childlike smile. Juliana felt a surge of affection for her big coarse maid. While most of the others in Stephen's household quailed in fear and shuttered their windows against the gypsies, Jillie embraced the novelty of the visitors. She had never been out of the shire, Juliana remembered. Perhaps the gypsies would bring a bit of the world to Jillie.

A few moments later, Laszlo entered the tent. He took one look at Juliana, and his swarthy face softened. "Look at you," he said in Russian, the language the two of them used when they were alone together. "I fled Novgorod with a frightened little orphan. When did you become a woman?"

Juliana smiled behind the veil. "I did it in secret, when you weren't looking."

He heaved a sigh. "And when did you begin to have a mind of your own? Ah, Juliana, why did you run off? What were you thinking of?"

"My future," she said simply, sprinkling herself with the rosewater Mandiva had given her. "I tried to tell you, but you wouldn't listen. I could never marry Rodion."

"I thought it was best. Time for you to settle down. To be a part of the *kumpania.*"

"I was never part of the *kumpania.* You know that, Laszlo. If I had wed Rodion, I would have had to give up trying to find justice for my family."

"That is a dream. You should leave go of it. Novgorod is half a world away. There is no way to go back."

Juliana took out her brooch and fastened it to her bodice in the center. "I think there is. Maybe now more than ever."

"With this pale, beardless Gajo?" Laszlo asked, contempt ringing in his voice. "How?"

"I haven't quite figured that out yet, but I will. Though neither of us asked for it, Stephen and I are man and wife. He is a peer of the realm."

"What is wrong with him, that he cannot find an Englishwoman to marry?"

"I don't know." Juliana thought of the moody Lord Wimberleigh, the pain in his eyes, the catch in his voice when he spoke of matters close to his heart. "I think one day I shall find out."

Laszlo took Juliana's hand. "For five years I have been your father. We have traveled many miles and seen many wonders. At first you were strange to me — a Gaja princess running for her life, helpless as a babe in a winter storm. But you changed, Juliana.

Grew straight and strong like a tree braving the blizzards of the steppes. I learned to see into your heart, and I discovered it was not so different from the heart of any gypsy. You are Gaja, and you will always be. But first you are a woman. First you are Juliana."

Tears pricked her eyes. From behind the veil she gazed at him, his dear face soft and diffuse, achingly familiar. "You have been good to me, Laszlo. When I triumph over the murderers of my family, you shall be rewarded."

He dropped her hand. "Always you cling to this idea of going back, taking revenge. Do you not see, little one? It is impossible. You wrote frantic messages to the family of your betrothed, Alexei Shuisky. I sent the messages by the means I knew — with a bit of gold to speed them on their way."

Juliana remembered. Once she and Laszlo had ridden a safe distance from Novgorod, each of four messengers had received a silver-and-garnet button from her cloak. Each was promised that, if he found his way to the Shuiskys of Muscovy, the wealthy boyar's family would add generously to the reward.

"Alexei's family never came for me," she whispered, half to herself. "I told them of our journey and our destination."

Laszlo spread his arms. "Five winters have passed. It was not meant to be. Your destiny is here, with the people who have become your family."

She studied the pattern of light from the bonfire flickering on the tent. For a moment she was back in the barn on her father's estate, her hand held out to Zara. *I see blood and fire, loss and reunion, and a love so great that neither time nor death can destroy it.*

"No," she said firmly, laying her fingers on Laszlo's sleeve. "You have been good to me, but I had to leave. I could not be trapped into servitude to Rodion. Perhaps it was wrong for me to go off on my own, but I had to take action. I did not tell you my plan because I knew you would argue against it."

"Of course I would argue against it!"

"I must follow my dream, not yours." She touched his somber face. "Why do you look at me so? Do you think I want too much?"

"Perhaps, little one, you want the wrong things."

"I don't know what you mean."

He jabbed his finger at the ruby. "Blood, vows and honor. All you do, all you live and breathe for, is revenge. I like it not. The desire acts like slow poison. When will you find contentment for Juliana?"

She bit her lip. "When I win back all that I lost."

"Ah!" He threw up his hands. "So you will revive your family by spilling the blood of others? Regain your honor by burning your soul to ashes on an impossible quest?"

"If that is what it takes," she said fiercely, "yes."

Laszlo hung his head. "I thought you had found peace. But perhaps there are some things a gypsy will never understand about the Gaje."

Sadness welled in her throat. He had given her everything it was in his power to give. Yet it was not enough, and he knew it. She hated herself for wanting — needing — more than the Romany people could offer.

The sounds of bells and tambours shrilled outside. Laszlo held out his hand. "It is time to go and receive your husband. Perhaps he can give you what I failed to provide. Or perhaps he can teach you what I failed to impart."

"And what is that?"

"The value of being simply Juliana." He kissed her lightly on the forehead. "Not of family honor. Not of revenge or even justice. Of you and you alone."

She thought of Wimberleigh, his brooding, impenetrable silences, the shadows that haunted him. "I doubt that, Laszlo," she said, but she took his hand as they left the pavilion.

"What in God's name am I doing here?" Stephen wondered aloud, speaking over the wild music of pipes and drums.

Standing beside him at the edge of the ring of light cast by the bonfire, Kit swallowed hard, his Adam's apple bobbing. "Getting married . . . again," he said simply.

"It's beyond me why I agreed to do this. I must have been moonstruck."

"You're doing it to please your lady." As Kit spoke, a girl bearing a basket of bread passed by, hips swaying, dark eyes smiling. He wet his lips. "What man wouldn't?"

"Indeed." Still, Stephen told himself he was going through the pagan ceremony only to placate Laszlo and speed the gypsies on their way. "Let's be about it, then."

He stepped into the circle of firelight. He wore his finest doublet and hose and his high Spanish boots from Córdoba. In his hands he held a bottle of muscatel wine wrapped in a length of bright silk and garlanded with a necklace of gold coins.

When Laszlo appeared on the opposite side of the snapping, hissing fire, the song of the pipes and tambours quieted to a low, steady drone.

Laszlo was flanked by two other men and behind him walked three women. The veiled, shadowy figure in the middle was Juliana.

Stephen's grip tightened on the bottle. This was madness. His soul would probably burn in hell for his part in the pagan ritual.

No matter, he thought wearily. He had damned himself long ago. Committing heresy with gypsies but a minor sin compared to his others.

A swarthy gypsy in blousy red trousers and green vest decked in tin bells shoved past Laszlo, his burning dark gaze fixed on Juliana.

"My lord," whispered Kit, " 'tis the one they call Rodion. The one she ran away from."

"How do you know all this, boy?" Stephen demanded in irritation. "What gossip have you heard?"

Kit did not answer; he didn't have to. The long wink he shared with the ripe gypsy girl nearby was explanation enough.

"She is my woman," Rodion stated in a booming voice.

"Oh, Christ." Stephen had not counted on dealing with a jilted lover.

Rodion clamped his hand around Juliana's

upper arm. "Come, wench. Rodion will teach you to run from your betrothed." In a swift movement, he crushed her against him, oblivious of the crowd. Pushing back her veil, he kissed her hard, his blunt fingers twining into her hair.

Stephen could neither move nor look away. The crude, elemental sensuality of the kiss, the air of sexual aggression that emanated from Rodion, held Stephen immobile with a sense of unfulfilled need. And a painful realization that he had denied himself what Rodion took so casually and openly now.

Even the throaty protest that came from Juliana mocked him. What a challenging little wildcat she would be in the hands of a lover. Not at all like —

"Devil take you!" The accented words burst from her. With an explosive motion of her arms, she shoved Rodion away.

Kit dug his elbow into Stephen's side. "My lord! You cannot let the clodpoll get away with that!"

Stephen swore again. Handing the wine bottle to Kit, he approached Rodion, who was reaching for Juliana once more. Stephen tapped the gypsy on the shoulder.

Rodion turned, a scowl blackening his roughly handsome face. "Ah," he said with a curl of his lip, "the Gajo bridegroom. Could you not find a mare of your own to ride, eh?"

"One more word," Stephen said in a soft, deadly whisper, "one more word out of you, my friend, and I shall string you out in pieces on a trotline across the Avon. Is that understood?"

"Ah, listen to the Ga—"

"That's more than one word," Stephen said, and with a great sigh of regret, he pounded his fist into Rodion's face. The impact of his bare knuckles on the gypsy's jaw was a sharp, clean pain that Stephen welcomed.

Rodion reeled back, senseless, and would have sprawled on the ground had not Jillie Egan broken his fall.

Stephen looked at Laszlo and found him grinning from ear to ear. "Let's get on with it," he muttered, taking his place again at the opposite side of the bonfire. *I wish you had taken her for your own,* Stephen thought as he passed the glowering Rodion. Yet even as he had the thought, he knew he lied.

His half-circle walk around the bonfire seemed endless. With an odd, tingling awareness, he noticed the pop of a pebble in the fire, the scent of burning grass, the low beating of a drum, subtle and steady as a heartthrob.

At the opposite side of the circle he met his host, holding out his offering of wine and coins in exchange for a wife he did not want.

Juliana stood before Stephen. A cairn of rocks was piled on the ground between them.

She was exotic and enigmatic behind the wispy veil, and she smelled of roses and feminine mystery. The firelight flashed over her petite form, briefly illuminating her wide, uncertain eyes shining through the gauzy fabric.

"You can save the playacting, princess," Stephen hissed at her. "You're getting exactly what you wanted."

She tilted her head at a haughty angle. "I don't recall wanting a horse's ass, my lord," she said sweetly.

Laszlo held out a curved piece of tile, probably pilfered from the roof of the spring house or the buttery. Stephen did not understand the significance, but they were required to break a piece of burnt earth between them.

He and Juliana each placed a hand on the tile, and together they lifted it. Stephen looked at her, a veiled illusion, a gypsy temptress, the price he had to pay for keeping his secrets.

In one motion, they brought the tile down hard on the crude cairn of rocks.

The tile broke, a cry went up and Laszlo shouted a command. The two women who had flanked Juliana came forward with the bread basket.

Remembering his instructions, Stephen tore the loaf in half, handing a piece to each woman.

The next part of the ceremony made him nervous. More than anything, this smacked of paganism. Men had been burned at the stake for lesser offenses.

Juliana took hold of her brooch and gave a tug. The cruciform top separated from the jeweled lower part. The small blade glittered in the firelight.

"Hold out your hand," came the whisper from behind the veil.

The drumbeat quickened and crescendoed. Stephen held out his hand. He barely felt the tiny blade score his palm. Barely felt the blood well up. Detached, he watched a single drop splash onto the bread held out by one of the gypsy women.

Then Juliana gave him the jeweled dagger, holding out her own slim hand. Stephen hesitated. Her flesh looked so soft, so pale. With all that he was, he did not want to hurt this woman.

She made a sound of impatience in her throat and lifted her hand to the thin blade. Blood beaded along the cut, bright droplets that caught the light with a sinister sparkle as a drop fell onto the second bit of bread.

"Are you ill?" Juliana whispered.

"No." His palm began to sting.

She put away the miniscule dagger.

The music grew wild, a whirling, hot, and airy melody. They traded the bits of bread. Stephen moved slowly as if bound up in a spell of enchantment, as if he were moving through warm, heavy water.

When Laszlo had explained the rite, it sounded simple enough. Yet it was not. It was as complex and mysterious as the human heart.

Stephen lifted the bread to his mouth and ate while Juliana did the same. There was something searingly intimate about exchanging anointed bread with his gypsy bride. The sensation seemed unbearably sensual, spinning a bond with the invisible strength of a blood vow. It was as if she became part of him, one with him, flesh of his flesh. One body. One heart. One soul.

A great shout went up. Hands clapped and feet stamped. With unsteady fingers, Stephen lifted Juliana's veil, draped it back over her head.

She appeared as pale as he felt. He bent slowly, wondering if he had been given some bizarre love potion, for she looked so beautiful, so desirable to him.

He pressed his hands upon her shoulders. She tilted her head up, fixing him with a gaze that seemed to hold all the ancient wisdom of the ages, yet at the same time bore an innocence that tore at his heart. Her lips were moist and full, parted very slightly, waiting. . . .

He had meant just to brush her mouth with his and have done with the farce. But the moment their lips touched, a devil of possessiveness swirled in his brain, melding with the memory of tasting her blood and pulsing with the drumbeats and bells of the musicians. He drew her into his arms, marveling at her supple, willow-slim body, and crushed his mouth down upon hers, opening his and letting his tongue go questing, tasting, searching for a treasure he could not name.

She tasted like some heady, unnameable sweetness and her lips were soft, unbearably soft. Stephen felt an explosion of sensations, like a man too long imprisoned and then too quickly freed.

She made a small sound in the back of

her throat — a helpless whimper, a plea for mercy. He came to his senses and stepped back, dropping his arms to his sides. She wore a bewildered expression; her lips were moist and bruised by his.

Stephen cleared his throat. "Is that it, then?" he asked, turning to Laszlo. "Is the rite concluded?"

Laszlo took the thick green wine bottle and hurled it into the fire. It shattered with a bright sound that clashed high above the cacophony of the music.

"There must be feasting and dancing," Laszlo explained, "and then you carry your bride off to bed."

To bed. The very thought made Stephen's throat go dry as dust. The clamor that had started in his body when he kissed her came back full force. He was on fire, suddenly full of dreams and desires he had long thought dead to him. He looked at his bride, a vision swathed in silks and redolent of rosewater. Aye, they all expected it of him, else Juliana would be shamed. They all expected him to carry her off to bed.

Duty called.

FIVE

Juliana needed to stall for time. She sat in the grass, drew her knees to her chest and stared into the heart of the great fire as if its hot core held the answers to all the unformed questions swirling inside her.

Stephen had endured the Romany ceremony gamely enough, though it was apparent he disapproved of what he considered pagan practices. She had witnessed gypsy weddings over the years, but never had she imagined herself as the bride exchanging vows of blood and eternity.

She found herself wishing that the marriage rite had not been a lie for both of them. She had lived with the gypsies long enough to feel the chill of superstition, to fear that something dire would happen as a result of their marriage. Part of her yearned to believe that the union was meant to be, perhaps ordained long ago by a fey woman in Novgorod.

But the stark truth was that Stephen had taken her the first time because the king had ordered it, and the second time out of a sense of obligation to Laszlo. She looked forward to ending their unholy alliance as much as he did.

"The stew's right tasty," said Jillie, joining Juliana on the trampled grass and sipping from a clay bowl. "The meat is so tender, I wonder what it is."

Juliana continued to stare into the glowing fire. "Hedgehog, I should think," she said absently.

Jillie gagged and set down the bowl. She put her sleeve to her mouth and scrubbed hard. "Blind me, that's a foul notion, milady."

A wicker jug passed into her hands from the long line of gypsies seated on the ground. Jillie closed one eye and peered into the bottle with the other. "Is this safe to drink?"

"It's probably just cider," said Juliana.

Jillie tipped back the jug and drank, the strong column of her neck moving lustily.

"On the other hand," Juliana said with studied nonchalance, "it could be fermented camel piss. An old gypsy fav—"

Jillie spewed a mouthful at the fire with an explosive hiss. Juliana laughed outright, pounding her bare feet on the ground.

Her face scarlet, Jillie glared at her mistress. Then she threw back her head and brayed with laughter. "Aye, me," she said, daubing at her eyes. "Before you came along, Lynacre was such a black, dour place."

"Was it?" Juliana plucked at a blade of grass and looked across the fire at Stephen. He stood with some of the men, his face stern as Laszlo spoke.

Standing slightly behind Stephen and to one side was the boy, Kit. To Juliana's amusement, Catriona walked past the dark-haired youth, her skirts swishing, her bangles chiming. Slack-jawed, Kit started to follow. Without looking around, Stephen reached out and grabbed the back of Kit's collar, pulling the lad back in line. Stephen did not even pause in his conversation.

Jillie chuckled. "His lordship knows the boy's mind."

Juliana nodded. "He promised Kit's father that he would keep the boy chaste. The lad seems equally determined to end his innocence."

"If it's a battle of wills, Lord Wimberleigh will prevail."

Juliana pondered this. Stephen was less a stranger to her than he had been at their first wedding, and she knew now that he was not a man easily crossed, nor easily dismissed. That had been clear enough when he had kissed her. She squeezed her eyes shut and relived the moment, the unique taste of him, the gentle possession of his mouth on hers.

"Tell me about that one," Jillie said, grabbing Juliana's arm. The maid pointed at a large, shadowy figure at the edge of the firelight. "The one his lordship laid out with a nice cuff to the jaw."

"Rodion," said Juliana, deciding instantly that Jillie need not know the details of their past. "He is the bearward and a captain of the *kumpania*."

"Lord, but he's a fine brute of a man," said Jillie.

Juliana tried to regard Rodion from Jillie's point of view. He was nearly as large as the maid and perhaps heavier. Dressed in hunter green and bright red, he possessed a rather crude, rough-hewn appeal and an air of swaggering confidence. He had recovered fully from Stephen's blow.

She shivered again, recalling the fire and ice in Stephen's eyes when he had attacked Rodion. Her husband, she decided, could be a dangerous man.

She noticed Jillie's rapt face and said,

"Would you like to meet him?"

Jillie lifted her apron and covered her face. "I couldn't!"

"Come." Juliana jumped up and took Jillie's hand. She dragged her over and presented her to Rodion. When he saw Juliana, his eyes narrowed in mistrust and resentment. Then he saw Jillie.

Juliana had never before witnessed the precise moment of an overwhelming attraction, yet when she watched the West Country maid and the gypsy bearward greet one another, she saw it happen — a meeting of the eyes, a touch of the hand. The expression on their faces was one of surprise, and then acknowledgment.

"Rodion, why don't you show Jillie the steps of the tambourine dance?" Juliana said.

He nodded, and together they entered the circle of light. Juliana looked wistfully after them.

"Does cruelty give you pleasure, Baroness?" Stephen asked, suddenly behind her.

She stiffened her spine. "I do not know what you mean."

He jerked his head at Rodion and Jillie. "Those two."

"They like each other."

"Exactly. And then what? Bring them

together, show them a glimpse of heaven, then tear them apart so that their hearts break."

"That is a sentimental statement coming from you, my lord. Why not let them know a little joy?"

"Because it cannot last."

"Why not? Do you think gypsies are inferior to the English?"

"Hardly. I merely see no point in lighting a fire that will burn to ashes in a short time."

"Then let them be happy — just for now."

"Just for now," he said in a mocking tone. He drained a cup of cider and set the empty mug down with a thud. "What about later?"

Juliana sniffed. "You always look on the dark side of life. I believe in capturing the moment." She looked off into the dusky distance, beyond the circle of firelight. "Joy is so fleeting. You never know when it might be snatched away." She blinked, coming back to herself. "Listen to me. Pretending to speak like a sage when I —"

"Perhaps you're right."

She was startled to see the shadow of a smile playing about his lips. A smile? On Stephen de Lacey?

"Dance for me, Juliana."

His request surprised her even more. The musicians had struck up a circle dance, and the women were joining hands.

The piper's tune raced up to a high, quavering note. For a moment, Juliana stood poised uncertainly between two worlds — the wild realm of the gypsy and the settled domain of the Gajo.

Then the rhythm sped through her blood. She swept off her veil and flung it aside. Her bare feet beat like a pulse against the bare earth. She raised her hands and clapped them together — once, twice, three times, turning her head to the side and sending a lazy, low-lidded glance at her bridegroom.

In the blink of an eye, Stephen saw Juliana change from bride to seductress. Without taking his eyes off her, he held out his hand. In it, someone placed a wicker jug. He hardly tasted the drink, for Juliana had captivated him. She moved in time to the heartbeat rhythm, her eyes smoky dark, her smile beguiling, her movements as fluid as warm oil poured from a jar. Her small bare feet skimmed the ground as she spun past him. The bells on her fingers laughed in the night air. The piper's tune was feral, skirling down like the wind from the chalk heights of the West Country.

Stephen had sat through endless court

entertainments. He had witnessed mummers and acrobats and jugglers by the hundreds. Yet never had he seen a performance quite like this one.

His wife was a coquette, drawing her hand across the lower part of her face and gazing at him through batting eyes. A moment later she was the temptress, her hands rising in a slow, sensual gesture high over her head. And finally she was the lover, her hips moving in suggestive circles, her slim fingers beckoning, her eyes beguiling. . . .

Then the song ended, and she stood flushed and panting before him, and she became neither coquette nor seductress, but simply Juliana. She bobbed a maidenly curtsey.

"That was —" Stephen swallowed, found the proper depth of his voice "— a most interesting performance."

"I'm glad you found it interesting." Did her silky tone mock him? It was hard to tell, given her accent and the natural huskiness of her voice.

"Now what?" Stephen asked.

She leaned toward him, and the fire flared behind her, limning her face with the precious hues of gold and bronze. "Now," she whispered, her hand brushing his sleeve, "I think you know what comes next, my lord."

■ ■ ■ ■

The gypsy bedding ceremony is not nearly so barbarous as that predicted by the English. Stephen recalled Laszlo's words vividly as he walked back to the manor house with Juliana.

Thank heaven for small mercies, he thought. In the Romany culture, the newlyweds were not escorted to bed by scores of drunken revelers. Instead, the groom merely had to produce evidence of the woman's loss of virginity the next morning.

He cut the thought short. It was ridiculous even to think of such things. Their marriage was one in name only. And so it would remain. There would be no evidence of conquest to display.

He glanced at the silent figure walking beside him up the graveled drive. A pair of torches at the foot of the front steps illuminated her small form, draped in layers of gypsy silk.

She had said nothing since they left the encampment. Stephen had no idea what she was thinking. She was like the moonless night, dark and mysterious, her secret dreams hidden from him.

They stepped into the quiet hall, lit only

by a scattering of embers in the hearth.

Juliana lifted her gaze to him at last. "Kit is still down by the river."

Stephen nodded. "I lacked the heart to make him leave before the festivities were over." He sighed wearily, feeling the mildly pleasant effects of the plum wine. "Jonathan has entrusted me to guard the lad's virtue. Do you think I should fetch him?"

She looked surprised that he would seek her advice. Stephen was surprised that he had asked. But the darkness seemed to allow them to speak across barriers, to be truthful for a while. "What is the best way to guard a boy's virtue?"

Against his will, Stephen felt a glimmer of humor. "The proper response is to say I must teach him right from wrong rather than restrict him in body."

She laughed. "Surely, my lord, you know that when a lad's blood is up, there is little chance he'll remember his lessons."

Stephen's breathing quickened. Just how innocent was his gypsy wife? He wished he could see her face. "And how would you know such a thing?"

"My lord, for five years I lived where privacy is — how do you Gaje say — where there are few intimacies I have not observed. The young, especially, hold self-restraint in small regard."

Stephen blew out his breath. "Then you do think I should fetch Kit."

Again he heard her low laughter floating through the shadowy hall. "You forget, my lord."

"Forget what?"

"Jillie is there. I told her to watch over Kit. If he misbehaves, she will toss him in the river."

Stephen felt an unfamiliar tugging at the corners of his mouth. Almost as if he were about to smile.

He glanced up at the main staircase at the screens at the end of the hall. The cavernous gloom yawned, waiting to swallow them.

"Let me show you something," he said, not stopping to wonder why he desired to entertain her. He walked over to the hearth and slowly lowered a lever.

"What am I supposed to see?" she asked.

"Top of the stairs."

Seconds later, a candle flared to life on the landing at the head of the stairs.

Juliana gasped and jumped back. "Black magic," she cried, twisting her fingers together in a sign against evil.

Stephen shook his head. "Hardly. It's a small convenience I rigged in order to light the way up the stairs."

She stared up at the tiny pinpoint of the flame and the yellow light that pooled around it. "A candle that lights itself, conduits that carry water through the house, curved glass that makes objects appear larger than they are . . . You do such remarkable things, Stephen."

"No, I don't," he said quickly. "I have a small skill for useful invention."

"I see." She went to the foot of the stairs and hesitated.

Once again Stephen felt a tug of amusement. "Remind me to show you exactly how it works in light of day so you won't suspect me of practicing black magic. Come." He took her hand and together they walked up the stairs. He stopped to light another taper from the flame and accompanied Juliana to her room.

Her room. When had he stopped thinking of it as Meg's?

"Pavlo!" she said as they stepped inside.

Paws in the air, the dog lay like a sultan amid the pillows and bolsters on the bed. He turned his head and blinked lazily at them.

With a huff of outrage, Juliana rapped out something in her foreign tongue. The huge dog laid his ears back and slunk off the bed, flopping down in the rushes.

For the third time since they had left the gypsy camp, Stephen felt like smiling. It must be something in the wine.

"For such a well-trained dog," she said, glaring in mock anger, "he has terrible manners."

Pavlo sighed, rested his long muzzle between his front paws, and closed his eyes.

"Well." Juliana turned to Stephen. Her hands clasped and unclasped in front of her as if she were uncertain. Or nervous. "Well."

He set the candle on the carved trunk at the foot of the bed. Perhaps it was the quality of the light or the lingering effects of the wine, but in that moment Juliana had never looked more enchanting to him. The veil was gone and her long hair draped like a brilliant mantle, dark as mystery, agleam with amber lights. Rose hues plumed in her cheeks. She looked pagan and ripe with a forbidden allure. Her eyes shone like jewels, only brighter, deeper, and yet he could not read her expression. What did he want, what did she expect from him?

She claimed to want the annulment, too. But he was cynical enough to know she would have changed her mind on seeing his rich estate.

The necklace of coins winked as she drew a small breath. Stephen glanced down and saw that her hands were curled into fists at her sides. The knuckles shone white.

The sight of those little hands, so honestly expressing her trepidation, caused his skepticism to heat and uncoil. He caught her in his arms, and this time there was no audience of gypsies expecting a performance. Now there was only Juliana, and he was only a man who had gone too long without her touch.

While his thumbs caressed the downy tendrils of hair at her temples, he regarded her wide, startled eyes and her soft, untried mouth. She swayed against him, her body pliant, and he remembered the way she had danced for him — her sinuous movements, the heat in her gaze — and his own yearning.

He closed his mouth over hers. She made a little gasp in the back of her throat. Then her hands smoothed up over his velvet doublet and slid around behind his neck. The force of his passion alone seemed to lift her off the floor, and her body melded and shaped itself to his, as if she were an empty vessel and he the liquid that filled it.

Even as he damned himself for a fool, Stephen laid her on the bed and pressed himself down on her, his mouth ravenous and his mind in a whirl. With one hand he found the hem of her layered skirts, and his palm brushed the smooth column of her leg, rising over the curve of her knee and along her inner thigh, higher yet to discover with dark, hot satisfaction that she wore no smallclothes.

"Ah, Stephen, Stephen," she whispered against his mouth, "is this what you meant by a glimpse of heaven?"

Her words made him remember. This was a chaste marriage. It had to be. Slowly, reluctantly, hating himself and trying to hate her, he dragged his lips from hers and stilled his hands. By an unfortunate play of the light he saw that her blouse had pulled taut, outlining the rounded swells of her breasts.

He swore and looked away.

"Stephen?" she whispered uncertainly into the semi-darkness.

It took all the power of his will to stand. "I told you from the start that this was to be a marriage in name only. Nothing has changed that. Nothing can ever change that. Not a gypsy ceremony, not a dancing bride, not plum wine from a jug."

He made himself look at her, into the wide, staring eyes that held a world of hurt — a hurt of his own making.

"Do you understand, Juliana?" he forced himself to ask.

"Yes, my lord," she replied in her most studied, precise English. "I understand perfectly."

Stephen traveled twenty miles and drank as many cups of ale in order to forget the look on Juliana's face when he had left her.

He failed. Even as he sat in the mangiest tavern in the city of Bath, amid tricksters and cardsharps and whores, he could not rid himself of the memory of her eyes, first heavy-lidded and smoky with passion, then tear-bright and startled when he pushed her away.

I told you from the start this was to be a marriage in name only.

What was it like, he wondered, for her to hear such words from a man who had just brought her to the brink of passion?

He glowered at the beaten earth floor until a shadow fell over him. "I'd call for more ale," said Jonathan Youngblood, "if I thought it would help. But I doubt that bousing a pint or two more would fix what's amiss."

Stephen lifted red, burning eyes to his friend. "What are you doing here? Go away."

With a great sigh of weariness, Jonathan settled himself on the stool opposite Stephen. "I believe I'll stay." He held up a coin. Seeing the color of his money, the carrier hastened over with a clay mug and a promise to keep it filled.

Stephen scowled at his friend. Though he feigned nonchalance, Jonathan could not quite manage to keep the concern from his eyes. “How did you find me?” Stephen’s tongue felt thick.

“I knew you’d gone to Bath, for it’s the closest place with appropriately seamy alehouses and ivy-bushes. After that, I simply asked around. You’re not exactly a commonplace drunkard.”

“Ah. Then I’m a most singular drunkard.”

“Nor are you easily forgotten, especially on that horse.”

“You’ve found me,” Stephen grumbled. “I’m not lying bleeding or dead in the mews, so you can leave now.”

Jonathan huffed out his breath, blowing the prongs of his big mustache. “I’ve not finished my ale. And you’ve not told me what’s troubling you.”

“Shall I make you a list? It might take awhile.”

Jonathan smiled. His kindness annoyed Stephen. It was so much easier to be wroth with a bastard.

“Kit said you took part in a gypsy wedding.”

Stephen nodded glumly and glared into

his ale. "Thought it would appease them, make them leave the vicinity more quickly."

"It was you who left. Why, Stephen?"

He tipped up his mug. It hovered uncertainly; then his mouth found the rim, and he sucked it dry. "Because of *her.*"

Jonathan lifted one eyebrow. "Her? You mean Juliana."

Stephen raised his empty cup. "Juliana Romanovna of all the Russias. A high eastern princess abased by the lowly and villainous English baron she was forced to wed."

Jonathan frowned and tugged at the end of his mustache. "Can you find no merit at all in her claims? She spoke excellent French to me."

"Tant pis pour elle."

"No, too bad for *you.* Don't mock the girl. Her table manners were excellent, and she seemed quite comfortable directing the servants. Could the gypsies have taught her the refinements, the social graces, the high French?"

"Teaching a female to speak another language is no great feat," Stephen said, slurring his words. "A far greater feat is to teach a woman to be silent."

"Ah. She talks too much. That is why you left her?"

"I left her," Stephen said, looking Jonathan square in the eye, "because I want her."

Jonathan whacked the table with the flat of his hand. "Such impeccable logic. It is time like this, my dear Stephen, when I remember why I am friends with you. You can be so amusing." He loosened the top button of his doublet. "So. You fled hearth and home because you desire your wife."

Simply put, it did seem ridiculous. Stephen's temper heated. "Damn it, Jonathan, you know the circumstances of our marriage. The king forced us together. I wed her to appease him. I hardly intend to make this a permanent arrangement."

"Why not?" Jonathan planted his elbows on the table. "Is it Meg, still, after all these years?"

Black memories swept like a death shroud over Stephen. Jonathan was right . . . and yet he was not. "When I choose another wife," Stephen said, "she shall not be a gypsy nor a false noblewoman nor anyone of the sort."

"She shall be someone prim and properly dull."

Like Meg was. Only Stephen knew different. "Can you not leave me to my own affairs?"

He rocked back on the stool and spread

his arms wide. "You manage them so well."

"There's naught wrong with me."

"Naught that a miracle couldn't cure." The front leg of Jonathan's stool clumped to the floor as he leaned forward. "Look, the girl is a mystery. But she's beautiful and accomplished. Let her into your life. You never know. She might banish that storm cloud that has been shadowing you all these years. Mayhap that's precisely what you fear."

"What I fear," said Stephen, "is that — that —" He broke off. He could not confess his true fears to his very best friend.

He amended, "I fear I shall get home and find my house looted, my offices robbed, and my tenants terrorized by my wife's gypsy friends."

"And what does the lady Juliana say in her own defense? I'd wager she harbors some small tenderness for you, too. You're a great yellow-haired brute of a fellow, but women seem to like you."

"She's a fool if she does." He had a defense against females who wanted to open their soft hearts to him. He had played the role many times. He knew it cold.

"You're a fool if you reject her."

Stephen looked away, idly watching the man at the next table cheating at cards. He was a Spaniard, inhaling the tobacco herb, a new fashion from far-off New Spain.

A beggar slipped into the tavern, unnoticed by the aleman. A mass of tattered clothes and running sores, he limped past the crowded tables and groups of idlers, heading straight for Stephen de Lacey.

Stephen looked into the almsman's good eye — the other was covered with a black patch — and stifled a sigh. No matter how stern and unapproachable he tried to appear, the beggars always spotted him for a gull.

With a sense of weary resignation, he peered into the beggar's clack dish. A few clipped coppers rattled piteously in the bottom. "Alms, sir?" the man rasped in a voice roughened by quantities of cheap green wine.

Jonathan started to wave the man away, but Stephen grabbed his friend's arm. He reached for his purse, then hesitated as an idea took shape.

Perhaps if he worked at it hard enough, Juliana would beg to leave Lynacre.

"I can do better than that, my poor unfortunate," he said to the beggar.

Jonathan's jaw went slack. "Stephen, you can't mean —"

"Ah, but I can," Stephen said darkly. "I

already have a band of gypsies at Lynacre. What's a few rogues and beggars added to that?"

Juliana hated herself for worrying about Stephen. Sweet St. Basil, she was a Romanov! Though he refused to believe it, Stephen had married far above his station. Why should she care that he held her in contempt?

Ah, but it hurt. Never one to deceive herself, she admitted that much. It hurt unspeakably to remember the compelling touch of his lips against hers. To feel his hands skim over her shoulders, her bare legs. And then to see him turn away, cold eyed and remorseless, unaffected by the fire he had touched off with his expert caresses.

I told you from the start this was to be a marriage in name only.

That was her agreement, too, and yet he had been so blunt, so heartless.

Did it give him pleasure, she wondered bitterly, to make her want him and then push her away like a beggarwoman? Dear God in heaven, what sort of man had she married?

Rather than wallow in melancholy, she decided to find out. Like a military strategist, she moved through the huge rambling house, seeking clues to the character of the man who had made her want him so desperately.

She started with the great chamber in the upper gallery. From Nance, she had learned that this was where Stephen slept — on the rare occasions he stayed home.

Feeling like a sneak thief, she pressed down the door latch and entered a big, high-ceilinged antechamber. Richly furnished and decorated with painted cloths on the walls, the room had a quantity of books and scrolled maps stored on shelves. In the middle of the room stood a great globe on a stand, its amber land masses identified in beautiful lettering, and the vast unknown seas embellished with dragons and serpents.

On a broad, low table with twisted legs lay a variety of unusual objects. Some looked like optical devices with thick lenses; others resembled a seafarer's or cosmographer's tools — an astrolabe and quadrant, calipers and protractors.

She studied the instruments for a moment, then looked at the rows and rows of books. Some were new printed works; others were hand copied and illuminated on vellum. Such books, she knew, had a value that could feed a peasant family for several years. She recognized a few works in Latin and French. There were many books in English, but at the moment she lacked the patience to decipher the titles.

She passed into the bedchamber proper. A massive bedstead, all hung with drapes and valances, dominated the room. An oriel window, projecting out over a breathtaking view of the main garden, let in great streams of light.

Everything, from the scholar's books and scientist's tools to the regally appointed bed, proclaimed this the domain of Stephen de Lacey — a man of knowledge, yet one who appreciated beauty and sensuality as well.

Juliana touched the heavy oak headboard of the bed, her fingers brushing the carved surface, finding the shapes of the letters *M* and *S*.

She wished she did not care, but she did. Stephen could not forget Margaret. When he kissed Juliana and carried her to the bed, he had probably imagined she was his beloved first wife. Then when she had spoken, her voice shattered the spell, and he had pushed her away.

She turned from the bed and glared down at the long, broad garden. Beyond the high-walled apple yard lay a tangled wilderness. For a moment, she fancied she saw a wisp of smoke rising from the heart of the distant forest, but decided she had imagined it.

Scowling, she brooded about her husband. He had more good sense than she. She was not supposed to be wandering about moonstruck because a man had offered her a few kisses. She was supposed to be concentrating on a way to find the killers of her family.

Her resolve firmed. With a proprietary air, she seated herself at the writing desk. She found a sheet of writing paper in the slim upper drawer, a quill and inkhorn in the stand above.

It felt strange to write with ink on paper. The skill was one the gypsies did not possess and found suspect.

She wrote the letter twice in case one copy got lost. Her message was simple. She told the Shuisky family where she was, calling herself a "guest" of Lord Wimberleigh.

She had written numerous such messages over the years. She doubted any had found their way one thousand leagues to Muscovy. This time might be different. This time she would stay in one place long enough for them to find her. This time she had the money to pay the messenger handsomely.

She prayed it would make a difference.

While searching the desk for sealing wax, she encountered a locked drawer.

The only obstacle to opening it was her conscience, and that didn't last long. She owed no loyalty to an English lord who could not bear to touch her.

The lock gave easily to her well-honed skills of pilfering, and she slid the drawer open. Inside lay nothing more than trinkets — a few whittled pen nibs, an ornate pair of scissors.

And then she saw the three small oval portraits. Limnings, they were called. Tiny paintings done on smooth ceramic.

With trembling hands, she laid them out before her. One was of the first baroness. From the portrait in the upper gallery, Juliana recognized the pale beauty with her demure eyes and aquiline features, the wispy white-blond hair.

The other two portraits were of children. Two boys, very young, perhaps merely four or five years of age. They looked similar — brothers, no doubt, with sweet red lips and pink cheeks, pale hair and blue eyes.

Eyes like Stephen's.

A chill skittered down Juliana's spine. *These were his children.*

Hastily she scooped up the limnings, replaced them in the drawer, and locked it. Children. Stephen had children. Two sons. So where were they now?

The most likely possibility raised a lump in her throat. Stephen's sons, like their mother, were dead.

Juliana took her letters and left the great chamber. She would give the missives to Laszlo, who would take them to Bristol and find a ship bound for the East. Then she would find Jillie and ask her about Stephen's sons.

She accomplished neither objective that day. Only moments after she closed the door to Stephen's chamber, she heard a commotion at the gate and rushed to the window to look out.

Her husband, with the most remarkable group of guests in tow, had come home.

Six

"Who are these people?" Juliana demanded, confronting Stephen in the hall.

He gave her a lopsided grin and winked a bloodshot eye. "Our guests, my dear." He gestured at the busy scenc in the huge room. "Shall I introduce you? That's Jack Sharpe, a master of card play. And the fellow with the eye patch is Penry Luck. The women are Lovey and Peg. Skilled at various forms of . . . entertainment."

Lovey's tightly laced bodice pushed her large breasts up so that they resembled twin half-moons above the dingy fabric of her blouse. She was pretty in a sly, coarse way, and she wore a smirk that made Juliana want to slap her.

"Our guests." Her temper smoldered. "And where, pray, did you find them?"

"In Bath."

"Apparently none of them washed in the waters there."

"My dear wife, you brought a tribe of gypsies to Lynacre. Why shouldn't I invite friends of my own?" With that, he left her standing by the screens at the end of the hall and went to join in the card game.

Lovey smiled and lowered herself to a stool next to him, leaning close to whisper in his ear.

Juliana's fist clenched with the need to box Stephen's ears. Curse him. The only way to rid the house of these vermin was to beat them at their own game.

She walked to the table, her chin proudly aloft. Five years with the gypsies, five years outsmarting the Gajo in order to survive, would serve her well this night. "Deal me in," she said, taking a seat opposite her husband.

Juliana was cheating at cards and had been for hours. Stephen was sure of it. He knew his companions were aware, as well, but not even Jack Sharpe could catch her out. She held her parchment cards close to the chest and kept her sleeves rolled back, baring her dainty wrists. Not once did she put her hands out of sight. How in God's name did she manage?

"Hell's bells," Stephen muttered, taking a sip of ale he did not need from the mug being passed around the table. "You have the winning hand once again, my dear."

She merely collected her markers and nodded at Sharpe, the dealer.

The wench called Lovey sighed and leaned her head on Stephen's shoulder. It used to be easy to dally with a lusty wench. Now he felt distaste, as if someone had added a purgative to the ale.

Lovey possessed a lazy indolence that kept her questions and demands at bay. Stephen had used women like her before. When a marriage prospect showed inordinate interest in him, he simply found a wench like Lovey. The tender young ladies always forgot their interest in him after that. It had worked every time.

Except with Juliana. She joined them with her game smile and her damnably quick hands. She cheated and bluffed her way to victory time and time again.

"I weary of this," Stephen said, slamming down his hand of cards.

"My lord, you've fallen so far behind in your winnings." Juliana aimed a wry look at the pile of coins she had amassed. "Fancy that. I have won everyone's money."

Jack and Penry exchanged disgruntled looks. Juliana touched a finger to her full lower lip. "My dear husband gives me everything I need. *Everything.*"

Stephen braced himself. He never knew what she was going to say. From the corner of his eye he saw Kit, Nance and Jillie gathered at the foot of the stairs. They wore nightclothes and sleepy expressions that turned quickly to avid interest.

"So I hardly need my winnings." With a shrug of nonchalance, she pushed the coins toward them. "Surely you can find good use for these . . . in Bath."

Her message rang clear and did not need repeating. Jack scooped up the money and hurried out of the hall, Penry and Peg trailing behind him, whining for their share. Nance shooed them out of the hall with an indignant flap of her nightrail.

Stephen regarded his wife with reluctant admiration. She had rid herself of them quite handily — and at his expense.

Lovey, however, proved more tenacious. "Let's to bed," she suggested, grabbing Stephen by the hand, standing and tugging him to his feet.

"You may either go with your friends to Bath, or bed down in the cow byre," Juliana said simply. She, too, stood up.

Jillie moved out of the shadow of the stairway, but Stephen saw Kit pull her back.

"Oh, ain't we the fancy one?" Lovey

taunted. "I'll take my ease where his lordship wills it."

Without so much as a glance at Stephen, Juliana said, "My husband thinks you should follow your friends."

"Mayhap we should let him answer for himself."

Stephen had no notion of what to say. Part of him wanted to laugh aloud; another part wanted to throttle one or the other of them. "I think —"

"Not hard enough, my lord," Juliana said mildly. Then she turned to Lovey, who had dropped Stephen's hand and stood with arms akimbo, glaring at Juliana.

Stephen had never seen such a small, beskirted female move so quickly. A slight form crashed into Lovey and shoved her back against the table.

Juliana barely seemed to touch her brooch, but in an instant, it was in her hand, the small sharp blade touching the hollow of Lovey's throat.

"Christ Almighty," Lovey shrieked. "She'll kill me."

"Only if you do not do as I say," Juliana said. "First, you'll give back the things your light fingers took."

"I took no —"

Juliana brought the blade down, slashing

an opening in Lovey's skirt. To Stephen's astonishment, she revealed a secret pocket. One by one, she removed a button, a pewter spoon and a silver coin.

"You're good," she said, "but not good enough. He did not notice your pilfering, but I did."

Lovey's face flushed red. "See here now —"

"No, *you* see here." Juliana leaned close. "You will leave this instant, or suffer the consequences. If you so much as breathe the air of Lynacre ever again, there will not be enough left of you to wipe the floor with."

Lovey uttered a word Juliana probably didn't understand and stormed out. Juliana calmly replaced the blade. Kit and Nance nudged each other, grinning like Bedlamites. Jillie beamed with the pride of a fencing master at a prized student.

"My lord," Juliana said, "this is the end of your doxies and gamblers and low-living scoundrels. I simply shan't tolerate jackfools."

"Tomfools," Stephen said, still inexplicably close to laughter.

She jabbed a tiny finger in his chest, punctuating each word. "I require a sober husband who does not make himself subject to beggars and thieves."

At last he found his voice. "And why, pray, is my character of such concern to you?"

From the corner of his eye he saw Nance and Jillie and Kit withdraw.

"Because I want your help."

He felt that unfamiliar twitching of his lips, and he realized how rare it was for him to smile. "Madam, you hardly seen to be a damsel in need of help."

"I want you to take me to Muscovy," she said.

He blinked. "Juliana. I have shown great restraint in allowing you to persist with your falsehoods and fantasies. But let us put an end to that, as well."

"No. You know I speak the truth. You know I was not born a gypsy. You know I am who I say I am."

"I know nothing of the sort."

"Then let me prove it to you. Take me to Muscovy. There are people there who knew my father, who would recognize me. They might try to kill me, of course, but you will not let them."

What an enigma she was, so small and earnest, and yet as fierce and courageous as a cornered vixen. Despite her wild claims, she was as sane a woman as Stephen had ever known. And lovely. Too lovely. His unreasoning desire returned, jolting through him, and he remembered why he had escaped to Bath in the first place. Now he realized bleakly that neither distance nor drink would keep his passion at bay.

"This place you speak of is one thousand leagues distant," he said. "Shall I go there simply to prove you're a fraud?"

"Ah. Then you did take pains to find out exactly where Novgorod is. The rewards will be great. Though you may try to deny it, you married far above your station."

"Such grandiose ideas, little comfit." Stephen took her by the shoulders. He had meant merely to steer her to her own chambers where she would trouble him no more.

Instead he felt himself drawing her close. Close enough to inhale her subtle scent of lavender, to see the individual bars of lucid light in her extraordinary eyes. To hunger for the taste of her full, unsmiling lips.

"Juliana, what the hell are you, a witch?" he demanded.

She shook her head, too wary or too startled to speak. Her teeth caught at her lower lip.

"How is it that you set a torch to my blood when all other women leave me cold?" The question was torn from him before he could stop it.

She tilted her head up so that her lips were

just inches from his. "A torch to your blood, husband?"

Husband. He wished like mad she had not called him that. He tightened his hands on her shoulders. "Don't play the innocent. I think I've guessed your game. You make me want you, then —"

"I do not 'make' you do anything. If I could, we would be on a ship bound for Archangel right now." She looked deep into his eyes, and he felt naked before her, stripped of his defenses and vulnerable. It was almost as if she could see the secrets he kept hidden.

"You'd best learn not to play with fire, princess, else you might be burned." He bent low and crushed his mouth to hers. She tasted unbearably sweet, of summer ripeness and feminine mystery, tastes he had forbidden himself for years and suddenly craved with an intensity that took his breath away.

She wrenched her mouth from his. "The last time you kissed me like that, you went to Bath and returned with a pack of thieves." She pressed her hands to his chest and stepped back. "This time I shall be the one to walk away."

" 'Woman is a necessary evil, a natural

temptation, a desirable calamity, a domestic peril, a deadly fascination and a painted ill.' " Forming the words with painstaking care, Juliana read aloud in a ringing voice.

Passing by the east flower garden on his way to the stables, Stephen paused in the shadow of an arbor to listen. Silent agreement rose up like a dark tide inside him. Aye, a deadly fascination indeed, and growing deadlier with each passing day.

"Nance, are you certain that is what this book says?" Juliana asked.

Stephen pulled aside a low-hanging branch to see his very own "domestic peril." She was with Nance and Jillie on a turf seat surrounded by soft grass. A basket of needlework and a stack of books in their midst. An open tome lay in Juliana's lap, and Nance paused in her sewing to point to the text. "Aye, in the words of Saint Chrysostom himself. He says the whole duty of a woman is to learn silence with all subjection."

"Saint Chrysostom." Juliana pronounced the name carefully.

A most excellent scholar, thought Stephen.

"A churl of the lowest order," Jillie Egan said with a scowl.

"Let us read something else, Nance," Juliana said, nodding vigorously in agreement. "I wish to learn to read English, not to learn to hate it!"

"Are gypsy men any different?" asked Nance. "By my reckoning, the wife is under the rod of the husband no matter what manner of man he be."

Juliana nodded glumly. "It is the same in Muscovy." She closed the book with a thud. "But at least there, the husband is not *afraid* of his wife."

Nance's wimple quivered in an errant breeze. "Ah, his lordship's not afraid of you, my lady. He's just . . ."

Don't say it, Nance Harbutt. Stephen almost shouted the warning at her. *Don't you dare say it.*

"Just what?" Juliana asked.

"I guess you might say he ain't eager to . . ." As if she'd sensed Stephen's fury from afar, Nance let her voice trail off and flipped to a new page in the book. "Maybe this one's more to your liking, milady. 'A dialogue defensive for women against malicious detractors.' "

Juliana drew her knees up and planted her small chin on them, looking charmingly girlish. "How is it that you know how to read so well, Nance?"

" 'Twas me own precious daughter what taught me. A right gift had my Kristine, and took vows back before the king broke with Rome. Ah, she were an excellent nun, all pious and never moved by the worldly temptations of the flesh."

"I did not know you had a daughter." Juliana left off her study of the book and measured a length of thread for her needle. "Nor a husband."

"I never had one of those," Nance said with a cackle of mirth. "Didn't you mark the words in that book? I'll be under no man's rod. Though time was, I weren't averse to having his rod *somewheres.*"

Jillie flung her apron over her face and, convulsing with laugher, collapsed backward on the lawn.

Stephen half hoped for a show of dainty outrage from his bride, but instead she joined in the laughter and gave Nance a hug. The sun through the leaves spattered them in rich gold.

"The company of women is so agreeable," Juliana said. "Why do we let a man ruin it?"

"It's on account of that rod," Jillie said, daubing at her eyes.

Nance fixed her with a censorious look. "And what would you be knowing about that, Jillie Egan? Just what have you been up to with that Egyptian fellow?"

His errand forgotten, Stephen listened in

fascination.

"Naught," Jillie said. "But not for want of trying. I like Rodion. He's . . . different. Makes *me* feel different, like anything is possible."

Nance sighed dramatically. "With the right man, anything *is* possible."

"Truly?" Juliana put aside her needlework, drew her knees to her chest and plucked wistfully at a blade of grass. "I wonder."

A terrible longing seized Stephen. He tried to tear his gaze away, but failed. She was wondrous; he could not deny it. Small and dainty as a rose she was, yet she had a steel inner core that commanded respect.

She had swept into his household with the authority of a castellan, running Lynacre Hall as if she had been trained from the cradle to perform the duties of a great lady. From dawn to dusk she held dominion over kitchen and buttery, stillroom and hall, directing servants and tenants. In the evening he was likely to find her at her devotions, repeating words and phrases over and over until she spoke like a West Country maid.

This same woman, he reminded himself, did not hesitate to draw a blade and hold it to a stranger's throat. The picture was imprinted on his brain, and there it lingered as he forced his feet along the path leading away from the garden.

In the weeks that followed, Stephen continued to disappear nightly. But never again to Bath, never far enough to be gone for long.

Some mornings Juliana would encounter him brooding in the hall, morose and uncommunicative.

A mistress was the only answer. The idea grew like a poisonous vine, choking her heart. He went to meet some woman, and judging by his moodiness, the relationship must not be going well.

She thought often of the limnings she had discovered in his chambers. She wanted to know more about Stephen's past, yet she kept silent, waiting for him to broach the topic.

Summer spun along in a string of lazy days. The gypsies camped in a forest meadow by the river Avon, keeping much to themselves and living off the bounty of the land, poaching the occasional coney or deer from the royal forest in Stephen's custodianship.

Juliana staved off a gnawing sense of impatience by delving into the workings of the estate. At one end of the hall were the estate offices. There, she had her own room, a tiny windowless cubbyhole. Stephen had seemed surprised that she would make use of the office. Apparently his first wife had not troubled herself with business.

One day at the peak of high summer, she came out of her office and nearly collided with Stephen in the open, colonnaded passageway. It was chilling the way he managed to look through her — as if she had no more substance than air.

"My lady," he said, inclining his head.

She tried not to notice how the sun struck his hair, tried not to notice the muscular shape of his legs. He wore plain hose and boots and tunic, for he worked as hard as any of his tenants. The day was warm, and the tunic was unlaced to the middle of his chest, revealing tanned skin glistening with sweat. Nonplussed, she looked into his eyes. The coldness there stopped her rising passion.

"Good day, my lord," she said.

For a moment, they stood facing each other. What could she possibly say to a man who had wed her so unwillingly, a man who preferred the company of doxies and gamblers to her own?

He seemed to have the same thought, for he nodded and stepped into his own offices. Juliana stood in the passageway, absently greeting the tenants who arrived to discuss their affairs with the lord of the manor.

They cloaked their curiosity about her in deference, tugging a forelock while greeting her, then stepping into the office. For a time, she stood listening to the murmur of voices inside, the occasional ripple of male laughter. Stephen was at ease with these people; he liked them and treated them fairly. She found herself thinking of her father, and a sudden sharp stab of yearning caught her unawares.

It was that ache of loneliness that made her enter the office after the tenants had left.

"Yes?" he asked without looking up. "What is it?"

"I . . . wanted to speak to you."

He glanced up swiftly, and the chill mask slid over his features. In that moment he resembled a marble god she had seen in the gardens of Richmond Palace. "Juliana, what do we possibly have to talk about?"

I want to know you better. I want to know your sadness and your anger. And, God help me, I want to see you smile.

She refused to be cowed by his brusque manner. Trying to appear nonchalant, she wandered to the middle of the room. "What are the markings on this table?" she asked, running her hand over the checkered surface.

"It makes tallying the accounts easier. I put markers on the squares to represent the sums. The notched markers stand for ten times the amount on the board."

She had always excelled at ciphering. "I could tally sums for you, and have no need of checkers and notches."

"I prefer to use the table."

"My lord, it is no great shame to admit you are deficient in —"

"I have my deficiencies," he cut in, "but not in ciphering. I use the table so my tenants can see each calculation. It puts their minds at ease."

"Oh." Had her father been a compassionate landlord? She could not remember. Self-conscious now, she walked over to a side table. "And what are these?" she asked, fascinated by the array of delicate-looking metal instruments.

Suddenly he was beside her, coming up swiftly and quietly, startling her. "Calipers for measuring bore sizes," he said. "And this is a scale. It's far more accurate than the brass balance used by most."

She glanced sideways at him. "You made all these things, didn't you?"

"Aye."

She thought of all the little conveniences she had noticed about the manor — a heat-driven spit in the kitchen, a lamp in a bowl of water to magnify the light, a rolling ladder in the larder, the conduits that carried water throughout the house. "Why?"

"I made them because I saw a need."

"You —" she frowned, retrieving he word "— you invented them. You have a marvelous talent, my lord."

"These are practical devices. I wouldn't call making them so great a gift." Turning sharply, he went back to the exchequer's table.

A tentative knock sounded at the door, and Stephen hastened to let in the caller.

A woman in a homespun gown and bare feet shuffled slowly, hesitantly, into the office. One of her thin arms was looped through the handle of a willow withe basket.

"Mistress Shane?" Stephen asked, his voice soft and gentle as if he had not just spoken so harshly to Juliana.

The shawl-covered head nodded, and she raised her eyes. Juliana's interest was caught by Mistress Shane's milk-pale skin, her hollowed cheeks, and deep, dark eyes. "Aye. Forgive the intrusion, my lord. I should have come when the others did, but —" A mewling cry came from the basket. She jiggled it, and the babe quieted. "The little one was fussy."

"Where's your husband, mistress?" Stephen asked.

"Died, he did, while you was gone to see the king."

Juliana watched in astonishment as compassion transformed her husband into a different man. His oak-hewn features changed, softened. His eyes warmed as he came around the table and took the young woman's hand as if she were the grandest of noblewomen.

"Sit down, mistress."

She lowered herself to the stool and settled the basket in her lap.

"Why didn't you tell me sooner?"

"It weren't rightly your problem, my lord."

Stephen's breath caught. "Why in God's name would you say that? How could you think I wouldn't care?"

"Tell us what happened," said Juliana.

The woman drew a deep breath, and Juliana recognized the shaking quality of it, the trembling effort to conquer grief. She had felt it so many times herself.

" 'Twas a fever. The same one what carried off me eldest boy a month before."

Juliana could tell Stephen had not been informed of that death, either. She pitied the reeve who was charged with keeping him informed of the tenants' doings.

"What sort of fever?" His voice sounded different. Harsh. As if invisible hands were strangling him.

Mistress Shane lifted her shadow-rimmed eyes. " 'Twas the lung fever, my lord."

The effect of the words on Stephen was startling. Juliana took his hand. His was rough and dry and cold. "Stephen?"

He seemed to shake himself then, blinking and all but ripping his hand from her grasp. "Mistress Shane, I deeply regret your loss. What land did your husband hold?"

"Three sections and a bit of water meadow by the river, my lord."

"Your rents are waived until further notice."

"Thank you, my lord!" She grabbed his hand and covered it with kisses.

Juliana thought he would snatch it away; he was so uncomfortable with displays of affection. But he stood still. With his free hand he lifted the woman's face and peered into her eyes.

"You'll need help with the work."

"But, my lord, there is no one."

"There are a dozen able-bodied men camped by the river," Juliana said gently.

Stephen frowned. "The gypsies mislike

working the land. 'Tis too constant for their natures."

"Gypsies!" Mistress Shane clutched the basket to her bosom. "They steal babies. I've heard they eats them and —"

"I assure you, they do not," Juliana said quickly. "And while gypsies do not like to work the land —" she sent Stephen a pointed look "— the men of Laszlo's tribe will help you."

The woman sought Stephen's gaze. "Is it true, my lord?"

He hesitated a moment, then said, "We'll see that you get your work done."

With a flurry of thanks and bobbing curtsies, she left. Juliana looked inquisitively at Stephen. "That was kind of you."

"Better to keep the land productive." He cleared his throat and turned to shuffle some papers on his desk.

Juliana hid a secret smile. Let him pretend he acted out of sheer pragmatism. She glanced at the estate map pegged to the wall over the table. "This is Lynacre?" she asked.

He nodded absently. The map showed the great bend in the river Avon, the curve that marked the fertile meadows the tenants occupied. It was fringed in fields and woods stamped with a portcullis device.

"What is this?" she asked.

"The king's hunting preserve."

"It takes up more than half the estate."

"Aye."

"And it simply lies idle unless the king wishes to hunt?"

"That is correct."

"Such a shameful waste." She traced her finger over Lynacre Hall, its H shape with the great chamber flanked by two gabled ends. Some distance away, there was a patch of empty green space. "What garden is this?"

"A forest." A tic of impatience started in his jaw.

"Where does it lead?" Juliana asked, pressing on.

"Nowhere. 'Tis long overgrown and useless even for hunting. No one ever goes there."

"Oh. Thank you for telling Mistress Shane about the gypsies," she said. Anything, please God, but this terrible silence. Anything to move him to something other than complete indifference.

He shot her a narrow-eyed look. "Does that surprise you?"

"Yes," she snapped, suddenly sick of his apathy. "As a matter of fact, it does, my lord. I was beginning to believe you had no heart at all."

In two strides he sprang across the room and faced her, close enough to kiss her. "Believe me, Juliana." His voice was taut with icy control. "Where you are concerned, I have no heart. My only burning desire is to see you gone."

She stared hard at his face, into his eyes. And there she saw the pain. The lie. The secrets.

It gave her the courage to touch him, to rest her palm on his cheek for a moment. "What is it, Stephen? What is it that tears at your heart, that makes you so tender with a grieving widow, so patient with Kit as he fumbles at the quintain and the archery butts? And then so callous with me?"

He flinched and drew away. "Damn you for a meddlesome busybody," he said. Then, turning on his heel, he stormed from the room.

SEVEN

No matter how fast he rode, Stephen could not escape the demons. Still he tried. Still he punished his beautiful swift mare at a brutal pace, needing no spurs save his own voice to urge Capria to her greatest speed.

Across the greening landscape she carried him, over windswept fells and scrubby downs. To the barren chalk heights and then down again. Dizzying leaps across streams and hedgerows and terraced fences of stone.

He found no escape. Even as the perils of hard riding leaped up around him, his mind clung to her image: Juliana, with her rich gleaming hair tumbling about her shoulders and her eyes on fire with wanting him, wanting his secrets, wanting his soul.

His heart slammed like a hammer against his breastbone. At last he knew what he feared.

That he could love again.

No. No. No. He pounded his heels against

the mare's sides. He drove her down to a hidden place that reminded him of exactly who he was and what he had done. A place that would help him freeze his emotions and keep his feelings for Juliana from devouring him whole.

When he reached his destination he was panting as if he, and not the mare, had raced for miles.

He threw the reins around a tree branch and approached the secluded spot. Aye, she was there, waiting for him, as always. Never changing, ever patient, biding her time. Sometimes he was able to stay away for weeks at a time and to go for days without thinking of her. But always he succumbed to her allure, her dark patience, her irresistible secrets.

Stephen was sweating now, his breath coming in great gusting pants as he fell to his knees before her, a supplicant begging indulgence from a deity.

He whispered her name, loud and harsh in the shadowy stillness. *"Meg!"*

Juliana used a sidesaddle when she rode. Her request for a lane saddle had scandalized Stephen's grooms. She thought it rather silly to ride sideways on a horse, but she gamely hooked her leg over the cantle, relaxed against the hindbow, and slapped the reins of the big dun mare.

"Let me escort you, milady," said Piers, tugging his forelock and gazing up at her with worshipful eyes.

"Thank you. That will not be necessary."

"But 'tis not safe abroad, milady. The hills and forests, they be crawling with cutthroats and gypsies —" He clapped his hand over his mouth and turned as red as a cherry. "Forgive me, milady. I didn't mean —"

She summoned a smile. "Insults sting but a little when they stem from a man's ignorance." With that, she quirted the horse and trotted out of the stable yard.

Stephen had told no one where he was going. He rarely did, or so the servants said, and he was never questioned. She followed his trail easily enough, finding the imprints of his mare's hooves in the bruised earth freshly moistened by a rain shower at dawn.

He had ridden hard and without direction for a time, leaping hedgerows and stiles and plunging through a wood.

The signs grew more subtle, but still she found them. She had learned to read *vurma* from the gypsies; her sharp-eyed glance picked out a hoofprint here, a broken twig there.

She emerged from the woods to find

herself on a broad slope that led down to a meandering stream. The remote, unfamiliar area was lush with reeds and forget-me-nots.

First she saw his horse tethered to a tree, placidly cropping at the clover and grass that grew thick and sweet in the spring-watered area.

Then, as she dismounted, her jaw dropped. The reins fell from her numb fingers. The dun mare seized the moment to sidle away. Juliana started after her, but the mare was off, trotting back toward the manor. With a shrug, Juliana returned her attention to the place by the stream.

The building was constructed of powdery yellow limestone. Though tiny, it had the same slim vertical lines that distinguished the large cathedrals at Salisbury and Westminster.

Yet this one — a chapel, was it? — would fit inside the stillroom at Lynacre Hall. Perhaps it was a shrine of some sort.

Filled with curiosity, she approached the chapel. It had only two small windows, no more than sidelights, actually, and a low-arched door that stood open.

Swallows flitted in and out of the eaves. Stopping outside the doorway, she looked inside and saw Stephen in profile.

He knelt with his head bowed, his clasped hands pressed to his brow. The light streaming through a high, cloverleaf-shaped window mantled him in gold.

Juliana felt a slight chill and a lurch of her stomach. She did not want to intrude upon a man at prayer. And yet at the same time she felt drawn to him and entranced by his pain, his need.

"Stephen?" She spoke his name softly.

He snapped to attention, coming to his feet and moving in front of something — or someone — as if to hide it. Or her.

"Is it not enough," he asked in a curiously weary voice, "that I have given you my name, a roof over your head, plenty to eat, new clothes?"

"No, Stephen. I do not suppose it is enough."

He seemed so huge in the small, shadowy space, the top of his head brushing the vaulted ceiling. And yet somehow, despite his size, despite the great golden strength of him, he looked vulnerable.

"Why?" he asked, his voice a harsh echo in the cavelike chapel. "For the love of God, Juliana, why must you meddle? Ask prying questions, follow me on private errands?"

She, too, had often wondered at her own insatiable curiosity about her husband.

"Something about you cries out to me. I know we were thrown together. I know we were not supposed to concern ourselves with each other. But I cannot help it. I want to know everything about you."

"No, you don't," he shot back, his voice ringing with clear certainty. "You won't like what you learn. Run along, Juliana." She bit her lip, and he seemed to relent. "I have given you all I am capable of giving. Please don't ask for more."

"Sometimes," she said, summoning her courage, "sometimes in my life I have been forced to take without asking." Before he could stop her, she entered the chapel.

It housed a pair of large effigy plaques of a woman and a small boy. The intricately molded brasswork was exquisite, set into the lids of two stone tombs.

"Oh," she whispered, cocking her head to view the brass more closely. Stephen's wife Margaret, Lady Wimberleigh. The artist had depicted a fair Plantagenet beauty — the thick-lidded eyes, the lyrical, aquiline cheekbones and nose, the firm and shapely thin lips.

Juliana said in a trembling voice, "I think it's time you told me about her." *I want to know why you still come here seven years after she has gone.* But she dared not go so far as to ask that.

His big hands clutched the back of a prayer stool until his knuckles shone white. "What is the point?"

"I am not certain. You are always so sad and distant. How much more can it hurt to talk about her?"

He blew out his breath. Again, she was struck by the impression of weariness. Grieving, for him, was an exhausting business. "Her name was Margaret." He spoke in lifeless tones and stared out the unglazed window, though his distant eyes seemed to see something other than the green hills and the treetops nodding in the breeze. "Lady Margaret Genet. I called her Meg. She was just fourteen when I married her, and I myself a mere fifteen."

Juliana nodded; her own match to Alexei Shuisky had been arranged mere hours after her birth. Margaret had grown up, wed and borne children before she had even reached Juliana's present age. The thought raised a shiver up her spine.

"So the marriage was planned by your parents."

"As is usually the case — when the king himself does not mandate it."

She refused to feel the barb of his words. "But you must have loved her."

"Why do you say that?"

He spoke so harshly that Juliana stepped back, half-afraid he would strike out. He made a menacing picture in his tight leather breeches and blousy white shirt, his golden hair falling about his massive shoulders, his big hands so tight on the back of the prayer stool that she feared the wood might snap.

The stance of restrained violence was meant to frighten her. She squared her shoulders. "So did you?"

"Did I what?"

"Love her very much."

With slow, deliberate movements he set the stool aside and placed his hands on his hips. "How can that possibly matter now?"

He seemed determined not to answer her question, so she let it pass. She brushed her fingers lightly over the smaller brass. "Which of your sons rests here?"

Stephen grabbed her by the shoulders, his fingers biting into her flesh, and his eyes — his usually pale, cool eyes — burned hot with rage.

"Witch!" he said, not shouting but almost whispering. "My God, what sort of unholy creature are you?"

He was truly afraid, she saw, though anger took the greater part. For no reason she could name, she felt perfectly safe with him.

Even when he was glaring at her as if he would like to set her aflame.

"I did not mean to upset you. I had no idea . . ." She swallowed. How was it that she had infuriated him? It was as if someone had burned him with a brand. "Is it so terrible, asking about your children? I just wondered which son —"

"I had only one son." He spoke through gritted teeth. It seemed to take a sheer effort of will for him to pry open his fingers and let go of her.

Juliana's thoughts raced. Stephen had fathered two sons. She had seen the limnings — one of Margaret, and two others, each of a small boy.

Perhaps each was a picture of the same child at different ages. Perhaps one was a relative, a nephew, a cousin.

"I'm sorry," she said, trying to cover her confusion. "I just assumed . . . there were two."

"Why?"

She had to answer carefully. If he truly did believe she was a witch, he could have her drowned or burned at the stake. "I just heard talk around the house."

"Talk? What talk?"

She shrugged elaborately. "I suppose I misheard. I am not a native speaker of

English, you know."

He glared at her for long moments. Then he made a visible effort to relax. "This is Richard's effigy," he said quietly. "Dickon, we called him. He died just two months before his mother — when he was six years old." A catch snagged his voice. "I loved him as hard as I could. Prayed and gambled the very surety of my soul, but the lad just got weaker and weaker. He died in my arms."

Juliana could not help herself. She took his hand. When he did not resist, she carried it to her lips and pressed a kiss to his palm.

He watched her as if in a state of astonishment. After a few moments, he pulled his hand away. She sensed no resentment in him.

"I am so sorry," she whispered. "I cannot imagine what it is like to lose your own son."

"It colors every thought I have. Every feeling. Every breath I take. There is no such thing as joy anymore." His hands were balled into fists, his eyes dark pits of sorrow.

She wanted to argue with him, to tell him he was wrong. But only a parent could gauge his grief. "Stephen? How did your wife die?"

"In childbirth."

Her senses came alert again. Then there had been more than one child. "The baby was a girl?"

"The baby is dead." Of all the statements he had made to her, that was the most chilling. The most final. "And now, my dear baroness," he said, his voice laced with familiar sarcasm, "you had best run along." With one hand firm at her back, he escorted her out of the chapel, out into sunlight diffused by evening mist and tinged with the green of summer leaves.

She turned and found herself very close to him, his chest inches from her. She did not know what to do with her hands, so she placed them in the crooks of his arms. "I know we are not supposed to like each other," she said. "But I have not always been one who does as she is supposed to do."

"What are you saying?" Again, that weary voice.

"That I am beginning to like you."

"Madam, that is a pity indeed."

She boldly touched his cheek. "Do not pity me for liking you. Pity yourself for not being able to accept my friendship."

They stood like figures in an artist's frieze, held captive by the golden evening sun. As she gazed up into his face, her senses came to a heightened awareness. She heard the low drone of bees buzzing in the dwarf thistle that glowed purple in its bed of green. She smelled the spicy scent of hawkweed and trefoil, and she felt the warm caress of the gentle breeze on her face. It was as if they stood alone at the center of the world, as if the beauty of the meadow existed for none but the two of them.

She liked being alone with him, close to him. Though he often glared at her and gnashed his teeth, he was still the man who helped a widow with her planting, who filled a beggar's belly, who counseled Kit when the young man sought his advice.

The world seemed to shift and tilt, and she realized it was because he had stepped even closer. Though a forbidding look darkened his face, his hands were gentle as they came to rest at her waist. His thumbs moved subtly upward, circling deliciously close to her breasts yet never quite touching them.

"Pity," he said, "has little to do with my feelings for you."

His gentle caress sparked a fierce yearning in her. She wanted to be closer to him, closer. Her slim arms went around his neck. She stood on tiptoe and still could not reach him. He met her halfway, bending, covering her mouth with his.

She was unprepared for her own reaction. Unprepared for the softness of his lips or the intriguing taste of him, the silkiness of his hair, the warm solidity of his back.

Juliana had seen her family slaughtered, had walked across a continent and spent five years with gypsies. She had the stoutest of hearts and yet Stephen's kiss startled her and turned her pliant and supple like a willow bending in the breeze.

She wanted the moment, the sharing, the letting down of defenses to go on forever. There was something exceedingly honest about the way he held her and kissed her. Much more honest than when he spoke with sarcasm or ignored her.

He lifted his mouth from hers, and she made a sound of protestation, for she did not want him to stop.

"This is insane," he whispered, and he looked dazed as if someone had just knocked him off a galloping horse.

"I do not know this word, *insane,*" she said.

His eyes smiled at her, one corner of his mouth turned up, and he had never looked so appealing to her. "Yes, you do, my gypsy." He brushed a lock of hair clear of her cheek. He bent to nibble at the pulse in her neck. "I assure you, you do."

The gentle flicking of his tongue, the grazing of his teeth in the sensitive spot made her forget to breathe. "Then it is not a bad thing, to be insane?"

Low laughter drifted from him as his mouth traveled downward, savoring the mounds of her breasts that rose above her stiff bodice.

"In this case, no." He straightened and took her hand. "Let us go, Juliana. This is a place of death and remembrance, hardly a spot for trysting." He looked idly at the tree where his horse was tethered and still cropping at the grass. "Your mount is gone."

Juliana muttered a gypsy oath. "The beast. She trotted off before I could tie her."

"She'll find her way back, for where else can she find honeyed oats?"

"And how am *I* supposed to find my way back?"

"Two can ride as one, Baroness." He took her hand and led her to the horse. "Didn't you know that?"

Sensing a deeper layer to his meaning, she felt no self-consciousness as she swung up and straddled Capria. Her skirts and petticoats, dyed crimson by Jillie's father, rucked up and bared her silk-stockinged legs.

Stephen mounted behind her, pressing

himself back against the hindbow. He took the reins in one hand, and the other went around her waist. As they started at a walk toward the manor, Juliana thought she only imagined that his hand was straying, first upward to brush the underside of her breasts, then down to slide along her thigh, nearly driving her mad as his clever fingers moved beneath the fabric of her skirts.

"What are you doing?" she managed to whisper.

"Just making certain you don't lose interest on the way back to the hall. Shall I stop?"

If she could have summoned the strength she would have laughed at the ridiculousness of the question. Stop? It would be like trying to douse a forest fire with a thimbleful of water.

"No," she said on a long sigh. "Do not stop, Stephen." She leaned her head back against his chest, baring her throat to him, and instantly his mouth moved there, nuzzling and tasting while his hand did the most delicious things to her breasts.

She felt a subtle coolness, and with idle lethargy realized that he had managed to free her breasts from the caged stiffness of the velvet bodice. His fingers played with them, rolling one rosy peak and then the other between thumb and forefinger.

A low soft moan escaped her. She felt helpless, vulnerable, trapped from behind in the velvet vise of his strong thighs, his circling arms, his clever, clever hands.

He quit his exploration and she would have wept, bereft, but he relinquished the reins to her in order to free both of his hands. With amazing delicacy, he lifted her skirts and touched the damp silk of her smallclothes in the most vulnerable spot of all. She felt wanton and free, with her skin bared and his hand never still, fingers flicking out and teasing her, and his mouth moist and warm on her throat.

Through a haze of wonder she watched the woods open to a shady lane leading to the manor. Some distance ahead, the lane joined the main road to the gatehouse.

Stephen's breath rasped harshly as if he was in pain. She wanted to say something, to ease his discomfort, but she was so caught up in the silken magic of his touch that she could not.

And then suddenly he spoke. "God's teeth!"

Juliana gasped, opened her glazed eyes, and saw what he was looking at.

"Havelock," he said through gritted teeth.

As Algernon Basset, the earl of Havelock, raced along the road toward them, Stephen made haste to tuck Juliana back into her bodice, to smooth her skirts down as best he could.

She swiveled around in the saddle. "What could he want? Surely he won't guess we've been, er, doing —"

He stared at her and seemed torn between horror and amusement. "A man would have to be blind to mistake that look on your face. If you look this much the well-tumbled wench after mere fondling, I wonder how you'll appear once I take you to the heights."

"Didn't you just do that?"

"Not by a mile, Baroness. Not by a bloody mile."

Stephen was appalled. How could he have so forgotten himself?

Juliana let out a quavering sigh and straightened her clothing. And he knew painfully how. She shifted gently, and he all but burst his cod laces.

With an effort he managed to drag the invisible barrier between them once again. The shield around his emotions had served him well for years.

Juliana alone, with naught but a soft-eyed look and a few whispered words, had breached it.

He clenched his teeth to keep from spitting an oath. He dismounted, reached up, and took her by the waist. He tried not to feel the sensual glide of her body against his as she slid to the ground. He tried not to feel regret as he stepped back to wait for Havelock. What kind of fool was he, anyway? This was no game, and Juliana was no plaything.

She seemed to sense his withdrawal. "Stephen?"

Damn it! Why did she have to look like a . . . a fresh new bride tumbling, very recently, from her marriage bed?

"Yes?" he asked impatiently. "What is it?"

A frown puckered her brow. "Your moods, my lord. One moment you hold me as if I were the only woman alive, and the next you act the stranger."

"Don't read any more than animal lust into the past few moments," he made himself say. "You've a talent for inspiring it."

She caught her breath. He wanted to touch her cheek, her proudly tilted chin, to tell her he did not mean what he had said, but that was simply too dangerous.

To her credit, she greeted the earl of Havelock with easy grace, waving as he slid his sweating horse to a halt.

And for once in his life, Algernon Basset was speechless. His mouth was a round *O,* his golden-brown curls bouncing as he leaned down to peer at Juliana. Had Stephen not been so disturbed by the forbidden intimacy with his wife, he would have laughed at the earl's gape-mouthed astonishment.

"Cat got your tongue, Algernon?" he asked archly.

Juliana offered her hand. "How charming to see you again, my lord." Her accent was as dark and enticing as spices from Byzantium. "Welcome."

"Madam," Havelock gasped, "the honor is mine, of course."

Stephen handed his reins to a groom who had rushed out to the gatehouse. Another lad waited for Algernon to relinquish his, but the earl shook his head. "I can't stay." His gaze, all but slavering with hunger, swept over Juliana. "To my eternal regret, I must be on my way. I simply came to deliver a message."

Suspicion trickled into Stephen's mind. "Haven't you retainers to deliver your messages, Algernon?"

"Yes, but this is too delectable." Again his eyes partook hungrily of Juliana. "Even better than I had thought."

Stephen waited. Algernon was given to dramatic pauses and knew just when he had taxed the patience of his listeners too long. "My dear lord of Wimberleigh," he said importantly, "you might want to put your hall in order and slaughter a pig or two. The king is coming to hunt at Lynacre Wood."

Stephen's breath gusted forth as if someone had punched him in the stomach. King . . . hunt . . . Lynacre Wood . . . He prayed he had heard wrong.

"Are you not honored?" Juliana asked, her eyes bright with excitement. "A royal visit is a great event."

Algernon lifted his heels to spur his horse. "I do hope you managed to do something about the gypsy camp," he said, laughing with his eyes. "And Stephen?"

"Yes?" he forced out.

One last time, Algernon's eyes fed on Juliana. "Lock up your valuables."

Eight

Stephen winced as heralds blew a salute, announcing the arrival of the king. The household retainers, decked in their best livery, waited in a military-style line behind him. He tried to pretend he was not bathed in sweat beneath his murrey doublet and shirt of white lawn. He prayed Juliana would have the sense to obey him and stay hidden.

King Henry, ponderous as a storm-swollen cloud in his great high-bowed saddle, entered through the main gate. Sunlight blazed around him, catching on his gold-braided doublet and chain of office. Retainers flanked him like lesser stars around the sun. Stephen recognized Sir Anthony Browne and Sir Francis Bryan, the king's young minions, and a host of others who had managed to snare the royal favor. Behind the king rode the sharp-eyed, pinch-faced Thomas Cromwell in his customary midnight black.

"A royal visit," whispered Nance Harbutt. "Why, we ain't had a royal visit since his lordship were newly married to our dearest Marg—"

"Nance." Stephen silenced her, furious that she had reminded him of that day. He had been naught but a gawking green youth, overwhelmed by the arrival of the king, who, in Stephen's credulous mind, had achieved the proportions of legend. Never was there so great a fool as Stephen de Lacey that day — fifteen and glowing with pride in his new wife, presenting her to Henry, watching her win the king's heart with a simple blushing smile, an innocent, murmured greeting. Or so he thought.

Stephen's life had changed irrevocably that day.

Now he was older, wiser, no longer gulled by the imposing splendor of the king. Now Stephen knew what to expect, and he had girded himself against the onslaught of royal intrigue.

He watched in bland dispassion as the king's attendants helped him dismount in the central courtyard. The task required no fewer than half a dozen strong men, yet Henry comported himself with a certain bulky dignity. Though his leg was swollen, he barely limped as he walked toward Stephen.

His heart thudding, his mind ablaze with hope that his ruse would work, Stephen made his obeisance.

Henry's small dark eyes took him apart. God, thought Stephen. He had grown shrewd as well as fat. Pray his lust for the wives of other men had diminished.

"How fares my lord of Wimberleigh?" Henry asked.

"High in health and good cheer," Stephen replied, feigning an eagerness to please his sovereign.

The king perused the household: Kit and the lads of the stable standing stiffly at attention, the household retainers and Nance Harbutt properly slack-jawed with awe. "And your bride, Wimberleigh. Where is your vagabond bride?"

Nance recognized her cue, thank God. She gave a wail of misery and lifted her apron to daub at her eyes.

The king, who missed nothing, thrust up his beard, a hound on the scent. "Answer me, Wimberleigh." He leaned forward and dropped his voice. "Have you done in this one, too?"

Stephen nearly snatched at the bait, nearly forfeited his life then and there by attacking the king's royal person. No. He was needed here. For how much longer, he could not say, but for the time being, he knew he must keep his temper in check.

"Alas, she has fallen ill, sire."

"Ill?" The king raised a skeptical eyebrow. "The wench looked hale when last I saw her. Flea-bitten, perhaps, but healthy as a nanny goat."

"The settled life does not agree with her. But sire, do not let her indisposition keep you from my hearth and table. I pray you —"

Kit Youngblood slapped his palm to his forehead and fell facedown in the yard.

Nance Harbutt plunged to her knees beside him. "Christ have mercy, the lad's done for. The sweat is at him!"

The men-at-arms recoiled, angling their pikestaffs at the invisible enemy.

William Stumpe, Stephen's steward, made a hissing sound to shush the weeping woman. Heedless, Nance crushed her face into her apron. " 'Tis the sweat. I'd know it anywhere. Same as the master's wife —"

"What?" Thomas Cromwell's voice cut her off like a pair of shears snipping a hedge. He planted himself in front of Stephen. "Your wife has the sweat?" Lord Privy Seal, who had honed the craft of lying to a fine

art, searched Stephen's face.

"Well, that's not certain," Stephen said, his head tilted, his eyes regretful. "I've yet to find a physician who'll go near her."

The king swore and took a lumbering step back. "By God, Wimberleigh, if you've got the sweat here . . ." Henry's face was death pale. For a moment Stephen almost felt sorry for him. Mortality was the only foe even King Henry could never vanquish.

Then Stephen remembered saintly Thomas More, Exeter, Neville and Nick Carew, all put to death because the king was at his most dangerous when he was afraid.

"Sire, I beg you. Just wait a little." Behind him, he could hear Nance fanning Kit with her apron. "If it is truly the sweat, my wife will be dead by morning. If she lives, then it wasn't that pestilence to begin with." He rubbed his chin thoughtfully. "How many Londoners were felled by the sweat last year . . . some several thousand, was it not?"

Without taking his eyes off Stephen, the king said, "Cromwell, send the heralds on to Hockley Hall. We shall pass the night with Algernon Basset, earl of Havelock."

"Immediately, sire."

As Sir Thomas turned to give instructions to the heralds, Stephen slowly and inconspicuously started to expel a sigh of relief. He still had half his indrawn breath to go when two royal wardens burst through the iron gates, shouting for assistance.

"Look what we caught poaching in the king's wood," Sir Bodely said.

Stephen's heart dropped with sickening speed to his knees. Between them, the guards held a furiously struggling gypsy.

"Rodion!" Juliana whispered, pedaling with her elbows to scoot even closer to the window in the tower.

"Rodion?" Her voice filled with concern, Jillie joined her in the recess of the window.

Juliana sent her maid a sidelong glance. "He chose the wrong time to poach a deer."

Jillie's chin trembled as the two of them lay belly-down in the window embrasure, watching the drama unfold in the courtyard.

It was musty in their high loft, and it smelled of dry timber, old stone and wood-smoke. Until a few moments ago, Juliana had been arguing heatedly against the necessity of staying hidden.

"I tell you, Jillie, I do not wish to cower like a thief in the night. And Steph— my lord husband has no right to force me to stay here. How dare he act like he's ashamed of me!"

Jillie, teary eyed from torn loyalties, had clutched the iron key that she used to lock the door. "I'm sorry, milady. 'Twas himself who ordered me to look after you. I'm not to let the king spy you at any cost."

"Stephen de Lacey is not my master!" Even as she shouted the declaration, Juliana was seized by memories of the afternoon she had spent with him, the desperate hunger of his kiss, the compelling touch of his hands. And her own ungovernable yearning . . .

"He said 'twas for your own good. And begging your pardon, but the master is seldom wrong."

"He is this time."

"Milady, please. There's something about the king, something he *does* . . . He's a danger. It might be like the last time he came to Lynacre."

"The last time? What happened then?"

Jillie had flushed an even deeper crimson shade than normal. She stared down at her large, thick hands, her fingers tightening around the key. "Can't rightly say. I were but a child of ten or twelve back then, but . . ."

"But what?" Juliana had forced herself to be patient. Jillie was not the sort to gossip and it was hard coaxing information from her. "Did the king hurt Stephen while he was here? Or the baroness?"

"Hurt?" Jillie's unhurried speech belied her quick and reliable mind. "Honest, my lady, I don't know. But after the king's visit, she were never the same, and he were a dark and brooding lord."

Juliana shivered. "She. The baroness?"

"Aye." Jillie dropped her voice to a whisper. "She were like a spring flower caught in a frost after that. Less laughter in the household. Less talk and merriment."

Juliana fell silent, remembering how she had found Stephen worshiping at the shrine of his first wife. How solemn he had been, mourning still, after all these years for his wife and child. One child. Only one had shared the crypt with his mother.

Why? *Why?*

And now Jillie was telling her that the laughter had gone out of Stephen even before he had lost Margaret and Dickon.

"God ha' mercy!" Jillie said, thumping Juliana in the ribs and startling her back to the present. "They're going to kill Rodion."

Juliana rubbed the side of her fist on the thick, lozenge-shaped windowpane. The king's men were tying each of Rodion's limbs to the saddlebows of four horses. Stephen had planted himself in front of King

Henry and was gesticulating wildly, his hand straying to the dress sword that slapped at his thigh.

"Mother Mary," she whispered in desperate, native Russian. "They are going to tear him apart."

She ducked out of the window embrasure and nearly tripped on her crimson velvet skirts. "Hurry, Jillie. Unlock the door. We must stop them."

Jillie did not hesitate. She tumbled the lock to the tower room door. With Juliana leading the way, they hurtled down the narrow, spiraling staircase and spilled out into the courtyard.

One look at Stephen's thunderous expression told Juliana she had made a grave mistake.

I'll kill her, Stephen thought as Juliana raced across the gravel path and plunged into a curtsy at the king's feet. *As soon as His Highness decamps, I will beat her raw and then strangle her with my naked hands.*

"Your Majesty, please, I beg you." Juliana looked up at the king from the lake of velvet skirts that surrounded her. "Have mercy on this man."

The king looked awestruck, his mouth a red slash in the middle of his beard. Even the inscrutable Cromwell seemed nonplussed, coughing vigorously into his sleeve.

"And who are you, my tenderling?" Henry extended his hand and drew her to her feet.

"Do you not remember, Your Serendipity?" White-faced, Juliana stumbled over her words. "Er, Seren— never mind. We have met before. My name is Juliana Romanov . . . de Lacey," she added almost as an afterthought.

"Good God," said the king, looking her up and down. "Marriage does agree with you."

Through sheer force of will, Stephen stopped himself from leaping between Juliana and King Henry to shield her from the king's lusty attention. He knew he would be better served if he pretended not to care.

Not to care. As the king complimented Stephen's wife, memories hurled Stephen into the past. He saw again a young beauty, dazzled by a king's favor. A vulnerable woman's heart and a slumbrous royal passion. A slim, pretty hand tucked in the crook of the king's proffered arm . . .

No. Stephen nearly spoke aloud, but he choked back his protest. Henry was like a child with a toy: he coveted what his neighbor possessed, then lost interest when he won the object for himself. If he had the faintest suspicion that Stephen was afflicted with a secret desire for his gypsy wife, Juliana would be no safer than a rose in a windstorm.

Henry glared at Stephen. "The sweat, was it, Wimberleigh?"

"It's a miracle! She's recovered, praise be to God!" From the corner of his eye, Stephen saw Kit jump up hastily, Nance brushing at his breeches and doublet.

Cromwell murmured in the king's ear. Henry grinned like a wolf — no humor, all hunger. "Very clever, Wimberleigh. Very clever indeed."

Stephen despised the verbal games of which Henry was so fond. He yearned for the days of his grandsire, when disputes were settled by force of arms and a man earned his own worth. He endured that penetrating royal stare, waiting and watching for the king's next move and silently cursing his wife.

The fool. Why couldn't she have trusted him, taking his word that she was better off staying hidden in the tower?

As she flashed a dazzling smile up at the king, Stephen's remembrances pounced on him again — a beautiful smile, a sidelong look . . .

Well, why not? he thought furiously. Why wouldn't she harbor a passion for the king? She would not be the first to crave the benefits of becoming mistress to the most powerful ruler in Christendom.

And, God knew, Stephen had given her precious little reason to be content at Lynacre.

"Your husband told us you were indisposed," Henry said.

"She was," Stephen said harshly, taking her by the shoulder. "You'd best return to your chambers before you suffer a relapse."

She put her wrist to her brow and swayed. "Lord Wimberleigh worries too much. I had a touch of the ague, that is all."

Cromwell and Henry exchanged a glance. She did not give them a chance to challenge her. "Surely, Your Serenity," she said, "you will take pity on my weakened state and grant a very small request."

A royal eyebrow lifted. "And what might that be, my lady?"

She gestured at Rodion, still struggling between the horses while Jillie Egan rolled up her sleeves, no doubt preparing to do battle with the men-at-arms.

"Sire, let that man go free," Juliana pleaded.

The king's men burst into a chorus of

protests. But Henry smiled, his expression an echo of the sincere young prince he had once been. "You plead so sweetly. Who is he to so great a lady?"

Juliana stepped back, clearly stung by the lash of the king's sarcasm. She clasped her hands together and studied the ground.

Chuckling, the king turned to Stephen. "Well, Wimberleigh. You've managed to dress it up, wash the stink off it. But have you turned it from gypsy to lady?"

Stephen crossed his arms. "She hasn't stolen any horses lately."

"I am proud to be Rom," Juliana blurted out. "Rodion belongs to the tribe that took me in when I was homeless. For that, I beg you to let him go free." She glanced at Jillie, who was turning a deeper shade of red by the minute.

"Besides," Juliana added with surprising good humor, "he is well-liked by my maid, and she never harmed a soul."

The king stroked his beard, then pointed a fat, beringed finger at the gutted carcass slung on a pole. "What of the deer he poached? Surely you understand its value. Not even my esteemed warden, Lord Wimberleigh, is allowed to hunt deer without a special license."

Juliana looked at Stephen. What a world

of emotion he saw in her beautiful face: pleading, regret, and a deep, steady pride. Without taking her eyes off him, she said, "Majesty, my lord husband will compensate you for the deer."

"A pretty speech," said Henry, while all present held a collective breath. "Well, Wimberleigh? You cannot marry this thief, as well. What will you give me to free the gypsy?"

Jaws dropped all around. Stephen turned himself to stone to keep from throttling his wife. First she proved him a liar when he had only lied to protect her. Then she humbled herself for Rodion — her gypsy lover, for all Stephen knew — when she should have known damned well he would not have allowed the poor sod to be yanked apart. *Now* she expected him to offer a fortune to save the gypsy's worthless skin.

And yet there was something in the way she was looking at him, something hypnotic, startling. Her spell drew his will from him and compelled him to say, "My steward will give you a hundred crowns, sire."

Gasps filled the air. That was ten times what the deer was worth.

"Done!" exclaimed the king, obviously delighted with Stephen, with Juliana, and with his own craftiness. "Let the Egyptian go, and make him leave my presence. Later, I expect the gypsies to give me reason to tolerate their proximity."

"They are great entertainers, Your Grace," Juliana said quickly.

He patted his girth, his eyes fixed upon her. "We'll sup on roast venison tonight," he said, "and I'll help myself to something sweeter for after."

Seated at King Henry's left side, Juliana watched in apprehension as he got steadily and determinedly drunk. Stephen sat on Henry's other side and stared straight ahead, drinking just as steadily but staying determinedly sober.

The hall teemed with the king's courtiers and retainers, all feasting at hastily set up tables. Their ringing laughter echoed off the magnificent woodwork of the ceiling beams. Iron coronas of candles hung from the rafters, joining with the roaring hearth fire to illuminate the great chamber. Above the dais, musicians played in a gallery.

For perhaps the hundredth time, Juliana stole a glance at her husband. She told herself Stephen was the same man who had held her in his arms and kissed her so ardently just this afternoon. She could not believe it. Only hours later, he was as cold and remote as the Russian steppes in the dead of winter.

And why shouldn't he be? she asked herself. He had whisked her to the tower room and asked her to stay hidden.

Now, as she felt the king's thick-fingered hand close around her knee, she knew why.

She stood abruptly, almost oversetting her narrow-backed chair. "Your Highness," she said as courteously as she could. "I would very much like to dance."

Stephen let out a snort of humorless laughter. Apparently he had convinced himself that she was throwing herself at the king. Laughter erupted, seemingly from the depths of the king's belly. "I want you to dance, my little tartlet. Alas, my bad leg plagues me." He jerked his head toward Stephen. "Dance with your husband, and I shall watch."

The prospect set her heart to thumping until she felt the pulse beat in her temples. Stephen blinked, took an idle sip of wine and said softly, "I have better things to do."

A flush rose in her cheeks, heated by the stares of the occupants of the hall. As nonchalantly as she could, she turned in the direction of Jonathan Youngblood. But the kindly man was facing away, deep in conversation with Thomas Cromwell. Perhaps

Kit . . . but the youth had slipped away as was his wont these days, no doubt to spy on the gypsies.

She stood helpless, furious and pitiful as a jilted maid. As she was trying to determine the most graceful way to return to her seat, a young man took her hand and bowed over it.

"Algernon!" she said.

His merry eyes smiled into hers. "The pavane is far and away my favorite. It would be an honor to partner you."

Juliana tried not to show her relief as she dropped her hand into his. She felt the eyes of both Stephen and the king on her. "Thank you, my dear lord of Havelock," she said as they stepped out onto the rush-strewn floor.

"The pleasure is mine," he said gallantly, lifting her hand and beginning the stately stroll around the perimeter of the hall. Then he ruined the gallantry by leaning over and adding, "I trow it was tempting to watch the drama play itself out. What *would* you have done had I not intervened, Juliana?"

She sniffed. "Believe me, my lord, I have faced graver humiliation before."

Havelock shook his curls and loosed a jolly laugh. "Do you know how delighted I am that Stephen has married such a singular woman? Our rustic life was so tiresome until you and your Egyptian friends came along."

Juliana seized her chance. "Tiresome?" She emphasized her accent to show her disbelief. "That is the last thing I expected to hear about Lord Wimberleigh's first wife."

To her astonishment, Algernon blushed. And stammered when he replied, "The lady Margaret was far from tiresome. But she's been gone a long time."

"Seven years," Juliana said.

Algernon lifted one eyebrow. "He speaks to you of Meg?"

"Seldom," she said, careful to betray nothing to the inveterate gossip. But Stephen's moods and his silences spoke loudly of his love for the young woman, of his obsession with her still.

The pavane ended and she turned to thank Algernon. She frowned when she spied the ornament he wore, an oval suspended from a black ribbon around his neck.

"What is this, Algernon?" she asked, touching the smooth limning.

"A bauble, no more," he said. To Juliana's amusement, he blushed.

"It is a portrait of you."

"Allow me a bit of vanity." He tugged at

the ribbon, but she held it fast.

She turned over the limning and saw the artist's name written in letters so tiny they must have been drawn with a single hair. N. Hilary. It was the same artist who had done the limnings of Stephen's first wife and children.

He sniffed and pushed the ornament down into his shirt. "I had it done last year."

She frowned. Last year? But Stephen had lost his son long before that. Had the artist painted the child from a description? It seemed strange to Juliana. Everything about Stephen seemed strange to her.

Just as she was about to return to her seat, Algernon took hold of her brooch. She wore it fastened on her bodice, the bloodred ruby and creamy pearls bright against the emerald velvet.

"Tit for tat, Jules, dear," he said. "I showed you mine, now you —" He broke off, astonished as the brooch came apart in his hand.

"God's death!" he whispered. Moving more quickly than she ever would have credited him for, he yanked her into the shadow of a window alcove.

"Give me that," Juliana said.

He held the dagger high out of her reach. The jewels caught the light from the coronas. "Not for a third ball," he said, frowning in rapt concentration at the blade.

"Algernon, please!" She hopped up and down, snatching at the dagger.

"Do you know the penalty for coming within a yard of the king with a concealed weapon?"

"It is probably something disgusting. Dismemberment? Amputation? A cossack could take lessons from you Englishmen."

He brought the dagger close to his face, angling it toward the light, and stared at the Romanov motto for so long that Juliana could have sworn he was reading it. Ridiculous, she told herself. She had not met a man in the whole of England who recognized Cyrillic characters. Certainly not a fool who thrived on gossip.

"Give it back," she snapped. "It is a family heirloom, not a weapon. If I'm arrested and minced into a pie, it will be your fault."

He leaned forward, poking his head out of the alcove. "I think I got us out of sight before anyone noticed. I am quick, you know. Your friend Laszlo has been teaching me the art of throwing daggers."

"Throwing daggers?" She almost laughed. "You?"

"I'm quite good. Shall I demonstrate?"

"No!" She grabbed his wrist. "My lord, I

must return to my table."

Algernon gave the blade one last look, then handed it back, and she secured it in its jeweled sheath. As she returned to the high table, she could not help but notice how quickly Algernon found his way to Thomas Cromwell. The little gossip. He was probably telling Lord Privy Seal that the baroness of Wimberleigh was an assassin.

The thought fled as her husband appeared, all solicitousness, holding out her chair at the table haute. Only Juliana could see the sharp sparks of fury in his eyes.

"Enjoy your little tryst, my lady?" he demanded in a low voice.

"Tryst?" She frowned down at her hands, then remembered the word from the writings of the loathesome Saint Chrysostom. "Ah, a secret meeting of lovers." She discovered an astonishing fact. Her husband was jealous.

She barely had time to ponder this amazing notion when she glanced at their royal guest and realized something else.

So was the king.

"By Christ's knees," Henry grumbled. "This is absurd, sitting in the damp cold outside. What is your wife about, Wimberleigh?"

Stephen feigned a grin of nonchalance. In truth he had no earthly idea. "She wished to see to Your Majesty's entertainment."

"Good. Lynacre's such a gloomy place. Where in God's name did you find those musicians? A charnel house?"

The royal entourage surrounded the king and they proceeded out into the west field, a grassy sward tucked into a broad bend of the river. Torchlight licked the darkness, and for a moment the orange flames were all Stephen could see. As his eyes adjusted, he realized what he was looking at.

"My God," someone whispered. "What madness is this?"

Juliana's madness, thought Stephen. The pitch torches were set in a half circle, close enough to the water's edge to reflect in the river so that, from a distance, the circle looked complete.

In the center of the makeshift stage stood Rodion, playing the pipes as a huge bear danced in circles. Most of the courtiers stood with mouths agape. The ranking members, starting with the king, filed toward the benches. Stephen saw Mandiva dart forward and furtively relieve Cromwell of his silver-gilt scent ball.

Henry slapped his thick thighs and barked with laughter. "Now that is entertainment!"

he declared, and the rest of the court joined his hearty applause. Stephen then began to understand. Whatever else she might be, Juliana was no fool.

The king expected the gypsies to give him reason to tolerate their presence. This, then, was her way of proving the worth of her people.

It might work, Stephen thought. The gypsies were accomplished performers, creating a vivid torchlit tapestry of juggling, saber dancing, sleight of hand, whirling skirts and acrobatic feats. The company oohed and aahed and occasionally huzzahed, and the king lifted his cup in a high salute.

Well done, little wife, Stephen thought grudgingly. Perhaps indeed the display would convince Henry to leave the gypsies in peace.

His silent compliment came a moment too soon. The crowd of gypsies parted and Juliana rode forth on an agile white pony.

Stephen's intake of breath was echoed by the gasps of the rest of the company. It was Juliana, and yet it was not. She had unbound her hair and dressed in Romany garb. Her feet were bare, her slim ankles circled by cheap tin bangles.

"Is she always this entertaining, Wimberleigh?" Henry asked.

Stephen thought of his strange wife: the horse thief, galloping off on Capria; the ragamuffin, sputtering like a wet cat in the millstream; the virago, furiously banishing gamblers from the hall; the gentle lady, offering her heart-melting sympathy; and finally, the lover, sighing and clinging to him with newfound passion.

He shook off the thought. "She is as wild and unpredictable as a spring storm, sire."

She rode as if the wind bore her, the light-stepping horse responding to the slightest tug of the reins, its movements as fluid as a banner of silk on a breeze. Gypsy music accompanied the pony tricks, the melody frenzied and underscored by the primal, raw thump of a skin drum. With one hand on the reins, she stood, her feet firm against the bare back of the horse. Her hair flowed out behind her, and Stephen thought of women like Boadicea, or Jeanne d'Arc, who faced peril with courage and panache.

Juliana delighted the crowd with a fluid dance on the back of a galloping horse. Pavlo entered the circle of light and loped along at the heels of the horse. She finished with a flourish worthy of a court reveler, bringing the horse to a sliding stop in front of the king. Stephen could see the horse's sides fanning in and out, the motion matched by the rise and fall of Juliana's chest, dewy with sweat above the bodice. A hunger gripped him, and he shifted uncomfortably, planting one foot on the bench and bringing his leg up to conceal an untimely swelling.

He could not help but think she caused the same discomfort to the other men present. Her cleverness had misfired. Perhaps the king would henceforth look more kindly on gypsies, but at what cost?

Juliana tossed her head and smiled boldly at the king, her eyes aglitter with reflected torchlight.

"My God, she doth give me a fright," muttered the king. He curled his lip in scorn. "She's only a gutter-born gypsy at heart." His dandified companions tucked their hands into their sleeves, no doubt making secret signs against evil.

And at that moment, Stephen realized she had triumphed.

Brava, my lady, he thought. *Bravissima.*

The horse executed a charming bow, its forelegs bending and head lowering. From her perch on its back, Juliana did likewise. Then she was gone as suddenly as she had come.

Cromwell shouldered his way through the crowd toward the king. In his wake came the pretty earl of Havelock, a smug look of triumph on his face.

Stephen grabbed his arm as he passed. "What are you up to, Algernon?"

His china-blue eyes widened in innocence. "I merely had some business with Lord Privy Seal. I've yet to be invited to court. I only hope to convince Cromwell of my value." With a mysterious smile, he moved off.

The king seemed distracted, almost startled when he saw Stephen. "Where did your wife go, my lord?"

"I'm never sure on a night like this, sire." He braced himself, awaiting the order to fetch her.

It never came. The king waved a distracted hand. "She's mad. You deserve each other. And now I must retire in haste, my lords. We leave at dawn."

Stephen struggled to conceal his relief. "So soon, my liege? What about your hunting?"

"Lord Privy Seal has remembered some business we must attend in London."

Unease nagged at Stephen. It had been a strange day at Lynacre, and he could not help but think the king's business had something to do with him — or his gypsy wife.

NINE

In the wake of the king's mercifully brief visit, an oddly agreeable domestic routine evolved at Lynacre. The days of high summer enveloped the manor in a golden, dreamlike haze. Stephen felt a sense of peace and rightness that was new to him.

Looking across the estate office and catching a smile from his wife, he tried not to acknowledge the reason for his most unexpected sense of tranquility.

He failed. Even in a heart grown as small and cold and fearful as his, he recognized the power of Juliana's appeal. In her most fleeting smile, there was a spark of joy that somehow had the power to burn through his doubts and his defenses.

It was incongruous to look upon such a fragile, dainty woman and see strength, and yet it was undeniable. Whether she was studying English books with Nance, teaching the cook to make a fermented drink out of spoiled milk or picking out a tune on the virginals, there was a firmness to her resolve that attracted him.

Only in the deepest hour of the night, when she cried out in fear at the nightmares that haunted her, did she show her vulnerability and her mystery. More and more, he dwelt upon her wild claim to be some lost Russian princess. He had begun to notice that she spoke differently to Laszlo than she did to the other gypsies. The words sounded harsher, more clipped. As if they conversed not in Romany but in a different tongue. But it would take a linguist to puzzle that one out, and Stephen did not relish taking his query to Algernon, who was so adept at foreign languages.

"If you stare at me much longer," Juliana said, intruding on his thoughts, "I shall have to ask Mandiva for a hex breaker."

Stephen leaned back in his chair and crossed his feet at the ankles. "You mean a man may not look at his wife?"

Color bloomed high in her cheeks, and she ducked her head. "Not in the way you were just looking at me."

He rose and walked around the desk to stand behind her chair. On the table in front of her lay his plans for a new winnowing box, which she had been studying with a critical eye. With his hand beneath her chin, he drew her gaze to his. Her skin was silky to the touch, and it took all his restraint to keep from placing his lips there, just to the side of her mouth. "And how," he asked, "was I looking at you?"

"In the way of a sorcerer putting a spell on his victim," she whispered. "You should not do that."

"Why not?"

"Because the spell is starting to work."

Her candor breathed new energy into the sparks that always seemed to dance invisibly between them. He removed his hand and stood upright, shamed at the ease with which he maneuvered her emotions, and even more disturbed by the instant, heated response of his body.

"You need fear no love charms from me," he assured her. To hide the evidence of his discomfiture, he turned hastily and walked toward the door. "Come, my lady. Master Stumpe wants to see me this morning. The king complained of the meager revenues from Lynacre, so I asked my steward to find a way to increase our yield."

Red to the ears, he led her out into a small yard enclosed by a high unmortared stone fence. It was a singular notion, including the lady of the house in the business of land management, but Stephen found himself involving her more and more in the routines of Lynacre.

William Stumpe had set up his table under a gnarled old plum tree. Lazy bees droned amid the ripening violet fruit, and from time to time Stumpe swatted at one of the pesky creatures by his ear.

Years earlier, a fever had robbed him of the ability to walk. Stephen vividly remembered his father's cold dismissal. Unable to work, Stumpe was given a fortnight to leave the manor.

Stephen, just twelve at the time, had implored his father to let the poor man stay on, rather than dragging himself to Bath for a life of begging. When his pleas had failed to move the former baron, Stephen had worked day and night to devise a vehicle for the steward.

The first one had been no more than a crude barrow. Over the years, Stephen had improved and refined his design. William Stumpe's present conveyance was a three-wheeled seat with handles on the two large side wheels so that Stumpe could propel himself. He sat the contraption like a king on a throne — proud and passionately independent.

Stumpe motioned Stephen to the table.

"Look here, my lord," he said, pointing at a parchment map. "If you enclose these acres for sheep, you could double the size of the flocks."

"No," Juliana blurted out before Stephen had a chance to speak. "We will not do that."

His aging dignity clearly offended, Will Stumpe directed a glare at her. "I beg my lady's pardon?" he said haughtily.

Juliana smiled. "Granted."

Stephen bit the inside of his cheek to keep from grinning. Sometimes her secondary knowledge of the nuances of English proved most charming.

"What I meant, dear baroness," said Stumpe, "was that I see no reason for you to object. Sheep grazing is the way to prosperity —"

"For whom?" she asked, propping her hands on her hips.

Surprise stirred within Stephen. His wife, it seemed, had more hidden depths than a winter bourne.

"Why, for his lordship." Stumpe spoke slowly, as if he were addressing a halfwit.

"I see. And what of the copyholders who raise crops on the land?" Juliana tapped the spot with a slim finger.

"They lose their leases —"

"— and go begging," Stephen broke in. "I won't have it, Will. Her ladyship is right."

Juliana's face lit with gratitude. "I am, aren't I?"

He felt a glow of something — he dared not call it affection — emanating from Juliana. Did it mean so much to her, then, to have his support?

He shook off the thought. "The land here is arable. It stays in the hands of the tenants."

"If *you* insist, my lord," Stumpe said.

"We *both* insist," Juliana said.

"I applaud your logic and your concern for the king's demands," Stephen said to Stumpe. "But I cannot increase the flocks without taking land from the tenants, and that I will not do."

"What of this section here?" Juliana asked, indicating a spot near the western bounds of the estate.

Stephen dropped his gaze to hide the blaze of apprehension in his eyes. *Why there?* he wondered, his mind boiling with secret worries. *Why there, of all places?* "I think not," he said quietly, lifting his eyes. "Nothing can be done there, nothing changed."

"Why not?" She tilted her head to one side.

"It is not suitable. It's rocky, forested land," Stephen said.

"Quite so, my lord," the steward agreed, sucking his tongue. That was another reason Stephen kept him on — Stumpe pretended to know every inch of the estate when in truth his disability kept him to the comfort of his own quarters and immediate gardens.

"The land there is not good for growing things?" Juliana inquired.

She could not know the pain and guilt her innocent query inspired. Stephen's heart beat with a dull, throbbing ache. "No," he said, suddenly wanting — *needing* — to touch someone warm and alive. He took her hand between his own and felt the smooth skin, the fragile bones. "It is not at all a good place for growing things."

Her eyes, clear as colored glass, focused on him for so long he grew uncomfortable and dropped his hands. Sending him a bewildered smile, Juliana folded her arms across her bosom, unconsciously drawing attention to her pale throat, the delicate structure of her collarbones.

"So, Master Stumpe, his lordship must prosper, yes?" she asked.

Stumpe shot her a suspicious look. "Yes, my lady, else he'll lose keepership of the royal woods."

"Why does he not prosper from the wool he already produces?"

With an excess of patience, Stumpe steepled his fingers. "Because the price of raw wool has fallen —"

"Raw wool," she said. "Fleece that has not been spun or woven. And yet the price of woven cloth soars."

Stephen was surprised she knew this; then he remembered she had spent the past years wandering the shires and had encountered plenty of opportunities to learn the worth of things. Meg never even knew the color of a shilling, much less the price of cloth.

Stephen studied his wife's thoughtful frown. Her mind was like a clockwork; he imagined he could see the wheels and cogs turning behind those green eyes.

"We must produce our own finished cloth," she said, so briskly that she obviously considered it a fait accompli.

Stumpe's mouth worked like a banked haddock's. "Produce finished cloth! But who . . . how . . . ?"

"The tenants. What do they do when the fields lie shallow —"

"Fallow," Stephen corrected. "They are idle."

"But we'd need looms," said Stumpe.

Stephen considered his special conduits,

the vented windows and rooftop cistern were clearly visible. Then he touched the back of the steward's wheeled cart. "My dear Stumpe, do you think I could not build a loom?"

"Of course, my lord." Stumpe slapped his thigh as enthusiasm took hold. Then his eyebrows crashed down into a scowl. "To turn a decent profit, we'd need a huge space. Bigger than the great hall of Lynacre. Not possible."

"That is not a problem," Juliana said.

"And why not, pray tell?" Stumpe asked, his impatience now mingling with frustration.

"We shall use the abandoned abbey church," she said. "Ever since it was destroyed by the Catholic-haters, it has sat idle."

"Malmesbury!" Stephen exclaimed, and then, inexplicably, he was picking her up, whirling her about with a whoop of gladness, throwing back his head, and shouting with laughter. Then he put her down, gave her a loud, smacking kiss on the lips, and said, "Stumpe, it's so simple only a crazy woman could have thought of it."

"The old abbey is a ruin —"

"Not for long," Juliana said, looking flustered by Stephen's outburst. "The tenants and gypsies will fix it up."

Stumpe bobbed his head vigorously and began chattering away about the endless possibilities of a cloth facture right here in the district. With his hands pedaling the wheels of his cart, he wandered away, already making plans. Stephen chuckled, his heart light and full.

Then he noticed Juliana staring at him in the oddest way.

"What?" he asked, unable to wipe the stupid grin off his face. "What is it, Baroness?"

"You," she whispered in a voice that was soft and full of wonder. She reached up, her hand trembling as she ran her thumb over his lower lip. "I have never seen you smile before, Stephen, never heard you laugh."

She was right, he realized with a start. The few smiles he had in him, he saved like a miser guarding his fortune. "Was it not you who insisted on a sober husband?"

"Yes. But this is different." She dropped her small hand, but not her wonder-filled gaze. The summer breeze lifted her hair like a veil, and he fought the urge to bury his hands in its velvety length. "The smile, the laughter. It makes you beautiful. Did you know that?"

To his chagrin, he felt his face redden. "If

that's true — and I sincerely doubt it is — I do not consider it a necessary virtue."

"Of course not, but . . ." She shrugged. "You have a glow of contentment that appeals to me." Her hands, light as bird's wings, pressed against the front of his jerkin. "Stephen?"

"Aye?" Just for a moment, he indulged his urge and touched her sable hair. Satin, but softer. Smoother. And redolent of summer herbs. *Jesu . . .*

"Stay with me after supper tonight. Do not go away as you always do."

The old fear leaped upon him then, and snatched away the last vestiges of mirth. Her request merely proved he could not live like other men.

And Juliana, with her laughing eyes and her heart-catching smile, was a threat to his necessary isolation.

"No," he forced himself to say, knowing he was hurting her. "You had a good idea, Juliana. You gave me a moment or two of mirth. And — God's teeth — you are a comely lass." He stepped back, out of her reach. "But do not think to weaken me into bedding you."

If someone had set fire to her backside, she could not have looked more outraged. "Bedding!" she shouted. "You think *that* is my purpose?"

Her show of temper made her more attractive than ever, heightening the color in her cheeks and intensifying the sparkle in her eyes. "When a woman begins groping at my clothing," he said, "I generally assume that to be her purpose."

She lunged like a striking adder. Even before he was aware that she was moving toward him, he felt the prick of the tiny blade at his neck. "And what," she said, "do you think my purpose is now, my lord?"

He wanted to swallow but feared the movement of his throat would do him injury. "Seems to be," he whispered, "murder."

"You should learn to tell the difference, my lord." With that, she put away her dagger, turned on her heel, and disappeared through the garden gate.

"Never," Rodion said to Juliana, thrusting out his bearded chin. "You'll not use this horse to haul and draw. He's made for show."

Juliana's heart sank. She had engaged the gypsies as laborers in the Malmesbury endeavor, and she desperately needed both Rodion and the horse to clear debris from the abandoned abbey.

"I'll pay extra wages for the horse," she offered, blowing a stray lock of hair off her damp brow.

"No, you won't," blustered Jillie Egan, walking toward them and turning back her sleeves. She planted herself in front of Rodion, standing nose to nose with him and glaring into his eyes. "You'll do the work, gypsy man, and so will your horse, else I'll . . . I'll . . ."

"You'll what?" Rodion asked.

Jillie leaned forward to whisper in his ear, then reached around and pinched the young man's backside. His scowl eased into a huge grin.

Five minutes later, the horse was harnessed and drawing a cartload of broken stonework out of the building. Juliana watched, bemused. What had Jillie said to him? Her familiar touch made Juliana suspect that Jillie and Rodion had become lovers. Was it that easy, then, to bring a man to heel?

Her mind full of intriguing possibilities, Juliana went into the church.

"Did so!" came a tiny, squeaking voice.

"Did not!" came the answer.

Juliana turned to see Sima, Mandiva's daughter, and Tam, the village chandler's lad, arguing in the apse.

"What is amiss?" she asked, lifting her skirts to hurry toward them.

"She stole my nest," said the lad, shoving out his lower lip.

"Did not!"

"Did so!"

"What nest?" Juliana asked in exasperation.

Tam said, "Master Stumpe told me I should climb up to the belfry, see, and 'twas there that I found a most wondrous bird's nest. I brought it down to take home, but when I turned my back, 'twas gone!" He poked a grimy finger at Sima. "She took it. Everybody knows gypsies are thieves."

"What do you know, you Gajo scutch-brain? I never even saw your stupid nest."

"Did so!"

"Did not!"

"Niddy noddy!"

"Bast—"

"Peace, I beg of you," said Stephen in a weary, half-amused voice. With athletic grace, he dropped the last few feet down from the rope that hung from the bell tower and strode toward them. "*I* took the nest."

The youngster blinked. "You did?"

"It wasn't yours to take." Stephen went down on one knee and gently squeezed the lad's thin shoulders. " 'Twas a rock dove's nest, and the birds return to the same spot every spring. How would you feel if you tried one day to go home, and your house was gone?"

Tam caught his breath. "I'd not like it in the least, my lord."

"I thought not." Stephen extracted a pouch from his belt and held out his hand. "Sugared almonds," he said, handing one to each child. "Now, I think Master Stumpe needs a pair of good workers to sort shuttles for him. Run along."

The children scampered out, holding hands, their mouths stuffed with sweets and their argument forgotten. Juliana said, "Since when does the baron of Wimberleigh carry sweets in his pocket?"

He shrugged. "Thanks to your plan to put both the gypsies and the villagers to work, there are plenty of children about."

She looked down the apse, through the wide-open doors at the end of the building. The villagers rushed back and forth with flywheels and battens, rollers and ratchets, the gypsies hauling stonework, and Laszlo at a makeshift forge, hammering out hinges and latches.

"It is a good plan," she stated.

"Aye," he said, and she was surprised, for she had expected an argument from him.

"It's a very good plan indeed, Juliana." He reached out and touched the tip of her nose. "You've a smudge of plaster here, my lady."

Juliana was so startled by his whimsical mood that she simply stood with mouth agape as he strode back down the aisle and walked out into the sunlight.

This project consumed her. Distracted her from pursuing her goal. Sometimes she went for days at a time without thinking about Novgorod and that horrible night.

It was most confusing, finding her heart divided by duty and revenge. On the one hand, she wanted to stay and help the insular but good-hearted people of Lynacre. Yet her soul still burned with the fire of her Romanov pride and the searing grief of her loss.

A most unexpected dilemma, and one further complicated by her increasingly ardent feelings for her husband. Sometimes he seemed accepting of her, grateful for her help and pleased by her abilities. In his more unpleasant moods he accused her of trying to entrap him into a permanent marriage.

Juliana sniffed. As if she, a princess from an ancient line, would even consider such a thing.

And yet she did consider it when she lay

alone at night, her body in flames as she remembered his touch, his kisses, the breeze of his breath on her neck, and the yearning that coursed through her veins. One moment he was the skeptic, jaded by a past he refused to reveal. The next he was tender and encouraging, working at her side, challenging her.

"Not a wise thing," she muttered, wiping her hands on her apron and hurrying to the high altar. "One does not challenge a Romanov."

To bring light into the abbey, the workmen had to remove the boards from the jewel-toned glass windows that flanked the apsidal chapels and blossomed high above the altar. Cromwell's iconoclasts, in their fit of reformatory zeal against Papists, had neglected to smash the windows.

Juliana was glad. When she looked at them, she saw not the evil trappings of popery, but relics of a forgotten age.

Using a system of ropes and pulleys, the workmen removed the boards from the last and highest window — a lovely cinquefoil allegory of Saint Agnes.

Stephen strode up the aisle, his pale eyes blank and cold. "That one's to be removed at once."

"But it's the prettiest of all."

"I want it gone." His voice was low, resonating with anger.

"It's too high up to reach," she protested.

Without sparing her another glance, he picked up a large chunk of limestone and held it over his head with both hands.

"Stephen, no —"

The stone smashed through the window, wrenching the frame. Glass and lead and bits of mortar exploded outward in a shower of ruby and sapphire, emerald and topaz.

The shattering sound echoed and died, and the ensuing silence was deep and ominous, punctuated only by the heavy rasp of Stephen's breathing.

He seemed so remote standing there, his eyes glazed with chilling hate and his big hands flexing and fisting as if he wished to wring someone's neck.

"Oh, Stephen," Juliana whispered.

Her voice seemed to snap the cord of his patience. A foul oath burst from him and he turned on his heel, stalking out of the church. She heard him bellow for his horse, and she knew he was lost to her, gone on another of his frequent, unexplained journeys to a place she could not follow.

She felt shaken as she looked at William Stumpe. "Why?" she asked simply. "Do you know?"

He caught his breath, then let it out loudly. "The window was a gift to his lordship's first wife."

"A gift? Then why would he destroy it?"

"Because it was given to the lady Margaret by the king."

A chill licked at her spine. "I see. I think I see." She had always known Stephen and King Henry hated each other. Now she knew why.

They had been rivals for Lady Margaret's heart.

One week later, uneasy villagers and wary gypsies stood at opposite sides of the greensward in front of the old abbey of Malmesbury. From the church porch, Juliana surveyed the people gathered for the celebration and wished Stephen would arrive. The sun had sunk to a single gold sliver on the horizon. What on earth was keeping him?

William Stumpe, who had responded to her idea first with slack-jawed disbelief and finally enthusiastic determination, sat in his wheeled cart beside her, uneasily cracking his knuckles.

"Think the bonfire be high enough, my lady?" he asked. The pile of wood and rubbish looked to be twice a man's height. The acrid scent of pine tar wafted from the heap, and on either side, tall torches awaited to spark the fire.

Juliana nodded absently. She looked to her left at the gypsies, who, for five years, had been her family. They had taught her woodcraft, storytelling and dancing, and the wisdom of their ancient way of life. In time, they had taught her to laugh again.

To her right stood the tenants and villagers, sturdy and forthright as the land they tilled, the prayers they said, and the vows they made. Since arriving at Lynacre, she had come to know them, had seen their children grow, had watched them marry their young and bury their dead.

And she realized, in the fever pitch of activity during which she had worked on turning the abandoned abbey into a weaving house, she often forgot about her vow. Muscovy seemed like a fantastic dream shrouded in silvery cobwebs, viewed through a distant frost. Lynacre was real and immediate.

"Oh, Will," she said, feeling the weight of the silent suspicion emanating from both factions. "Now that the work is done, they are strangers again. Even after laboring side by side, they do not trust each other."

"Nay," he said, thumping his fist on the

arm of his cart, "they simply don't know each other. Say a few words in a toast, my lady. They'll come around."

With a tremulous smile, she turned and directed a nod at Kit, who waited at a trestle table set up on the lawn. He poured a cup of ale and brought it to her. His eyes shone at her for a moment, then strayed down to Catriona, the gypsy girl, who looked boldly back.

Juliana wished Stephen would arrive, but since the matter of the window he had been absent even more often than usual.

With sudden, bitter resolve, she decided not to wait. She lifted the cup of ale and said, "Let this drink celebrate the work we have all done. May the blessings of wisdom and courage be shared by all, and may God be with us."

The brewer thumped his wooden mug on the head of his barrel and then, unsmiling and hesitant, he raised his cup.

Laszlo responded to Juliana's pleading look by clapping together the heels of his boots and lifting his own tin mug. Smiles appeared on faces one after the other, like the first stars of evening winking on.

Kit and Catriona each took down a torch and touched the flaming heads to the base of the bonfire. The tar-soaked wood caught with an airy roar. The sun-yellow flames rolled up to the sky, painting the twilight in deep, rich gold.

Lyle, Stephen's chief musician, blew a fanfare on his trumpet. Not to be outdone, Troka, the gypsy piper, echoed the melody with his reed pipe. Then both Rom and Gajo joined in, creating a wildly spontaneous cacophony of pipes, drums, trumpets and gitterns.

Feet began to tap out the irresistible rhythm. Sima, the little gypsy girl, stepped boldly across the greensward and twirled elaborately in front of Tam, the lad who had stolen the nest from the bell tower. He caught both her hands and together, laughing, they danced down the length of the greensward.

Both of the bells in the tower began to ring, the deep brassy sound reverberating across the land. Stephen had designed special wheels for the bells so that the tolling went on unceasingly, underscoring the sound of music and laughter.

"I thought this project would be impossible," said William Stumpe. "And you made it happen, my lady."

She swallowed past an unexpected heat in her throat. "No. They all made it happen, Will —"

With a hearty laugh and a swift, powerful motion, he tugged her onto his lap and aimed his chair down the ramp constructed especially for him. Juliana shrieked and clung to his neck as William Stumpe, once declared useless by small-minded men, led her in a most singular dance of glad triumph.

"Do you see what I see?" Algernon Basset asked his companions.

Jonathan Youngblood rubbed his eyes as if to make certain he was awake. His jaw dropped as he gazed at the roaring bonfire with flames and sparks climbing high into the night, the wheeling dancers caught up in a storm of motion, the milling crowd drunk on ale and good cheer.

Stephen alone showed no surprise. He was growing accustomed to the changes his wife brought about in all that she touched. Juliana had worked her magic once again. Had turned an abandoned abbey into a place where men and women could prosper, had drawn villager and gypsy together with a unity of purpose that had seemed impossible to everyone else.

"Stephen," Jonathan said as they rode closer to the abbey, "your wife is a wonder."

Stephen gave a snort of derision even as

his gaze caught and clung to Juliana. "My wonder of a wife has been moonstruck." He tried to ignore the feeling that jolted through him at the sight of her. Tried to swallow the thickness in his throat and still the clamor in his heart.

He could not. God help him, he could not.

She was like a summer rose brought to full flower by the heat and light of the sun. She sat in Stumpe's lap, one arm hooked behind his neck, her feet in the air and her bare ankles and legs shamelessly displayed.

While Stumpe wheeled himself about to the quick pace of the dance tune, Juliana threw back her head, hair streaming down, her full-throated laughter riding the night wind.

"God, she is lovely," said Algernon, sending Stephen a sidelong glance. "Though I suppose you consider such hurdy-gurdy beneath the dignity of a baroness."

"To Juliana, it matters not at all what I consider."

Jonathan chuckled. "Too much woman for you, Wimberleigh?" With a deep belly laugh, he spurred his horse. He and Algernon galloped into the midst of the revelry.

Stephen sat for a moment absorbing the sting of Jonathan's words. The full moon showed its mottled face in a purple sky pierced by stars. It was the sweetest of nights — bright and clear, the air cool yet tinged at its very edges with the latent warmth of summer.

Too much woman for you?

The words pounded at the wall of reserve Stephen had built around himself, his sole defense against his strange and captivating wife.

Even as he told himself he should go back to his hall and get quietly drunk in the dark, he felt his blood stir, felt a devil of knavery leap to life inside him.

TEN

Stephen's heels dug into Capria's velvety sides. The mare surged forward, thundering across the field to the abbey. Pavlo barked madly, and Juliana left William Stumpe and walked to the edge of the firelit greensward. Despite the pumping motion of the galloping horse, Stephen could see her with remarkable clarity.

Though clad in simple, workaday homespun, his wife made an elegant figure — slim and strong, lit from behind by the bonfire, with loose tendrils of her hair lifting on the breeze.

He slid his horse to a stop in front of her. For a moment, words failed him. Then he uttered the first inanity that occurred to him. "Isn't the fire a bit grand, Baroness?"

She tossed her head and planted her hands on her hips. " 'Tis said a bonfire keeps away dragons."

He slapped the reins on his palm. "Idle

nonsense."

"Do you see any dragons about, my lord?"

"No. Of course not."

"See?" Laughter danced in her eyes. "It works."

A man could only endure so much. There she stood, laughing up at him. He felt drawn into the glittering depths of her eyes, spellbound by her subtle enchantment.

As if in a dream, he watched her gesture with her hand and call out a command. A Romany lad brought forth one of the gypsy horses. The animal's muscular flanks gleamed bloodred in the firelight. Her nimble bare foot found a stirrup, and in a flutter of layered skirts she landed high astride the horse's back. She leaned across to Stephen and whispered, "Ride with me tonight. I want to go very fast and very far."

Ride with me.

She used no spurs. The jab of her naked heels and the low, guttural command in an alien tongue were all the encouragement the stallion needed.

The gypsy horse's mane and tail were braided with bright ribbons that streamed back in the wind. Stephen had no idea what destination she planned, yet he could no more keep himself from following than the tide could resist the pull of the moon. With a soft clicking of his tongue, he sent Capria in pursuit.

Juliana's laughter floated back as she shot across the broad meadow between the south wood and the Chippenham road. The grass glistened with dew, risen in secret in the lightless moments between evening and night. Like diamonds, droplets flew up in the wake of pounding hooves. Faster and faster she rode, as skilled a rider as he had ever seen.

To his surprise, he found that he enjoyed the challenge of a race. Catching her, snaring her, would not be easy.

He loved the speed, the wind screaming past his ears, the rapid heartbeat of hooves striking the earth, the hiss and snort of the horses' panting. He felt the animal beneath him, hot and lathered, her perfectly conditioned body extending and contracting in sinewy rhythm.

He watched his own shadow racing across the moonlit ground, swift as a storm-driven cloud, toward Juliana.

Too late, he realized where she was headed.

She had chosen a path that led to a hidden byway known only to a very few, and a half mile from that was —

He pounded in the spurs. Capria charged

forward and sallied up beside Juliana. Her head whipped toward him and he saw the flash of a dazzling smile.

He nearly pressed his chest to Capria's pumping neck in his effort to coax the mare to greater speed. He passed Juliana, then prayed his mare would respond to the maneuver.

He angled in close to Juliana. With his hands high on the neck and the reins choked short, he tugged at one side. Capria neatly severed the path of the stallion.

The gypsy-trained horse behaved differently from an ordinary one. Rather than veering off on a new path, the stallion reared.

Polished hooves raked the night air. The animal's eyes rolled, showing white. Its lips peeled back and it let out a squeal.

"Juliana!" Stephen yelled, sawing at the reins to stop his mare.

Juliana clung like a limpet as the stallion rose up to his full vertical height. When the horse came down, Stephen heard a *whoosh* of breath as the impact emptied her lungs.

"Hang on," he called, dismounting and pounding across the field toward her. "Jesu, please hang on. Keep your seat."

The stallion's blood was up, though. The instant its forelegs touched the ground, its rear legs took to the air, snapping up and out. Back and forth it went, like a slender tree harried by a gale force.

Each time Stephen moved toward the tearing hooves, he was forced back. The stallion was like a warhorse of old, trained to fight as fiercely as its master in battle.

An eternity seemed to pass, not merely seconds, yet Stephen died a hundred shameful deaths as he watched his wife fighting for her life. He called her name again and again while helplessness clawed at him.

Have you done in this one, too? King Henry's mocking words echoed in his memory.

And then, like a storm skirling out to sea, the tumult subsided. Juliana's quick, clever hands worked the reins, and the stallion settled, head down and sides fanning like a smithy's bellows.

She brushed the flying hair out of her face and looked at Stephen. He braced himself for the tempest of her anger.

Instead, she laughed. Her hearty shouts of mirth rang out as she spread her arms, reaching out to embrace the very air around her.

"That was marvelous," she called. "I had no idea you could be such fun, my lord."

"Fun!" he exploded. His emotions were

like the horse — out of control despite his efforts to grapple them into submission.

She dismounted gracefully, her skirts billowing around her and settling on the dew-wet grass. "In Novgorod, we played such a game. Papa insisted it was a war game suited only for boys, but the horse master often let me join in."

Stephen stalked across the grass, grabbed her by the shoulders, and hauled her close against his pounding heart. She lifted her smiling face to his.

And then, with a passion heated by long-denied yearning, he kissed her. Even as he touched his lips to hers, he told himself to resist. Yet he felt such a powerful need that caution flew upward and disappeared like sparks in the sky.

She brought her arms around his neck and sighed against his mouth. This only sharpened his wild hunger, and he traced her lips with his tongue, tantalizing himself with the shape and the softness of her mouth, tasting the wine she had drunk and drawing small urgent cries from the back of her throat.

He sank down on one knee, pulling her with him. She came willingly, seeming to melt in warm compliance, as if she had been awaiting this moment.

"You've set me on fire," he whispered

against her mouth. The confession came easily. He kissed her again, harder, and they sank onto the dewy grass, peppery with the scent of wildflowers. No pallet of swans down could have felt more sumptuous.

Stephen reveled in the warmth radiating through him, causing the tension in his chest to ease. His tongue probed her soft mouth as if the intimate search would yield the key to her soul. His need ran far deeper than fleshly cravings. He wanted to revere her, to cherish her, to give her pleasure.

She clung to him, and her almost desperate intensity intrigued him. She was a creature of many facets, and at her core dwelt a reserve of wild passion he wanted to explore. He touched her hair, indulging an urge he had often fought. Like silk it was, fine as gossamer and unbelievably soft, spilling like warm liquid through his outspread fingers.

"Smoother than sable," he whispered, drawing a wavy lock across his lips. "I knew it would be."

Her head fell back and moonlight showered the arc of her throat. He touched his lips to the pulse leaping there, tasted her skin with his tongue. He loosened the laces of her blouse, and a brush of his fingers pushed it off her shoulders. Her breasts were bathed in pale starlight. Stephen felt a jolt of astonishment tinged with a deliciously forbidden edge of superstition, for no woman had ever looked so beautiful to him. His hand shook as he cupped it first over one breast and then the other.

God. He had forgotten the satiny weight of a woman's breast in his hand. The sensation was alien and exotic to a man made of hard muscle and tanned flesh, a man accustomed to keeping himself numb to all feeling.

He felt the peak draw tight, and he bent his head, brushing his lips gently back and forth, feeling the delicate, velvety texture and glorying in her gasp of surprise and delight.

Her back arched, and in the moonglow she looked like a pagan offering, mysterious, delectable, irresistible. He took the bud of her breast into his mouth and whisked it with his tongue. And even as desire burned hot at his core, he felt an unbidden tenderness wash over him. He knew with fierce and satisfying certainty that he was the first to bring her to this state of breath-held, bewildered anticipation.

And through it all, a part of him sat back in judgment and warned that he was going too far with his in-name-only wife. Yet he ignored the caution and control he had schooled into himself over the past years. He was bringing a new part of Juliana to life. He sensed that part had been slumbering inside her for years: the dark passion, the sexual yearning, the womanly desire she had kept at bay . . . until he had come into her life. And into her arms. It was a wonder she could want him.

"Stephen?" she said, her hands clutching his shoulders. "What are you . . . are we . . ."

"Hush." It almost hurt to speak; his throat ached so. He lifted the corner of his mouth in a half smile. "You choose an awkward moment to protest, Baroness."

She touched her finger to his lower lip where the taste of her still lingered. "But we both agreed it would be best to —"

"Hush," he said again, not wanting to hear his own cold rationality flung back in his face. "There are things I will not take from you, Juliana. And I will not do anything that can't be undone." He hoped she understood. "But let me . . ." He nuzzled her neck while his leg brushed against hers. "I can give you something."

"I do not understand."

"I'm not sure I myself understand." *And I need to touch you,* he admitted, but only to himself. For weeks, the tension had been building between them, and it was time to ease it. At least for her.

She did not argue further, this woman who usually would dispute with him whether it was day or night. She turned her head to kiss him, and she was so sweet and pliant that he forgot his vow. Forgot they were adversaries in a marriage of convenience, forgot what had brought them together and what would ultimately tear them apart.

For now, she was the woman in his arms, and he gave in to his urge to please her. He fondled and suckled her breasts until he heard her breath come in short gasps, felt her legs stir restlessly with need. Catching her moist, open mouth with his, he moved his hand lower, finding the hem of her skirts. He brushed aside the dew-damp fabric and slid his hand upward, finding the shape of her knee and the soft firm flesh of her thigh.

She gasped, and though she could not know it, he smiled against her lips. It no longer mattered to him whether she was a conniving gypsy or vagabond princess. Right now, she was a woman who desperately wanted the sweet release he could give her.

He shushed her with soothing whispers. His hands caressed, and she responded with a willingness that renewed his faith in the honesty of physical lust. He pressed her thighs apart and found the nest of curls, the flesh there tender with her wanting. He knew he had pushed her past maidenly modesty, past caring about why she was here and what the future would hold. In her naïveté, she could not know where his touch would take her.

Ah, but he knew. He knew and he craved it for her. In all ways but one, this would be the death of her innocence. After tonight she would know the dark velvety byways of carnal pleasure. The endless moment of beautiful dying and the breath-held burst of pleasure. There was something selfish in giving her this; he needed to know, at last, that he had never forgotten the brief but fiery power of intimacy.

He knew instinctively where to please her, where to ease the pressure and where to apply it. She held her entire body taut as a drawn bow, quivering. He found himself holding his breath with her as if he awaited the same rapture.

And then, just as suddenly, a convulsive movement rocked her, and he felt the rush of her pleasure, heard the half-bewildered, half-exultant cry of her completion. She seemed to melt in his arms as if her bones had turned to water, and Stephen let out his breath, held her close, listened with inexplicable satisfaction to the beating of their hearts.

"Stephen?" she asked, her voice thready and uncertain.

He stretched out in the grass beside her, brushed his lips over her damp temple, and tried to ignore the searing pain of self-denial. "Hmm?"

"What did you . . . did we . . . ?"

He smiled into her soft hair. "What do you think, Juliana?"

She stirred beside him, pulling up her blouse, pulling down her skirts. But she stayed beside him, pushing her shoulder into the crook of his arm. "I did not know . . . had no idea. I think you just made love to me. But it seemed a bit . . . one-sided. Perhaps I should —"

"Juliana, no." He made himself stop kissing her hair, stop stroking her shoulder, and forced a mocking laugh. "My dear, you read entirely too much into our little tumble."

She propped herself on her elbows and stared straight into his eyes, searching so deeply that he felt certain she could see down to his core, to the shivering soul that hid there behind the bluff facade.

"Do I?" she asked, never blinking, never

taking her eyes off him.

"Aye," he lied, dry-mouthed. "There was that tension between us." He touched her cheek, pretending it was a casual, almost dismissive gesture, knowing it was not. "You pleased me, Juliana, with your idea for turning the abbey into a weaving house. There was a wildness in us both but —"

"Yes?"

He could see her holding her breath, waiting for him to declare his true feelings, silently begging him not to hurt her. "But no more," he said, looking away. "The moment has passed."

"No," she said, striking him lightly on the chest and forcing his gaze back to hers. "Stephen, you know my body better than I do. You knew just how to touch me, just when. Something happened here. I do not begin to understand it, for Laszlo has been very protective of me. I've not been privy to the intimacies between a man and a woman. But I refuse to believe you would use this as a way of — of rewarding me or pleasing me."

"For God's sake." She was getting too close, seeing too much. He thrust her aside and jumped up. "You make much of this when in truth it is so trivial."

"Trivial?" She sat up and drew her knees

to her chest.

"So small," he said, pacing, trying not to wince at the mocking ache in his loins. "Unimportant."

She tilted her head to glare up at him. "After tonight I will never look at you — at myself — in quite the same way. That is small? Unimportant?"

"To me it is," he snapped. Then he put his fingers to his mouth and whistled for his horse. In truth he wanted her so much that his blood was aflame. He was so hard that it created a burning pain in every nerve, every cell. He wanted her so much that his very teeth ached with it.

He snared Capria's trailing reins. "Look. Men and women do this all the time. How could you think I would possibly be moved by a few moments of idle lust?"

She jumped to her feet. "Damn you, Stephen de Lacey!"

"No," he said. "Damn *you,* Baroness. Damn *you* for seeking meaning where none was intended." He would not look at her as he boosted her onto his horse and mounted behind, trying not to wince at the fiery discomfort. He did not want to see her face, for he knew she would read the lies in his own.

■ ■ ■ ■

It was a day of dappled sunshine and clouds melting into the green horizon, yet Juliana's heart felt as cold as winter, as barren as a blighted field. Lost in bewilderment, she watched her husband at work by the river. The large, squarish hands that had brought her such unspeakable pleasure last night now labored over his latest invention.

"Right ingenious is his lordship," Jillie said. "Why, with that contraption, we'll be able to bring the wool to the weavers twice as fast."

"Do you think so?" Juliana asked absently. She leaned her elbows on the fence rail and propped her chin in her hands.

Some yards away, Stephen and William Stumpe, Laszlo and Rodion worked the seines for bundling wool. The seines would be put in the river and drawn downstream from the sheepfolds to the abbey. In that fashion, the raw wool would get a preliminary washing, and the oils could be collected for making soaps and salves.

"The best ideas are always simple," said Jillie.

"Really?" Juliana asked, only half attending. She kept her attention fixed on her husband, and while her body responded with a warm spasm of remembered pleasure, her mind brooded on his harsh dismissal.

He had lied to her about his feelings. Surely he had. No man could bring a woman so close to heaven and feel nothing himself.

She held the thought to her heart and caressed him with her gaze. He wore rough workman's garb — a tunic and jerkin and knee-high boots. Watching him work, she felt a sense of contentment. The feeling took her by surprise, for she had always thought that happiness could never be hers until she avenged her family.

Jillie was still speaking, but Juliana stopped even pretending to listen. Stephen de Lacey held a never-ending fascination for her. No matter how long she looked at him, she never ceased to see something fresh, some bright new facet.

Though the group of workmen made bluff and merry company, she sensed a melancholy about her husband. Subtle as the undercurrents beneath a placid stream, his discontent lay hidden, visible only to those who looked for it.

As she watched, he put aside his bundled seines and stopped to watch a group of children at play. With tattered tunics, skinny brown legs, and dirty faces, they careened along the riverbank. Their laughter rose like swifts to the sun-dappled treetops, and they chased a pig-bladder ball with the determined abandon of a horde of barbarians.

With no notion he was being watched, he had let down his guard. What she glimpsed was the ache of loss, or perhaps the sadness of a promise betrayed, tinged with the winter hues of hopelessness. It was that almost hidden mournfulness that held him apart from others even when he stood in their midst. He had built his anguish into a wall no one could breach.

And perhaps in the end, Juliana thought, stepping through the fence gate and moving slowly toward her husband, this was what made her care for him, what made her forgive the harsh lashing of his words. Not just the heat of his kisses, the gentleness of his caresses, the explosive ecstasy he had shown her. Those made her hunger for him. But the other qualities awakened her tenderness — the challenge of his melancholy, the mystique of his isolation.

The lure of his secrets.

"Stephen." She spoke his name quietly.

Startled, he looked away from the children. For a second, pleasure flickered in his eyes; then he fixed a polite expression on his face and gave a courteous nod. "My lady."

My lady. How formal he was. How distant. As if he had never chased her across a moonlit field and kissed her. As if he had never lain with her upon the dew-wet grass and brought her to a state of insane completion.

Her cheeks heated. "I wanted to applaud your work here, my lord."

"I work not to win admiration," he said, glancing at the laborers, "but for those who had their lands taken when the king enclosed the forest."

"Of course." She searched his face for a sign of the man who had held her the night before. The man who had looked at her with his heart in his eyes.

Instead she saw a cold stranger. "My lord, yestereve —"

" 'Tis best forgotten," he snapped.

She drew him away from the workmen. His arm felt hard and slick with sweat, and the tenseness of the muscles beneath her fingers brought a fresh wave of remembrance. Beneath the low, spreading branches of an ancient oak tree, she planted herself in front of him, standing on tiptoe to bring herself nose to nose with him. "Tell me you have forgotten."

"I have forgotten."

"You lie."

A lock of his hair fell over his brow, making him look more devilishly handsome than she could bear. His mouth curved in a mirthless smile. "I assure you, tupping a wench in an open field was nothing out of the ordinary for me. I'm flattered that it was for you."

"Do not think," she whispered furiously, "that you can ever put me off so easily, Stephen de Lacey. I may be inexperienced in bed sport, but I am not stupid."

"Then why do you wish to discuss last night?"

"It was new to me. I tend to dwell on new experiences. Like the first time I ate sturgeon eggs or drove a troika —"

"A what?"

"Troika. Sleds pulled by stout ponies. And do not roll your eyes like that, my lord, for I will not argue any more about my past. I merely wish to explain that I am not hesitant to try out new adventures."

"Aye, you made that lack of hesitation clear enough."

"And what is *that* supposed to mean?"

"Only that you are a creature of the senses. I mean nothing ill by it." He lifted his hand as if to touch her, then seemed to think better of it. "I made a mistake. There is no reason in the world for us to be intimate. Good God, what if we were to make a child?"

"That's no sin between man and wife."

"We are playacting," he said with an infuriating excess of patience. "We have every reason to keep our urges in check. Soon the king will forget his jest, and we shall get this marriage annulled. We both agree on that, do we not?"

"Something made us forget." She tried to steady the catch in her voice.

"Then we should take care not to complicate the problem. You're a winsome female. It would be so easy to —" He clamped his mouth shut and looked away, at the women at the water's edge gathering the lanolin foaming up from the submerged wool.

"Easy to what?"

A shutter seemed to drop over his eyes. "Easy to tumble you like a ha'penny whore," he said. "You do not lack for wanton willingness."

Even before he finished speaking, she had her hand drawn back to slap him. But she made herself resist, made herself lower her arm. He wanted her to hate him.

"You're afraid," she said, her voice soft

with wonder.

"Don't be foolish."

"You are afraid," she said, speaking now with firm conviction. "You're beginning to care about me."

"I've not time for a woman's fanciful notions." He stepped back and turned sharply, stalking away to lose himself in work.

Juliana folded her arms across her bosom. Her husband's facade was growing thin. If she probed a little deeper into his life, into his heart, she might begin to understand.

For today, she would not ask herself why it mattered. She merely told herself that she was tired of being married to a stranger.

She leaned against the rough trunk of the tree and watched as a tiny girl ran up to Stephen and tugged on his hand. He turned swiftly, as if in anger, and grasped her beneath the arms. While the child shrieked with joy, Stephen swung her high in the air, up and up until her laughing face was framed against the blue summer sky.

Ah, tonight, Juliana resolved with her heart in her throat, she would learn the secret of Stephen de Lacey.

ELEVEN

Stephen blew out his breath, long and loud, as he waited for Nance to fill a scrip in the pantry that evening. With an idle eye, he watched the self-turning spit he had fashioned after the cook's favorite spit runner, an ill-mannered terrier, had singed its fur and refused to go near the contraption again. The new design was rotated with a turbine propelled by the force of the heat rising up the chimney.

"You barely touched your supper, my lord," Nance called through the open half door of the pantry, adding a twist of marchpane to the sack. "Ate no more than a Lenten eve groom. Was the fare not to your liking?"

He picked up a bottle of cider and inspected it for impurities. Finding it clear, he handed it to Nance. "Supper was fine," he murmured distractedly.

"Fine, was it? Then why didn't you eat?"

"I wasn't hungry."
"Aye, you were." Nance gave him a broad wink. "But for a woman's breasts and thighs, not a capon's."
"Christ," he muttered. "Not you, too."
"You mean someone else noticed?"
He rotated his shoulders, feeling the weariness there. It had been a long day of work, and a longer night lay ahead. "Juliana. There's something about her, Nance."
"Something." Her doughy face creased into a merry smile. "A caring heart, I'd call it. I was the first to have my doubts when you brought her here all lousy with vermin and needing a bath, but I've been wrong before." Her chubby elbow jabbed him in the ribs. "Remember you, my lord, that scutch-brained apothecary what sold me the love philter —"
"Nance, it's getting late."
"— all in a flurry I dropped it on the ground and that fat gander ate it —"
"Nance."
"Never did shed myself of that gander but with the kitchen ax." Shaking her head, she drew up the string of the parcel and jabbed a finger at him. "Now, don't you be getting any ideas about that ax. Is that so very awful, my lord? To find a lady who cares about you, about your —"

"Yes," he hurled at her. "For Christ's sake, you of all people should know that."

"Sometimes I wonder, my lord. Would it be such a high catastrophe if you was to tell her —" She broke off at his murderous look and crossed herself.

"That's enough, Nance. Juliana must never, ever know." He felt the burn of distrust in his throat. "I'd kill her. I'd die myself."

It was on nights like this, Juliana thought with a certain grim satisfaction, that Pavlo was at his best. Since coming to Lynacre, the dog had led a life of ease, but tracking was what the windhound was born to do.

At twilight she had pleaded fatigue, retired early from the hall, and pretended to tumble into bed in an exhausted heap.

Now she stood wide awake at the farthest end of the main garden, having dressed in a plain gown and slipped away, barefoot, with only the *borzoya* dog for company. Wind-torn clouds raced across the night sky, and shadows loomed in the gatehouse and walls encircling the garden.

It felt vaguely and uncomfortably criminal, sneaking out, straying far from the hall in search of her husband. No, she told herself, watching Pavlo streaking down the length of the seemingly endless wall, nose to the ground and tail waving high. It was Stephen's fault. Stephen's secrets. Stephen's lies.

His presence was everywhere; each corner of the manor bore the stamp of his inventive mind. The park was fenced with paling and buttressed walls designed by Stephen. The turf seats built around a wych-elm tree had enchanted beds of chamomile and pennyroyal growing at their base. The trellis work was intricate, twined with climbing roses, and in the center of a long bed of herbs was an escutcheon bearing Stephen's banner — a Lacey knot and border of the entwined initials *M* and *S*.

For Margaret, he had fashioned a crest of flowers. For Juliana, he had made a vow to banish her from his life.

She gave a tight smile as Pavlo paused and lifted his leg on the base of the escutcheon. Then she murmured a Russian command. The hour was late, her business pressing. Her newfound pride forbade that she allow her husband to stray even one more night.

The dog ranged farther and farther from the manor, past knot gardens and along pebbled paths, down to where the grass grew thick and tall and the scent of lavender spiced the air.

Impatient, Juliana began to wonder if the hound understood her goal, even though she had prompted him with one of Stephen's neckcloths pilfered from the laundry.

Pavlo trotted along beside a tall hedgerow of quickthorn, snuffling at broom plant and herbs. They had nearly reached the end of the vast park when the dog stopped and whined softly. Half expecting to find the burrow of a hedgehog, Juliana went to see what he had unearthed.

She hesitated, suddenly afraid of what she might find. Then she forced herself to part the plumes of a broom plant and saw that there was a break in the hedge. The thorny branches had been pruned to reveal a low gate, all but invisible to the casual eye. She caught her breath, then gave the gate a push. The low door swung open smoothly and quietly, as if someone kept the hinges oiled.

Pavlo slipped through and Juliana followed, then paused to get her bearings. She had thought this section of the estate to be a thick, wild woodland. Now she realized the tangled growth concealed a strange network of passageways.

"Sweet Saint Peter," she whispered, slipping into Russian and pressing back against the gate. "What is this place?"

The moon had not yet risen, so she had to rely on starlight and the keen vision of Pavlo. She was at the entrance to a maze.

A very large maze, the hedges no less than eight feet high and pruned so thick that they were as impenetrable as brick walls. Branches formed almost solid arches overhead.

A secret maze, she thought with a shudder. Why would Stephen keep such a thing hidden?

Because he had something dreadful to hide? A corpse, perhaps, or a den of thieves?

Steeling her nerves, she uttered a quiet command to Pavlo. The dog lowered his head, found the scent again, and trotted along a twisting path. Juliana took a deep breath and followed.

A half hour later, she began to imagine herself dying here. She had followed the dog through at least three miles of twisting, curving paths, and the search had yielded nothing save more winding endless byways. She pictured her bones lying undiscovered along one of the sinister lanes, her flesh picked clean by ravens and rooks.

She shivered and kept her gaze trained on Pavlo's waving tail. How would she be remembered? The folk of Wiltshire would dub her that crazy gypsy who had been forced to choose between hanging and marriage to an English lord. She had never proven her identity to the satisfaction of anyone who mattered. No one save Laszlo believed she was a Romanov.

A pity, she thought. Then she realized that, to a corpse, rank and bloodlines mattered not. Hardly a comforting thought.

The hem of her skirt snagged on a hedge, and she yanked at it. A bit of fabric stuck fast to a thorn. "The *vurma,*" she whispered into the darkness. She should have been leaving a trail all along. Too much luxury was making her forget sensible Romany ways.

Squaring her shoulders, she started off again, her footsteps quickened by anger. She began to mark her way with strands of hair and bits of thread from the weave of her torn skirt. Pavlo never faltered, never hesitated when the paths diverged.

Her bare feet ached from hurrying over the packed earth. Just as she was about to give up and find her way back, Pavlo whined. She reached the juncture of two paths. Here, the foliage over the maze was thinner; the light shone brighter. The hedges no longer arched together, and the moon appeared fat and butter-white.

A few steps farther, and she emerged from

the maze . . . into an enchanted garden.

Damn her to hell.

From the second story, Stephen glared at the round, rising moon. Though he was not far from Lynacre Hall, he felt as if he had traveled many leagues.

He wondered why he wanted Juliana, why her smile seemed to light up a room when she entered it, why his arms ached to hold her — and her alone. Not even for Meg had he felt this constant yearning, this unquiet emptiness in his soul that only seemed to fill when his wife was close.

He had spent the past seven years teaching himself not to feel, and now in just a few short months Juliana had brought it all back to him — the fierce joy, the sweet anguish, the passion, and the heat.

She made him want it again — all of it, the pain and the ecstasy, the caring and the hushed, fragile knowledge of heart-deep love.

Stephen stared at the single flame of the candle on the windowsill and told himself he could have none of it.

He could not have Juliana, for his life was ruled by dread. A seeping, conniving dread that had a life of its own; in seconds it could render him helpless, invading his body like quick poison.

He lived in hell. Loving Juliana would only condemn her to the same fate.

He returned to his vigil in the darkened room.

Gooseflesh rose on Juliana's arms. Wide-eyed in the darkness, she took in the shadowy profusion of herbs and flowers tumbling along winding paths. Here and there stood a bench or resting stool, all but smothered in rampant gilliflowers or snapdragons.

Rising out of the wild splendor of the garden was a grassy mound surrounded by a menagerie of fantastical beasts: a unicorn, a griffin, and a dragon. They were covered in small-leafed ivy, and the breeze made them stir as if half-alive.

Pavlo stood as stiff as a palace guard, the hairs at the scruff of his neck standing on end, a growl of suspicion rumbling in his throat. He took a few steps forward, then feinted nimbly back.

At the top of the mound was a fountain embellished with four roses that spouted streams of water. The streams in turn sprayed into the open mouths of laughing frogs. Water from the basin of the fountain spilled down a conduit, and the rivulets powered a water wheel that turned slowly and soundlessly — and seemingly without purpose.

Moving like one in a dream, Juliana climbed the mound to the fountain. She put a tentative finger into the scallop-shaped basin, then touched it to her lips. Yet even the taste of the cool, sweet water did not dispel the magic.

Aye, it was a magical place, one she had thought to exist only in nursery tales or deep in the dreams of sleeping children. The riot of flowers, the cavorting beasts, the burbling fountain, were all too wondrous to be real.

But they were, and she knew just where they had come from.

"Stephen," she whispered. She had long been aware of his genius for creating things, but his inventions at Lynacre had always been of a practical nature. In this garden lay the fruits of a whimsical imagination she hadn't known he possessed. It was like looking through a window into his soul — and seeing the enchanted prince trapped inside his gruff exterior.

What was this place?

Pavlo gave the topiary beasts a wide berth and trotted through an arbor that led to a small, snug building. Hurrying after the dog, Juliana saw that it had chimneys, a bank of small windows on both the first and second stories. A kitchen garden grew on the south side, the rows of greens and herbs as neat as a regiment of soldiers.

And high in one window on the second story, a single candle burned.

She stood spellbound by the solitary flame. Suddenly she wished she had not come. She did not want to be here, did not want to know who shared the elegant little cottage with her husband.

And then, as Juliana stood watching, the candle flickered as if disturbed by someone brushing past. For some reason, the slight change in the light awakened her Romanov soul — the place where passion dwelt deep, where rage and pride overcame fear and uncertainty.

Damn Stephen de Lacey. And damn the woman who was fool enough to think she could dally with the husband of Juliana Romanovna.

She touched her brooch and the small dagger slipped free, the jewel-encrusted hilt solid in her hand. She did not pause to consider why she had armed herself. Simple instinct told her not to go defenseless to her husband and his mistress.

"His mistress." She hissed the words into the gloom. Then, motioning for Pavlo to stay, she crept toward the house. Its hidden location made locks unnecessary, and Juliana gained entry simply by lifting the latch of the main door in the front.

She stepped blindly into a dark room. Moon shadow created a pattern of diamonds on the floor. She paused to let her eyes adjust. A strange odor of porridge and herbs hung in the air. It was not a pleasant smell. Stephen's mistress must be a woman of no taste at all.

Except in her choice of lovers.

Aye, Juliana could finally admit it to herself. Stephen was that rarity among men: one who could be both tender and masterful, shamelessly romantic and coldly logical. A man of common sense and airy whimsy. A man whose touch had the power to lift her into rapture.

The remembrance of his kisses and her response to them seared her with anger. Her hand tightened around the hilt of the dagger. Her eyes picked out the way to the stairwell.

As she moved across the hall, she had only vague impressions of her surroundings. The entire room was unusual. Tables and chairs seemed to have shorter than normal legs and backs. Ceiling beams seemed uncomfortably close to the top of her head.

She put down the flaws to the inferiority of the unknown woman's character and started for the stairs. They were made of solid masonry, narrow and spiraling upward.

Her skirts brushed the stone as she moved soundlessly up and found herself in a low, vaulted corridor. A single gold filament of light glowed in an outline around one of the three doors.

Juliana went toward it. Now she could hear sounds coming from the room. Her hair stood on end when she identified the noise: rough, ragged breaths from a man in the throes of lust.

As her resentment burgeoned, Stephen's hoarse sounds of passion drifted out into the passageway to torment her.

"I am your *wife,* damn you," she whispered. Still clutching the knife, she quietly pushed open the door and stepped into the room.

And stopped as if the very hand of God had turned her to stone.

Stephen had his back to her, and he had not heard her enter. Contrary to the lust-ridden vision she had formed in her mind, he was fully dressed and kneeling on the floor.

Nothing could have prepared her for this.

His shoulders shook, not with the tremors

of passion, but with sobs of heart-deep grief. His head bent, he crouched beside a tester bed. His big hands clutched convulsively into the coverlet as if they would rend the fabric into shreds.

And in the bed, sound asleep and oblivious to Stephen's wild grief, lay a beautiful, golden-haired child.

In a flash, Juliana remembered the limnings she had discovered in her husband's room. She had found portraits of two children, half-grown, though Stephen had sworn one died at birth.

In the moments since she had entered the room, she had forgotten to move. To breathe. Her mind filled with the image before her: Stephen, her magnificent husband who was always so full of swaggering confidence, hunched like a defeated man over this sleeping angel of a child.

Juliana finally found her voice. "S-Stephen?"

In one swift motion he stood and turned, his face stark with shock, wet with tears, ravaged with grief. And deep in his eyes burned a violent fire of pure hatred.

"Get out," he said, his voice deadly yet low, for even in his state of grief he seemed mindful of the sleeping child. "Get out, Juliana, before I kill you."

■ ■ ■ ■

Stephen had never made a more sincere threat in his life, and he knew his intent was evident in his voice, in his smarting eyes. And so he waited for Juliana to flee for her life. Just as everyone else fled from his wrath.

Instead, she remained standing inside the door. Her small figure caught the light from the long golden flame of the taper. She wore a net coif, but strands of her hair escaped it, making a frame of sable curls for her pale face. And she looked at him, truly looked at him in that unique and unsettling way she had, taking him apart by inches, probing deep, seeing all the way into his soul.

Finally she moved. She did not flee, but glanced down at the small knife in her hand. "I shall not be needing this after all," she said, half to herself, and put the blade back into the jeweled sheath pinned to her bodice.

She took a step toward him.

"By all that I have, Juliana," he said, "I mean that. I command you to leave. I want you to forget about this place. I want you out of my house, Juliana. Out of my life. Forever."

She winced, and he felt a twinge of regret. He was not by nature a cruel man, but a moment of pain was preferable to inviting this ravishing stranger into his heart.

"I will not leave," she said. "Not yet, at least." Then she did the unthinkable. She went and sank to the floor beside the bed, her skirts pooling around her.

"Stay away from him!" Stephen hissed through his teeth.

She did not even look up. Her low-lidded gaze was fixed on the child. "What is your son's name?"

Shaken, Stephen looked at his beautiful child. His beautiful, dying child.

"His name is Oliver, and if you don't get away from him, I'll remove you by the scruff of the neck."

She brushed her fingers over the little lad's brow, the gesture so sweetly maternal that Stephen's throat filled with fresh sorrow. Meg had never even held him in her arms. The golden head stirred a little.

"Remove me?" Juliana murmured. "A moment ago you were going to kill me. We are making progress, my lord."

"Damn it." He grabbed her shoulder and pulled her to her feet. "I do not permit anyone to touch him."

She jerked away from him, and defiance

blazed in her eyes. “This child is feverish, Stephen.”

“Do you think I don’t know that, you meddlesome bitch? He’s feverish nearly every night, damn your eyes —”

“Stephen,” she whispered, “you are hurting me.”

He glanced down at his hands. His strong fingers dug deep into the flesh of her upper arms. With an effort of will and a sigh of self-loathing, he released her.

“You shouldn’t have come here,” he said wearily.

“I had a right to come here. I am your wife, and I grew tired of your disappearances each night.” A tiny smile tugged at one corner of her mouth. “Believe me, Oliver is the last person I expected to find with you.”

He remembered her drawn knife. “Just what did you suppose?”

“Another woman. A mistress.”

He almost laughed. “Would you have used the dagger on me, or on her?”

“You will never know, my lord.” She gazed down, misty-eyed, at Oliver. The lad stirred, coughing softly and then turning on his side and tucking his hand up under his chin.

How thin and frail he was, thought Stephen with a lurch of his stomach. He thought of the robust village children with their bright eyes and muddy bare feet. Even the poorest tinker's child outweighed Oliver.

Before Stephen could stop her, Juliana bent and pressed a kiss on Oliver's brow. Her lips lingered there, and for a moment she squeezed her eyes shut and caught her breath.

Then, serene and in control, she picked up the candle in its holder. "Come below, my lord. I wish to talk to you."

Stephen told himself to grab the candle and send her on her way. But he kept seeing the look on her face when she had kissed Oliver. The tightly clenched eyes, the expression of heartfelt concern. In that moment, she had conquered something inside him, some fearful part of him that for years had not even let him speak of Oliver.

His mind was ablaze with wonder: Juliana had found out about Oliver, and the world had not come to an end.

"What is that herb I smell?" she asked. "It was very strong in his hair."

"Borage," said Stephen. He moved like the walking wounded, mindlessly following the light in her hand. "It is supposed to correct the imbalance of black bile and yellow bile."

They reached the hall. Juliana set down the candle and faced him. The amber light imbued her features with a diffuse glow, flickering like a caress of fire across her high, proud cheekbones and the dainty wisps of hair brushing her neck. "So you have consulted a physician."

"Of course."

"And is your son getting better?"

Stephen did not speak for a moment. He merely stared at Juliana, who stood only inches away, her face soft with a compassion so deep and real that his knees nearly gave way. Then, without thinking, he caught her against him. God, how exquisite she felt, how warm and vibrant. Somehow, she gave him the strength to speak the truth.

"Juliana," he whispered into her hair, "my son is dying. It is only a matter of time."

He heard her breath snag in her throat. Then she pulled back and raised herself on tiptoe. Her kiss was soft and brief, a glimmer of healing warmth against his dry mouth. "Are you certain?"

Stephen nodded. "My first son, Dickon, had the same affliction. Most doctors and astrologers agree that the disease is an asthmatic fever of the lungs. Eventually Oliver will suffocate, as Dickon did." The cold, unemotional words belied the raw soreness of grief in Stephen's throat. "Dickon died in my arms. I could not slay that dragon for him. No matter how much I loved him, no matter how many prayers I said or candles I lit or doctors I consulted, I could not save him."

"Ah, Stephen." She touched his cheek. "You take too much upon yourself. Why do you keep Oliver's existence a secret? Why do you let everyone believe he died at birth?"

"To protect him," Stephen said fiercely. "My first son was summoned to court to serve as a page. Half a year later, he was dead. The rigors of court life drained the last of his strength."

"And you fear Oliver will suffer the same fate."

"Aye."

"Then you did a wise thing."

"No, I fear I did a very foolish thing."

Dropping her hand, she picked up a wooden whirligig from a shelf on the wall. He had made it for Oliver's fifth name day. "What do you mean by that?" she asked, watching the wooden blades spin.

"I'm not certain. Somehow, King Henry knows about Oliver." Bitterness twisted Stephen's mouth into a parody of a smile. "Haven't you figured it out by now, Baroness? The threat to summon Oliver to court is the ax hanging over my head. It is the reason I married you."

She dropped the whirligig with a clatter. "You mean the king is using that poor child as a threat against you?"

"Compassion is one of His Majesty's lesser virtues."

She sank to a cushioned stool. In the wavering light of the candle, her hands trembled. Faintly from above came the sound of Oliver coughing. Stephen's shoulders burned with helpless tension. Then the coughing subsided.

Juliana raised her troubled eyes to him. "You should have told me."

He let out a bark of mirthless laughter. " 'Twould have served nothing."

"I would have understood." She reached for his hands and clasped them in hers, drawing him down to the stool next to her. "I want to understand."

He blew out a long, quavering breath. "After Dickon died, my wife perished giving birth to Oliver, our second son. From the very first breath he took, I heard the wheezing, and I knew he had the same affliction as his brother. It seemed simpler to allow everyone to believe Oliver had died at birth. That is the report that went out by mistake and I took no pains to correct it."

"Who else knows of him?"

"Only my most trusted retainers. Old Nance Harbutt and her daughter Kristine, who lives here. She is an herbalist, convent trained and exceedingly learned. She oversees the place and tends to Oliver's needs."

Juliana glanced at the stairway. "She never leaves him?"

"No. Nor does she ever want to. She took her vows to heart, and the king's break with Rome offended her deeply. Here, she can dedicate herself to study and prayer."

"How did the king find out your son lives?"

Propping his elbow on his knee, Stephen winnowed his fingers into his hair. "Though Nance and Kristine and Dr. Strong swear they have kept their counsel, one of them must have let the secret slip."

"Where is Kristine now?"

"She's gone to fetch Dr. Strong from Chippenham. The fever worries me."

As if prompted by the words, Oliver began to cough. Stephen grabbed the candle to light his way. His ears were sharply attuned to the sound, and he was on his feet and climbing the stairs in an instant. *Don't think. Don't feel.*

He heard the whisper of skirts on the stair

behind him. "Stay back," he ordered gruffly. "Seeing a stranger will only upset him if he wakes."

Resentment flared in her eyes but she nodded curtly and hung back in the shadows outside Oliver's chamber.

"Hush, son," he whispered to the small figure on the bed. He lit a flame beneath the brazier. As he hurried to the cupboard, he saw from the corner of his eye that Oliver had lifted his hand, reaching for him.

"Lie still," Stephen muttered, even as some invisible part of him leaped toward the boy. Dr. Strong advised that Oliver not be touched or squeezed in any way, save when he was being bled. Resisting his own instinct to hold Oliver close until the spell passed, Stephen went to work. The routine was painfully familiar — chamomile, chopped and dried, ground arrowroot, and white vinegar that sizzled when it touched the charing bowl over the brazier flame. Though the smoke was noxious, the doctor swore it was beneficial to the lungs.

Thankfully, a full-blown attack did not ensue. Oliver stopped coughing and never fully awakened, although for a second, his eyes opened and he stared dully at his father. Stephen's heart twisted with helpless love, but he made no move toward the lad, not wishing to excite him. Best to keep his feelings in check. His emotions numb. His hopes ruthlessly suppressed.

Oliver shut his eyes. He was twitchy and restless, but within a few minutes he was asleep. Stephen snatched up the candle and left the room.

Juliana waited, her fist pressed to her mouth and her eyes shining with tears. She looked as if her heart were breaking.

"You should have gone back to the house," Stephen said, leading the way down the stairs. "I'll thank you to leave now. Do not come here again."

She followed him meekly enough, but stopped in the hall. "When I was ill as a child, my nurse always pulled me into her lap and told me stories. I thought it strange that you did not touch your son, kiss him and tell him it will be all right."

"That, dear Baroness, would be a lie," Stephen said furiously. He went to the door.

Her face flushed. "I thought you left each night to visit a mistress." She glanced at the stairwell. The strong herbal smell was beginning to pervade the house. "I had no idea, Stephen."

"You were not meant to."

"But if I had known, I would not have thought ill of you."

Suddenly the urge to hold her was so great that it scared him. It would be too easy to bring Juliana into his world, into his heart. Too easy to repeat the mistakes of the past — to sell his soul to a beautiful woman.

With an effort of will, he pointedly yanked the door open. "Juliana," he said, injecting a lethal dose of venom into his voice, "by now you should know that I care not at all what you think of me."

A son. Stephen had a living son. The thought had kept pace with Juliana as she made her way back through the maze to the manor. She took the idea to bed with her and awoke with the image of the fair-haired child in her mind.

She knew what she must do. "I will be away most of the day, Jillie."

The burly maid looped Juliana's long hair into a net coif. "Working at the weaving house again, milady?"

"No." Juliana stepped into a pair of velvet slippers. "Perhaps your father could use your help in the dye shop."

"I trow he could. Since the weaving's begun, he's got work aplenty."

"Go, then. I'll have no need of you today." Juliana waited until Jillie left, then took out a large tapestry bag. In it she placed a lute, a book and a gypsy tambourine.

Then, when she felt certain no one was observing her, she went down through the long garden, out the gate and through the break in the hedge.

A sense of resolve quickened her steps. For years her sole purpose had been to avenge the murder of her family. That had been a dark and furious goal, one that sapped her strength and sometimes frightened her.

This was different. It was a task lit by the brightness of compassion and warmed by the radiance of hope. Her heart felt feather light as she and Pavlo made their way through the tangled maze and emerged into the sun-filled garden of the cottage.

By day it was even more fantastical than it had been in moonlight. The creatures seemed ready to spring to life as they stood in eternal vigil by the fountain.

She pushed open the door to the cottage and stepped into the room where she had left Stephen. There were the stools where they had held hands, where he had finally told her of his past, his voice shaking, his eyes haunted by darkness.

It was here that she had faced the truth: she had fallen deeply in love with her handsome, tormented husband.

And it was here that he had cut her off, so swiftly and so brutally.

I care not at all what you think of me.

She winced at the memory. Then she cast it aside, squared her shoulders and prepared to climb the stairs.

A crash sounded from above, making her jump.

"I won't eat it!" came a shrill, angry voice. "I will not, and you can't make me!"

A feminine murmur came in reply.

"You dare not!" said the child. "If you do, I'll — I'll tell my father you pinched me."

Juliana mounted the steps and went to Oliver's chamber. The door was ajar. Oliver sat up in bed, the color high in his cheeks as he glared mutinously at the young, black-clad woman. Beside the bed lay the pieces of a crockery bowl, and grayish gruel oozed over the floorboards.

"Master Oliver, please —"

"Go and find him something else to break his fast," Juliana suggested, stepping into the room.

The woman gasped. The boy stared.

"I am Juliana de Lacey," she said calmly. "His lordship's wife. And you must be —"

"Dame Kristine Harbutt," the woman said, her mouth agape as she bumbled through a curtsy. Like so many of the West

Country women, she was strong of limb and broad of feature. She wore her rich chestnut hair scraped back into a plain coif, and not a single ornament graced her drab costume save the heavy rosary beads at her waist. As she recovered from her surprise, keen intelligence shone in her face.

"Nance told me about you," Juliana said. "It is an honor to meet you. You may leave us now."

"But — but his lordship said —"

"I am his wife, and I wish to acquaint myself with my stepson. Please."

Pale and shaken, Dame Kristine picked up the broken bits of pottery and hurried out.

Juliana set down her bag and paused for a moment, looking about the room. Everywhere she saw gifts from Stephen — little clockwork animals, a chess table, stacks and stacks of precious books. A copybook lay open on a table; Oliver had been practicing his penmanship. At the end of the page the careful penstrokes had dissolved into a frustrated scrawl, and the lad had written *Papa is a pysse-potte.*

Trying to look pleasant yet unamused, she crossed the room and pressed at the window latch to open it.

"I'm not to breathe the outdoor air," said

a glum, suspicious voice behind her.

"Nonsense," Juliana said over her shoulder, pounding at the edge with the heels of her hands. The limewash crumbled and finally gave way, and the dormer window swung open. "It is a glorious day, and the herbs and flowers in the garden smell delicious."

She went to the bed and sat on the edge, smiling into the boy's startled face. "So," she said lightly, "you are Oliver de Lacey."

He seemed leery of answering her. He continued to stare, and she was amazed at how very like his father he was. Though Oliver's hair was several shades lighter than Stephen's, it seemed to be of the same texture, thick and wavy as a lion's mane. Equally reminiscent of Stephen were the chiseled shape of the face, the serious mouth. And the strange, cold, moonstone eyes.

Oh, God, she thought, *he has his father's eyes.*

"You're not supposed to be here," he said at last. He had a raspy, little-boy voice, both wary and petulant.

"Of course I am supposed to be here." Juliana took care not to smile, for she knew at once that this was a proud, serious little boy who would not care to be patronized.

"I am your stepmother."

"Dame Krissie said my father had married a filthy gypsy."

"I am gypsy by adoption. And I know many gypsies. They are no cleaner or dirtier than anyone else."

Oliver coughed absently. "You talk funny."

"Then you should laugh at me."

"Not that sort of funny," he said impatiently. "I mean you sound odd."

"English is not my mother tongue. I first spoke Russian, and then Romany, the language of the gypsies. Some of your words are hard for me to say. Perhaps you could help me."

He narrowed his eyes. "Why should I?"

"Everyone needs help, Oliver. We should all help each other."

"I don't want a mother," he said abruptly.

"Everyone needs a mother, too."

His fingers, with the nails chewed low, plucked at the counterpane. "I've never had a mother."

"Well, I have never had a little boy. Perhaps we should not worry about that. Perhaps we should simply agree to be friends."

He tucked his chin against his chest and mumbled something.

"What did you say?" she asked, beginning

to ache at the way he huddled on the bed, pale and withdrawn and distant.

He drew a deep breath, then wheezed a little as he tried to expel it. He glared. "I said, I've never had a friend, either."

Juliana caught her breath. She looked quickly away, blinking fast to conquer the tears that pressed at the backs of her eyes. And even as she fought to subdue her sadness, she felt a little lick of rage leap to life inside her. What in God's name could Stephen be thinking, hiding the lad away like this?

She tamped down her anger, tucked it away to unfurl later, when she would not frighten the boy.

"Oh, Oliver," she whispered, and she barely got the words past the lump in her throat. She had failed to get hold of herself after all. When words deserted her, she did the only thing she knew to give comfort. She hugged him hard and close, his warm cheek against her chest. Her heart broke for this strange, pitiful boy who lived alone in a world of his own. "Oliver, what is the matter?"

"Don't . . . touch . . . me!" he half shouted, half wheezed. His eyes were bright, the color a more vivid blue than they had been a moment earlier. With a great whoop, he sucked in air, then seemed to struggle to let it out. A thin wheeze escaped him, yet he still seemed to be struggling to exhale.

The lad was air-hungry, strangling; his eyes lost focus and rolled while a gurgling sound rose in his throat. He tore off his bed-shirt as if the garment were a prison. With each desperate breath, he sucked in the skin below his breastbone and between his ribs.

"Dame Kristine!" Juliana shouted. "Come quickly! Oliver needs you!"

Dame Kristine pounded up the stairs, burst into the room and rushed to the cupboard. Bottles and crockery clinked as she gathered up medicines and instruments.

Still gasping, Oliver shrank against the headboard. Horrendous hives peppered his neck and chest. It was not simply inhaled air that he was trying to expel, but the panic, too, as if it were a demon to be exorcised.

Dame Kristine shot an outraged look at the wide-open window and slammed it shut, the panes shaking. Then she set a flame to a bag of herbs in the brazier by the bed. Noxious smoke filled the air, and around the smoldering leaves she placed three small, shallow glass cups.

"What set him off?" she asked briskly.

Juliana coughed at the rank odor of the

burning herbs. "I — I embraced him."

Dame Kristine scowled through the thickening smoke. "What do you mean, you embraced him?"

Juliana crossed to the bed. Some of Oliver's exhalations were long and labored; others were short and shallow. She had never in her life felt so helpless. Despite what had happened earlier, she yearned to smooth a white-blond lock of hair from his brow.

"I held him close." She dropped to her knees and gazed intently into his eyes. The terror was buried so deep she knew she could not reach him. "I am sorry, Oliver," she whispered while the voice inside her begged him to stay with her, pleaded with him not to be sucked down by the fear.

"Oliver, I have never met a boy like you. I didn't know you did not like to be touched. Dame Kristine is here and she is fixing some medicine. Come back to us." Juliana stayed there until her knees ached. She stayed until they went numb. She kept up a gentle endless patter reminiscent of the way she would speak if she were trying to calm a skittish colt.

Oliver's fear-filled gaze clung to her, and she dared not even blink for fear of losing him.

Then she felt a hand on her shoulder.

"My lady, it is over."

No! Juliana screamed inside. "He cannot be . . ." She choked back a sob.

"The attack, my lady. Master Oliver's breathing is better now."

At last Juliana began to understand what Stephen endured every minute of every day. The unbearable apprehension, the uncertainty. A careless word by a servant could send Stephen into a panic.

"Oliver?" she whispered. "You are feeling better, yes?"

"Yes," he said in a thin voice.

Dame Kristine busied herself with the tray of instruments. Oliver's face showed only blank disinterest as he lowered the twisted bedclothes and turned over on his stomach. His ribs stood out like a starveling's, and his skin was nearly as pale as the bleached linen sheets. Horrid scars in a sinister pattern scored his back. He turned his head to the side and asked, "Is it to be the leeches or the cups this time, Dame Kristine?"

Dame Kristine sucked her tongue, her manner brisk. "Cupping, I think. Lie still now. . . ."

She worked with the deftness of long habit, drawing a thin knife along Oliver's left shoulder and placing a hot cup over the wound. Juliana stayed on her knees in a state of horror and awe as Dame Kristine made two more cuts.

The herbal smoke hung like a blue-gray shroud over the room. A pounding began in Juliana's ears and a soft moan escaped her.

"Never seen a cupping before?" Oliver asked in a flat, chillingly adult tone.

"No."

"You look greensick." Mischief gleamed in his eyes. "Maybe Dame Kristine has something in the cupboard for you."

Realizing that this was an attempt at jesting, Juliana forced herself to smile. "Not today. I think my humors are properly balanced."

He drifted off to sleep, and the hives on his skin faded away. Dame Kristine put up her medicaments.

"Will he be all right?" Juliana whispered.

Dame Kristine gave a curt nod. "The spell passed more quickly than usual. He seemed to like having you here, talking to him."

Juliana tucked the coverlet over him. "Do you truly think it was my fault? He fought me when I touched him."

"He's a prickly little thing. Hard to say what set him off." They sat in the tidy kitchen, sipping small ale while Dame Kristine talked. For the past seven years, Oliver had lived here, visited nightly by his father and on occasion by an eminent physician. The lad had been bled, leeched, purged, dosed and bathed in every concoction imaginable, but none of the treatments seemed to stop the attacks.

Stephen gave him toys and books and amusements — mechanical soldiers, a skin horse that made a whinnying sound, a model castle with a working catapult, a puppet theatre and a variety of games. The lad lived in a fairyland with every magical gift Stephen could bestow upon him.

And yet Juliana was struck by the conviction that Stephen withheld the one thing the boy needed most — a father's love.

Jillie practically had to wrestle her into submission to keep her still long enough to dress her for supper.

"Now, that's a rare shade," the maid said, touching Juliana's cheek. "I've no label for it, but were I to give it a name, I'd not be far wrong to call it choler. What's amiss, my lady?"

Juliana patted her coif. "I must speak to his lordship about a matter. And it is impertinent of you to ask."

Jillie mumbled something under her breath.

"What did you say?"

In clumsy Romany, Jillie said, "Everyone doth something know which you have yet to learn." Grinning, she reverted to English. "Now, if you'll not be needing me again, milady . . ."

Juliana could not help smiling. She squeezed her maid's hand. "Go on with you, Jillie." After she had left, Juliana's smile lingered. Jillie Egan had never ventured farther than the village of Chippenham. But Rodion, it seemed, was bringing the world to her.

She recalled Stephen's warning about allowing Jillie to dally with a man who might break her heart. Indeed. As if her husband were an expert on the vagaries of romance.

"Ah, Stephen," she whispered to the empty room, " 'tis you who have much to learn."

She squared her shoulders and went to find him.

TWELVE

Stephen had been unable to concentrate all day. In his routine meetings with his steward and reeve, he had been vague and unfocused, barely attending to the details of management that usually fascinated him. Even his latest contraption — a pulley to open the main gate unattended — failed to hold his attention.

A persistent dread had taken up lodging in him, and he could think of nothing save the reason why.

Juliana had found out about Oliver.

Against his will, Stephen remembered the day King Henry had revealed that he knew the secret.

"It comes to me that you've been hiding something, my lord," King Henry had said, his voice ringing to the rafters of the Presence Chamber.

With his insides knotting, Stephen had knelt before the gold-canopied throne and waited for the king to continue.

Henry waved a jeweled hand to banish his courtiers from the dais. He dropped his voice low and said, "Why did you not tell me that Meg's son still lives?"

Stephen had yearned to deny it, to tell the king he was mistaken. But the look on Henry's face — stern, all-knowing, and just at the edge of royal fury — convinced him that it was time for the truth to emerge.

"I . . . The lad is sickly. The physicians do not expect him to survive." *Oliver, Jesu, Oliver, forgive me.*

Henry had been silent for a few moments; then a look of cruelty hardened his black eyes. "Meg's son. And is he your son, as well, my lord of Wimberleigh?"

The question seared Stephen like a glowing brand. He longed to spring up and throttle his sovereign king. Instead, he held Henry's attention with an unwavering stare.

"The boy is mine, sire."

"Ah. And yet you gave it out that the child had perished when Meg died birthing him."

Stephen nodded, full of the old familiar feelings of shame. "I . . . it seemed simpler that way, sire. There was little chance that he would live. Even when he did, he was always so sickly that I feared each day would be his last."

Henry's thick fingers had drummed on the figured wooden arm of his chair. "Indeed. And now, my lord?"

"Oliver is deathly ill." He narrowed his eyes and hoped to hide the glint of defiance. "His condition is the same . . . as Dickon's was."

"Dickon. Named for the usurper, Richard of the house of York." Henry's fingers fell still. "My lord, you'll doubt this, but I truly am sorry for what befell your elder son."

"You're right, sire. I do doubt it."

"Marry, I thought you might. Still, I did not summon you here to reopen that old wound, but to discuss your other boy. Oliver, is that his name?"

Stephen nodded. He burned to know who had told the king.

"Oliver is the son of one of my most powerful barons," Henry said, stroking his red beard. "He should not be exempt from royal service. If other nobles found out, they, too, would demand special treatment."

"Sire, it is not beneath me to beg for mercy," Stephen had said.

"Beg for what?"

A light, feminine voice hauled him from the dark depths of memory. He leaped to his feet as Juliana stepped into the room.

"Madam," he said icily, furious that he

had spoken his remembered words aloud.

She closed the door behind her. She looked, he could not help but notice, particularly comely in a peacock-colored skirt and matching bodice. Her hair was swept into a gold net to reveal the length and delicacy of her neck. "We must do something about Oliver."

"You are not to speak of him." Stephen measured his words, aware that to betray too much emotion would give her even more power over him. "Not to me," he continued, "not to your gypsy friends and most especially not to anyone at Lynacre."

Three brisk steps forward brought her to the edge of the table. "He is your son, my lord, and my stepson. I intend to speak of him anytime I wish."

He stood and grasped her shoulders, wrenching an exclamation of surprise from her. "I forbid it."

Rather than shrink from him as he expected her to do, she leaned closer still, so that their noses nearly touched. "Why?" she demanded.

"Because the world isn't safe for a boy like Oliver." The black violence of rage swirled like a storm inside him. With an explosive motion of his arms, Stephen thrust her back.

She stumbled, then regained her balance. He could not believe he had handled her so savagely. He felt the urge to apologize, yet she seemed unperturbed. Calm, even.

"Stephen. I want to understand. What do you mean, the world is not safe for him?"

"Life is hard enough for a strong, hale lad. If people knew about Oliver, there would be . . . expectations."

"What sort of expectations?"

"He'd be required to go to court. It's bad enough that the king knows. If Cromwell ever found out, he'd goad Henry into summoning Oliver."

"That seems quite an honor. Court —"

"— is what killed his brother, you meddlesome harpy. I told you that. Dickon was smaller than the other boys. They played cruel tricks on him, teased him about his weakness. If Dickon ever felt the honor of serving at court, it was crushed by petty rivalries that would challenge even a healthy boy."

Stephen turned sharply away, pounding his fist on the window embrasure and staring furiously at the rolling landscape beyond. Far in the distance, Kit and a gypsy girl in a red skirt rode bareback across the fells. There were moments when he hated Jonathan Youngblood's son, hated the boy's high good health, his easy, athletic grace. Yet at the same time he thanked God for Kit, who was living proof of the sweetness of life.

He heard Juliana walk closer to him and felt a jolt of surprise. He had expected her to depart. In tears. Why shouldn't she, after the insult he had flung at her?

Instead, she touched him. At first Stephen was too startled to react. Her warm hands found the small of his back and traveled upward slowly, tenderly, until they found the knots of tension in his shoulders. Her caress was compelling, her hands deft and sure. She knew the soothing power of a human touch on aching flesh. Knew the strange bond that formed when two creatures united in mutual need, one hurting, the other healing.

"Stop," he said in a low, outraged whisper.

"No."

"Juliana . . ."

"Turn and look at me, Stephen. Turn and tell me you want me to go away."

He swung around, and her hands migrated to the tops of his shoulders and the sides of his neck. His tongue felt thick, and he forgot what she wanted him to say.

"I command you to forget Oliver. Leave him to those who have cared for him all these years. He's *dying,* Juliana."

"We are all dying, Stephen. No one has ever escaped this world with his mortal life."

He had no ready answer for that. He found himself caught in the depths of her eyes. How green they were — not a hard emerald or jade but soft and luminous like new leaves with the sun glowing behind them.

"Stephen?"

He blinked, realizing he had been staring into her eyes as if deep within her dwelt a place he yearned to go. Only with great effort did he summon the words that would distance him from her once again.

"The matter of my son is closed, Juliana. He is to remain as he is, and you are to forget you ever saw him."

"Forget I have a stepson?" The simplicity of her question rendered Stephen's command ridiculous.

He raked a hand through his hair. "What I mean is, leave him be. Let him have peace, Juliana."

"My lord, I can't claim to know a great deal about little boys. But I do know that they do not crave peace."

Her words awakened memories in Stephen — of Oliver's first toothless smile, his first wobbly steps, his first words. But the milestones were slain by the darker remembrances: the episodes of wheezing that left the lad exhausted and weak, the fevers that raged for days and nights. The illness was like a demon, lurking in the shadows and then springing out to fling Stephen into black, impenetrable despair.

"I know what is best for my son," he said through gritted teeth. "You are not to interfere with him."

"He lives like a hermit."

"He has everything a boy could want and more," Stephen snapped. "A garden. A houseful of playthings. A caring, attentive and learned servant."

"And a father?" Juliana asked in a voice so soft Stephen thought he had heard wrong. "Does he have a father?"

"Of course he has a father!" The words exploded from him, causing her to jump back. "I go to him every evening and sometimes during the day, as well. Were I like most men, I'd foster him out to some other family and see him only once a twelvemonth."

"If you were like most fathers," she shot back, "you would touch him, hold him close instead of keeping him hidden away!" She poked a small finger at his shoulder. "How long has it been, my lord, since you took that child in your arms, kissed him and told him that you love him?"

The words lashed at Stephen. *Never.* The truth gave a razor edge to the sting. How could he show a rough-and-tumble affection for Oliver? The boy was too fragile, too excitable. He could die during one of his attacks.

"I won't be judged by you," Stephen said furiously. "This illness could take him at any moment. It will claim him all the sooner if you persist in meddling with him."

"He is sick. I know that. But he is also a boy. He wants desperately to be treated like a boy. To be loved — not with lavish and expensive gifts, but with your heart. Let me love him if you will not."

Her soft plea scourged him like a knotted whip. "Madam," he said, whispering to keep himself in control, "if you knew how close I am to throttling you, you would be diving for cover on the instant."

She threw back her shoulders and tipped up her chin. "How can you keep him at a distance — your own flesh and blood, the child of the woman you love beyond the grave?"

Stephen was taken aback. He wondered where she had gotten that notion. Then he remembered the day Juliana had found him at the shrine. Good God, could she truly think he went there out of love? In truth, he went to the shrine because he knew no way to remedy a *failed* love.

The grief of losing his wife and elder son had never healed. Sometimes he bore it; other times he would hear the furious roar of a storm and only belatedly realize it was the tempest inside him. A part of him had been torn away. Oliver was the only intact portion of the past, and Stephen was terrified of the day the pattern would be altered by the lad's passing.

"I treat my son like a prince," he said.

"You treat him like he is on his deathbed! He spends every day waiting to die! Each day he lives should be a gift, Stephen. Why can you not understand? He is alive now. Every life is precious. Every hour, every minute, every breath Oliver takes. Each day should be a celebration, not a vigil. Not endless hours waiting for death to come." Her accent became more pronounced and her breathing quickened. How could she care so compassionately for a boy she did not even know?

"You speak a pretty case, Juliana," Stephen said harshly. "However, your pleas impress me not. I know my son. Oliver is simply too fragile to celebrate life, whatever that means. Unbridled revelries would only hasten his death."

Vivid color shot to her cheeks. She stood on tiptoe, her small fists gripping the front of his jerkin. "The way you entomb your son in that hideaway, my lord, he already *is* dead."

Juliana Romanov de Lacey lived a double life. With her husband she was distant yet decorous, as a proper lady in a loveless marriage should be. She accepted his interdict against acknowledging the existence of Oliver.

Yet each day, she defied Stephen in thought and in deed. Flouting the dictates of her husband, she wended her way through the maze and visited Oliver.

At first they simply talked, for he was as wary and skittish as an untamed colt.

"Your father must not know I come to see you," she had said on her first visit, only minutes after her hurtful argument with Stephen. "Dame Kristine agrees with me."

She did not mention what it had cost her to extract that agreement. For the rest of her days, she would owe indulgences to the Roman church.

Oliver had glared at her through narrowed eyes. "I might tell him."

"That would be a pity." She heaved a great sigh. "I was going to bring Pavlo to meet you —"

"Who is Pavlo?" Oliver had asked, struggling to appear uninterested.

Juliana had eyed him mysteriously. "The strongest, swiftest and bravest friend in all the world. But I needn't say more, since you're going to tell your papa —"

"I never said I'd tell."

Juliana had hidden a smile of satisfaction. The promise of meeting Pavlo had been enough to buy Oliver's complicity.

On her next visit, she found the lad as usual, lying in his darkened room, a painted chessboard on his knees and a scowl of ill humor on his pale face. A bowl of gruel sat untouched on a tray beside the bed. Dame Kristine dozed in the box chair in the next room.

Oliver looked up at Juliana. "Where's Pavlo?" he asked.

She took a deep breath. "He will be up anon."

"You *said* you'd bring him."

"I wanted to make certain you were . . . awake."

"You mean alive," the boy said baldly, without censure.

Juliana was glad for the darkness in the

room, for she knew her eyes would betray her alarm. "Were you not hungry?"

He wrinkled his nose. "I hate gruel. Hate blancmange, hate watered wine and ale, hate mashed turnips. That's all she gives me. She says anything else makes me wheeze or gives me a rash."

Juliana took a warm, ripe plum from her apron pouch. "Try this."

He eyed the fruit suspiciously. "What is it?"

"A plum." She held her breath. Dear God, what if she was wrong? What if the fruit did bring on an attack?

"I don't want it," he said.

"Well," she said airily, "if you will not eat it, then there is only one thing to do."

"What?" He glared through narrowed eyes.

"Juggle." She took two more plums from her apron pouch and tossed them from hand to hand. Within seconds, three fruits were spinning in a tall arc while Oliver watched in rapt fascination.

"Where did you learn that?"

She plunged her hand into the apron and added a fourth plum to the whirling fruit. "From Rollo of the gypsies. He's much better at it than I. You could see him someday, but . . ." She let her voice trail off.

"I want to!"

"Then perhaps you will." She caught one plum in her teeth, biting into the soft flesh and letting the juice run down her chin while she caught the other three.

"You're not like any baroness I ever heard of," Oliver muttered.

"Goodness, I should hope not. In Novgorod, my mother used to have a great baroness as a friend. She smelled of camphor and never smiled. And her eyes were all twitchy, like this." Juliana blinked to demonstrate. Oliver smothered a giggle. She took another bite. "Are you certain you won't try one?"

He took a plum from her and cupped it in his small hands, seeming to enjoy the warmth and smoothness of it.

"You should not eat it," she said. "Only smell it."

He brought the plum to his nose, closed his eyes, and inhaled. Then, with a defiant smirk, he bit into it, and his eyes opened wide. " 'Tis sweet and tart all at once." The juice dribbled down his neck. Juliana watched him closely as he devoured the plum. She saw no sign of labored breathing, heard no warning rasp in his throat.

"Why did you think eating fruit would make you wheeze?" she asked.

He rubbed his stick hands on the counterpane. "Dr. Strong said so. My humors are unbalanced." Oliver seemed eerily adult when he discussed his condition. "Dr. Strong said I have too much blood on my left side, and eating red foods would only make it worse."

"I see. Well, perhaps your humors are better balanced of late." She put her hand over his and watched his face. For a moment he sat frozen; then he turned his hand palm up and squeezed hers.

"Oliver?"

"Yes?"

"Do you like living here?"

"Of course I do. It is my own world here. Dame Krissie is ever so learned, and she's never cross with me. And Papa — well, he comes every night, and he always brings presents."

She remembered the insult Oliver had scrawled on his writing tablet. "Does your papa ever get cross with you?"

"No. Well . . ."

"Yes?"

"Sometimes when I'm wheezing, he makes a fist like so." Oliver clenched his. "And he slams it against the wall."

"I see." She tried to appear pleasantly

interested, though the image broke her heart.

"My illness makes him cross," Oliver said.

"No," she said quickly. "He is frustrated, because he wants to help you."

"Perhaps." Oliver shrugged.

"Do you never wish to go to the manor house? To see other boys and play with them?"

He tugged idly at his lower lip. "I think not. I can't run and play."

"Why not?"

He rolled his eyes, clearly thinking her an idiot. "Because I am sick. I could fall down dead any instant. That's what happened to Dickon."

"Your brother."

"Aye. Dame Krissie says my father didn't speak for weeks afterward."

"He must have loved Dickon very much." Juliana ducked her head to hide the bleakness in her eyes. "Would you like to meet Pavlo now?"

Even in the dim amber shadows she could see his teeth flash as he grinned. "Oh, yes!" Then he seemed to catch himself and slid back into insolence. "I suppose so."

"Pavlo doesn't like the dark." Juliana crossed to the first shuttered dormer window.

"But I'm not supposed to —"

"You're not the only one in this room," Juliana said over her shoulder. "Do not be selfish." She spoke lightly, though her entire body thrummed with nervous anticipation. What if she were wrong?

But she had been right about the plum. She would pit her common sense and instinct against the wisdom of Dr. Strong any day, her knowledge of gypsy cures against those of any alchemist.

"I'll go fetch Pavlo," she said, turning to look around the light-flooded room.

More *things*. Poppet dolls, whistles, games, books and every manner of plaything a boy could desire.

Then why did the room seem so empty?

Putting aside the depressing thought, she went to the top of the stairs and whistled. Pavlo came bounding up, a streak of shimmery white.

He trotted down the hall beside her, and when he entered the room, Juliana wished suddenly that she knew how to draw pictures. The expression on Oliver's young face was priceless — shocked beyond words, sharply fascinated, and infused with intense, boyish yearning.

"*That* is Pavlo?" he whispered, pointing a shaking finger.

"Indeed it is."
"I thought he was a person."
"I never said that."
Juliana patted her thigh. "Come, Pavlo," she said in Russian. The dog had always adored children. Eagerly he leaped on the bed, a slim foreleg on each side of Oliver, a long pink tongue lapping at the lad's face.
"No! Help! He's trying to eat me up!"
"Do not be foolish." Juliana smiled. For the dog, at least, it was love at first sight. "He is saying hello."
"I — I'm having an attack," Oliver gasped. "Get him off me. I demand that you get this brute off me!"
Horrified, she started forward.
A firm hand held her back. She turned to see Dame Kristine, her face alight with interest. "Leave them, my lady," she whispered.
"But Oliver says —"
"Hush. Look at him."
Juliana looked. The lad grappled vigorously with the huge dog. Thinking it a merry game, Pavlo yelped in delight and nuzzled Oliver's forehead.
"He is not wheezing or coughing," Dame Kristine said. "His color is a healthy pink."
"Off!" Oliver shrieked. "Get him off! He'll kill me!" But the boy's shouts dissolved,

suddenly and sweetly, into helpless giggles. Within moments, he was hugging the dog fiercely, laughing into his furry neck and looking for all the world like a boy who had found a long-lost friend.

Juliana looked around the room again, and now it did not seem empty at all.

"Where is that dog of yours, Juliana?" Stephen asked one day. She was with him at the village well, where he and the smith had set up a rather strange, screwlike pump to draw water. "I've not seen the beast for a fortnight or so."

Juliana dropped her gaze, pretending close inspection of a cog at the top of the pump. "Pavlo is never far, my lord. Perhaps he is down with the gypsies." It had not been a fortnight, she reflected, but three weeks since she had taken the dog to visit Oliver. She closed her eyes for a moment, remembering the lad's surprise and delight. They played for hours each day, and she noticed a new vigor in Oliver.

"It's a high wonder to me," Stephen said, only half attending his own words as he worked the windlass of the pump, "that the great beast manages to find his way home each night to sleep in your bed."

Juliana slid a tentative glance at him. At

moments like this she found him most fascinating, when he forgot he was lord of the manor, when his whole attention was absorbed by some invention. He seemed heedless of the water-cooled breeze stirred by the pump even though the wind lifted his golden hair away from his face and neck. "Since when do you trouble yourself over who — or what — sleeps in my bed?"

He did not even glance up at her, but she saw the sun-browned flesh draw tight over his cheekbones. "Whether we like it or not, you are my baroness, and I won't have my good name besmirched."

"The fact that I sleep with a *borzoya* dog would make for very choice gossip indeed," she said with a sniff.

Stephen scooped up a handful of water and drank. He looked up at her for a moment, his face bland and inhumanly handsome; then he set to work on the pump again, muttering something about a Greek named Archimedes. Honestly, he could be as infuriating as his son.

Juliana wished she could discuss her progress with the boy. She had, item by item, put an end to Oliver's lackluster diet of gruel and watered ale. Now he dined on oranges, salad, fresh meat and mare's milk. The new food added girth to his painfully thin frame. She managed to coax him out into the garden at least once a day, and the sunshine put color in his pale cheeks. A tea made from a special herb called ephedra, brought by gypsy sea-traders from remote Asia, eased his breathing.

She and Dame Kristine hardly dared speak of it, but Oliver had suffered only a few attacks of late, and those seemed to pass quickly.

She wondered if Stephen noticed the improvement. Probably not. Though he visited his son frequently, he took pains to avoid discussing Oliver's health. According to Dame Kristine, Stephen heard nothing but gloomy predictions from visiting physicians and herbalists.

The thought made her angry, the deception uncomfortable. Perhaps now was the time to admit she had been interfering with Oliver's treatment.

"My lord," she said, "about your son —"

Still he did not look up, but she noticed with some satisfaction that his shoulders tensed. "We agreed not to spcak of the boy."

"The boy has a name. It's Oliver, or have you forgotten?"

He glanced up at last, and his eyes were dead. "I have not forgotten. Damn you to hell, Juliana."

She faced him, hoping she looked braver than she felt. "I think you are damning yourself. For pity's sake, Stephen. Let yourself love him."

"Why?"

And then she understood clearly. Stephen was afraid. Terrified of losing Oliver. How deeply Stephen must have grieved when his wife and first son had died; now, it seemed, he meant to spare himself if anything happened to Oliver.

She must not let herself pity him. Must not begin to think like him. Oliver was alive *now.* He should not suffer because his father was afraid of losing him.

"Stephen, do you remember the horse fair in Chippenham Tuesday last?" she asked.

He frowned, no doubt confounded by her change of subject. "Of course I remember it."

"And the roan mare Laszlo bought?"

"Aye, half-dead on her feet she was."

"To you, that is how it looked. Come." She took his hand and led him away from the village, pausing now and then to greet people. A cheery atmosphere pervaded the cluster of half-timbered cottages. The weaving house had received a large order from Flanders, and the looms worked constantly these days.

Stephen and Juliana descended toward the clearing by the river where the gypsies camped. The day was sweet and clear, the grass dry and crackling beneath their feet, the changing leaves creating a riot of color against the marbled blue sky.

A glorious day, she thought. A good day to be in love.

They reached the gypsy camp and she brought him to the horse run where animals on long tethers grazed.

"There is your half-dead horse, my lord."

Stephen stared at the mare, and Juliana savored the progression of expressions that transformed his face: surprise, disbelief and finally open wonder.

He touched the gleaming neck of the roan. "What in God's name did he do?"

"The Romany people have a talent for curing illnesses of horses that others discard. The farmer who sold this mare thought she was ready for the knacker's yard."

"Yet Laszlo healed her."

"Yes. Perhaps she will never be perfect. She will never run races like your Capria. But she will prove useful and be content enough." She chanced a squeeze of his hand. "Don't you see? What one man has discarded as hopeless, rejecting any chance of healing, another has made whole."

Stephen yanked his hand away. "It's not the same. My son is not a goddamned horse."

"Exactly." She refused to flinch from his cold fury. "He is a little boy. You have given him everything he needs except the one thing he truly wants — your love."

"What possible difference can that make?"

Juliana now knew the answer to that. At first she had merely brushed Oliver's hand with hers. Then, while he was giggling at Pavlo's trick of balancing a crust of bread on his muzzle, she had squeezed his shoulder. Day by day, hour by hour, she moved closer to him until they were embracing, his cheek against her bosom and his little hands clinging around her waist.

"I think it would make a great deal of difference — to your son . . . and to you." Juliana stroked the thin horse. The animal flattened its ears, and she spoke to it in Romany, the language that had been used to train gypsy horses since time out of mind. The horse dropped its head and snuffled into her shoulder. She turned and smiled at Stephen. "I think it would make a very big difference indeed."

"Damn you," he said through his teeth. "All my boy wants to do is *breathe,* and I can't help him. I would give my entire fortune and my very life — the surety of my soul — to heal him. If I thought owning the moon were a cure, I would devise some way to snare it. How dare you imply that I am withholding something from my son?"

"You are." How fearsome he looked, his eyes as cold and shining as marble, his face flushed with fury and his fists clenched hard. And yet she did not fear him. He could hurt her, aye, and she had no doubt that he would — but not with his fists.

"My lord," she said, leaning against the horse's neck for support, "there is something you haven't given him. Your unconditional love and the chance to live a normal life."

He bent so that his face was very close to hers. "And since when, pray, has love been proven to have healing powers?"

His anger was so fierce, so tangible, that the horse snorted and sidled away, its hide twitching as if to dispel flies.

Juliana folded her arms and glared at Stephen. "Maybe loving Oliver will not cure his affliction. But it might give hope and meaning to his days." She wanted to say more — wanted to say that when the lad started wheezing and she held him close, his breathing seemed to ease. His exhalations came with less desperate effort, and he seemed more in control. But she could not tell Stephen that, for he had forbidden her to see his son.

"Hope and meaning," Stephen repeated cynically. "Had I the power to create such things, I would. You believe me a hard and hateful man. Fortunately for you, you will not have to endure me much longer."

She blinked, taken by surprise. "What do you mean?"

"The bishop of Bath has received my request for an annulment. The king has sent an emissary to meet the niece of the duke of Cleves, and there might be a wedding in the offing. No doubt he's lost interest in tormenting me."

Suddenly, inexplicably, she felt the burn of tears in her throat. "What are you saying?"

A joyless smile curved his mouth. "Come, Juliana, your understanding of English has always been remarkable. I'm saying you'll soon be free to go."

The thought struck her silent. At one time, she had wanted nothing more than to be away from this bucolic manor with its brooding lord, but of late she had thought little of escape. Now she felt a sense of frustration, almost desperation. She had just begun to understand Oliver. And she needed . . .

Juliana swallowed and made herself look at Stephen. She needed *him.*

"I cannot go," she whispered.

For a moment, heat flashed in his eyes. Hope? Surprise? Triumph? It was too fleeting to tell, and he quickly concealed his emotions. "Why not? I thought you were a Russian princess with a blood oath to fulfill."

"I *am,*" she shouted, almost hating him for the mockery in his voice. Then with a will, she tempered her ire. "I still have work to do here. The weaving house —"

"William Stumpe has that all very well in hand."

"Then I —"

He held up a hand to silence her. "Enough, Juliana. We both agreed this would be a marriage in name only. That it would be temporary." He reached out and cupped her chin in his hand. His thumb skimmed over her lower lip, and the look in his eyes was almost regretful as he said, "The pretense is up, Juliana. This forced marriage will be over soon."

THIRTEEN

Three weeks had slipped by since Stephen first gave Juliana the news about the annulment. Of late, time seemed to pass in the blink of an eye. With Juliana around, one day was never like the last. She upset his routine. He was likely to find her teaching mime to country folk on the village green, doing pony tricks for children in the stableyard or finding some means to coax game out of the royal forest in order to put food on a poor man's table.

He should have been annoyed but instead found himself entranced, watching her, wondering what she would do next.

Alone, he tromped through the maze one afternoon, the autumn sun warm upon his neck, and the feeling in his heart as bleak as winter's barren hopelessness.

He rarely visited Oliver during the day; their meetings were too strained and formal. Neither father nor son dared to breach the invisible distance between them. But the maze needed tending. The correct path was well worn, while the byways to dead ends had become overgrown from disuse. With heavy steps of his booted feet, he trod the paths and used a set of clippers to trim the dense, thorny hedges.

The clippers were a device of his own invention, long-handled to reach the topmost places, worked with a cord-and-pulley system. He clipped the hedges with a steady, dogged rhythm, comforting in its mindlessness.

Three weeks. A letter from Bath lay upon his desk. He had but to sign his name to paper. Then he would be free. Free of Juliana. Never to see her again. Never to watch her eyes light with amazement at one of his inventions. Never to hear the unexpected chime of her laughter. Never to return her challenging glare across the supper table. Never to comfort her in the night when she cried out in terror at the bloody visions in her dreams.

Never again to touch her.

He snapped the clippers with a savage jerk. God, if she knew.

If she knew, she would eat you alive, he assured himself.

Jesu. When they had last spoken alone,

amid the gypsy horses, it had taken all of his restraint to keep from sweeping her into his arms, burying his face in her hair and — God forgive him — holding out his heart to her in both hands.

He prowled through the maze, snipping viciously at a branch here, a twig there. A witch. That's what she was. An evil enchantress. God knew what she was sprinkling on his food. What strange incantations she mumbled while he slept. But it was working, damn her. He wanted her. Badly. Badly enough to —

He cut the thought short, for he found himself standing at the edge of Oliver's garden.

How long has it been, my lord, since you took that child in your arms and told him that you love him?

Juliana's words tormented him still. It was ridiculous, he told himself. He had loved Dickon, and Dickon had died. Dickon had taken his father's heart; Meg had taken Stephen's soul and battered it with guilt. There was nothing left for Oliver.

Neither did Oliver, in his strange and silent little world, seem to need anything from Stephen. The painful thought entered his mind as he stopped at the garden well to wash off the sweat and hedge clippings.

Stephen's meetings with Oliver were stiffly decorous, the boy reciting his Latin lesson or demonstrating his swiftness at figuring sums while Stephen gave his awkward approval. Oliver was a grave lad content in the tightly bounded place Stephen had created for him.

Or was he?

Every once in a while there was a rebellion, as if a small tempest swept into the snug house. Oliver would hurl something, shout in anger, break one of his toys. But the infrequent storms were quickly over and forgotten.

Shaking off water like a large dog, Stephen entered the house quietly and stopped in the kitchen. As he was drying himself off with a linen towel, he was surprised to see a most interesting array of foods. Carrots and parsnips. Sprigs of salad greens and fennel. A bowl of fresh apples. A fat roasted capon on a cutting board.

Dame Kristine must have quite an appetite these days. Stephen wrenched a leg off the capon and bit into it. Delicious. It was a pity Oliver couldn't —

He forbade himself to finish the thought. Oliver's diet had to be severely restricted. The regimen of gruel and foul medicines finally seemed to be helping. In the past few weeks the lad had put on a bit of weight, and the color in his cheeks seemed better.

As Stephen turned to go up the stairs, his foot encountered a well-gnawed bone. What could Dame Kristine be thinking? He had never known her to be careless in her housekeeping. He would speak to her at once.

His tread was slow on the stairs. He had to gird himself for each visit like a warrior on the verge of pitched battle. Yet no matter how hard he tried to armor himself, one part of him always lay exposed.

His heart.

Coming in the daytime was even riskier than visiting at night. At midday Oliver was likely to be more wakeful, harder to resist. And lately, these past few weeks, need had shone more acutely in his eyes.

As if the lad had finally become aware of a great emptiness in his sheltered life.

At night, in those twilight moments between wakefulness and sleep, Stephen could hold him and inhale his little-boy scent and pretend, just for a moment, that Oliver was healthy and strong. That in the morning he would bound out of bed to go riding at the quintain with Kit, to play hoodman blind with the village children.

Stephen paused outside the chamber door

to marshal his nerves. It was quiet within; perhaps the boy was napping. Lately Oliver fell asleep more readily, as if exhausted by his day.

The thought chilled Stephen. Perhaps the fatigue portended the worst. Perhaps, despite his increasing girth, Oliver was failing.

Stephen pressed his forehead against the door frame and squeezed his eyes shut. Last winter, while in the grip of a high fever, Oliver had fixed his bright eyes on Stephen and said, "I want to be an angel. I'd make a very good angel, don't you think Papa?"

And the worst of it was, the boy spoke truly. Stephen had said nothing, only turned away to hide the agony in his face. Then he had gone on a hunt for boar, savagely killing the luckless beast like a pagan performing a sacrifice, pleading to the gods for mercy.

Haunted by the grim memory, Stephen pressed the latch and stepped into the room.

He was unprepared for the flood of sunlight that greeted him. Dr. Strong had expressly forbidden direct sunlight; it unbalanced the humors grossly. Stephen looked at the bed, and his heart fell still.

Empty. Oliver's bed was empty.

Stephen crossed the room swiftly, crushing unseen toys beneath his feet. The bedclothes were all in a mess — as if the boy had been snatched up in haste.

No, please God, no . . . His heart jolted back into a painful rhythm as he threw back his head and screamed, "Dame Kristine!"

The woman was nowhere to be found. Doubtless she was off searching for him to deliver the news he had been dreading for years.

The house and garden and maze passed in a blur as he raced back toward Lynacre Hall. Fighting a bloodred haze of furious grief, he tried to be rational, tried to stay calm.

He had known from the moment of Oliver's birth that this day would come. He had had years to prepare himself. He would not let himself be destroyed by this passing.

And yet as he ran, he could not shut out the memories. With each ragged breath he took, each hammerlike thud of his heart, he remembered. Holding Oliver's warm newborn body in the crook of his arm while clutching Meg's lifeless hand. Savoring the joy of his son's first smile and plummeting into despair over his first blue-lipped attack of wheezing. Practicing blatant deception to shield Oliver from the world. Watching him toddle his first steps, hearing him speak his first words, seeing him reach with chubby hands for his father.

What a fool I have been, Stephen acknowledged as he rushed to the main gate of the manor. He slammed his back against the gatehouse wall. Breathing hard, he stared up at the crisp autumn blue sky. *I have loved him all along. His death is going to pound me into dust.*

As he covered the distance to the hall to search for Dame Kristine, he felt a furnace of rage building inside him. Its destructive force threatened to erupt, yet he beat it back, certain that once unleashed the anger would devour his sanity. And in the midst of all the wild, whirling, red-hot fury, he found himself wanting Juliana, wanting to bury himself in her sweetness, wanting, with the foolishness of a callow youth, for her to comfort him.

Though he stormed through every room and office of Lynacre Hall, he could not find Kristine. Frustrated, he went to the kitchen in search of Nance Harbutt, only to learn from a cringing scullion that she had gone down to the gypsy camp to get a pot repaired.

This from a woman who swore gypsies were at the root of every plague and crop failure in the past hundred years.

Moving with the relentlessness of a siege

engine, he stalked to the stables. While the grooms ducked for cover, Stephen leaped upon Capria's bare back and jabbed in his heels. The large, powerful mare could be dangerous when ridden in such a fashion, but Stephen didn't see how his own safety could matter now.

He galloped down to the river meadows and wished that numbness would overcome him. He wished he did not see and hear and feel so clearly, and yet he could not escape the riot of images that lay before him as he entered the camp. The skirl of pipes and the chime of bells, the laughter on the autumn wind. The sight of Juliana clapping her hands in pure joy as a gaggle of gypsy children raced past in pursuit of a bouncing ball. The jubilant yelps of Pavlo and several mongrels cavorting in their midst.

It was a scene of unabashed revelry — smiling faces, bright music, strong-limbed gypsies. The dark force inside Stephen made him yearn to hurl himself straight at Juliana. To shake her and shout at her: *My son is gone, damn you!*

Instead he moved with the stiff-necked dignity of simmering wrath, dismounting to stride across the muddy track that ran lengthwise through the gypsy camp.

He could not trust his voice to greet her.

He merely planted himself in front of her and said, "I came looking for Nance Harbutt."

Juliana's face blanched. Her gaze darted to the throng of racing children and dogs. Then she looked back at Stephen. Her smile had a forced quality. "She is somewhere about, my lord." She grasped his sleeve and gave it a tug as if she were eager to pull him away from the area. "Come, I think she is with the tinker —"

At that moment a large ball made of an inflated bladder and beslimed with fresh mud struck him with a great splat on the side of his head.

Stunned silence fell over the camp. Juliana, her own face bearing a few droplets of mud, stared in horror at him. And the light in her eyes danced like new leaves in a breeze, bright with mirth she dared not indulge.

"My lord," she said in a tight-throated whisper, " 'twas an acc—"

"Who threw that ball?" Laszlo bellowed. "By God, I will tan him like a butchered ram!"

Juliana pressed her lips together. Laughing at him. She was laughing at him.

With a shaking hand he scraped the mud from the side of his face and wiped his fingers on his cloak. He felt it again — that same killing rage that had gripped him the night Juliana had discovered Oliver.

As from a great distance, Stephen heard Laszlo repeat his question.

"*I* threw it," said a high, clear voice.

"Oh, no." Ducking her head, Juliana whispered something foreign under her breath.

Shaken to his core, Stephen turned toward the familiar voice. He expected to encounter a ghost. Instead, he saw a pack of ragtag children, their eyes round and white in contrast to their mud-streaked faces.

Skinny bare legs and feet coated in mud. Impish grins shining with mirth.

And one of the urchins, the lad who had spoken, stepped to the fore as if he were their acknowledged leader.

Stephen thought he had gone mad. He blinked, certain he was seeing things. *"Oliver?"*

The lad nodded. " 'Twas I who threw the ball." He showed no shame, only a fierce and heartbreaking sense of pride.

Stephen sank to one knee. Oliver wore nothing more than a broad grin and a tunic of rough brown homespun. Before Stephen knew what he was doing, he grasped Oliver's thin shoulders and pulled him against his chest, heedless of the mud and the crushed grass beneath his knees. Then he lifted Oliver and began striding toward his horse.

The boy squirmed, all bony elbows and knees. "Papa, I can walk —"

"Hush. I'll take you home where you'll be safe."

"I don't *want* to go home!" With surprising strength, Oliver jabbed his elbow into Stephen's side. "I want to stay and play!"

"Nonsense, lad, you must hie yourself back to bed. You can't play —" Even as the words came out, Stephen realized what he was saying. "Oliver —"

His son's thin body snapped like a bow. The familiar deadly wheezing sound eked from his throat. His eyes flared unnaturally bright. His hands convulsed. His cheeks faded to the color of chalk clay.

Stephen had suffered through Oliver's attacks countless times before. But never in broad daylight. Never before an audience of gypsies.

Juliana rushed forward, fumbling for something within the folds of her skirt. She held out a damp white cloth.

"Try this, my lord. 'Tis ephedra, and sometimes it helps."

A witch's cure. Stephen slapped it away. The cloth landed in the dirt. He glared at

Juliana. "You're responsible for this. What in God's name did you hope to prove by exposing Oliver to danger?"

She started to speak, but the lad's mouth began to work as he wheezed. His eyes had taken on a wide-flown, helpless look. When an attack came, Dr. Strong had instructed, the lad must be shut up in his room, the braziers stoked with herbs, and the shutters drawn against noxious sunlight and garden air.

But here, in the dazzling clear autumn day in the midst of a broad riverside meadow, Stephen had no notion of what to do.

"Lay your cloak on the grass, my lord." Juliana spoke from behind him.

"J . . . J . . . Jul . . ." Oliver stretched his arms toward her.

Stephen nearly came undone. The lad was using the last of his strength to reach for the woman who had dragged him out of his secure little world and thrust him amid unwashed strangers.

For want of a better plan, Stephen did as she suggested, placing his small son upon the cloak she spread on the soft meadow grass. He stepped back to watch . . . and to pray for his son's life.

Juliana sent him an odd look, then dropped to the ground. She gathered Oliver close, stroking his muddied cheek, pressing her lips to his pale hair, holding the herb-soaked cloth to his nose.

At first Stephen was too stunned to move. To breathe. The picture they made turned his world upside down. She was a madonna, her face suffused with terror and soul-deep love. Oliver's hands clutched desperately at her. His chest convulsed in a sharp, irregular rhythm. And his gaze stayed focused on her face.

She began to croon lightly, a foreign lay that held the echoes of an ancient melody. Her hands caressed him — his back, his arms, his struggling chest.

"Jesu, what are you doing?" Stephen demanded, finding his voice at last. "You'll smother the lad." He knelt beside her. "Goddamn you," he whispered through gritted teeth. "Leave my son alone. The physicians told me he needs space. Move back and give him room to expel the bad humors."

Still she ignored Stephen, her loving gaze fixed on Oliver's red, contorted face, her gentle hands stroking and stroking, echoing the slow and subtle rhythm of the gypsy song.

Stephen had no notion what to do. He could not very well grab the boy away from her — but neither could he sit by and watch her suffocate his son with her good intentions.

"Please," he whispered. "Juliana —" The words stopped in his throat, for something was happening with Oliver. An abatement of the strained wheezing. A calmness in the silver-blue eyes. A gentling in his chest.

After only moments of suffering, the lad was breathing easier. Normally he took hours to recover. It was a miracle. A bloody miracle.

"Son?" Stephen whispered. He reached out, caught himself, and dropped his hand. "Oliver? Are you better?"

Oliver expelled a grateful breath of air. "Better now, Papa." He lay relaxed, looking curiously wise and adult.

"Juliana." Stephen spoke past a thickness in his throat. "That attack ended so quickly." The whirling fury of his emotions nearly overwhelmed him. In the span of an hour, he had gone from painful grief to cautious, shining joy.

"Holding him close seems to calm him. The gypsy herb works far better than leeching and cupping. I know it is contrary to the doctor's orders, but Dame Kristine has noticed it, too."

Oliver stood. He wobbled slightly. Stephen

reached out to grab him, but Juliana held his hand back.

"Look what I can do, Papa!" The lad went to the middle of the camp where the children had already resumed their game. Appalled, Stephen started after him.

"No, wait," Juliana said. "He knows he must not play too hard after an attack. Trust him, Stephen."

"You've done this before." His anger was alive and writhing, choking him. *How dare she?* "How long have you been playing me for a fool, Juliana?"

"Do you mean, how long have I been taking care of my stepson?" she shot back. "From the very day I discovered that you keep the poor child hidden like a dirty little secret. I have banished all those nasty quack-salver remedies and all that terrible food. I have held your son close, laughed with him and wept with him."

"And come close to killing him," Stephen said.

She flinched as if he had jabbed her with a pin. "Have I?" she demanded. "Look at him, Stephen. Look at him for a moment and tell me he is close to death."

Oliver had joined in the game in a modified fashion. Rather than running for the ball, he flung out an arm and shouted something. Pavlo streaked amid the running children.

"What's that he said?" Stephen asked.

"Go fetch. I am teaching him Russian."

Jesu. She was teaching his son bloody Russian.

Pavlo dove into the herd of running children. Canine yelps and merry laughter erupted from the brood. Then the dog broke free, returning with the ball to Oliver.

Oliver laughed with a clear, sweet voice. Lustily. Joyously. As if he had not just survived a life-threatening attack.

She had done it, Stephen thought in wonder. When doctors and astrologers and alchemists had failed, she had found a way to bring the episode to a fast end. He was not so foolish as to believe Oliver was cured, but she had shown him that a loving touch alone could be more healing than any medicine.

As Stephen turned to Juliana, he knew his face was naked, knew his heart was in his eyes, knew his smile was ablaze with gratitude and amazement. And before he could stop himself, the words burst forth from the depths of his soul.

"I love you, Juliana," he said.

"I hate you, Papa!" Oliver said in his most

churlish tone. "You always put everything your way. I want my bed *here.*" He planted his skinny leg on a sun-flooded spot beside the oriel window of his new bedchamber.

Stephen gritted his teeth. Bringing Oliver to live at Lynacre Hall was something he had never dared to contemplate. Yet here he stood in the room Juliana had chosen. It was an airy little chamber situated in the upper level of the hall, off the center of the open walkway. His long muzzle between his paws, Pavlo lazed on the floor in a bar of sunlight.

Juliana had convinced Stephen that this move would help Oliver feel less like an invalid.

Oliver was doing his best to behave like an infuriating, ungovernable little boy.

"Now, son," Stephen said, his voice rusty with repressed impatience, "that's too close to the window. You'll catch a chill on cold nights."

Oliver thrust out his lower lip. "I like being by the window. I *want* to be by the window. I *hate* y—"

"What an impossible little snot you are being." Juliana breezed into the room like a breath of spring after a dark winter. She looked particularly ravishing this morning in a gown of blue-flowered damask and a pretty winged coif. At moments like this, Stephen believed she could actually be the princess she claimed, and he realized he did not care one way or the other.

I love you. Had he really spoken those words to her only the day before?

Aye, and the jewel-bright feeling came rushing back. Had Oliver not been present, Stephen would have spoken them yet again. He would have swept her up into his arms, twirled her around, and shouted his declaration a hundred times.

She kissed the top of Oliver's white-blond head even as she scolded, "Of course you may not have the bed right next to the window, brat."

Oliver licked the palm of his hand and smashed down his cowlick. "Why not?"

She dropped her voice to an ominous note and said something in Romany or Russian; Stephen could not tell which.

Oliver's mouth dropped open. "Truly?"

"Truly. Now, take Pavlo and help Dame Kristine at the garden gate. I just saw her arrive with a barrowload of your toys."

"Yes, ma'am." Oliver patted his thigh and spoke in Russian. Pavlo lurched to his feet. The boy and the dog raced from the room and clumped down the stairs.

Stephen scratched his head. "What did

you tell him to make him so agreeable?"

She laughed. "Something my grandmother Luba told me when I was very small. If a child sleeps too close to a window, a demon will come and snatch his soul out through his nostrils."

"Oh, that's helpful."

"It was a bald lie. I knew it when I was small, and Oliver knows it."

"Then why did he give in to you?"

"Because I did not dictate to him nor try to force my will on him. I gave him a reason to agree without losing his pride."

Stephen went to the window and pressed the latch. Oliver and Pavlo cavorted near the garden wall while Dame Kristine ordered retainers about.

"I've much to learn about my son," he said.

"I do not know all the answers, Stephen."

"He says he hates me."

"He adores you. Trust me."

"We're awkward together." He turned from the window. "We don't . . . fit."

"That takes time. And patience and understanding." She leaned her cheek against the carved bedpost and looked at him with the world in her eyes.

I love you. The words sang out from his heart and seemed to hang, still unspoken, between them. It was as if they both saw them written in the air.

"Juliana, what I said yesterday . . ."

"Yes?"

"It was the wrong time." Aye, the right words, spoken at the wrong time. "I had no call . . . I should not have said it."

"Why not?" She regarded him placidly, as if she did not care what his answer was.

He flexed his hands, feeling clumsy with his unwieldy emotions. "I promised you an annulment. Is that what you still want?"

She bit her lip. "Is it what *you* want?"

"I don't know," he said honestly. "We never got a chance to speak in all the excitement over bringing Oliver to live at the hall."

Her mouth curved in a smile that did not reach her eyes. "It took you half the night to explain to the servants and convince them that I am not a witch who simply conjured Oliver out of thin air." She pushed away from the bedpost and took a step toward him. "Stephen, what will happen now that everyone knows you have a living son?"

"You ask that now." Bitterness flavored his words. "You should have wondered that before announcing Oliver's presence to the world."

"You can still protect him. If he is summoned to court, you can simply refuse."

A bark of ill humor escaped him. "Nothing is simple where King Henry and Thomas Cromwell are concerned."

"Never mind the king and Cromwell. You and Oliver must learn to get on together."

He narrowed his eyes at her. "Everything is simple to you."

Shouts came from below. They heard footfalls on the stair and the clicking of Pavlo's nails.

Juliana seemed relieved by the interruption. "We will find time to speak of this later. For now, think of your son. The two of you are strangers." She regarded him thoughtfully. "The gypsies could help, I think."

"For the love of God, Juliana, then tell —"

"Look at this!" Oliver stopped in the doorway. He formed a hoop of his arms and yelled a command. Pavlo leaped through the hoop, knocking the boy to the floor. Stepping over the giggling boy, servants arrived with more of Oliver's belongings.

"Later," Juliana said, and laughter danced in her eyes.

Stephen could not believe he had agreed to Juliana's mad plan. Mounting his horse in the stableyard, he felt his stomach churn at the thought of the solemn Romany rite he was about to perform. The gut-deep feeling reminded him of his pagan marriage. Though all his moral instincts and Christian principles clamored a denial, he felt himself being drawn into the mystique of the ceremony.

As he rode Capria out through the postern gate, he could not escape an onslaught of memories. It was as if each part of the estate now held a memory of her. Of Juliana.

It wasn't supposed to be that way. She was his temporary bride. He was supposed to recover from his feelings for her and then be immune forever. He should not be thinking of her at all.

Yet as he rode along the ridge of a hill, he recalled her first glimpse of Lynacre Hall. He had expected the slack-jawed awe of a beggar for her betters. Instead he had gotten a cool, faintly disdainful acceptance. As if Lynacre were less grand than manors she was accustomed to.

To the northwest he could just make out the spires of Malmesbury. Only a few short months ago it had been an abandoned abbey crumbling to ruin. Thanks to Juliana's inspiration, the abbey was now a prosperous weaving factory.

He passed the copyhold of the widow Shane. The fields were neatly cut and gleaned, awaiting the autumn sowing, thanks to the gypsy laborers. Stephen had no idea how Juliana had wrung the toil from them. Normally they fled from farm labor like demons from red garlic.

Though it never should have happened, Juliana had become part of Lynacre. The imprint of her accomplishments would last long after she left. Stephen would forever remember the one brilliant summer of the gypsies, a rare time of hope and possibility — when he had dared to love again.

He tried to banish his thoughts as the gypsy camp came into view, but the panorama only inspired a fresh wave of aching memories.

He had agreed to the gypsy wedding because he had known the pagan ritual would mean nothing to a God-fearing Christian.

Instead, it had been a surprise. It had touched him in places he had never explored within himself. He remembered it as if it were yesterday — his veiled bride, unhesitatingly shedding a drop of blood onto a bit of bread. She had danced for him as though he were the only man alive. Something mystical had happened that night. Aye, the ritual had been pagan, but the magic had been real.

And that, he told himself, riding into the camp, was why he had agreed to the ceremony today. Because he and Oliver desperately needed the magic.

"Are you ready, Gajo?" asked Laszlo as Stephen dismounted.

"Aye." He tossed his reins to a lad. "Should I have brought anything?"

"Nothing but your own flesh and blood." Laszlo made a broad showman's gesture toward the people milling about. "The Rom believe a man must acknowledge his son before the world. It is simple enough to know a child's mother; there can be little mistaking that. But to identify the father . . ." Laszlo sent Stephen a sidelong glance. "Ah, that, my friend, is an act of faith."

A sudden chill rippled through Stephen's blood. *To identify the father . . . an act of faith.*

"Gajo?" Laszlo interrupted his thoughts. "You look pale as a ghost."

Stephen cleared his throat. "Let's get on with it. Shall I —"

He never finished, for as he turned he saw the most amazing sight. Lined up at the edge of the camp were his friends and household retainers. He had not expected them.

He knew he should feel embarrassed to be seen participating in yet another Romany rite, but instead he grinned and walked over, nodding at Jonathan and Kit and Algernon.

"I should apologize," he said to Jonathan.

Jonathan scratched his head. "Apologize?"

"I won your sympathy because you thought I was childless. You sent Kit to me for fostering to fill that void in my life."

Jonathan's eyes crinkled at the corners, and he gave his son an affectionate cuff on the head. "Mayhap I sent the baggage to you because he gave me a pain in the neck."

Stephen smiled, grateful Jonathan was willing to make light of the deception. "I misled you. I am not a liar by nature, and I especially mislike lying to a friend."

Jonathan Youngblood blew out his breath, the air lifting the prongs of his moustache. "I could not have asked for better fostering for Kit." He whacked his son between the shoulder blades. Kit, who had been gawking at the luscious Catriona, choked and came to attention.

"Isn't that right, Kit?" his father demanded.

"Er, yes, sir, whatever you say."

With a snort of amused disgust, Jonathan shoved the youth toward Catriona. "You can look but don't touch. In the eyes of a true gentleman, all females are ladies."

"Yes, sir." Kit stumbled off.

Stephen released a long sigh of relief. He had feared that Kit would be resentful or jealous upon learning of Oliver.

"By God's grace, Wimberleigh," Jonathan asked, "how the devil have you kept such a secret?"

"Aye, do tell," Algernon said eagerly, bouncing on the balls of his feet. "You have us all agog."

"The moment he was born," Stephen said, "it was clear to me that he bore the same affliction as my first son, Richard."

"Dickon — the one who died after serving at court," Jonathan said gently.

"Yes." Stephen closed his eyes as Dickon came back like a flood of sunlight into his arms. He recalled the golden hair, the sun-washed scent, the frail body, the huge eyes far too beautiful to belong to a lad.

"A lovely boy," said Algernon. "So like Meg, he was."

"I could not let the same fate befall Oliver. And so — God forgive me — when the news went out that the babe had perished with his dam, I took no pains to correct it.

Only Nance Harbutt and her daughter Kristine, the midwife, knew the truth. I sent Oliver to be cared for by Kristine. His existence was a secret — or so I thought."

"Someone found out?" Jonathan beetled his thick eyebrows.

Algernon made a strange little *eep* in his throat, then studied the toe of his boot.

"King Henry found out," Stephen said, his voice low with long-held anger. "That was why I was compelled to wed Juliana. If I refused, Henry would have summoned Oliver to court."

"Oliver would be a tempting game piece for our king," Jonathan said. "How did he find out? Surely Nance —"

"It wasn't her." Algernon Basset spoke softly yet firmly.

With a sick twisting of his gut, Stephen stared at his neighbor. "My God, Algernon."

Havelock raised pleading eyes to Stephen. "I'm sorry —"

"I knew you for a wag tongue." With all the force of his sudden, hot rage, Stephen smacked his fist into the palm of his hand. "I knew you had ambitions to advance yourself at court, but I had no idea you'd stoop to using sick children as pawns."

"I meant no ill, Stephen." Algernon sounded desperate, his voice shaking with fear and remorse. "I had no idea about Dickon. I truly did not!"

"How did you learn about Oliver?" Stephen demanded.

Algernon shuffled his feet. Then he grasped the enameled badge that clasped his cloak at the shoulder and tore the bauble free. " 'Twas the limning artist. Nicholas Hilary. The same artist remarked that he had also painted his lordship's sons. Both of them."

Stephen remembered. It had been a foolish risk, but the traveling artist did glorious work. He had preserved the images of Meg and Dickon like precious jewels. Several years later the artist had called at Lynacre again. Oliver had been so frail. . . . Stephen had hated himself for thinking it, but if he lost the boy he would have nothing to remember him by.

"I commissioned him last summer and paid him to keep silent," he said, glowering at Algernon. "I assume he called at Hockley Hall after he finished here."

"I employed him, as well," said Algernon. "Found he had a taste for fortified wine. And one night he described the lad you had hired him to paint. Said the lad chattered like a magpie all through the sittings. Oliver de Lacey." Algernon lifted miserable eyes to

Stephen. "Your son. God help me, I told Lord Privy Seal that the babe your wife died birthing lives."

Jonathan curled his fist into the lace at Algernon's throat. He gave one tug, and Havelock's feet nearly left the ground. "You just couldn't leave well enough alone. You had to fly to the king with the rumor. And did it win you an invitation to court like you'd hoped?"

"No," Algernon said miserably. "Stephen, if I had known how weak the boy was —"

"You little puff of froth," Jonathan burst out. "I ought to show you how a *man* repays such a disloyalty."

An ancient weariness pressed down on Stephen as he pulled Jonathan away from the trembling earl of Havelock. "Not now. 'Tis done. You're an unctuous little varlet, Algernon, but I cannot change what has happened. Henry's nobles will learn of Oliver. I can only wait and see what the king will do."

Algernon backed away. "I don't deserve your forgiveness."

Stephen could summon nothing but bleak emptiness. " 'Tis too soon to ask for it, Algernon. We'll speak of it later."

Havelock bit his lip, seeming more nervous than ever. "I must go. I'm expecting news from London." The shadows swallowed him up.

Jonathan looked after him with eyes narrowed in speculation. "London, eh? Now what mischief is he about?"

FOURTEEN

"I don't want to go."

Juliana took Oliver's small, cold hand in hers and gave it a squeeze. "Of course you don't." She sank down on one knee and looked him in the eye. "The music is loud and all sorts of people are arriving. I do not blame you for being afraid."

The pointed little chin shot up. "Afraid? Who said I was afraid?"

She shrugged and peered over his shoulder. Beyond the tent flap Stephen waited stiffly by the bonfire. How alone he looked, despite the presence of Jonathan, Kit and the people of Lynacre. Her husband's great shoulders seemed tense with anticipation, and in the flaming glow from the fire his handsome face appeared ravaged by uncertainty.

"No," she whispered in Oliver's ear. "Your papa is the one who is afraid."

He craned his neck to see Stephen. "Papa?

How can Papa be afraid? He's the biggest, strongest man here. The biggest and strongest in all of Wiltshire."

"Yes, he is. But the biggest, strongest man in the world can be afraid because he can love." She lowered her gaze. "And love can hurt you, no matter how big and strong you are."

Oliver fiddled with the laces of his new velvet doublet. "I don't understand."

"You will one day. For now, I want you to understand that he needs to know that you love him and you want him to be your papa."

"Then why didn't he just say so?"

Juliana laughed, steering Oliver out of the tent and into the firelight. Someday, this lad would comprehend male pride. And probably would possess it in excess. She took his face between her hands and turned him toward Stephen. "He is saying so right now."

Oliver stared across the leaping fire at his father. In his curiously sage, adult fashion, he nodded and patted Juliana's hand. Then he bit his lip. "Will it hurt?"

She shook her head and hugged him. *Not in the way you think, little one. Not in the way you think.*

The pipes skirled up to a shrill note, and the bulb-nosed shawm drew out a long, spine-shivering tone.

Juliana took Oliver by the hand. As they walked toward Stephen, she suffered a moment of misgiving. Oliver was still a very sick little boy, and no Romany rite could mend that. But it was too late to turn back now. In the circle of firelight stood the gypsy tribe and the people of Lynacre. And in front of them all was Stephen — vast and vulnerable, the firelight flickering across his unsmiling face.

The ceremony was only a symbolic act, Juliana told herself as she walked toward Stephen around the climbing fire. Nothing more. The magic had to come from father and son.

She stopped before him. The music shimmered, soft and liquid like a warm rain. It seemed they stood there for the longest time, staring at each other — Oliver pressed back against her skirts, and she with her face raised to Stephen's while tiny sparks from the hazelwood fire flew between them.

Her hands rested on Oliver's shoulders. She felt the evenness of his breathing and gave silent thanks. His bothersome cough persisted, but he had not suffered a full-blown attack in several days.

Laszlo placed a blanket on the ground between Stephen and Oliver. He held up a hand to silence the music. In Romany, Laszlo said, "If this child be flesh of your flesh and blood of your blood, then claim him."

Stephen knelt at the edge of the blanket. He kept his gaze fixed on Oliver.

Juliana wondered how she could ever have thought Stephen's eyes to be cold and emotionless. They were quite beautiful now — blue as the heart of a flame and blazing with fierce love and hope.

"You are Oliver de Lacey," he said, drawing out his dagger and pulling the blade across his palm. "You are my son. Flesh of my flesh, blood of my blood." He made a fist and held it over the blanket, letting a few drops fall onto the bleached fabric.

Juliana felt Oliver's shoulders draw tight, then relax as Stephen put away the dagger. He picked up the blanket, holding a corner in each hand.

Oliver stood like a soldier at attention. Juliana wanted to shove him forward, but she resisted the impulse. Oliver had to go to his father on his own.

"Please, son." Stephen's whisper was faint and racked with pain.

The gypsy musicians began to play again. The strange, sinuous song rippled up Juliana's spine. The counterpoint of shawm and pipes, guitar and tambour, haunted the evening air, and the melody was as mysterious as the ineluctable bond between father and son.

Oliver took a step forward. Stephen caught the boy against his chest, wrapping the anointed blanket around him and holding on tight.

A cheer went up from the people. The tempo of the music rushed into a dance tune. Stephen swept Oliver up, higher and higher into the air, and whirled him around while the boy shouted with laughter.

For as long as she lived, Juliana would remember them thus, laughing into one another's faces, whirling around and around while all the world seemed to smile at them.

And though she smiled, too, it was not without a pang of regret. In all the excitement over Oliver, Stephen had made no further mention of the annulment. Yet she knew the papers were there on his desk, waiting for a decision. And the worst of it was, she no longer knew what she wanted — a life here with Stephen, or the chance to find out who was responsible for that night in Novgorod.

Rodion grabbed Jillie around the waist and led her in a high-stepping jig. Laszlo clapped his heels together smartly and bowed to Nance Harbutt, who blushed, fanned her face with her apron and shook her head vigorously.

Laszlo shrugged and started to turn away. Nance grabbed him by the arm, pulled him back, and they joined the dancers. Those who did not partner off simply joined hands and reeled in a circle around the fire.

Juliana watched through a blur of tears. Her rising joy crested, aching and bittersweet, in her throat. She had come to love them all, to cherish both their triumphs and their pain. And yet she stood apart, a stranger watching from afar, because long ago she had made a blood vow, and she was bound to fulfill it.

But not yet, not tonight. Tonight was not a night for revenge, but one for love and healing. She found herself facing Stephen, her breath coming quickly and her heart in her eyes. Oliver sat on his shoulders, skinny legs hooked beneath his father's arms, hands tangled in his hair.

As Stephen bent forward in an exaggerated courtly bow, Oliver shrieked with delight. Then the three of them joined the dancing, laughing while the firelight bathed their faces.

"Shhh." Stephen put his fingers to his lips as he settled the sleeping boy into his bed.

Juliana brushed her hand over the pale, tousled hair and bent to kiss Oliver's brow. Sweet, sharp affection welled up in her, and she hesitated with her head bent, the night shadows hiding the emotion in her face.

Stephen kissed the boy, too; then their eyes met when he straightened. "I used to kiss him only while he slept," he whispered.

The searing honesty of his words touched Juliana's heart. "I think he always knew," she said, tucking the blanket under Oliver's chin. "But I think, too, that you and your son are strangers who must come to know each other. Day by day."

He caught her hand in his. "Moment by moment." He brought her hand to his lips. "It is how I came to know you, Juliana."

I love you. Somehow she heard the words he did not say, the question he did not ask, and she gave him the answer she knew he sought.

"Stephen, yes."

He swept her into his arms, up and up with graceful strength. She tucked her head against his shoulder as he left the room, stepping over the sleeping Pavlo and the fantastical toys he had made for his son, forgotten now that Oliver was permitted to play with other children.

They went directly to Stephen's chamber.

She felt a warm flood of excitement flow through her. As the evening had progressed, she had sensed an inevitability about this night. They would make love; the knowledge had come to her slowly and in secret as if he had whispered his intention into her ear.

He had said nothing, but the message was there in a long, half-lidded look, in a brush of a hand on a thigh, in a private shared smile.

The one thing she had not expected was that he would carry her to his private chamber.

Embers burned low in the brazier. The subtle orange light mingled with moonglow streaming through the window. Swaying shadows from the breeze-blown trees danced across the floor and flickered upon the painted wall hangings. The bed, with its filmy summer draperies, seemed shrouded in mystery.

Stephen set her gently down. The rushes stirred softly under her bare feet. He caught her face between his hands.

"This is madness," he said. "Tell me to stop, Juliana."

"Tell you to stop?" she whispered, still not wholly convinced that she wasn't dreaming. Very deliberately, she freed her hair from its coif so that it toppled down around her hips. "Now *that,* my lord, would be madness."

His rich, alluring chuckle drifted from the darkness. Then she heard a rustling sound as he shed his doublet, letting it drop to the floor.

"You're no help at all, Baroness." He bent to kiss her. First his lips brushed hers, light and delicate as a breath of wind. The graze of his lips made hers tingle, and the sensation spread downward, touching the tips of her breasts, the pit of her belly, the place between her legs.

"Please," she said, pressing close, seeking release from the delicious ache inside her. "Oh, Stephen. Let it not be like before, that night in the field, when you made me soar and yet took none of your own pleasure."

He laughed again, the sound oddly thrilling, for it was so rare. "I can manage that but once. You're doomed tonight, my sweet."

He deepened the kiss, and she felt the warmth of his tongue, evocative and tender as it slipped in and out of her mouth. She let her neck arch back while her hands ran up his chest, over the smooth fabric of his shirt. She inhaled deeply; he had a spice all his own, as intoxicating as vintage wine.

She had forgotten how clever he could be with his hands. How inventive. Now he reminded her, disengaging her sleeves, sliding his fingers up under the laces of her bodice, and pulling the garment loose with a single long tug. Within seconds, he had her skirt and petticoats drifting to the floor, and then she stood before him clad only in her shift.

He lifted his mouth from hers and touched her mouth with one finger, tracing the moist curve of her lower lip. Then he took her hand and drew her closer to the bed.

"Good God in heaven," he whispered as she stepped into the pooling moonlight. "You *are* a witch."

She tilted her head to one side, feeling the weight of her unbound hair and glad for its concealing length. "Why do you say that?"

He pressed one hand over her breast and cupped the other hand behind her neck, pulling her firmly against him. "That is what you do to me, my gypsy bride, and I know of no other word for it than witchcraft."

"Call it what you will," she whispered and moved closer still, nearly undone by the rich sensation of his hand on her breast.

"Ah, Juliana. Do you know how hard it's been for me to stay away from you? Knowing you were my wife and not being able to have you?"

"Yes," she said, her fingers finding the

laces of his codpiece. “I think I might have a vague idea.”

He groaned as her fingers brushed against him, loosening his trunk hose. “You know, don’t you, that this night will change everything between us.”

For the moment, she did not pause to consider what he meant. “It had better,” she said, pressing her lips to the hollow of his throat, intoxicated by the taste of him.

“Why do you say that?”

“Because I have fallen in love with you, Stephen de Lacey.”

As he lifted her off the floor and spun her about, the sound that escaped him was one of mingled joy and frustration. She threw back her head and watched the play of light and shadow whirling, whirling, as enchanting as the faceted lamp chimney he had made for Oliver.

When he set her down, her back was against one of the thick bedposts, and she stood breathless, waiting, her skin on fire with wanting.

Stephen gave a secretive smile as he bent low. He kissed her earlobe and then the side of her neck. His tongue flicked out and touched the sensitive skin there, and then his teeth were nipping, nibbling, as if she were a feast and he a man on the verge of starvation.

He clasped his hands around the pillar, imprisoning her between himself and the great, waiting bed. Soft laughter vibrated in his throat as he bent lower still and took hold of the ribbons of her shift with his teeth and pulled back. The bow came loose and the shift shivered down, baring her body inch by inch until she stood in a spellbound state of helpless anticipation.

"Ah, Juliana," he said, his voice wavering over her name. "Ah, love, you can't know how it makes me feel to look upon you — all of you." He brushed aside a tendril of her hair and lowered his head to kiss her breast. "Sweetheart, you come to me so clean and new, all innocent."

"And so do you, my beloved," she whispered. "For in truth you seem a different man of late."

"You taught me to hope again," he said, scooping her up and laying her on the puffy velvet counterpane.

Living among gypsies had taught Juliana that lovemaking was a frantic, furtive affair enacted in the dark to the discordant rhythm of uneven breathing, the occasional muffled shout and the creak of wagon springs.

Being with Stephen in the massive bed corrected that notion. Though a fire blazed in his eyes, he took his time with her, lowering himself beside her and kissing her lips, her throat, her breasts, then pulling back to watch her like an artist surveying his handiwork.

He said little and his infrequent whispered phrases were disjointed, but his meaning was clear. From the depths of her being he summoned passion and tenderness and the jewel-bright conviction that she belonged here, in his arms. She felt as if she had reached the end of a long journey.

And then he left her with her body bathed in firelight and moonglow. She gave a little cry of dismay and came up on her knees, reaching into the shadows.

He laughed quietly, cupping her chin in his hand. "Patience, love." Bracing one hand on the bedpost, he removed his boots, his hose and trunks. He stood there for a moment in only his large, blousy shirt. His gaze touched her like a caress.

He needed her. She saw it in his eyes as clearly as if he had admitted it aloud. His unguarded expression made her tremble.

"You are afraid," he whispered.

"No, I . . ." She looked away. "Yes."

He captured her chin again and made her look at him. " 'Twill hurt."

"Perhaps."

"Do you want me to stop?"

"No!" She clenched her hands into his shirt. "It is as if, all my life, I have been searching, seeking. Without quite knowing what I sought." Her hands drifted down to the hem of his shirt. "And it is not just the heat of your body next to mine that I need, but something more. Something deeper. Something I begin to believe I can find with you, and you only."

He made a strange, low sound in his throat. She studied his face, and what she saw surprised her. "You are afraid, too."

He gave her an endearingly crooked grin. "It's not every day that I bring a wife to bed."

"I am a woman, no different in essence from any other. And you've had so many —"

"Hush." He kissed her briefly, firmly. "First of all, you are very different indeed. I daresay you are the most singular baroness in all of England. And second of all, I think you should know that there has been no one since Meg."

She shook her head in disbelief. "Please don't lie to me. Not tonight. You are notorious, Stephen. Your love affairs with lightskirts are common gossip."

"Pure invention, love. It was a way to

chase off unwanted betrothals."

"Truly?"

"Truly." He winnowed his fingers into her hair. "There is no greater intimacy than this, Juliana. Some take it lightly. I do not. I never have."

"I love you," she whispered.

His mouth hardened, just for a heartbeat. Just long enough to shadow her heart with doubt and make her blurt, "Stephen, did you love your first wife? Did you love Meg?"

He hesitated, his fingers ceasing their exploration. "Must we speak of her now?"

" 'Tis a thing I have long wondered — ever since I first saw the shrine you built to her memory."

He rolled his eyes. As if the ceiling were a higher authority, he asked it. "Why do women always want to know these things?" Then he looked down. "Sweetheart, you do use words as a bucket of ice water."

She stifled a giggle and brushed her hand over his. "By knowing what you cherished, I learn to know you."

Stephen heaved a great sigh and sat on the edge of the bed, clutching his head in his hands. "She was chosen for me in the same manner my first horse was selected. We wed as children, and at first it seemed we were only playing at being married. How could I have loved her if I did not even think she was real?"

Juliana clutched the bedclothes to her chest and sat forward. She had no answer, so she simply listened, trying to picture a much younger Stephen, a Stephen untouched by sorrow.

"Of course, the world changed, and I changed. My father died and the estate fell to me. Meg was delivered of a son — Dickon."

"And did that change her?" Juliana whispered.

"Oddly, it did not. She was as childlike as ever, playing with Dickon like a little girl with a poppet. I suppose, when I saw them together, I felt gratitude and something warm in my heart that might be called love, but that feeling was slain quickly enough."

"By Dickon's illness?"

"Aye, that, and —" he lifted his head, and his hands curled into fists on his knees "— my inability to forgive her."

Juliana closed her eyes and remembered the heavy stone Stephen had hurled. She saw it all again, the stone smashing through the exquisite colored window, the gift to Meg from King Henry.

Suddenly Stephen turned to her, grasped her by the shoulders. "I am an unforgiving man, Juliana, but I am no liar. What you took for my devotion to Meg was guilt. Before I could forgive her, before I could make myself understand why she became the king's lover, she died. She died cursing me, and cursing the children we had made. It has not made for blissful memories."

"But there is hope in you now. I see it shining in your eyes when you watch Oliver. I know it is why you brought me here tonight." She kissed him again, long and lingeringly.

He looked slightly dazed when she lifted her mouth from his. "I think," he said, "I have recovered from the ice water." He stood and reached down, pulling the shirt over his head and letting it drift to the floor.

"Oh, my." It was all she could manage. She cupped her palms on his shoulders, glorying in the feel of his warm skin, then slid her hands inward, mapping the contours of his chest. He made a hissing sound as if she had burned him.

She took her hands away quickly. He grabbed her wrists. "Jesu, don't stop," he said.

With a cry of delight, she flung her arms around his neck, and he came to her, tumbling with her until they were spread crosswise on the huge bed, the velvet counterpane nuzzling their flesh.

How delicious he tasted — of plum wine and male sweetness and hot desire. She explored his body with increasing boldness, daring at last to touch him intimately. The heat and hardness beneath the warm silk of his skin startled her, and she forgot to be afraid.

She moved her hips, tilting them upward, and his hand and fingers led her closer and closer to the dark release, the addictive pleasure.

"Minx," he whispered in her ear. His breath was ragged, uneven; he sounded as if he was about to explode. "I'm trying to go slowly, but I'm not made of stone."

He pressed her back against the bolsters and bent to kiss her breasts. His hand slid down between her thighs, brushing them apart, seeking and probing with a refined tenderness that took her breath away.

"Ah, Stephen," she said, "what are you doing to me?"

Stephen smiled at the naïveté of her question. God, she was sweet, so pliant and warm, so lacking in feigned modesty. "Loving you," he said in a soothing tone. "Just be at ease."

There were a thousand reasons he should

not be with her, touching her. But for the life of him, he could not think of a single one. And then he acknowledged, with a rare lightening of his heart, that it was useless to think at all. He skimmed his hand along her inner thigh. Warm alabaster it was, deliciously smooth. His fingers brushed lower, and her eyes flew open. He saw in their depths the bewildered anticipation of a woman on the verge of a shining discovery.

"Yes, love," he said, nipping at her ear. "Let me touch you here . . . and here . . . and then here, as well." With each word he caressed her more deeply, and she gasped until at last she shuddered, and a hot flush swept over her body. The look in her eyes turned from anticipation to the smoky satisfaction of fulfillment. A thin cry escaped her, and she threw back her head. Never had he seen ecstasy engulf a woman so completely.

As he bent to kiss her lips, he knew a moment of regret. A tiny ache flared in his chest. This would be the end of her innocence.

The thought passed in a blur; he was fast losing his will to postpone his own pleasure. She clasped him against her, so close he could feel her racing heart, and her legs slipped around him.

"Don't move," he begged her.

She moved. Bless the girl, she lifted her hips and finished the job, and the sound that escaped her was more a shout of gladness than a cry of pain. Swept past self-control, Stephen buried himself to the hilt in her.

"No," he ground out in a last futile protest, but his long-denied desires, kindled by the months of unbearable tension, overcame him. "Ah, Juliana." He spoke in the voice of a stranger, the voice of a man who was learning to feel again, and learning that feeling did not always have to hurt.

Long moments later, he lifted his awestruck face from the thick silken tangles of her hair. "Jesu," he said.

She blinked. "What is wrong?"

He tried to shape the feeling into words. "I saw heaven. I swear to God, I did. That's never happened to me before. Jesu." He kissed her forehead, her cheeks, her lips. "I had no idea."

"This is good, yes?"

He laughed, and his body reminded him that they were still deeply and intimately joined. He could not remember such a feeling of joy. "No," he said, "this is not good."

She looked crestfallen.

"This is wondrous, magical." And frightening as hell, said a little voice in the back of his mind. Now what are you going to do with her?

"I'm going to do it again." The stranger he had become spoke without volition.

Her eyes opened wide. "Do what? Stephen, you are acting very oddly. Do what again?"

"This," he said, lowering his mouth to the bud of her breast, lingering there, tasting her dulcet essence. "And this." He slid lower still, savoring the raw sweet musk of their loving.

She began to pray in Russian.

"And this," he continued, until she could not speak at all.

FIFTEEN

A crisp breeze through the partially opened window teased Stephen to wakefulness. The wind carried the music of lark song and the scent of ripe apples, and for a moment he felt so content that he was certain he was still dreaming.

A sinuous movement in the crook of his arm assured him that he was not. And more than just his mind came awake when he felt her move against him, her body satin-soft and sleep warm.

Juliana. His heart called her name.

He turned his head to brush his lips over the downy disarray of her curls and the delicate skin of her temple. His hand skimmed up her arm to her shoulder, and he remembered.

He had known his share of beautiful women. He had married one. He had courted many others.

But none of them, neither Meg nor the

refined beauties of court, nor yet the women Cromwell paraded before the king, had Juliana's gifts.

He could not name precisely the special quality she possessed. A glow. An exuberance. An aggressive and determined joy that gave her the courage to push past his defenses, to confront him with unflinching courage, to look into his heart and to see something there worth fighting for.

When he regarded her, he saw more than a beautiful woman. He saw himself reflected in her eyes, with all his pain and fear and fierce pride and passion. And the love he was learning, day by day, to give freely.

Juliana. Her name was a silent song on his lips. Her love was like a circle in the water, radiating ever outward, inevitably encompassing even the remotest of hearts.

And he'd thought he had the power to resist her.

As the brightening dawn made a play of rainbows over the bed, Stephen de Lacey dared to dream. He studied her face, a delicate oval within its frame of pure sable curls. He saw the sable gone white as winter ermine, the face delicately etched with the tracery of passing years, and he realized that he wanted to grow old with her by his side, in his arms.

He wanted to fall in love again.

The idea dragged a gasp of amazement from him. And a cold fear gripped his heart.

If he begged her to stay with him, she would bear his children.

Children like Dickon. Children like Oliver. Children destined to blaze like bright flames, to be snuffed out by the inevitable, accursed disease, leaving only the charred remains of their parents' hearts.

Juliana had never endured that loss. She had never held a dying child in her arms, had never shaken her fist at God in helpless frustration, had never felt the huge, gaping ache of sorrow as that precious life suffocates in her arms.

No children, he decided resolutely. He should practice abstinence.

He nearly laughed aloud at his own foolishness. Abstinence indeed, after such a night.

His arms tightened around her. God. He had taken her again and again, with the single-mindedness of a madman. No wonder she was sleeping so soundly.

Just the memory of her eager passion, her smoldering hunger, her unbridled ecstasy, made him hard with wanting her. Very well, he told himself. Abstinence was not a possibility. Perhaps he would avail himself of those French sheaths. Aye, some likened their use to bathing with one's boots on, but in the name of protecting Juliana's precious heart from grief, the discomfort was a small price to pay.

"What is a small price to pay?" she asked, brushing the sleep from her eyes.

Stephen nearly leaped out of his skin. "What?"

"You said, ' 'Tis a small price to pay.' "

"I did not."

"I heard you." She braced up on her elbows and shook back her hair. The motion bared her breasts and made Stephen's throat go dry while his mind emptied of thought.

Without looking, he groped for the jar of fresh water he kept on the bedside table. He took a long, cooling drink. "I must have been thinking aloud."

She sat up and took the jug from him. He watched in rapt fascination as her throat undulated with swallowing. She set the jar aside. "Why do you look at me like that?"

He shifted so that he lay between her legs and kissed her moist mouth and then the tips of her breasts. His water-cooled tongue brought the peaks to hardness, and a cry leaped from her throat.

"*That* is why, Juliana," he said.

"I do not understand."

His lips moved from one breast to the other, teeth grazing and nipping while short gasps escaped her. "Can you guess yet?" he asked, his fingers dipping down and parting her thighs.

A soft moan was his only answer.

His mouth skimmed lower, down over her taut flat belly. "Just make a guess, my comfit. Why —" his searingly intimate kiss made her body arch like a drawn bow "— would I regard my naked wife in such a way?"

He expected no reply, nor did he get one, save that of her wonderfully expressive body and the wordless cries that escaped her as his hands and mouth brought her to ecstasy. And then he could not help himself; despite the vow he had made, he joined with her, reveling in the welcome of her body, in the gloriously evocative tightening of her female muscles.

Much later, when they lay sated and replete, listening to the lark song and letting the breeze caress their naked bodies, he felt dazed with love and wonder. Like a groggy sleeper coming awake, he blinked and smiled.

"Does that answer you, my lady?"

She blinked back at him, looking equally

dazed. "It probably does, my lord. But I do not remember the question."

The season was dying, but Juliana had never felt more alive. Her every sense hummed with awareness as she worked the cider press in the apple yard. She was aware of the ripe, heavy scent of apples, the chilly tang of winter on the breeze. From the porter's gate in the distance, she heard a call and remembered that Stephen was expecting a shipment of goods from France. Oliver's shrill voice called out, bringing a smile to her lips.

Every day was a new adventure for Oliver. She adored watching his first tentative overtures of friendship with the children of the village and manor, and taking him to see the weaving house in the old abbey of Malmesbury. She even relished the bitter-sweet agony of love when she held him through an attack of wheezing.

And every night — with a dreamy mist in her eyes, Juliana turned her thoughts to her husband as she emptied another bushel of apples into the cider press while Jillie worked the windlass. Every night was another sort of adventure altogether. Hours and hours of lovemaking with Stephen, as inventive in the bedchamber as he was at his drawing board. What joy they found in the intimacy, the sharing, the love that held nothing back, the lack of sleep, the aching . . .

"Ooh, look at her ladyship," said a bright, teasing voice. "Off in dreamland again."

Juliana blinked and grinned at Nance Harbutt. "I have been at work on the cider since dawn. I'm entitled to a rest."

Jillie jabbed Nance in the ribs. "Bet she weren't thinking of rest at all, were you, my lady? Come, tell us what put the roses in your cheeks."

"Never," Juliana declared. "You are a maiden, Jillie Egan."

"Not by choice." She brushed her yellow hair out of her eyes and cast a wistful glance down toward the river. There, Rodion was working with the gypsy horses. He had stripped off his shirt, and sunlight bathed him in gold.

Nance sucked her tongue in disgust. "Pining after that Egyptian fellow," she scolded. "He'll lead you to heartbreak, you mark my words."

"What's all this gossip?" Stephen boomed, walking up to them with Oliver riding high upon his shoulders.

Juliana felt a spasm of elation at the sight of her husband. In truth, he was the same man who had, long ago, caught her stealing his horse. Yet the subtle differences shone clear to her. No longer a brooding, secretive lord, he was frank and affectionate, with laughter in his eyes and a broad grin on his face.

Oliver waved a drinking cup in his fist. "Look what came from France! It's got a picture of a naked woman in the bottom of it."

"Give me that." Juliana snatched it, looked inside, and laughed, then showed it to Nance and Jillie. The nude was Bathsheba, modestly clad in bunches of grapes and fig leaves, a crown of laurels on her head.

The women oohed and aahed until, with mock severity, Stephen said, "You're supposed to be working."

"We are not slaves, my lord," Juliana said pertly.

"Are, too!" piped Oliver. "I heard Papa talking to Uncle Jonathan. Told him he made you a slave to fashion."

Juliana cocked her head. "To fashion?"

Stephen's ears went red.

"To passion," Nance declared, shaking a finger in Stephen's face. "You've the devil's own tongue, my lord, to be talking that way in front of a tyke."

"I'm not a tyke," Oliver roared, sliding

down his father as if Stephen were a tree trunk. "I'm a spy! Yes! A *spy* like Uncle Algernon!" With a savage war cry he summoned the widow Shane's lad from his labors gleaning apples, and the two of them scampered out of the apple yard.

Juliana jumped up on a wobbly stool so that she could face her husband eye to eye, nose to nose. As if running for shelter from a gathering storm, Jillie and Nance disappeared, closing the gate firmly behind them.

"A slave to passion, am I?" Juliana demanded, quivering with feminine outrage.

Feigning nonchalance, Stephen took an apple and bit into it, chewing slowly. " 'Tis unfortunate the lad overheard, but I trow 'tis the awful truth."

"It is insulting," she declared. "And you are arrogant."

He took another bite and carefully held the white flesh of the apple between his teeth. Leaning forward, he offered her a bite.

She hesitated. He curled his hand around the back of her head and drew her forward. With a wicked little laugh she took the bait and would have pulled back, but he was quicker. He crushed his mouth against hers and with a single deft motion gathered her hard against him.

She knew then that she had no defenses and wanted none. He could make her — raised amid age-old wealth and privilege — forget that she was a Romanov. In broad daylight, he carried her to a thatch-roofed shed made of fieldstone. There, amid clay bottles and wooden vats of cider, he stripped her bare and made love to her on her shawl spread out on the packed-earth floor. She did not make one word of protest when he grasped her hands and held them high over her head, when he entered her swiftly and, while moving within her, somehow managed to anoint her breasts and belly with frothing apple cider, then drank the nectar from her bare skin.

Lying replete in his arms, she admitted, "You are right. I am a slave to passion."

He kissed her with his apple-flavored lips. "I would have you no other way." Rolling to one side, he reached for the pouch hanging from his discarded baldric.

"Stephen?" she asked. "What is it?"

"A sheath. It's from France. It was made to . . . prevent certain things."

"To prevent us from making a baby," she said. "How dare you?"

"Juliana." He took her firmly by the shoulders. "Listen to me. I have sired two sons. One died in my arms. The other is sickly still. I mean to spare you —"

"Spare me!" With a violent jerk of her body, she wrenched away from him. "Who are you to make that decision?"

He flung up his chin and squared his shoulders. She had nearly forgotten how imposing he could be when possessed by a fine rage. His bare chest loomed like a wall before her. "I am a man whose beautiful son died in agony. A man whose other son might well meet the same fate. I can't suffer that again, Juliana. I won't. And I will not have you know such sorrow. If you refuse to use the sheath, then we will practice abstinence."

"Ab—" The word was unfamiliar to her.

He pulled her close. His knuckle under her chin forced her to look into his stone blue eyes, into those icy wells of pain. "Think of it, Juliana. Never to feel my caresses." His hand drifted down to touch her throat and breasts. "Nor my kisses." He bent and brushed his mouth back and forth over hers. "To sleep alone in your room, night after night."

For long moments she stood spellbound, on fire with a need he could arouse with no more than a low-lidded glanced across the great hall. When he added the touch of his lips and hands to that, it was putting a torch to fresh pitch.

She pushed at his chest. "Damn you, Stephen de Lacey. Damn you for a selfish rogue."

"Denying myself the full pleasure of making love to you is selfish?" With jerky, frustrated movements, he donned his clothes. "How so, Baroness?"

The cruel lash of his irony stung her. "You want me on your terms. You seek to alter fate. What about all the times we did not use the sheath, Stephen? Even now, I could be carrying your child."

His face drained of color. He looked panicked, a cornered animal, scared and dangerous. "Get rid of it," he said in a frantic whisper. "The midwife can help you, or perhaps the gypsies have a remedy for —"

"Remedy?" she shouted. "A child in the womb is not a sickness, but a blessing from heaven."

"It is a curse, damn your eyes!"

She turned her head to the side as if he had slapped her. "I thought I had found happiness with you." She jumped up, backing toward the door of the shed. "I thought I could abandon my quest to find the killers of my family. I was willing to give up my identity and my need for justice — everything I have lived for for the past five years. For you, Stephen. I would have given it all up for you."

"Never sacrifice for me." He stuffed his feet into his boots. "You should know better than that."

"Yes, I should. You still have the annulment papers, don't you?" She drew a deep breath, then spoke from the bitterness in her heart. "I want out of this unnatural marriage."

He raised his arm, and his hand closed in the empty air between them. "Juliana —"

"Your lordship!" The garden gate creaked open. "Your lordship!"

Juliana rushed out of the shed. Stephen pushed past her.

Skirts hiked to her knees, chubby legs pumping, Nance raced across the apple yard toward them. "Oh, do come. 'Tis Master Oliver. He's collapsed and cannot breathe!"

Stephen sent Juliana a look that was as fleeting and lethal as lightning. Then he raced toward the hall.

Juliana paced the passageway outside Oliver's bedchamber. Stephen had been in there for hours. The door was half-open and she could see him through the light fog of camphor mist, sitting against the headboard of the bed with Oliver limp and gasping in his arms.

Stephen's head was bent, his golden hair obscuring his face. His big hands stroked the boy's back, his shoulders, his frail, convulsing chest.

Agony squeezed her heart. Stephen had stunned her with his insistence that she remain childless. Now she began to understand his terror. This was the worst attack Oliver had suffered since she had known him. Simply watching was torment.

My beautiful son died in my arms.

Her mother's heart, awakened by her love for Oliver, rose into her throat at the thought of losing him as Stephen had lost Dickon. She closed her arms protectively across her middle.

No. No. No.

In truth she did not know whether or not she was quick with child. Her menses might simply be late. Foolishly, she had never thought to count the weeks.

Get rid of it.

How could he? How dare he pronounce a death sentence on his own child? Surely he could not mean it. Surely, surely not.

"My lady?" Pale, with a tuck of worry in his brow, Kit approached her. "There's a royal messenger in the hall."

Juliana's blood ran cold with apprehension. "What does he want?"

"He has a summons for his lordship." Kit started into the room.

Juliana hauled him back by the arm. "You are not to disturb him, Kit. Do you understand? He is not even to know the messenger has come."

"But it's a summons from the king."

"I said no, Kit. My husband has worries enough without this. I shall deal with the messenger myself."

Kit scuffed his feet in the rushes. "Are you asking me to keep this a secret?"

"No. I am commanding you to." She saw his stricken look and softened. "Oliver is very sick. Stephen is doing his best to help him through it. It takes concentration. It takes all the love in his heart. If he is distracted for one moment, and something happens to Oliver, who will he blame, Kit? Who?"

"Himself."

"Now do you understand?"

"Aye, my lady."

She went down to the hall and she heard the message. And when it was done, she knew what she had to do.

She said her farewells to Lynacre in secret.

No one save Kit knew she was leaving, and she had sworn the youth to silence.

In the garden, she felt the cold bite of the coming winter. Leaves scurried across her path, and a brisk wind tore seed pods from the flowers.

She had so many memories bound up in this place. There, far in the distance, was Malmesbury. She remembered Stephen dropping down from the bell rope to settle a dispute between two children, then hurling a brick at the window King Henry had given the first baroness.

At the river's edge, long pens were ready for the spring shearing, and down the lane was the tall hedgerow and wall that had once hidden the maze. Now the gate always stood open, and the maze and Oliver's garden had become a favorite playground for the village children.

Just for a moment, she paused to look into the apple yard. The low door to the shed hung open, and she watched a heatless light creep across the area where they had last made love. She closed that memory into her heart, for it was the last time she would feel the touch of his lips and his hands, the last time their bodies would join in fierce unity.

She had thought, when she lost her family, that she had found a pain beyond enduring, but somehow this was even worse.

She moved swiftly to leave, extracting herself from Lynacre like a thorn from tender flesh. If she hesitated, she would talk herself out of doing what she knew was best for all of them.

All the way to London, with Laszlo riding at her side, she held the tears at bay. She did not shed them in her grand chamber of honor at Hampton Court. Dry-eyed, she accepted a bath and the fussy ministrations of the handmaids sent by the duchess of Bedford.

And a majordomo conducted her to the Privy Chamber, where only the best-favored guests were permitted. Ignoring incredulous whispers from robed councillors and silk-clothed nobles, she made a graceful obeisance to the king.

King Henry was at the zenith of his majesty, in full royal regalia — ermine collar, heavy gold chains, jewels on his fingers, clothing of figured silk and embroidered batiste. By some happy chance, rays of winter sunlight slanted through a high cloverleaf-shaped window and gilded him like a halo.

"What manner of man is your husband, madam," Henry demanded, "that he would send you to court alone?"

"My husband did not receive your summons. *I* did."

A rustle of interest swept the courtiers. Henry made a flinging gesture with his hand and sent them scattering like seeds broadcast to the wind. "Fools," he muttered, glaring at his retreating counselors. "They want me to marry again. Cromwell has some Flanders mare in mind. A kinswoman of the duke of Cleves."

There was an awkward silence; then Henry seemed to shake off his thoughts. He aimed his imperious glare at Juliana.

"Your coming here alone was a foolish thing to do."

"Your summons," she countered, "was heartless."

"Since when has a king needed to have a heart?"

She would have laughed if he had not seemed so deadly serious. "I thought one was required of every great prince."

"It is required of a prince's subjects to obey!"

She suffered the blast of his temper with stony calm. It was as if Stephen had taken all of her emotions and locked them away in some sort of magic box, to be taken out at his whim, not hers.

"Your Grace," she said, "you summoned

Oliver de Lacey to court. Why?"

"I need not answer to you, nor to anyone." For the first time, she noticed that the king was nervous, his eyes darting every few seconds toward a side door of the Privy Chamber. "So long as Wimberleigh kept his son hidden away, I saw no need to force my will upon him."

"Then why —"

"Silence!" Like a dragon's flame, his roar filled the chamber. "It came to me that the lad — Oliver, is that his name? — is improving in health."

"Not so much that he could tolerate —"

"Wimberleigh's heir gets no special treatment. If I allowed that, my nobles would revolt. The lad *will* serve at court."

A knock came from the side door. To Juliana's amazement, the king's florid face paled. "Come," he said quietly, his manner subdued, almost deferential.

A page in green-and-white livery scurried over, followed by a man in a long, stark black robe. A physician.

The doctor whispered to the king. Henry's chest rose and fell quickly, and Juliana felt a jolt of recognition. It was the same fear and panic she had seen on Stephen's face when Oliver fell ill.

"It is the prince, yes?" she whispered when

the physician had withdrawn.

"Yes." He seemed shocked. Numb with terror. And suddenly less like a king and more like a man.

"Your Grace, why do you not go to him? Children heal best with a loving parent near."

"How so?" His black eyes pleaded with her.

"I saw this with Oliver. He needed touching and nearness. Every child does." She bit her lip, wondering if she dared to refer to Henry's beloved Queen Jane. "Especially a child without a mother."

The king winced. "You're saying I should fawn all over the Prince of Wales? His household is the richest in the realm, second only to my own. He has an army of physicians. Nurses, tutors, servants —"

"He has only one father, Your Grace."

For a moment, Henry sat as still as a statue, save for the flash of the gold Tudor rose pendant on his chest, which lifted and fell with his breathing. Then he nodded once, curtly. His meaty hand grasped a summons bell and rang it.

"You Romanovs are a loud, impertinent lot," he said.

While his gentleman pensioners scurried in to assist him in rising from his throne,

Juliana stared in amazement. "When did Your Grace decide to believe I am a Romanov?"

Henry grunted as a pair of gentlemen gripped his arms and helped him to his feet. The layers of bandages on his bad leg made a bulge in his hose, and he touched his foot gingerly to the floor.

"Havelock told us about that, too." He poked a fat finger at her brooch. "Cromwell did some digging. Turns out the design and motto are indeed Romanov."

"Blood, vows and honor." Juliana spoke the words in Russian.

"Not only that," Henry said. "I've another surprise for you. I think you'll be pleased. I know I was. Cromwell!" he shouted as he limped toward the door.

As if he had been in the antechamber listening at the door, Thomas Cromwell slipped into the room.

"Show our guest to the river garden," said the king.

Though Juliana badgered Lord Privy Seal with questions, she got no answers. He led her out through a door, and a cold wind struck her face. She stood at the top of the garden. A terraced hill, laced with paths and arbors, slanted down to the river where barges and lighters plied the Thames.

Juliana glanced back, a question on her lips, but the dour, secretive Cromwell had withdrawn. The garden seemed empty, barren, the trees skeletal, and the evergreen shrubs dulled by a coating of London smoke.

A movement down the terraced steps caught her eye.

A man stood with his back to her, facing the river. His booted feet were planted wide, his crimson cloak thrown back over one shoulder. The late-afternoon sunlight glinted off his black hair.

For a moment Juliana simply stared. The tops of the man's boots were folded down below his knees. A bright design of Byzantine crosses decked the bloodred lining of the cloak.

Her stomach churned. The world went out of kilter. A flash of awareness streaked like fire through her, and she must have made some sound — a gasp or squeak of disbelief — for the man turned.

She saw jeweled buttons on his chest. She saw gleaming dark eyes and a jet curl of hair tumbling down over a noble brow. She saw a handsome, familiar face light up with a smile.

As if in a dream, Juliana walked toward him. She tried to speak, but the only word she was able to form was his name.

"Alexei!"

SIXTEEN

"God help me, Jonathan, I miss her." Blowing out his breath in frustration, Stephen scraped the edge of his rapier against the whetstone. Due to a sudden, early snowfall, he had canceled Kit's fencing practice. The three men were in the armory, cleaning weapons and drinking ale. Oliver had recovered from his attack. Stephen could hear him outside in the armory, playing with his dog.

Jonathan Youngblood's mug thunked with a clatter onto the worktable. Kit, who was washing a set of spurs in a basin of vinegar and sand, jumped at the sound. For the past several days, the lad had been uncharacteristically nervous.

"Sorry," Jonathan said, using his fingers to wring out his bushy moustache. "That ale must be stronger than I realized. I thought I heard you say you missed your wife."

Stephen scowled at the gleaming damascened blade. "I do. I know it's crazy. We fought constantly —"

"Constantly?" Jonathan lifted an eyebrow.

A hot rush of memories engulfed Stephen. Her silken limbs wrapped around him. Her soft voice whispering in his ear. "Almost constantly," he said.

Jonathan sighted down the thin length of his Spanish rapier. "You should not have run her off, then."

Stephen slammed his fist on the table, sending the whetstone to its death. Bits of shattered pumice littered the flagged floor of the armory. "I did not run her off."

He lied, and he knew it. He remembered with stark clarity the awful hurt in her eyes, the disbelief, and then the utter devastation when he said he did not want her baby. He would have tried to make her understand the fear and grief in his heart, but then there was the emergency with Oliver. Afterward Jillie, with an accusing glare, had reported that Juliana had gone off somewhere with Laszlo.

Perhaps her gypsy blood ran true after all. She could not stay in one place.

No. She could not stay with him. With a man who placed no trust in love, no faith in the future.

Where had she gone? What had she been thinking?

"She'll cool her heels and be back," Jonathan said consolingly. "Though in sooth I thought it would be before now." With a playful grin, he touched his son's ear with the very tip of the sword. "A fortnight, it's been, eh, Kit?"

The youth ducked his head and swirled the spurs in the basin. Before he could answer, Pavlo barked a sharp alarm outside the armory. Algernon Basset burst into the room. His cheeks bright red from the cold, his curls bouncing beneath a velvet Venetian cap, he paused inside the door.

Stephen eyed him coldly. "Havelock. Ever the loyal friend. Betrayed any good secrets lately?"

Algernon ducked beneath a beam over the entranceway. Battered helmets and shields from forgotten battles hung from the timber. "Stephen, I know better than to expect your forgiveness, though I do crave it." He took off his gloves and shook his reddened fingers. "I have another confession to make."

"Oh, this should be jolly good," Jonathan muttered. He stood, flexing his rapier and eyeing Algernon wolfishly.

Algernon licked his lips. "It's about your wife, Stephen. I told Thomas Cromwell about her brooch. The Romanov ruby, the family motto."

"My," said Stephen, "you have been busy."

" 'Twas months ago, and I merely thought I was passing on a harmless bit of gossip."

"You son and heir of a mongrel bitch," Stephen said as the rage boiled up inside him. "First you used a sick little boy to ingratiate yourself to the king because you could not win his attention on your own. And now this — this —" He cursed bitterly and turned away.

"What is this about a brooch?" Jonathan demanded.

"The one Lady Juliana always wore. Having some small measure of competency as a linguist, I recognized the markings on the bauble. I thought it would help you save face, proving that you'd married a foreign princess, not a gypsy."

Stephen planted his palms flat on the table and leaned across. "Since when have I been concerned about my *face,* dear Algernon?"

Havelock swallowed. "As it turns out, Cromwell arranged for a Russian ambassador to come to England."

Stephen's glance flicked to the narrow, unglazed window of the armory. Tiny windblown snowflakes obscured the view. A chill touched the base of his spine. "He'll have no luck locating her. She's run off with Laszlo. Add that to your stockpile of scandals."

"Don't you think we'd best try to find her?" Algernon asked. "After all, we don't know what sort of man this Russian is."

"The little pestilence does have a point," Jonathan said.

"I don't have the first idea where they might have gone," said Stephen.

"My lord?" Kit stood, his hands shaking.

"We'll organize a search," Stephen said, feeling more alive than he had in days. "Jonathan, you get a party of men from the village. Kit, you —"

"I know where Lady Juliana went, my lord," Kit said. His lips looked dry, almost bloodless.

"What?"

"Your wife. May God forgive me, I have known from the start."

"Where?"

"To London, my lord." Miserable guilt pinched the youth's features taut. "To the royal court."

Slumped over on her knees, her hands clutching the rim of a clay chamber pot, Juliana heaved violently. When her stomach had emptied itself, she came shakily to her feet and walked to the basin of fresh water on the table. She bathed her face and then bent to rest her forehead against the cool edge of the basin.

A fortnight earlier, she would have rejoiced over her symptoms. Now her heart was in anguish, her mind whirling with doubts. She could take no delight in the news that she carried Stephen's child.

And yet . . . She straightened and let her open hand rest protectively over her lower belly. From deep inside her, a woman's secret joy rose up like a fount of warmth. She had not been prepared for the intensity of her feelings for this small, unformed life so completely within her care.

Get rid of it.

Stephen's cold command echoed through time and across the miles.

She plunged her face into the basin of water before the tears could start.

A half hour later she emerged from her elegant chamber in Hampton Court and headed toward the royal lodgings. She was bathed, coiffed, gowned . . . and smiling.

One did that at the court of Henry VIII. She had learned the custom quickly. No matter what misery tore at one's heart, one smiled and played the gay courtier.

As she walked through frosty courtyards and down wind-filled, cloistered passageways, she wished she knew where Laszlo had gone. Moments after she had told him the news about the miracle of Alexei's survival, the gypsy had slipped away; she had not heard from him since. He was bound to be as uncomfortable as he was unwelcome at Hampton Court with its imposing gatehouses and walled yards, its guards armed with fearsome weapons.

She had not seen Alexei, either, yet she knew he was about. The ladies of court chattered on about his handsomeness, his exotic, mysterious allure. Since he claimed to remember nothing of the slaughter at Novgorod, Juliana was content to avoid him.

She braced herself for the day to come. Ending her full week of waiting, a herald had come to announce that the king would see her.

The delay had not been a time of idleness for Juliana. She used the days to acquaint herself with King Henry's court. The task turned out to be simpler than she had anticipated. She found many similarities to her father's ducal household in Novgorod — the ceremony, the secrecy, the gossip, the pageantry.

By listening carefully and discreetly in the ladies' salon, she learned some of King Henry's predilections. He enjoyed *being* king, yet performing a king's duties was burdensome and tedious to him. Henry devoted only two hours each morning to ruling the realm. It was whispered that he did not even like signing his name to official decrees and documents. He used a stamp for that purpose. A very official, unique stamp with the raised impression of his seal and signature.

Designed, years earlier, by a loyal baron called Stephen de Lacey.

Each time she thought of Stephen, the wave of longing that swept over her was so vast and deep that it took her breath away. She told herself she should not miss him, but her heart wouldn't listen.

After each brief morning meeting with his council, the king left matters in the ruthlessly capable hands of Cromwell. Henry's fondness for sport and entertainment was indulged through the rest of the day.

And today, thanks to the cold, hissing rain, which in the night had hardened to pelting snow flurries, the king would indulge in indoor sport.

A far more deadly game than hunting or archery.

The courtly whirl was in full swing in the Presence Chamber. Long tables lined the walls. Wine and ale flowed as copiously as gossip from Havelock's lips. And at the very center, like the hub of an ever-spinning wheel, sat King Henry himself.

A troupe of mummers was performing. Juliana lost sight of the herald and stopped in the shadow of a wall sconce. Foolishly, she had neglected to break her fast, and a sudden hunger burned her stomach. She moved on unsteady feet to a table, but the smells of ale and meat reawakened her nausea.

Her head spinning, she turned toward the door to leave and found herself facing Lord Spencer Merrifield, whom she had met some days before. A distinguished older gentleman with an air of splendid melancholy about him, he looked incongruous in full-court dress while jiggling a baby on his hip.

Giving Lord Spencer a weak, polite smile, Juliana turned her attention to the play. It must be a daring troupe indeed, for it did not take Juliana long to divine that the farce being enacted was a familiar one.

A ponderous fellow wearing a cockeyed crown pantomimed an argument with a stiff-backed older woman. She shook a rosary of exaggerated size in his face until he threw up his hands in disgust and turned to face the sloe-eyed beauty waiting in the shadows behind him.

The moment she handed him a poppet with bright orange hair, he flung it away and in the same motion, lopped off the head of the young beauty. A paste-and-paper head with a startled, openmouthed face painted on it rolled across the floor.

The huge crowd burst into gales of laughter, but only for a moment. It became evident that His Majesty was not amused and so, one by one, like candles being snuffed, the nobles stopped laughing.

The baby in Spencer's arms mewed. He jiggled her and whispered, "Hush, Lark."

"Her name is Lark?" Juliana asked.

" 'Tis truly Guinivere Beatrice Leticia Rutledge Merrifield. Lark suits her."

Feeling the fascination of an expectant mother, Juliana peered at the baby. She had skin of ivory and roses, hair of the blackest down. "She's charming, my lord. Your granddaughter?"

He half turned to her, a smile of bitter irony curving his lips. "No. She is my wife."

"Your *wife?*"

"Aye, but that's another story entirely, and long in the telling." Lord Spencer turned his attention back to the players.

Juliana blushed, ashamed of herself for prying.

With an imperious command, King Henry ordered the mummers out of the court.

"Will they be punished?" Juliana asked Spencer.

"A day in the stocks. If the fools don't freeze to death, they'll be free to go."

"Didn't they know better than to lampoon the marriage woes of the king?"

"They're Irish." Apparently in Spencer's mind, that explained everything. When Juliana gave him a quizzical look, he said, "All Irish are fools. And they hate the English from the king down." He pointed at the retreating mummers. "That one's the biggest fool of all. Claims he had a vision. Claims he'll found a line of Irish noblemen and that one of that line will sit in the lap of the English monarch. Pah!" Spencer spat into the rushes. "An Irishman's visions have no more substance than vows made in wine."

Alexei and his hard-faced Russian gentlemen entered the chamber.

"Indeed," she murmured. "My compliments to you, my lord, and to your, er, wife." Awkwardly she patted the infant's downy black head and hurried to greet Alexei.

As she wove a path through the milling crowd, she wondered anew at the strange workings of fate. The prophecy of the gypsy called Zara had been but a faint echo of memory, yet today it came rushing back in all its dark mystery.

True, Juliana had traveled far in both time and distance, and yet something did not fit. When she looked at Alexei, she saw a sharply handsome, proud Russian boyar. He had many things, yet he was not the man she loved.

But was Stephen?

In a quandary, she greeted Alexei with a polite smile. His minions fell back. One of them stepped into a pool of torchlight, and the glow flickered off a shiny scar on his cheek. The sight raised the hair on Juliana's arms, and for a blink of time, she faltered. She attributed her dizziness to her persistent mother-sickness.

Alexei clapped his booted heels together and bowed. The torchlight caught some ornament he wore, and for a moment Juliana's eyes were dazzled. She blinked, then saw the buttons on the front of his Russian jacket.

Garnet buttons.

"Alexei?" she asked.

He brushed his knuckle under her chin. "I had always imagined you would be agreeable to look at," he said, his cultured Russian a song in her ears. “I never dared to dream you would be so beautiful, and yet you are.”

His words made her shiver. She could not take her eyes off those buttons.

“You received my messages!”

He slashed a dark brow up at her. “Messages?”

“All of them,” she said, suspicion rising like bile in her throat. “I sent one button with each message to your family, knowing they would pay in gold for my token.”

He took her arm, seemingly with gentleness, but Juliana could feel the secret bite of his strong fingers grasping her just above the elbow.

“You must have gotten the first one four years ago or more. Alexei, why did you wait so long to find me?” she asked.

Still he did not answer, did not stop walking until he reached the dais where the king waited.

Juliana could scarcely think for the confusion in her mind. Whirling, swirling thoughts, crystallizing and then disappearing like snowflakes on the water.

“My good and loyal ambassador from all the Russias,” Henry said expansively. “You don’t know how glad I am to receive you.” His speech was florid with diplomatic niceties; Juliana recognized the high flattery from her girlhood, when she and her brothers used to hide beneath the marble stairs at Novgorod and listen to their father and the other boyars.

The sudden memory of Boris and Misha made her eyes burn. She forced herself to listen to the conversation.

"Prince Ivan is a boy child, only eight years of age," Alexei was saying in his heavy, slow English. "His dear mother, the princess Elena, died earlier this year. But one day he will be strong. A prince for all the Russias. My father is his chief adviser."

The Shuiskys used to be a minor family. How had they risen to such power in just five years? Suspicions crowded into Juliana's mind.

"Your reunion with Lady Juliana is a most happy occasion," the king said, and with the relish of a gifted bard, he told the court a tale of young lovers torn asunder by tragedy, separated by leagues and years, and finally and joyfully reunited in the presence of a powerful and benevolent king.

Except I feel no joy, she thought.

"Lord Privy Seal assures me your marriage is bound to form a matchless dynasty," the king concluded.

"Marriage!" The word burst on a wave of

disbelief from Juliana. "But —"

"I assure you, the wishes of your father, the great boyar Gregor Romanov, will be honored at last."

"But —"

"And in the interest of cementing our new trade agreements with the Russias," Henry blithely continued, "the nuptials will take place here at my court, with full honors."

Juliana could not believe her ears. Nausea pushed bile up to the back of her throat. If Alexei had not been holding her arm in a death grip, she would have slid to the floor. Vaguely she became aware of a commotion behind her: a voice raised in harsh protest, gasps of outrage, and finally the clink and whir of spurs as heavy footsteps strode toward the dais.

The king's face hardened until he looked like a graven image. "I did not hear you announced, Wimberleigh," he drawled in a bored voice.

Juliana wrenched free of Alexei and whirled to face Stephen. "Oliver," she whispered, sick with dread.

"Recovered," he said simply. With icy hatred in his eyes, he looked at her, then at Alexei and finally he bowed to the king.

"Forgive me, sire," he said in a voice that was anything but apologetic. "I've come to fetch my wife."

"Wife," Alexei said in Russian, speaking through clenched teeth. "What is the meaning of this?"

"Excellent timing," Henry said, seeming to find a perverse satisfaction in the situation. "We were just discussing your predicament, Wimberleigh. It seems Lady Juliana has been betrothed to Lord Alexei for many years."

An ironic smile curved Stephen's mouth. "Most interesting. But surely the betrothal ended when, at your royal edict, the lady wedded me."

Outside, the winter wind shrieked through the courtyard. Juliana looked from her husband to the man her father had chosen for her so long ago. Stephen's tawny good looks, enhanced by redness from the cold, contrasted sharply with Alexei's dark, lean handsomeness. Like day and night they were, one golden, one dark, both pinning her where she stood with their fierce, possessive stares.

"A marriage entered into so blithely is easily ended." Henry drummed his fingers on his chest. "Now. Will it be an annulment, or divorce?"

"Neither," Stephen snapped. "We were wed in the eyes of the state and the church and —" He stopped himself. Juliana knew he was remembering their gypsy wedding. "The union is as strong and inviolable as a bond of blood." His hand, clad in a rough leather gauntlet, tightened around her wrist.

King Henry's grin was deceptively casual. "Are you saying, my dear lord of Wimberleigh, that I lack the authority to declare a marriage null and void?"

The silence was heavy and filled with the words the king did not need to say. He had defied the pope in order to dissolve a twenty-year marriage to Catherine of Aragon. A man who could fly in the face of hundreds of years of tradition need not justify himself to a minor noble.

Henry gave his stomach a satisfied pat and beamed at Alexei. "He who has been wronged shall find restitution in our court. You may marry Lady Juliana as soon as arrangements are made."

Stephen lunged toward the dais. "Your Grace, I —"

The razor tip of a blade at his throat stopped him cold. A woman screamed and fainted in a rustle of skirts. Juliana felt the color drain from her face.

Stephen did not flinch as a filament of blood scored his neck. For a moment, no one even breathed.

Then, with frosty calm, Stephen placed one gloved thumb on the wickedly curved tip of the blade, moved it aside, and stared impassively at Alexei. Juliana recognized the fire in Stephen's eyes. He was spoiling for a fight.

"By God's body, that was rude of you, sir," he said.

Alexei's nostrils flared. "In my country, one does not challenge one's sovereign."

Stephen's smile was as thin as a sickle. "Nor do we in England. However." Without taking his eyes off Alexei, he bit down on his middle finger and tugged at his glove. "We do," he said, removing the glove one finger at a time, "challenge foreign, wife-stealing upstarts."

The gauntlet sailed through the air and struck Alexei on the chest, right atop the garnet buttons. Then the glove hit the floor with a gentle slap.

Alexei's eyes blazed with rage. He lifted his booted foot and ground his heel down on the gauntlet. "You are a fool, my lord."

"Do I take that as an acceptance?"

"Immediately."

"No!" Juliana snapped, covering her fear with anger. "My fate will not be decided by fools on the field of combat." She felt someone — a gentleman pensioner — grasp her arm to hold her back.

The king lifted his hand. "Peace, madam. Let us have done with the sport."

With a regal wave, he set the game in motion. Courtiers fled to the inner courtyard where the swordplay would take place. Manly cheers went up from Alexei's entourage.

Juliana wrenched away from the pensioner and latched onto Stephen's arm. "Do not do this," she whispered. A shiver of foreboding caused her fingers to tremble. For no good reason save the sick foreboding in her heart, she did not trust Alexei.

Stephen stared at her for a long moment. Something flickered in his stone-blue eyes. Confusion. Pain. Yearning. He had all but cast her bodily out of his life and yet —

"Don't worry, madam," he said crisply, his face expressionless. "I might humiliate your precious Alexei, but I won't kill him. If I did that," he muttered, striding away, "I might have to keep you."

The short days of deep winter reminded Laszlo of the old country, when the sun would hide after only a few hours of daylight. The waning light, combined with Russian voices in the tavern, peeled away the years.

Fixing a genial smile on his face and eyeing his drinking companions with secret scorn, Laszlo went to work. He was barred from the palace by gypsy-hating officials, so carousing with Alexei Shuisky's entourage was the only way he could keep watch over Juliana.

And what easy Gajo louts they were, surrendering information with the eagerness of overaged brides on their wedding night.

Over the first round of ale, Laszlo learned that the four members of Alexei Shuisky's entourage had been members of a forced labor party on a Baltic trading ship.

"What kind of man lets another man force him to work?" Laszlo mumbled into his cup as he drained it.

He had his answer by the third round of ale, and the answer made him nervous. Feigning admiration, he grinned through his beard. "Convicts, you say? Convicted of what, gentlemen?"

The Russians laughed and nudged each other.

Laszlo called for more ale. "Ah, I am just a stupid gypsy. It is beyond my grasp why a great ambassador should surround himself with convicts."

His companions' laugher crescendoed. "Stupid as an Englishman, is he not, Dmitri?" one of them said. "Lord Alexei has everyone from the king down believing he's the ambassador."

Though Laszlo's every instinct told him to flee, he forced himself to paste on an idiotic grin. "You mean Alexei Shuisky is not the ambassador from Muscovy?"

Dmitri picked up the flagon and peered, disappointed, into the emptiness. "Dead," he muttered. "Didn't even reach the gates of the Kremlin."

As the laughter of murderers rang to the timbers, Laszlo told them he needed to piss, and excused himself from the table.

Striking steel clanged and echoed in the snow-covered courtyard. Juliana stood watching with her hands pressed protectively against her middle. She ignored the activity around her: men tossing back cups of hot wine, courtiers placing bets on the outcome of the duel. She was only vaguely aware of a commotion at the gate between the inner and outer yards.

Her rapt attention was fixed on the two men who were trying to kill each other. With all her might, she tried to summon the fierce gypsy she had become during the five years of hardship. Juliana of the gypsies would have flung herself between them, screamed at them to stop. But she was different now. Nauseated, light-headed, confused. Her spirit seemed made of thin crystal sheltering the tiny life inside her. She felt that if she moved, she would shatter into pieces.

"You stupid, stupid fools," she whispered, her breath puffing in the icy air.

The combatants were both winded and panting. Alexei wielded his rapier in one hand and a short stabbing dagger in the other. He fought with the cool, taut skill of a seasoned warrior. Stephen used his sword and poniard with equal skill but a good deal more passion. He took risks, lunging recklessly and feinting back only inches from the Russian's razor-sharp blade.

The king called for refreshments and remarked expansively on the skill of the fighting men. Laughing with glee, he sat in the royal litter, a snow king with a red face and a hunger for blood sport.

Juliana wished Laszlo were here or at least near. She stood alone and shivering, apart from the loud-mouthed nobles. When the daylight waned, bearers brought torches and set them in sconces along the walls. The orange glow gave the snow-clad yard a look of eerie familiarity.

And that, more than anything, caused fear to rise in her chest. She moaned softly and swayed. The day had been long and eventful. She was pregnant. She was tired.

Stephen and Alexei were killing each other.

She could not forget the look on Stephen's face when she had touched him. It was clear to her that he believed she had fled to meet Alexei.

She flinched as the Russian's blade lopped off Stephen's sleeve. With his left leg boldly leading, Stephen slashed back. Alexei's dagger stabbed at the basket hilt of his opponent's sword.

She started forward, but a strong hand held her back. She turned to see Jonathan Youngblood, who looked grim and travel weary. "He's holding his own," said Jonathan. "Don't humiliate him any more than you already have."

"I? Humiliate Stephen de Lacey?"

"You intercepted a royal summons and came racing to court to be with your Russian lover. In the eyes of most, that is something of an embarrassment."

"I had no idca Alexei would be here," she protested. "I'd had no contact with him in five years. He —"

"By God's body!" Jonathan scowled at the distant, towering gatehouse. "That's Kit coming in the gate."

For a moment Juliana looked away from the swordsmen. An amazing sight greeted her.

Good God in heaven, they had all come. They resembled a troupe of traveling players, some in gypsy wagons, others on horseback. She saw Kit riding in the lead like a captain of the vanguard with Pavlo running at the stirrup. Then came Rodion on horseback with Jillie on pillion behind him, and even from a distance Juliana could see her bossy maid giving directions, pointing ahead while her mouth worked ceaselessly.

In the wagon Dame Kristine and Nance Harbutt sat beside William Stumpe. And between them sat a small, pale-haired Oliver.

Oh, no, she thought, her worst fears hardening in her gut. *Please God, no. This will kill him.*

"A pox on my son," Jonathan muttered. "I told him to stay in Wiltshire."

A grunt of surprise diverted her attention. She looked at the duelists in time to see Alexei recovering from a lunge. His smile was a cruel red slash in his beard.

Stephen wore a look of shock and agony. The entire side of his face ran red with blood.

With a sob, Juliana surged forward once

again. And once again, Jonathan grabbed her. " 'Tis not so bad as it looks. Head wounds, even shallow ones, bleed copiously."

"Do not be ridiculous. He must yield to Alexei."

Jonathan gave her a little shake. "Damn it, woman, what will it take to make you understand?"

"Understand what?"

"He'll die before he yields."

She pressed her fist to her mouth and inhaled deeply. The smells of burning pitch and new-fallen snow wafted on the frosty air. She forced herself to watch. The combatants circled each other. Stephen's cold eyes tracked his opponent with pinpoint sharpness, and she knew he was looking for the slightest hole in Alexei's defense. Stephen sighted down his rapier, readying himself for a lunge. Alexei put up his own blade in defense while his gauntleted left hand hung low, beckoning. Taunting.

Stephen thrust with the swiftness of a lashing whip. Alexei's blade came up and parried the blow. Stephen was already in retreat, backing toward the makeshift pavilion where the king and his court sat enraptured.

Alexei followed, his rapier whipping little

rings in the air.

"Aye, come for me, you rank Russian pestilence," Stephen said through his teeth, his gaze never leaving the circling blade. "I make a big target, and you can see I already bleed."

"In my country," Alexei said, "there is no dishonor in conceding the battle at first blood." His sword thrust in and out like a bolt of lightning, but Stephen eluded it, backing toward the towering wall.

"This is about a woman," Alexei said. "Truly, my lord, is she worth dying for?"

The bald question caused the merest crack in Stephen's defense. In the blink of an eye, Alexei had him plastered against the wall, the deadly point of his rapier tickling Stephen's throat.

Stephen froze. So did the crowd. The only sounds were the shallow rasp of his breathing and the distant jangle of harness as the party from Lynacre approached.

"Yield or die!" Alexei shouted.

Stephen's mouth curved into a smile. Then his booted foot came up and out, thudding against Alexei's chest.

Alexei stumbled back, then recovered into a defensive stance. But he had changed the terms of the battle. He had meddled with the alchemy of Stephen's emotions and set loose a volatile mixture of passion, rage and injured pride.

Stephen's blade slashed in wide, relentless strokes. Back and back went Alexei, displaying real fear for the first time. His dark eyes showed white around the centers as he struggled to meet every slash and thrust.

Stephen was like an animal toying with its prey, opening a wound in Alexei's left arm, his right shoulder, his thigh. It happened so fast that Juliana saw the bleeding rather than the blow.

Her husband was like a man wielding a scythe, hacking with unceasing rhythmical blows as Alexei grew more and more disoriented.

Juliana's mind played one of its tricks again. Stephen and Alexei were both raining blood upon the snow. In the torchlight their shadows loomed huge and menacing as demons. She was back in Novgorod again, under a snow-draped bush while soldiers butchered her family. She put her hands to her mouth to stifle a moan.

A clattering sound broke the spell. Alexei's sword went skittering across the snow-crusted courtyard and came to rest against a flight of squat stone steps.

Stephen drew back his blade for the coup de grace.

"No!" Juliana heard herself scream. "I beg you, Stephen, do not kill him!" She was not sure why she begged for mercy for Alexei. Perhaps because she knew the act of vengeance would make a murderer of Stephen and haunt him for the rest of his days.

He lowered his blade. "I suppose," he said calmly, between panting breaths, "we should have asked the lady to settle this in the first place. 'Twould have spared us a heap of trouble."

Alexei sank, bleeding and groaning, to the ground. Juliana started toward Stephen. The mother-sickness threatened to drive her to her knees, but she stumbled forward. She wanted to explain. She had so much to tell him that the words crowded into her throat.

And then, before she reached him, the nightmare came to vivid, terrifying life.

It was heralded by the furious bark of a dog.

Alexei dove to reclaim his weapon. Like a creature possessed, he sprang forth out of the snow and shadows, shouting, *"Be damned to hell!"*

Suddenly Juliana *knew.* It was the same voice she had heard all those years ago. The same words.

The present became a mirror of the past: bloodred fire on new-fallen snow. The flashing sword slicing the air with a high-pitched whine.

A hoarsely shouted curse. A deadly blade going down and down . . .

Stephen must have heard Juliana's formless cry of horror.

He spun around, but he was too late. Alexei's blade drove closer and closer. A canine snarl broke the moment. A streak of ivory lightning lashed at Alexei, knocking him sideways and pinning him to the icy ground.

The world had gone crazy. And yet everything made perfect, terrible sense. Juliana felt faint, struck down by shock and rage and memory.

Seventeen

Stephen paced like a sentry in the passageway outside his wife's chamber door. Evening had slipped into night, when Hampton Court became a maze of cramped, torchlit corridors and draughty halls.

"Damnation, Jonathan!" He winced as the cut on his face pulled taut. "What can be taking so long?"

"Woman things. Do not try to fathom them. They are a danger to a man's sanity."

Stephen pounded his fist on the smooth stone wall. He was sore in every bone and muscle from the sword-fight. "She dropped like a felled sapling. She was like a corpse when they carried her off. It's been hours."

"She swooned, Stephen. Now, to you and me that is a foreign notion, but women do it all the time. Doubtless she was overcome by the sight of her beloved in peril."

"Alexei Shuisky was never in peril," Stephen snapped. "That dog wouldn't have killed him."

"I wasn't speaking of the Russian," Jonathan said, slapping his ample girth. "I meant you, good brother."

A foolish leap of hope surged in Stephen. Ruthlessly he beat it back. "I am no witling. She fled Lynacre because the king sent word that the Russian had come for her."

"Are you certain that's why she left?"

Pained remembrances of their quarrel ached in him. He had all but driven her away.

Nance appeared and bobbed a curtsy. "Has she awakened, my lord?"

Stephen shook his head. "Dame Kristine is with her still. How fares my son?"

"Well, my lord. He is already fast friends with tiny Prince Edward. They are both asleep in the royal nursery."

Stephen had been shocked by the appearance of Oliver at Hampton Court. Come the morrow, he would thrash the brat within an inch of his life. No, he would not. He would hug the boy and try to find a way to explain why Juliana would never come back to Lynacre.

"I wonder what the king has to say about the duel," Jonathan said.

Nance poked a finger under her wimple

and scratched her head. " 'Twas a curious thing, my lord. His Majesty called a privy meeting, he did." She shrugged. "The ways of princes be a great confounding bother to my brain, but even such as myself knows —"

"She sleeps," Dame Kristine whispered, coming out of the chamber. "She came around just for a moment or two. Spoke in that foreign tongue of hers. Something about the Russian prince."

"Alexei Shuisky." Stephen tasted the bitterness of his rival's name. "I shan't disturb her. I just want to sit with her awhile." He turned to Nance. "Go to the nursery and watch over Oliver. If he so much as coughs, come and fetch me."

He stepped into the darkened room and closed the door behind him. The only illumination came from the glow of embers in a brazier beside the bed. Crossing to the window, he opened the shutters, letting in a stream of indigo winter moonlight.

He saw, with a tingling of dread, a vigil stool beside the bedstead. Such a stool had been his constant perch while he had watched Meg bleed to death after the birth of Oliver.

He set the stool aside and parted the bed-curtains.

The moonlight fell slantwise across the sleeping form of Juliana. The bluish quality of the light gave her face a fairy glow that pierced his heart with tenderness.

God's teeth, he loved her.

The stark certainty of it filled him with a terrible joy. He had vowed never to love again, never to lay his heart open to agony. Never to make himself vulnerable to the emotional vagaries of another.

And yet in just a few short months, Juliana had made him fall in love twice: with his son, and with her.

That love had crystallized into a sense of purpose he had thought lost to him forever. He stood looking at her, with her skin as pale and smooth as cream, bruised shadows under her eyes, her hair a halo of dark silk spreading out over the pillow.

She had come like a whirlwind into his life, stripping away his defenses with more precision than a gifted swordsman. From the first moment he had seen her — a grubby, beloused horse thief — a part of him had somehow understood that their destinies were inevitably entwined.

And now he stood to lose her.

"No." He spoke the vow aloud to the silence. He would beg her on his knees if need be. Generations of stern de Lacey

pride flew out the window. His life was empty without Juliana.

The thought ran through his head as he banked the embers in the brazier and then stretched out on the bed beside her. To his shameless gratification she turned to him and snuggled close.

"Aye, beloved, you belong here, right here in my arms," he whispered in a stranger's voice. "And when you awaken, that is the first thing I shall say to you."

"I love you."

The words came to Juliana from out of a dream. She smiled in her sleep and curled closer to the warm, long-bodied man in the bed beside her. She inhaled his scent of fresh air and leather and the faint hint of wood-smoke that clung to his hair. A stray lace from his shirt tickled her cheek.

She brushed it away and came awake to complete amazement. "Stephen!"

His warm lips pressed against her temple. "I didn't mean to wake you."

She raised herself on one elbow and blinked at the darkness. He loomed very close, an inky shadow against the curtain enclosing the bed. He angled his head toward her, and the sleepy glow of moonlight glinted in his eyes.

"What are you doing here?" she asked.

His shoulders went rigid. "I had to make certain you were well. Are you?"

"Yes. I had not eaten all day, and the winter air made me light-headed. I am fine now." The half-truth burned in her throat. She was quick with a babe he did not want. And somewhere in the palace slept the murderer of her family.

She nearly confessed all to Stephen — about the baby, about Alexei. But now she knew the value of caution and the imprudence of Stephen's temper. If she told him that Alexei had murdered her family, Stephen would challenge the Russian again. And this time Alexei might prevail.

The thought of losing Stephen made her shiver. It was her fight, her revenge. Hers alone.

"Cold?" he asked. Without waiting for an answer, he parted the curtains and dragged the brazier on its brass stand closer to the bed. He stared at her for a long moment, then seemed to come to some decision.

In one swift movement, he pulled off his shirt. Juliana tried not to look at him, tried not to see the beloved lines of his profile, tried not to feel the love rise inside her. Her contentment with Stephen must wait until she had confronted Alexei and brought him to justice.

Stephen turned to her and cradled her face in his hands. "How beautiful you look in the moonlight," he whispered. His thumb caressed her cheek and then her lower lip, slipping inside to touch the moistness there. "Juliana, I do love you."

She was unprepared for the blaze of joy that swept over her, leaving her breathless. Until this moment, she hadn't realized how badly she had needed him to love her. Certain he would know she was hiding something, she sat up and turned away. "I thought I'd dreamed hearing you say that," she heard herself whisper.

" 'Twas no dream." He moved close to her from behind, lifted the hair away from the nape of her neck, and traced his tongue over her sensitive skin. A hot tingle of pleasure shimmered up her spine.

"Stephen?" Her voice held a low thrum of yearning.

"Do you want me to stop, love?" He loosened her chemise and bared her back inch by inch, his lips following in the wake of the wispy fabric. "If you're still feeling unwell, I'll stop."

"No, I feel fine," she said hastily, greedy for him.

His hands cradled her breasts, gently

caressing, bringing her to a state of mindless passion.

"I want . . . I . . ."

"Yes?" The chemise pooled at her waist, and he turned her, placing his mouth where his hands had been. "Say it, sweetheart."

Her desire for him was one thing she could not hide. "I want you."

As soft and startling as the beat of a moth's wings, his lips moved lower, awakening every inch of her flesh, parting her legs for a kiss so intimate that she was certain she was close to dying. Her response was swift and blinding, a profound splintering sensation followed by a breathless moment of oblivion. In a half-dazed state she drew him up and embraced him fiercely until they were fully and deeply joined.

His climax was as lightning-sharp as hers had been, and she loved him for the honest wonder she saw in his face when he cried out her name. For all of his carnal accomplishments, he still seemed to find something new and shining and delightful about making love to her.

Like the calm after a storm, passion subsided and they lay replete in each other's arms. Stephen drew the thick layers of blankets over them and pressed her cheek to his chest. "Sleep, Juliana," he whispered, his voice thick with slumber. "On the morrow we'll speak of . . . everything."

She knew he meant Alexei, and that thought kept her awake long after he had drifted into contented sleep.

When she felt certain he was deeply asleep, she slipped from the bed, dressed in the dark, and extracted Stephen's sword from its sheath. Before leaving, she paused to look at him, his face relaxed and unbearably appealing in the pale moonlight. He said that he loved her.

She clasped the thought close to her heart as she went alone, into the night, to confront the demon of her past.

"Bloody hell!" Stephen sat up in the big draped bedstead. He had awakened to empty arms and an empty bed.

Where in God's name had Juliana gone?

He ripped back the covers and sat on the edge of the bed, blinking at the early dawn light and shoving his feet into his boots.

A skin of ice had formed on the surface of the water in the basin. Without a moment's hesitation, he cracked the ice and scooped frigid water over his face.

Swearing, he came up for air and dried his face on his sleeve. As he dressed hastily, memories of the previous night came pouring back. How sweet she had been, coaxing forth a tenderness he had not known he possessed, assuring him that falling in love was not the disaster he'd always thought it.

And then panic took hold. Where was she? Had she had second thoughts? No, he trusted her love now.

But something was amiss.

He jerked open the door and pounded through the passageway, swinging down a coiled stairwell and along a cloistered walkway to the royal lodgings. Vaguely he heard house wardens challenging him, but he raced past, not stopping until he reached the antechamber to the king's privy apartment.

He was about to yank open the heavy door when a black-clad figure appeared at his side.

"Looking for your wife, Wimberleigh?" asked Thomas Cromwell.

Infuriated by Lord Privy Seal's smugness, Stephen demanded, "Where is she? Damn it, Thomas —"

"Gone."

Stephen's heart skipped a beat. "Gone where?"

"Fled to the coast, most likely. With her Russian lover."

■ ■ ■ ■

She was their prisoner.

"Alexei, you have no honor," Juliana said, covering her fear with bravado.

"Shut up," he said over his shoulder. He bent lower over the horse's neck and jammed in the spurs.

Juliana tried to twist her wrists free of the cord that bound them, but the sudden increased speed of the horse jolted her against Alexei's back. By craning her neck she could see his retainers — three dark, silent riders behind and two in the vanguard.

Hatred seared her heart. This man had butchered her family in cold blood. His act of inhuman cruelty had driven her from her home, forced her to cross treacherous miles and churning seas to live in poverty amid gypsies.

And she had trusted him. She had grieved for him.

Seeking refuge from her despair, she remembered her moments with Stephen. He had taken her in his arms and said he loved her. His ardor had filled her with a boundless, breathless joy.

Why, in God's name, had she thought

winning his love would not be enough?

She should have told Stephen what she knew — that Alexei was the man in her nightmare. Instead, she had refused to relinquish her blood vow and had taken matters into her own hands. Wrapped in a cloak fastened with her brooch, the rage of revenge burning high in her heart, she had burst into Alexei's quarters.

And fallen right into his trap.

She would never forget the look of supreme satisfaction on his face. "I have been waiting for you," he said, snatching the sword from her grasp. "Your Romanov pride has delivered you right into my hands."

A staccato command from Alexei had roused his lackeys from their slumber in the antechamber. In seconds she had been bound, gagged, and dragged to the riverfront. They bore her away in a swift wherry that cut through the chunks of ice in the Thames.

That had been hours earlier. They had gone to a remote riverside wood where horses were waiting, and now they were heading eastward, into the rising sun, to a destination Alexei would not disclose.

What was his purpose? She clawed at the twine that bound her wrists; her skin had already been rubbed raw from chafing. She squirmed in the saddle, provoking a bark of anger from Alexei.

"In the Lord's name, be still, you little hellcat," he commanded.

"Then stop," she said, knowing every minute took her farther away from Stephen. "I need to rest."

He muttered a curse and called out to his men. They took a high path that led up and away from the banks of the Thames and into a Kentish forest. By using her foot, she managed to snag the hem of her cloak on scrubby bushes here and there, hoping the gypsies, at least, would recognize the signs of her passing.

They stopped in a clearing surrounded by winter-bare trees with skeletal branches clawing at the bleak sky. There, four more Russians awaited, and they had a hurried conference about a cog that awaited the tide at Gravesend.

For the first time, Juliana faced the truth. She would either die or be spirited back to Muscovy with a group of assassins.

"We shall be at sea within the hour." Alexei's quiet, sly voice sounded in her ear as he helped her dismount.

She spun around, her nerves and her temper out of control. "I want to know why, Alexei. Why! Why did you murder my family and burn my home?"

He lifted an eyebrow in surprise.

"For years I thought you had perished while defending my family," she said, so filled with hate that she could barely speak. "But that is not what happened at all, is it?"

"What does it matter what happened so long ago?"

"You came to my father's house, ate at his table, slept under his roof, claimed his daughter's hand, all to cover your evil purpose. How long did you search for me that night?"

"Not long enough." Dry laughter rustled in his throat. "Your father was a fool. On his deathbed, Prince Vasily sought to strip the nobles of their rights. Us! His boyars, who fought his wars for him —"

"And took your share of the booty," she retorted. "My father knew that once Vasily was dead, you would beggar the peasants and turn the farmers off their lands."

"He should have known better than to align himself with a dying prince whose sole legacy was that puling infant, Ivan, and Ivan's half-witted brother, Yuri."

Prince Ivan. The lad was not nearly old enough to rule, only to be used as a puppet of the grasping nobles.

"Why did you come all this way?"

"When I learned you had proven your identity to the king of England, I knew I had to . . . find you." He brushed his lips over her cheek. "I could love you, Juliana. You've a fire in you, a sense of pride. You would be an ornament to my family."

She felt a wave of nausea rise from deep in her belly. He was mad to think she would ever accept him, ever sleep with the man who had murdered her family. "What became of my father's estate?" she forced herself to ask.

He shrugged. "Fallen into a derelict state. A fitting tomb for your father, no?"

It took all her willpower not to lunge at him. She hated him, aye, enough to kill him, but not now. Not with his vigilant men standing sentinel nearby.

"They were not shriven and buried?" she asked.

"They died like pigs and lay as fodder for wolves and carrion birds."

"You treacherous corruption," she said in a deadly voice. "*You* are the carrion bird. A coward, striking at night, slaughtering women and children and feeding on their defenseless flesh. You make me sick."

He struck with the swiftness of an able killer, his leather-gloved hand cracking against her face. At first she felt only numbness. Then pain drove away the chill and spread across her cheek. She tasted blood in her mouth.

As quickly as he had struck her, he recovered and spoke almost placatingly. "Forgive me. I want to love you, Juliana, but you must obey me. Do not lament the estate. After we're married, we'll restore it, keep it as a summer retreat."

"Married!" A light-headed feeling overcame her. She swayed, then backed against the rough trunk of a linden tree to steady herself. "I have been wed at the king's command to an English nobleman."

Alexei sent her a silky smile. "Who is to say you're not widowed by now?"

She absorbed his statement like a physical blow. Could it be? Could he or his men have murdered Stephen while he slept?

No, she told herself firmly. If Stephen were dead, she would surely sense the loss. He was that much a part of her now, the keeper of her heart, the guardian of her dreams. They had been enemies at first, but gradually she had found her way into his empty life. They had been helpmeets equally concerned with the estate. They had been parents, anxious about Oliver and fiercely proud of his accomplishments. And they had been lovers in the fullest sense of the word, sharing the secrets of their souls as well as the pleasures of their bodies — and finally, they shared the ultimate bond.

The babe that grew inside her.

"You lie. And I love Stephen de Lacey."

A wolfish smile slashed his beard. "Love is an English malady that strikes the faint at heart."

"One of the greatest acts of courage Stephen ever committed was to love me."

Alexei spat on the ground. "In Russia a man knows better than to put his stock in sentiment." Snakelike, his arm shot out and he fingered a lock of her hair. "Like sable, it is. And until we are joined, I want you to wear it as you do now. Unbound, like a virgin's."

"If you seek to wed a virgin," she said, "you had best look elsewhere."

His hand, still entangled in her hair, clenched into a fist. "It is a pity that the English swine claimed you. But once we are back in Muscovy, it will be as if this had never happened. We will be betrothed and wed as our parents intended."

"Not quite," she whispered, her bound hands straying low to press her gently rounding belly. "I carry a reminder."

He gave his hand a jerk, snapping her head back and forcing her to look at him.

"You had best be lying, my little whore. I will not play father to any Englishman's get. I'll beat it out of you —"

"You wouldn't dare!"

"If you're with child, then I cannot marry you."

Before she could release a breath of relief, he added, "If you're with child, I'll have to kill you."

"You've not been invited into our presence, Wimberleigh," the king said in a bland voice. He studied his fingernails with rapt attention. His half-eaten breakfast lay on a salver on the massive table and he sat in a box chair, his swollen leg propped on a tuffet.

Stephen did not flinch at the censure. He gave the most cursory of bows and reached to remove his hat, only to find that he had forgotten it in his haste. The gentlemen of the bedchamber moved discreetly about their morning duties, readying the king's toilette and his raiments for the day.

Stephen was not surprised to see Algernon among the men. His wagging tongue had finally won him a place of privilege in the royal household. Apparently he cared not that he had destroyed Stephen's marriage in the process.

"I came to beg leave to depart," Stephen said to the king.

Interest flashed in Henry's black currant eyes. "Did the Russian displace you so easily, then?"

Algernon, who had been pouring small ale from a ewer, dropped the cup. The pewter vessel thunked into the rushes and rolled bumpily to a stop at Stephen's feet.

"Your pardon," Algernon murmured, stooping to retrieve the vessel. As he rose, he whispered, "Stephen, I must speak with you."

"Good God, Havelock!" Henry said. "Have I engaged a fool? I thought Will Somers served that function. Now, Wimberleigh, where were we? Ah. Your wife has decamped with our dear ambassador from Muscovy. A pity he left in such haste. I had such tantalizing trade agreements in mind."

"Your Majesty!" Algernon interrupted the king and bravely awaited the royal wrath. "There is something you should know about the man who presented himself to you as the Russian ambassador."

Stephen came instantly alert. Nothing short of mortal danger would compel Algernon to risk the king's displeasure.

"That will be all, Havelock." Thomas Cromwell hastened across the room, a black-winged figure with an ominous scowl. "You may seek your own chambers now."

"That *will* be all," Algernon said, his curls bobbing like a lion's mane. "You said you'd tell Stephen the news brought by the gypsy Laszlo."

"What news?" Stephen demanded. "Where is Laszlo?"

Cromwell glared at Algernon. "My lord, if you value your position, you will keep silent."

"If my position is at your side, Thomas Cromwell," Algernon said, "then I value it not at all."

A discreet jerk of Lord Privy Seal's head brought forth a pair of men-at-arms.

Stephen planted himself in their way. "Havelock has something to say. Let him speak."

The guards looked at the king. Henry merely steepled his fingers and watched with sharp interest.

"Stephen," Algernon said, "I have been a party to the worst sort of treachery —"

"You sniveling little varlet." Cromwell beckoned to the men-at-arms. "Take him away!"

"Sire, I beg you, hear me out," Algernon shouted over his shoulder. "Thomas Cromwell swore he would tell Stephen the news from Laszlo, but he has not, he —"

His captors shoved the door open, and there stood Nance Harbutt, wringing her hands, her face soaked with tears.

"Good God, Nance, what's amiss?" Stephen asked as Algernon was dragged off.

" 'Tis your son, my lord." She raised her voice over Havelock's shouts. " 'Tis little Oliver."

Stephen froze. "Another attack?"

Her wimple flapping, Nance nodded vigorously. "I've never seen him like this. I fear this time he'll die. He —"

Stephen did not hear the rest. Borne by his worst nightmares, he raced to the nursery.

As he sat in the small bed, cradling his son in his arms, Stephen was hurled back across the years to the nightmare day when Dickon had died.

"Not again," he whispered, pressing kisses on Oliver's sweat-dampened hair. "Please God, don't do this to me again."

Oliver dragged in a breath of air. The spasms in his chest prevented him from expelling it. His desperate convulsions caused a raw pain deep inside Stephen. The agony smoldered and then took fire, burning his heart to ashes.

Please God, not again.

Oliver's hands clutched at Stephen's shirt. The lad's eyes were wide and glassy. "Jul . . . Jul . . ."

"She's not here, son." And with all his soul, Stephen wished that she were. Only one thing in the world could have held him back from going after her — Oliver.

Stephen felt torn to shreds by indecision. He needed her. Oliver needed her. She had the most magical, calming effect on the lad. Her presence and her touch seemed to soothe him. When all the medical wisdom in England had failed to control Oliver's attacks, she had managed to increase his strength, to give him confidence, to make him part of a world he had once only watched from his window.

She had taught Stephen to love again. Had taught him that to retreat, to build walls to shield his heart, was the way of a coward. She had given him back his son.

"Want Jul . . ." Oliver wheezed.

"Son, she had to go away." The words tasted like bile on his tongue.

"You go!" The shout nearly sapped the lad of his strength. He lay still, ghost pale, his white-gold hair framing his colorless face like a halo.

No.

Oliver's body shuddered like a kettle releasing steam.

"My lord, I think you should fetch her," Nance said solemnly. "I've seen the way it is with her and the lad. She calms him."

"Damn it, Nance, I cannot leave him in this state."

"What good will it do to hold him while he dies?" Nance said in a defiant whisper. "He needs her. She is his mother in all ways save the least important one."

"You've done all you can, my lord," said Dame Kristine. "My mother is right. You should fetch your wife."

Damn it, Stephen thought, why had she left? She had loved Oliver. How could she leave him?

"Wimberleigh." The king had entered the nursery and spoke quietly. "I order you — I command you — to go after your wife."

"Sire, I cannot —"

"Listen to His Majesty, Stephen." Algernon rushed into the room. His doublet had been torn open. His hat was missing, his curls mussed from his struggle with the guards.

"I decided to hear what Havelock had to say," Henry stated. He avoided looking at Oliver, as if he could not bear the sight of an ailing child. "You should hear it, too,

Wimberleigh."

Stephen stepped away from the bed, leaving Nance and Kristine to press cool cloths to Oliver's brow. "I'm listening."

"Alexei Shuisky is not the man sent from the court of Prince Ivan. The gypsy, Laszlo, found out the truth. He told me and Lord Privy Seal this morning. He speaks the Russian tongue, and over many cups of ale made friends with some of Alexei's retainers. Last night he coaxed the truth from these men. Alexei overtook the ambassador, murdered him and his escort and came here in his place."

A shiver twisted along Stephen's spine. "Why would he do that?"

Algernon's face lost all color save a sick bluish tinge around his lips. "Alexei Shuisky led the massacre of Juliana's family."

Henry stroked his beard. "I sensed something sly about Alexei right from the first. Lady Juliana's dog always seemed the most docile of creatures. Yet he hurled himself at Prince Alexei, did he not? They say dogs and horses never forget."

"Juliana is with him," Stephen whispered. "Juliana has ridden off with the man who murdered her family."

"I fear so," Algernon said.

Stephen swore between his teeth. He

glanced at the chamber door, then at his son who lay gasping on the low bed.

"My lord of Wimberleigh." The king spoke in a strangely gentle tone. "I am not proud of — all I have done to you."

Stephen's jaw nearly dropped. Henry, apologizing? And for what? For Meg, who in her ignorance had become his lover? For all the betrothals besmirched by his lust? For putting Juliana in the hands of a killer?

"I know you feel you must stay with your poor son," Henry went on. "But Lady Juliana needs you more."

If she still lives. Stephen failed to stop the thought from forming.

His mouth dry as ashes, he said, "Are you certain the charges against Alexei are true?"

"Why would he leave so furtively, and in such haste, if he were a man of honor?"

Nance fell with a thud to her knees and began praying in Latin and the vernacular as if unsure which the Lord would heed.

Stephen pictured Juliana spirited off by a man driven by hatred to find her. And then he looked at Oliver, barely breathing, the air a thin, strangled whine between his teeth.

Jesu, what if the poor lad died while he was away?

"Please," Oliver whispered between panting breaths. "Bring her back, Papa."

"The boy's fate is in God's hands," Henry said. "But the fate of your wife might yet be up to you."

Dame Kristine wiped her hands nervously on her apron. " 'Tis dangerous for her to go galloping off, and her in that condition."

"Condition?" Suppressing the tempest of emotion inside him, Stephen approached the young woman. "Condition?"

Dame Kristine nodded. "My lord, I thought you knew. Your wife is with child."

EIGHTEEN

And so it was that Stephen de Lacey, baron of Wimberleigh, found himself riding hard for the coast at the head of the most singular army in Christendom.

Jonathan Youngblood served as lieutenant, showing the bluff command and backbone he had exhibited in the Scots wars. His son Kit possessed both his father's unwavering loyalty and the fruits of Stephen's excellent training.

Behind them rode Algernon Basset, curls bouncing beneath a battered helm and wearing a breastplate with the air of a penitent in a hair shirt. In the wide leather baldric around his waist he carried a short-sword and a selection of daggers.

And all around them, in a formation no military tactician had ever imagined, ranged the gypsies and one notable addition: Jillie Egan.

Dark thoughts nipped at Stephen's mind

as he forged ahead at a merciless pace. He had left his son's bedside. He could only pray he had made the right choice in going after the mother Oliver had come to love.

Stephen cursed himself a hundred times for a fool. He had let Juliana slip through his fingers. Now she was a captive of the man who had murdered her family.

And she was carrying Stephen's child.

Blessed Savior, he had as good as told her he wanted no more children. Doubtless she had not dared to tell him.

With London twenty miles behind them, they reached a crossroads. Stephen drew up his mount and studied the lay of the land. To his left rose a rock-strewn path that led to a high point on the Kentish coast. To his right was a muddy track winding down toward the mouth of the Thames.

He jerked his head to the right. "We'll take that way."

"No." Laszlo trotted up on his nimble gypsy pony. "They went that way." Stephen frowned, and Laszlo sidled his mount over to the edge of the road. Leaning down, he scooped up a small bit of blue fabric. "She left signs along the way."

Gratitude welled up inside Stephen. "Bless you, Laszlo," he murmured, motioning for the company to follow him up the path.

The raspy blowing of the horses, the thump of hooves, and the creak of saddle leather filled the cold silence of the winter woods. With a twist of irony, Stephen thought of all the odd tools and devices he had invented over the years. There was no implement to help him now, only his wits and determination.

Juliana. Like an image from a dream, she filled his mind. Just as she had filled his life. She was beauty and grace and nobility personified.

And because of his own stubborn refusal to trust in his love for her, she was in mortal danger.

With his heart in despair, he guided his horse along the hoof-torn track and emerged upon a level ground where the path disappeared into a grove of trees.

He turned to look at Laszlo to ask if he had spotted any more signs. Before he could speak, a crossbow bolt whizzed out of the woods and thudded into a tree behind Laszlo, missing him by mere inches.

A foreign curse broke from the gypsy.

"Take cover," Stephen yelled at the others, and they fell back down the path. "Gentlemen."

Jillie cleared her throat.

"And my lady. I think we've found ourselves a fight."

"Kill Stephen de Lacey first," Alexei instructed his men. "The rest will scatter. I'll take the woman down to the shore, and from there we'll make for the harbor."

"Alexei," Juliana said, her hands once again tied helplessly around his waist. "I beg you, don't hurt my husband."

A bitter yelp of laughter broke from him. "A Romanov, begging? Perhaps there is hope for you yet, Juliana."

"You're a coward," she shouted. "You would steal a woman like a cossack and leave underlings to do your fighting."

Alexei twisted around in the saddle. "A regrettable thing to say, my dear. I have a long memory and a terrible temper." He addressed his lieutenant again. "Do as I say. Let no one follow us."

As he spurred the horse, Juliana cast a frantic glance back. What she saw astonished her. Stephen galloped forth on Capria, horse and rider showing vivid gold and silver in the winter-gray woods. In their wake rode Kit, Jonathan, Algernon, and the gypsy men. With her braids and wimple flying, Jillie brought up the rear.

Three men armed with crossbows took aim.

"No!" Juliana screamed, but her frantic cry was lost amid the whir of crossbow bolts and the thunder of hooves.

"Only three of them discharged their crossbows," Jonathan called out to Stephen. They stopped and pulled into a shelter created by a stand of trees.

"That leaves six who wait with their weapons loaded and ready." Stephen said. He took a deep breath, thanking God Juliana was alive. At the same time, panic seared him, for she rode with Alexei, the most dangerous of the lot.

"Who is with me?" he asked loudly. "These men are trained killers. No one will think ill of you if you turn back now."

Not even Algernon flinched, and for the first time, Stephen thought about forgiving him.

"What about the woman?" Laszlo cast a dubious glance at Jillie, flushed and steely-eyed on her pony, with naught save a hastily grabbed mucking rake for a weapon.

"I think you should wait for us here," Stephen said.

"So you said back at Hampton Court, yet here I am." She glared at him. "I think you should protect your own arse, my lord, else I'll tan it for you."

"Can't you control your woman?" he demanded of Rodion.

"No more than you can control yours," Rodion shot back.

Unwilling to waste more time arguing, Stephen guided his horse back toward the clearing. "Ride swiftly and stay low," he cautioned.

Almost immediately, one of the deadly bolts found living flesh. Stephen heard an equine squeal, saw a gypsy horse rear and rake the air with its hooves. A thick bolt protruded from the animal's flank. The rider, a dark Romany youth, vaulted from the saddle and landed as if it were a planned trick. The horse galloped off in pain-hazed fright.

An ominous whir sped past Stephen's head. Cold purpose froze out all fear for himself, and he merely bent lower, urging his horse faster.

In moments he was among them — nine fur-clad Russians with strange squared-off beards and the dispassionate authority of seasoned assassins.

Stephen heard the click of their gear as they put away their crossbows and drew steel.

He reined in, sensing rather than seeing the small company gather behind him. His eyes were fixed on the fleeing figure of a man and woman on horseback. All that stood between him and Juliana was this wall of cold-blooded killers.

"You are a fool," the leader said in rough English. "Only a craven fool would bring gypsies and women to a man's fight. We do not want to hurt you. We just want you to go home."

Stephen and Jonathan exchanged a glance. If the words were meant to persuade, they weren't working.

Not even on Algernon. Reaching into his baldric, he selected a short, pointed dagger.

The Russian's long blade flashed. "What will you do with that, pretty man?"

"This," said Algernon. His dagger sped through the air and embedded itself in the Russian's arm. The man screamed and dropped his reins. The horse reared, pouring the helpless victim backward onto the ground. He writhed and clutched at his arm.

Stephen quickly decided that Havelock had redeemed himself.

Algernon drew a second dagger. "Any more questions?"

The leader bellowed a command and surged forward. Stephen met him halfway. Guiding Capria with only his knees, he drew his sword.

Their blades clashed and sang as steel ran along steel. Stephen's arm quivered with the impact. From the corner of his eye he saw Rodion dismount and stalk another swordsman. Ducking beneath a swinging Russian blade, he grasped the man's wrist and dragged him to the ground. Jillie Egan brought her rake crashing down on the Russian's head.

Looking apprehensive and frighteningly youthful, Kit rode toward the left flank of the Russians. As a tribute to Stephen's training in the tilting yard, he struck with precise aim and timing, sending his opponent toppling.

With his sword still locked against his opponent's, Stephen saw Juliana and Alexei drop from sight down the other side of the hill.

"Go after her, Stephen," Jonathan yelled. "We'll take care of this lot."

Stephen aimed his mare into the ranks of Russians. He felt a rush of blood on one arm, felt the sting of a thrown dagger in his shoulder. The pain was nothing. Shouting Juliana's name like a battle cry, he broke through the fray and headed down the path toward the shore.

Juliana could feel the jeweled pommel of

Alexei's sword rubbing against her hands. Her fingers were nearly numb from the tight hemp binding.

Alexei's gelding was no match for Capria. In seconds Stephen rode abreast of them, his sword drawn, his golden hair sailing out behind him, and a look of stark fury on his face.

"For the love of God, I beg you to let her go," he called to Alexei. "Let this fight be between us."

In that instant, she felt the depth of Stephen's love, and her heart sang with bittersweet joy. She knew a moment of fierce, bright elation, and whatever happened now, no one could take that from her.

Alexei reached for his sword. Almost without thinking, Juliana moved her wrists. As the blade whined from its scabbard, she let it slice through the ropes that bound her. She felt a gush of red warmth, but she did not care. Her hands were free. She raised her fists to pummel Alexei's back.

"Treacherous bitch!" He swung out with his sword, and a yelp of triumph broke from him. His blow had broken Stephen's blade.

As Alexei wheeled his horse around to go in for the kill, Juliana reached down for a stirrup, hoping to unseat him. Alexei only laughed and spurred the gelding again. He raised his sword, aiming at Capria's vulnerable belly.

"You have always been a coward," Juliana said through her teeth. She plucked the dagger from her brooch. Time seemed to slow, and she saw again her family — her father's lifeblood seeping into the snow. Boris's chest exploding from a gunshot. Her mother's hair streaming in the wind as she screamed. Misha sobbing, begging for mercy, only to be silenced forever by a curved blade.

Juliana was a Romanov. She had lived for this moment.

She drew back the knife and prepared to plunge it into Alexei's back.

And hesitated. Could the taking of another life bring her family back? Could more bloodshed rid her of nightmares?

Stephen shouted something she did not understand. She brought the blade down just as Alexei hit her arm. The dagger plunged through the saddle blanket and pricked the gelding's hide.

Another shout from Stephen rent the air.

The horse reared. Though all her instincts urged her to hold fast to Alexei, Juliana forced herself to slide backward over the high back of the saddle, down over the rump of the pain-maddened horse. She knew this trick; she had performed it countless times for rapt audiences who tossed coins to the gypsies.

When she neared the ground, she leaped free, landing on her feet. She welcomed the damp, solid sand beneath her. She still held her dagger. With a shaking hand, she put it away.

Stephen shot her a look of astonishment. Alexei cursed, hauling on the reins. The bit sawed back and forth in the injured horse's mouth.

The gelding snapped its head back, and the sharp ridge of its neck caught Alexei full in the face. The panicked animal raced across the pebbled beach, barreling toward a mudflat. The brown mud sucked at the horse's hooves, halting its frantic flight.

The sudden stop hurled Alexei up and over the horse's head. End over end he flew, seemingly borne on the high winter wind. With a terrible cracking sound he struck the ground and lay still. Reins trailing in the surf, the horse ran off, kicking back with its hind legs and tossing its head.

Stephen leaped off Capria and raced to Juliana, pulling her into his arms.

"Ah, beloved." She could hear his breath coming in fast rasps. "Are you all right?"

She nodded against his chest. "And you?"

"A flesh wound, no more." He touched her bleeding wrist.

" 'Tis not deep. Alexei?" Her voice was muffled by his jerkin.

He swept her up into his arms, and she was glad of his strength, for her knees had suddenly gone weak.

Stephen walked slowly toward Alexei.

She forced herself to look at the figure on the ground.

Alexei Shuisky, the murderer, had died with his eyes wide open, a look of eternal disbelief on his face.

"His neck is broken," Stephen said.

She shuddered. "He is the one who killed my family."

"I know."

The waves raced up to lick at the sand. She lifted her face to his. "You knew?"

"Only since this morning. Laszlo found out."

She hugged his neck tighter. "I wanted him dead. Did I kill him, Stephen?"

He pressed a kiss to her temple. "He killed himself. The moment he led his men against your family, he slew whatever good might have been in him. He has been driving toward his destiny ever since."

" 'Destiny falls like a stone into still water,' " Juliana said, remembering Zara, and the soldiers, and the fire casting blood-red shadows on the snow. She had lost everything that night — her home, her family, all the things that made her a Romanov.

Yet the tears in her eyes when she looked up at Stephen burned with a welcome heat. She had traded her plans for revenge for something far more lasting and hopeful and bright. Out of the darkness had come this man, this love, this life.

Stephen was looking at her oddly. " 'Destiny falls . . . ?' "

A chill wind blew in from the sea. "Something I heard once, long ago. A gypsy prophecy. I am still not certain I understand, but I think, somehow, she knew. Zara knew."

Juliana glanced one last time at Alexei. "Yet I wonder if I ever had the power to stop it. If I had not drawn my knife, caused the horse to rear —"

"Then I would have killed him myself. Willingly." He turned and walked away from Alexei Shuisky. When they reached Capria, Stephen set Juliana gently on her feet and cradled her face between his hands.

"Juliana, you are my world. I told you so last night. Why did you leave me?"

"I did not want you to have to fight Alexei again." She touched his stubbled cheek and felt a surge of tenderness.

His shoulders trembled. "It's my fault. I gave you little reason to trust me. I can't blame you for telling me nothing of Alexei. Or of the baby."

She caught her breath in surprise and fear. "You know of that, too?"

"Aye. Ah, Juliana, would that I could take back my harsh words. A child is a gift from God to be cherished whether it be flawed or perfect. I will love our child as I have come to love Oliver — as you taught me to love him."

She heard the catch in his voice. "Stephen? Is Oliver well?"

"He had an attack. A bad one. He only seemed to improve when I promised to find you. He was calmer after that."

"We'd best go and see, then."

A faint shout drifted down from the bank above the shore. Juliana looked up. There, on the edge, stood Laszlo and Jonathan and their mismatched company of gypsies. All in a line, linked by the necks with rope, stood the defeated Russians.

The gypsy warriors raised their fists with a shout of triumph. Rodion drew Jillie into an ardent embrace.

Juliana smiled at her husband. "At last I think our adventures are over."

He kissed her, warming the chill salt air from her lips, and she felt the love crest inside her like a wave, breaking over her and showering her with an aching tenderness.

Stephen lifted his mouth from hers, and his hand stole inside her cloak to caress the place, where, warm within her, a new life grew.

"No, my love," he whispered, "they are just beginning."

Epilogue

Summer 1548

"God have mercy on us all, my lord, he's done it again!" Puffing with exertion, Nance Harbutt burst into the garden. Once hidden by a dark maze, the cottage and yard now lay wide open to the world.

"Who's done what?" With his firstborn daughter tugging at his hand and his youngest child riding high on his broad shoulders, Stephen walked toward Nance. He passed his twin sons, Simon and Sebastian, who were busy playing Muscovy Company with toy ships in the fishpond. Nine years earlier, King Henry had placed Stephen at the head of the trading venture.

The housekeeper flapped her apron vigorously to fan her flushed cheeks. "Got himself sent down from Cambridge again, he did, and brought that lot of outlaws home with him! Didn't I tell you, my lord, the lad was trouble? Delving and donging and —"

"Nance." Stephen bit back a smile.

"— swiving wenches like there's no tomorrow —"

"Nance."

She thrust up her chin, knocking her wimple askew. Natalya, who rode Stephen's shoulders, giggled.

"Aye, my lord?" the housekeeper asked.

"Mind your tongue around the girls."

She quivered with indignation. "I speak naught but the truth. Marry, my lord, what's the world coming to, with a puling boy on the throne and those Anabaptists mocking the sacraments? Why, no wonder your big lout of a son has no shred of moral —"

"Oliver!" Belinda, the elder daughter, squealed and sped down the lane toward a small train of lumbering caravans. Hard on her heels were Simon and Sebastian. Natalya squirmed her way down from Stephen's shoulders and joined her brothers and sister.

Scolding for all she was worth, Nance stalked after the herd of running children.

Stephen leaned against the basin of the fountain to wait. Some joyous, ineffable impulse caused him to look back at the cottage in time to see Juliana emerge with Laszlo. The aging gypsy man had given up the wandering life to settle in the snug house.

They were flanked by four elegant wind-hounds, all sired by Pavlo on a dam brought to England from one of the early voyages to Russia.

Juliana walked toward Stephen. Lush, heavy roses bloomed in the arbor that arched over the path, creating a frame for her silk-clad form. Bearing his children had thickened her waist, and he cherished every single extra inch.

"By God," he said, holding out his hand for her, "you do dim the beauty of roses, my love."

She smiled as he drew her to his side. The fountain burbled quietly into the fragrant stillness, and a warm wind rustled through the ivy that grew thick upon the whimsical topiary beasts Stephen had made so long ago for a boy who hid from the world.

The memory brought a sudden thickness to his throat. Now he watched Oliver, vast and golden as a young god, leap down from the gypsy wagon and greet his half brothers and sisters.

From the second wagon, the children of Jillie and Rodion poured like an army of ants and joined in the fray.

"What has your son done this time?" Juliana asked.

"*My* son?" Stephen glared at her with

mock indignation. "Why is he always *my* son when trouble arises?"

"Surely he gets his penchant for mischief from you."

"Indeed? I think it was the fact that he was raised by a gypsy horse thief who refused to bathe —"

"Until you gave me a dunking in the millstream," she reminded him.

He laughed and pressed his lips to her silky, sun-warmed hair. "We are both at fault. The boy's as spoiled as last year's cider."

But as they watched Oliver cavorting with the little ones on the dusty road, neither regretted indulging him. He had weathered a hellish sickness, and then, when he had begun to sprout his first beard, the attacks had almost ceased. Now only on the rarest of occasions did the illness plague him.

Juliana trailed her hand in the water. "You had best find out his latest offense and prescribe a suitable penance. I wonder what he did. I hope it doesn't involve the provost's wife this time."

"Or stealing the statuary in King's College."

"Or singing bawdy songs at chapel."

They both tried to summon anger, and they both failed. Oliver was on his hands and knees now, surrounded by squirming children and barking dogs.

"Ah, love," Stephen said, letting the music of his children's laughter fill his ears. "Perhaps he simply needs a good woman to tame him."

She smiled and shook her hand dry, then slid her arms around his neck. "Perhaps," she whispered. "It worked for you."

As he bent to kiss her, the wind swept a rain of petals down into the fountain, and he saw himself reflected there with his wife, a shimmering image lit by the sun glinting off clear water, the ever-widening ripples enclosing them in the circle of eternity.

AUTHOR'S NOTE

In Tudor times, asthma was a misunderstood and poorly defined disease, which accounts for the often brutal and almost universally ineffective treatments endured by sufferers such as the fictional Oliver.

The symptoms of asthma had, however, been successfully treated for millennia by the Chinese and by the ancient Romans with medicine made from the shrub called ephedra. Although the use of ephedra disappeared with the fall of Rome and was not rediscovered until the nineteenth century, the medicine was still common in the east.

Itinerant gypsies, their population flung from Kashmir to the British Isles, might have encountered the ephedra plant, called *mahuang* by the Chinese.

Ephedrine, derived from the shrub, is still used today in the treatment of asthma.

Dear Reader,

Something old is new again. I'm very proud to bring you a brand-new edition of the Tudor Rose trilogy, first published about fifteen years ago.

These books were researched and written when the information superhighway was a mere goat track. But the themes and story lines are timeless, exemplifying the things that have always been important to me, both as a reader and a writer: fiercely honest emotion, ordinary people experiencing extraordinary challenges, passion and adventure, and of course, a satisfying ending.

In addition to being revised, the books have been given a new lease on life with fresh titles. Book One, originally titled *Circle in the Water* and now called *At the King's Command,* was the winner of a Holt Medallion. Book Two, originally called *Vows Made in Wine,* is now *The Maiden's Hand,* and was a finalist for a RITA® Award. Book Three, also a RITA® Award finalist, was titled *Dancing on Air* and is now *At the Queen's Summons.*

It is with pleasure that I invite you to step back in time, into a vanished world of court intrigue, where sovereigns ruled by the scaffold, and men and women dared to risk everything for love.

Susan Wiggs
2009

The employees of Thorndike Press hope you have enjoyed this Large Print book. All our Thorndike, Wheeler, and Kennebec Large Print titles are designed for easy reading, and all our books are made to last. Other Thorndike Press Large Print books are available at your library, through selected bookstores, or directly from us.

For information about titles, please call:

(800) 223-1244

or visit our Web site at:

http://gale.cengage.com/thorndike

To share your comments, please write:

Publisher
Thorndike Press
295 Kennedy Memorial Drive
Waterville, ME 04901